After taking a Modern Languages degree at Oxford, Elizabeth James taught at various comprehensive schools and also worked with maladjusted children. She then ran a bookshop with her husband in Essex but since 1987 has been writing full-time.

By the same author

Life Class

ELIZABETH JAMES

Life Lines

GRAFTON BOOKS

A Division of the Collins Publishing Group

LONDON GLASGOW
TORONTO SYDNEY AUCKLAND

Grafton Books
A Division of the Collins Publishing Group
8 Grafton Street, London W1X 3LA

A Grafton Paperback Original 1988

ISBN 0-586-07334-5

Printed and bound in Great Britain by
Collins, Glasgow

Set in Times

For D.J., Cath and Matthew.
With my love.

Part One

1

'So we don't go to war after all.'

Flopped on a blanket, propped on one elbow, her bare, pale legs stretched out in front of her, Dominique David looked round at the rest of them. Voicing the thought that was uppermost in all their minds she felt impatient, almost aggressive. How terribly restrained they all were. Arriving at Maggie's with Robert and Sarah she'd expected fireworks. But they hadn't hugged one another or exclaimed with shaky relief. Instead, Maggie had led them quietly through to the mellow, autumnal garden, settled them on the lawn in the sun, and poured chilled Muscadet into green-stemmed glasses.

'Dominique likes to state the obvious.' There was mild hostility in Robert Lessing's grey eyes. He seemed vaguely out of sorts with her. Increasingly nowadays that seemed the case. He held his glass up to the sun and peered through it. 'An honourable peace.' His flat, south London tones were effectively scathing.

'You'd rather have war, Robert?' Maggie asked gently.

He looked sideways at her, bland. 'Not me.' A pause. 'Cannon-fodder. That's the phrase I keep thinking of these last two weeks.'

'What sickens me is all this jubilation and thanking of God and peace in our time.' Sarah leaned forward in her deck chair, resting her elbows on her black-trousered knees. 'Nobody wants war. We all know that. But let's not pretend we've got peace with honour. We should be walking around like whipped curs, ashamed to meet each other's eyes . . .'

'He's given that bastard Hitler everything he wanted and then he comes home like a bloody conquering hero.' Robert raised his glass in a sardonic toast. 'To bloody Chamberlain!'

'All the same, I've got a craven, cringing sense of relief.' Sarah hugged her knees, drawing up her shoulders in a kind of shudder.

Maggie looked at her. 'Haven't we all?'

'What are you going to do with your gas mask now, Maggie?' Robert asked wryly. 'Grow plants in it?'

Dominique leaned back on the tartan rug and watched them all, strangely detached from the situation. As a French national she felt the matter hardly concerned her. She imagined, of course, that conversations like these would be taking place all over France, but she wasn't there to hear them.

If anything, she had to admit to a childish tinge of disappointment. It wasn't exactly that she wanted a war. It was just that the possibility had held a hint of excitement, of change, perhaps. And now it was nipped in the bud and everything had gone back to normal.

'Dominique?'

She turned to Robert. He was offering her a cigarette. She didn't like them much, but smoked one now and again for practice. Perhaps one day she would need to pretend sophistication and coughing and spluttering on a cigarette would destroy the illusion. She took one and Robert lit it for her, smiling directly at her. He looked friendlier now. He always liked her when she seemed remote and thoughtful.

'Penny for them?'

The odd English expression always amused her. But it

never occurred to her to tell her true thoughts. 'I'm thinking whether I've forgotten my toothbrush,' she teased him.

'More than likely,' he said with an affectionate, forbearing sigh.

She lay back on the rug, one hand behind her head, blowing out smoke-rings, as Robert had taught her, with careful insouciance. She'd visited Maggie only once before, but she liked it here. The spacious house, with its arched, pointed windows, sloping lawns and muted, coral-coloured brickwork was wholly welcoming. Maggie had the knack of conferring on her surroundings a kind of homely elegance that Dominique thought very English. Her hospitality was carefully planned, yet warm and apparently effortless. Maggie had two little boys aged four and five. Dominique could hear their piping voices from inside the house, along with the bossier tones of Ruth, Sarah's ten-year-old daughter. Ilya, Maggie's husband, worked in the theatre and was expected home later.

Sarah and Robert were still discussing the narrowly averted war with Germany. Dominique watched them without taking in their words. She admired Sarah and was proud of the friendship that was growing between the two of them. The older woman was everything Dominique hoped to be when she reached the unthinkable age of thirty-five. Sarah was chic and slim in her black shirt and trousers. She approached people with a kind of teasing irony, both friendly and self-contained, poised and natural. She had an absorbing career as a painter and she worked hard at it.

But I'll never be like that, Dominique thought, with a rueful flash of self-recognition. I just haven't got the discipline.

11

'What do you think of all this political talk, Dominique?' Maggie smiled down at her, offering more wine.

Dominique held out her glass. 'I saw some barrage balloons yesterday,' she said. 'Over Hampstead Heath. They looked like big, stuffed fish.' Knowing that her French accent – which she deliberately emphasized – would make the observation irresistible. Sure enough, an abrupt and spontaneous burst of laughter from the three others followed her words. Robert leaned towards her on the rug and kissed her on the cheek, then turned to Sarah to share his amusement, as though Dominique were a precocious child and he a proud parent.

Robert's relationship with Sarah intrigued Dominique. It seemed odd to her, this friendship between a woman of thirty-five and a boy of twenty-one. Robert simply ignored the difference in their ages, treating Sarah as he would any one of his contemporaries. As far as Dominique could see there was no element of sexual attraction in their relationship. They were more like affectionate, squabbling brother and sister.

Sarah was a widow. In fact she'd been married twice. Once, briefly, in her late teens. It had ended in divorce. Later she'd wed a writer called Stephen Law who had committed suicide ten years or so ago rather than face a slow death from serious illness. His books had been savage and radical and more appreciated after his death than in his lifetime. Now he was something of a legend among earnest left-wing students. Robert admired his work inordinately and had written a letter to Sarah two years ago telling her so and asking to meet her. She'd liked the note and had agreed to see the unknown young man. Their friendship was unpretentious. Neither made demands or asked for explanations. They accepted one another.

12

Robert turned back to Dominique and touched her shoulder. 'D'you want to come for a walk across the fields? I'll show you that little ruined lock-house I told you about.' There was a secret, vulnerable look in his eye, belying the nonchalance of the question.

Dominique knew he wanted to be alone with her, and she was pleased. But she felt contrary. Once or twice that afternoon Robert had shown flashes of hostility, impatience.

'No.' She pouted her lips playfully, shaking her head. Her mussed red-blonde hair brushed her shoulders. 'I don't want to go.' Knowing full well the refusal would hurt him.

Abruptly she stood up and slipped her bare feet into her blue shoes which lay discarded next to the tartan rug. 'I'm going inside. To find the children.'

Sarah leaned back luxuriously in her deck chair, enjoying the feel of the October sun on her face. In autumn its rays seemed especially precious. In the nature of things there wouldn't be many more days like this. At the end of the long sweep of lawn a huge sycamore showed a sprinkling of yellow leaves. A drift of deep blue-mauve Michaelmas daisies shone from the herbaceous border. How she loved this place. In every detail. From the pots of red geraniums on the rickety bench under the kitchen window to the yellow tricycle lying abandoned at the margin of the flowerbed, and Natasha, the black Labrador bitch dozing on the flagstones outside the back door. Today all the beauty of it seemed sharper, more poignant than ever with her awareness of the catastrophe so narrowly avoided.

Determinedly she pushed away the thought of war and the guilty knowledge that in beleaguered, abandoned

13

Czechoslovakia this kind of quiet enjoyment had suddenly become a pleasant memory.

They were here for the wedding anniversary of Sarah's oldest friend, Maggie. It was eight years now since she and Ilya had been married, though they'd lived together for longer.

Sarah shook her head wonderingly. 'It can't be eight years. You've miscalculated.' Smiling affectionately at her friend. 'Two years, maybe. Three at a pinch . . .' Her words were accompanied by a flash of remembrance. If Stephen had lived, she, Sarah, would have been married for more than ten. The realization merely brushed her. She had long since steeled herself implacably against pain at such thoughts.

'I'm beginning to feel like a matriarch.' A self-mocking grin crossed Maggie's sweet face. 'But I don't think I mind.'

'You don't look like one.' To Sarah her friend seemed unchanged from the day of her cheerful, bohemian wedding all those years ago in Notting Hill. In those days Ilya had called himself a scenery painter. Success had conferred on him the title of theatrical designer. He was a Russian by birth, but naturalized now, an Englishman.

Sarah could still picture Maggie in a home-made dress, sewn from material she'd printed herself with a blue and yellow Mondrian design, a yellow scarf tied gypsy-fashion round her head instead of a hat, and earrings made from tap washers, her face lit-up and live as a candle flame. Today her appearance was just as picturesque. Above a burgundy smock, vaguely medieval in its lines, her long, dark hair was pulled back into a black chenille snood. Her face was thinner now perhaps, subtly transformed from prettiness to the gravity of beauty.

But basically Maggie was the same. It was her habitat

14

that had changed. After a series of more or less eccentric cold-water flats she and Ilya had settled here in the quiet village of Alder near St Albans. And what could be more classic and established than this spaciously proportioned house with its roses and lavender and centuries-old trees? Yet somehow Maggie suited it perfectly, loved it, cherished it, with all the passionate visual flair she'd had since their days together at art school.

'To be honest, I think I'm happier now, here, than I've ever been.' Maggie gestured vaguely at the house and the sunlit garden. 'Isn't that dull of me?' Always she seemed to have known what was right for her and calmly followed her own path. She had a kind of fragile toughness. To Sarah, Maggie had always represented the essence of sanity.

'I envy you.' Sarah hesitated. 'In some ways.'

Maggie was scornful. 'No you don't. My life wouldn't be your cup of tea at all.'

Deep down Sarah knew that it was true. Maggie had never shared her fascination with the act of painting, the constant, almost physical drive to clarify her own vision on canvas, her total absorption in confronting the problems that arose during the process. Her daughter Ruth apart, this was the enduring passion in Sarah's life.

Maggie was different. She had talent in abundance, but she put it into her everyday life. Adoring Ilya and their solemn, dark-haired little boys, her pleasure lay in creating an environment for them. The artist in her was satisfied by caring for a garden, knitting subtly coloured Fair-Isle sweaters for her children, or building a papier-mâché castle for them on the garage floor. She gained as much joy from these activities as Sarah did from the prospect of a day's painting with no domestic obligations to interrupt and rob her of her time.

15

Robert had gone quiet, Sarah noticed. He was lying on his back, arms folded behind his head, his sharp, intelligent profile turned towards the sky. She guessed that he was brooding on Dominique's casual snub, but knew with an absolute certainty that Dominique would by now have totally forgotten it.

There was a delighted and fearful squeaking from the direction of the back door. Sacha and Stephen, Maggie's boys, burst through the opening, closely followed by the leggy figure of Ruth, her blonde hair flying. Natasha, the dog, was rudely woken from sleep. Shrill, threatening sounds came from inside the house. The children rushed giggling to hide behind a nearby laurel bush.

Then Dominique emerged from the house, uttering manic, sinister laughter, her hands curved like claws. On her head was a cardboard witch's hat Maggie had once made for Ruth. She pretended not to see the children, searching for them everywhere but in the right place.

'Where are they?' she cackled. 'I'll have zere guts for garters!' A phrase Sarah guessed she'd learnt from Robert. Sacha, she could see, was jumping up and down, crimson-faced with merriment. Ruth had knelt behind Stephen, the youngest, with her thin arms round his waist to reassure him in case the fright became too real.

Finally, like a ham actor in a silent film, Dominique made a play of sighting the huddled children. She advanced on them slowly, with a narrow-eyed menace. Their laughter rose to a hysterical crescendo.

Then, just before she reached the laurel bush where they were hiding, Dominique threw off the lopsided hat and resumed her normal persona, hugging the small figure of Stephen and lifting him up to show that she meant him no harm. Her red-gold hair stuck out frizzily where she'd pushed off the hat. There was a broad, unselfconscious grin on her face and her grey-green eyes were narrowed with laughter.

Now she held Stephen against her blue-patterned, puff-sleeved frock, cooing, 'It's only me. It's your Auntie Dominique.' Her feet were bare again. She was totally without the chic her countrywomen were supposed to possess, Sarah thought. But she had a vibrant, unique vitality that became at times an almost overpowering magnetism.

Robert watched her intently. His expression was blank, but the avidity of his gaze betrayed his fascination. It was odd for Sarah to see him at a loss. Quick, irreverent and acid-tongued as he was, he was used to having the upper hand with women-friends. But the French girl was not to be dominated. She moved through life on her own terms and Robert could accept them or not, as he pleased.

An economics student, Robert flirted with communism while lacking the dedication to become seriously involved. That spring, though, he'd volunteered to fight in Spain with the International Brigade against Franco's militia. Sarah had been touched by his raw, youthful fervour.

He'd been captured, briefly imprisoned, deported, and was back in London within a couple of months. This exploit had made him a hero among the earnest, politically conscious young women he normally frequented, but Dominique just teased him about what she called his Spanish holiday. She *was* impressed, Sarah guessed, but felt the need to stand apart from his band of dewy-eyed admirers.

'Don't they just love her?' Sarah indicated Dominique and the gleeful youngsters.

Robert nodded without looking at her. 'Don't they just.' He found it painful to see Dominique make much of anyone but himself, jealous even of three small children.

17

2

Ruth sat quietly on a divan in one corner of Maggie's living room. Leaning back on a pile of patchwork cushions, one arm round the sleeping figure of four-year-old Stephen, named for her own dead father. On a small table at her elbow stood the half glass of champagne that Sarah had allowed her to toast Maggie and Ilya's wedding anniversary. The pale liquid had gone warm and flat. Ruth was pleased to have been offered such a grown-up drink, but thought the taste nasty and metallic.

This evening the room was lit by candles. Maggie had bought two twisted blue glass candlesticks at a local jumble sale and seemed very proud of them. When dinner had been cleared away she'd stood them on a carved oak chest at one end of the room. 'Let's christen these.' The lights had been switched off and the four long candles in each holder lit.

'Pure Lalique,' Ilya had said, laughing at Maggie and cuddling her at the same time. The room was so cosy. The glow from the flames moved and flickered as though it were alive.

Too sleepy now to say much, Ruth watched the adults laughing and talking a few feet away from her, their chairs turned inward in a rough semi-circle. Michael was bending towards her mother and smiling at something she said to him. He was one of Sarah's oldest friends and always had a special smile for her, and a sort of kindness in his eyes.

'I'm happy,' Ruth thought drowsily. Often at Maggie's she felt this. Most of your life you never really noticed.

There were lots of reasons. Like the warmth of Stephen's little body against her arm. And the candlelight, and being up so late. And the grown-ups in a laughing mood, the sort of mood that meant they wouldn't get cross whatever you said or did.

Best of all, she could pretend to herself that Maggie and Ilya and the boys were family. She envied the other children at school with their casual mention of aunties and grandmas and cousins, as if everyone had them. Sometimes she even talked about Sacha and Stephen as 'my little cousins', crossing her fingers as she did so to wipe out the lie. Dominique would make a good auntie too.

Stephen opened his eyes for a second, sightlessly. Then his head fell forward again in sleep.

Robert and Dominique were friends again. They were in a giggly, excited mood. The last few days, with war a threatening, incredible reality, had been taut and breathless. Now the tension was released. Between the two of them there was a sort of high-spirited complicity at being young among people in their thirties.

Michael, back from a trip to New York, had brought with him a stack of swing records. He'd put on 'One O'Clock Jump' by the Benny Goodman Orchestra.

'On your feet, Dominique.' Robert had pulled her by the hand. To the delight of Ruth and the boys they'd performed a crazy, clowning dance before collapsing into an armchair, breathless and laughing. Dominique draped herself across Robert's lap. The rest had applauded riotously.

'Oh, I feel old.' Behind his moustache Ilya had pulled a comic-rueful face. 'Cavorting like that. I'd have put my back out.'

19

'Not true, not true.' On the battered chesterfield Sarah had patted his arm reassuringly. 'There's life in you yet.'

But suddenly she envied the young couple their nervous high spirits, even the constant abrasive edginess of their relationship. They were so . . . alive.

In the aftermath of her husband Stephen's death Sarah had fought desperately to prevent her pain from turning to bitterness. She had cultivated a teasing, gently ironic façade, suppressing feelings that could cause her hurt. Now she wondered whether there was anything left to suppress and whether the façade had not become reality.

'You're so *raisonnable*,' Dominique had said to her once. A compliment, but tinged with impatience.

There was affection in her life, plenty of it, warm, enduring, and stable – from Maggie, Michael, Ilya. Even Robert, though with him she played the tolerant aunt and he the wayward, slightly shocking nephew. And there was passion of a sort. For her work, and for Ruth. The mere sight of her daughter's leggy frame, her flying blonde hair and grave, immature features could make Sarah's heart contract with pride and an aching love. But would she ever again feel anything as unsettling and intense as Robert's infatuation for Dominique? Did she even want to?

'So pensive, Sarah.' Michael looked up from where he was sitting on the floor, leafing through a stack of records in search of a Billie Holiday song that he wanted them all to hear. He gave her that special, intimate smile, a smile of friendship and acceptance.

She shook her head, returning to the here and now. 'I'm getting morbid. It must be the political climate.'

'Ah, got it!' He selected a disc from the pile and slipped off its paper sleeve, then hauled his long body upright and crossed to the gramophone. 'Sarah's latest favourite.'

20

There was a second of silence, broken only by the slight crackling of the needle trundling through the grooves. Then the opening bars, newly familiar to her, of the haunting 'I'll Never Be The Same'.

He bent over Sarah, teasing. 'You'll do me the honour?'

She stood up, facing him. They moved easily, having danced together time without number. Michael was gangling and slightly awkward physically, but surprisingly the awkwardness vanished on the dance-floor. He moved like an American, as if the music belonged to him, Sarah thought, without the inflexibility of some of his fellow-Englishmen. 'This could have been our first dance of the war. Think of that. I forget, and then it hits me all over again.'

Michael turned down the corners of his mouth briefly. 'I hate postponement. It's like having an examination cancelled and being told to present yourself again in a week's time. War'll come, I'm certain of it.'

'Maybe,' she conceded. 'Well, probably. But let's not think about that tonight. We've been let off the hook. Let's enjoy it.'

As they circled she noticed that Ruth had now fallen asleep propped on the pile of cushions, pale in the candlelight, still cuddling Stephen. Sarah smiled. 'Look, babes in the wood.' When the record was over it'd be time to put her daughter to bed.

The song had a raw, yearning quality that brought her out in gooseflesh. It was rare that Sarah permitted herself the luxury of an emotional response to words and music, but . . . 'there is such an ache in my heart . . .' The voice and phrasing of Billie Holiday, restrained, yet totally heart-breaking. There was a magic in the melancholy which Sarah allowed to pervade her body and linger in

21

her head. Michael smiled down at her as though he could read her mood. 'I'd like to talk to you later. On your own. In the garden or somewhere. Could we?' His face was earnest and slightly flushed from alcohol. A lock of hair fell across his forehead. How nice he was.

'Yes, of course. I'll put Ruth to bed, then we'll slip out. We could walk down the lane. It's a gorgeous night. Cold . . . but gorgeous.'

The music ended. Gently Maggie extricated Stephen from Ruth's arms and carried him up to his room. Sacha had long since opted for bed voluntarily. Sarah roused her daughter sufficiently to take her upstairs.

In the little attic room where she and Sarah always slept when they came to Maggie's, Ruth undressed, still half-asleep, then slipped under the fleecy red blanket that covered the camp bed. There was no electricity this high in the house. On a chest of drawers that Maggie had painted with bizarre, Picassoesque nursery-rhyme figures stood a dim bicycle lamp run by batteries. It was the only lighting. Ruth liked the torch left on until Sarah came to bed.

'Goodnight, darling.' She bent to kiss her daughter's smooth lips. 'I won't be more than an hour or so.'

'Mummy.' A small, sleepy voice as Sarah reached for the door-latch.

'What is it, love?' She turned towards the pale blur that was Ruth's face and hair.

The soft voice came again. 'Does Michael love you?'

'What?' Sarah was seriously taken aback.

'Does he love you? Michael?' With the child's drowsiness the question was almost expressionless.

Sarah blinked with surprise. Why spring such a question now, when her friendship with Michael had been a fact for all of Ruth's life? Last term at school there'd been a craze for sweethearts between the boys and girls in her class. Perhaps this explained the quaint inquisition.

She hesitated. 'Yes, he does. Like a friend. Like you love Sacha and little Stephen and I love Maggie. But he's not my sweetheart.'

'Oh.' The reply was so sleepy that Sarah wasn't sure her answer had been heard.

In fact her words had been an over-simplification. Wherever possible Sarah believed in telling Ruth the whole truth. But on this point, she thought, her daughter was too young to appreciate shades of meaning.

In the main what she'd said had been true. She and Michael *were* friends from way back. Even now she could picture their meeting in New Mexico over ten years ago, when Stephen had still been alive. She could see his tall figure walking towards her across the flat stretch of scrub outside their cabin. He'd been flushed with the heat, an expectant smile on his face, his sandy hair looking lighter in the glare of the sun. She remembered how surprised she'd been to hear his clipped British tones in that remote spot. But she and Stephen had taken to him immediately. He had introduced himself as a journalist, there to write a piece on the art colony of Taos. He had a letter of introduction from Maggie in his pocket, and he was en route for Hollywood where his sister had a steady career in the movies.

At that time Sarah had been at a crucial stage in her development as a painter. After false starts and dead-ends and months of inactivity she had finally learnt to trust her own vision and work in her own way rather than be influenced by contemporary whims and fashions. She'd been energetic and receptive, painting prolifically and passionately, even in the wake of Ruth's birth.

At that time the mere act of painting had satisfied her. She'd had no thought of selling her work. Michael had been excited by her canvases and had offered, diffidently, to try and market them through contacts of his in England. She'd agreed. His venture had been wildly successful and a few months later he'd sent her newspaper clippings from London with enthusiastic reviews of her work by critics she respected. He'd enclosed a couple of sizeable cheques and requests for further canvases to be shipped home.

Then Stephen had died and Sarah had come back to Britain with Ruth still a baby in arms. The pain inside her had been made bleaker by the greyness of that first winter. After the strong, clear light of New Mexico there seemed a perpetually jaundiced, doomsday look to the world. She'd found a furnished flat in Camden Town – she could still picture its floral mince-coloured carpet and distempered yellow dado. If it hadn't been for Maggie and Ilya – and Michael – she was certain that she would have foundered in clinical depression.

She remembered long days at home with Ruth in the cold flat, trying to paint during the increasingly short periods the child would sleep or stay contentedly in her playpen. She remembered protracted walks with the pram through cheerless streets to amuse her daughter and – she hoped – to tire her out so that she, Sarah, could get some work done.

Michael had been a rock. A discreet, self-effacing rock. He'd never pushed or pulled, but merely nudged her little by little into taking up the reins of her career again. He'd taken her to exhibitions, introduced her to some useful contacts, asked her to do some reviewing for an arts magazine called *Liaisons* which he was trying to get off the ground. Insignificant things in themselves, but gradually they gave Sarah the feeling that she was back in circulation.

Then she'd found an unfurnished ground-floor flat in Fulham Road, quite close to where Michael lived. It was roomy and homely, with a small backyard that Ruth could play in. Best of all, there was Maud upstairs, a good-hearted, middle-aged woman with a high colour and a girlish giggle, whose husband worked all day on the buses and whose children were grown. Ruth adored her and Maud offered to look after the child each morning from eight to twelve. It meant that Sarah was free to paint without interruption for four hours each day.

She found it surprisingly easy to get back into the rhythm of work. Her paintings were lower in tone than the vibrant canvases she'd produced in New Mexico. The muted English light decreed it. But the direct, passionate vision she'd discovered over there had stayed with her. There was fascination in her own neighbourhood with its solid, monumental architecture under whitish skies, the small, chaotic shops, stumpy, pollarded trees. She painted the local streets in all their aspects, almost obsessively.

Sarah began to experience a kind of fragile contentment again. Having Michael close by was a large part of it. Often they spent Saturdays or Sundays together, motoring to the seaside or playing with Ruth in the local park. Michael became a trusted figure in her daughter's life.

About eighteen months after her return to England there was an exhibition of Sarah's work. It was held, ironically, at a gallery in Camden Town, where she'd spent her first listless winter. But this time Camden Town turned up trumps. The exhibition was a success, building on the reputation she'd made with her New Mexico canvases. From then on, her career had its own momentum. But in the incestuous art world her professional life and Michael's overlapped constantly and their friendship was deepened by the interests and acquaintances they had in common.

During the mid-thirties both she and Michael sat on a committee concerned with the plight of the increasing number of artists who'd fled Hitler's Germany and gone into exile in London. The idea was to raise funds and organize showings of their work. Sarah was friendly with a shy young German painter called Albrecht who shared a room in a house a few doors away from her. He was forced to work as a waiter to earn his living and had virtually no time for painting. The committee was important to her and to Michael, but some of its older members were more interested in the sound of their own voices, it seemed, than in achieving anything positive.

She recalled one cold evening in the autumn of 1935, three years ago now, when she and Michael had sat through a particularly vexing session. Sarah's chief bugbear, a grey-haired, bulbous-eyed bore called Thornton, who travelled up from St Ives for each meeting, monopolized the gathering, huffing and puffing over trifles so that the main business of the evening was hardly touched on and a hasty emergency meeting had to be arranged.

It had poured with rain as they left and Sarah and Michael arrived back at her flat like a couple of drowned rats. They lit a fire, made coffee and dried their hair. Then they sat in the firelight, railing against Thornton until their frustration turned to wild and mildly shame-faced laughter.

Suddenly Michael said, 'I wish you'd marry me. We could have such a good time together.'

The warm, pale light of the flames made him look young and earnest as he leaned forward in his chair, elbows on knees, cradling an earthenware coffee mug in his large hands. It seemed to Sarah then as though everything stopped around her and stood temporarily suspended and hushed. Oddly, she wasn't surprised by his words, although the thought of marriage with Michael had never occurred to her until now. But in that sharp, breathless moment her mind reviewed the idea in a kind of shorthand and rejected it outright. ·

If she'd weighed up his proposal, taking points for and against one by one, there would have been overwhelming reasons in its favour – their shared tastes and sense of humour, their frank liking for one another, Ruth's fondness for him. But her refusal was a gut reaction. It was only later that she had time to analyse – and come to the same conclusion.

She said slowly, 'Yes, we could have a good time. And I like you so much that I almost love you.' Reaching out to touch one of his hands. 'But I can't marry you. I'm sorry, Michael.'

He nodded. 'I thought you'd say that.' It was a point of honour with him not to let personal feelings show. 'But I had to be sure.'

There was no breath of rancour. He was sure enough of her regard not to feel ashamed, and he'd never danced attendance on her. With his well-bred good looks and quiet humour he was considered highly eligible.

There was a silence between them, then Sarah said quietly, 'Michael.' She hesitated. 'I'd hate this to affect our friendship. It's always been so very valuable to me.'

'It won't, I promise.' He'd smiled ruefully, the lopsided smile she liked, and had been as good as his word.

In the days that followed Sarah thought a lot about Michael's proposal. And always – in spite of her fondness for him – she knew that her decision had been the right one. She was content now to be on her own with Ruth, independent and, in the foreseeable future, financially secure.

Just occasionally, even now, a passionate sense of loss would penetrate her guard, temporarily devaluing the life she'd made for herself, making it appear arid and solitary compared to the years she and Stephen had spent together. But always she'd re-arm, determinedly banish the creeping regrets and get out oils and canvas, absorbing herself in the abstract problems of painting. Or she'd take Ruth out to the park or the pictures. The activity would restore her sense of balance, and the real world would regain its importance. She was content. It would take a great deal now to tempt her to change the basis of her life.

Downstairs Maggie was washing up glasses in the kitchen. Ilya dried and polished them, brandishing a soft cloth with a flourish like a waiter. Michael lounged against the door-jamb, talking to them. Sarah passed through the dim adjoining living room to reach them. As she walked towards the lighted doorway, she was briefly aware of the tableau made by Robert and Dominique.

The French girl was still sitting on his lap. With one hand at the nape of her neck Robert was talking to her, low and insistently. As she listened, Dominique stared straight ahead of her, white-skinned and inscrutable, her eyes in shadow. Her stillness was striking. With her tousled red-gold hair curling round her face, she had a wild beauty. Neither she nor Robert appeared to notice Sarah as she walked by.

Michael looked over his shoulder as she approached. 'Ready?' She nodded, smiling.

'Ruth all right?' Maggie turned from the sink, wiping her hands on a striped cloth.

'She's fine. You know how she loves it here.' Sarah stood beside Michael and linked her arm in his. 'Maggie, Ilya, we're just going for a walk down the lane. I don't suppose we'll be long. If you two want to go to bed, we'll lock up.'

Outside it was clear and cold, the stars sharply visible. Sarah sank her hands thankfully into her jacket pockets, looking up at the immense dark sky bordered by the blacker shapes of the trees. 'All this would look just the same even if jackbooted Nazi hordes were clumping down the lane.'

'When the life you live is threatened it makes you think about what's important to you.' At times Michael had a hesitation in his speech, then the following words would come in a little rush. It happened now. Usually it meant he was nervous and Sarah wondered why that should be.

'I feel a terrible sense of indignation – helpless indignation – at Ruth's childhood being threatened,' she said.

'Ours was.'

'I know. That's what's so stupid. It was so God-awful last time. Why should anyone want to repeat the experience?'

'The inevitability of history?' He spoke politely, without great interest.

'That's all very well. But who do you know that actually wants to go to war?' She could sense that from his point of view they'd got off the point. There was something Michael wanted to talk about. That was why they were here. She prodded. 'Did you decide, Michael?'

'Decide what?'

'What it was that was important to you . . . under threat of war?'

'Yes, I did.'

They reached a slatted bench by the side of the footpath. There was a metal plate screwed to it that read 'Rest and be thankful'. It was too dark now for it to be legible.

Michael took her arm. 'Shall we sit down?'

They became aware of the silence around them. From somewhere they could hear a trickle of water, and there was a rustling in the leaves, a sound not unlike soft rain. Apart from that, nothing. On the opposite side of the path was a jagged, blasted tree. Ruth had once said its shape reminded her of the prow of a Viking ship. Sarah was about to tell Michael so, but stopped herself. She must leave him to get to the point without interruption. She could see his shape dimly next to her, his hands plunged deep into his pockets, long legs stretched out in front of him, his head bowed as though in thought. She sat patiently.

Then he turned towards her. 'Sarah, do you remember that night ages ago when I mentioned the idea of your marrying me?' Again the speech hesitation, but then she could sense him grinning as he added, 'What on earth am I saying, do you remember? If you've forgotten I might just as well crawl away on the spot and die.'

'Michael, what a question.' She laughed back at the mock-dejection in his voice, then said softly, 'I was proud. Really.' She took his hand. 'The strange thing is, I was thinking about that night myself just half an hour ago. Less. Something Ruth said . . .'

'The point is, I made light of it.' Michael ploughed on as though determined to get the thing off his chest. 'I thought you'd say no, so I played it down as if it were an amusing suggestion. As if it was pretty well the same to me either way.'

'I didn't see it in that light.' But what he said had a certain truth. The conversation had been strangely incon-

30

sequential, quickly over and done with. At the time she'd thought it tactful of him.

'It's the *vice anglais*. You know. Never make an embarrassing scene.'

She smiled. 'I should just think not.'

'But then I've wondered. Often. Supposing I'd been honest. Supposing I'd showed you how much the question really meant to me . . .'

A lone figure passed. A man in a flat cap, carrying a torch. Michael stopped talking until he was gone.

'Then yesterday I thought, sod it, I'm going to stop being so bloody discreet. I'll disturb the status quo. I think it was the war scare that decided me. Panic focuses the mind a treat.'

'So what are you saying?' The silence, the darkness somehow intensified their exchange.

'I'm saying that I love you. And that I want to marry you. And that after tonight I'll never ask you again.'

He delivered the speech with uncharacteristic vehemence. Michael was usually mild and humorous in his manner. There was almost a trace of aggression in the words as though he were venting some private frustration. The echo hung between them on the night air, shaking Sarah out of her self-possession.

'I don't . . .'

'Sarah, think about it.' Michael spoke simultaneously, and his greater intensity carried the day. 'You're going to say no, but think about it. Wait a bit. Think about the life we could have. We could have wonderful times. We're on the same wavelength. We laugh at the same jokes. We've got so many hundreds of things in common.' He was quietly persuasive. 'Look, Sarah, I'm giving you reasons. For you. I don't need these reasons. You see, I love you, and for me that's enough.'

Suddenly Sarah found herself terribly moved. She had never thought to wrench such feeling from teasing, civilized Michael. She folded her arms across her body as though she were cold. 'I'd love to say yes, Michael.' For a moment she could feel tears stinging. 'You know how fond I am of you. I'd almost like to say yes to please you, to make you happy. I can almost imagine doing so.' She shivered. 'But it wouldn't be right. It'd be a mistake.'

'Yes.' He spoke as if to himself.

She knew he was hurt. And briefly she wondered if she were merely being obstinate in refusing all the solid, valuable reasons that could bind her to Michael. *It's not like it was with Stephen*. That was the phrase that came to her if ever she was tempted to lower her guard and admit someone closer. *It's not the same*. It never was. There had been a current, strong and live, between herself and Stephen. A powerful sexual attraction, certainly, but something else, a kind of recognition. It had never been like that with anyone else. But perhaps she was wrong to expect emotions to repeat themselves. Might there not be other ways of loving? Still something in her rebelled. She would not admit it.

'So that's your last word.'

She nodded, dying inside.

In the silence between them an owl hooted, some way away in the direction of Alder village.

'Well, that's that out of the way, then.' There was a trace of bitterness in his tone, but even now he held any further emotion under control.

'I can't help myself, Michael.'

He placed one hand over hers in a gesture of conciliation. They sat quietly for a time in the closeness that follows intimate conversation. Then Michael said, 'There's something else I want to talk to you about.'

'Go on. I'm all ears.'

'You see, Sarah, I seem to have reached an age where I've got the urge for a home and family. I've felt it for some time, but the last few days, well, they've brought it home to me just how much I want them.'

She nodded encouragingly. Michael sounded if anything even more reluctant than earlier, as though what he had to say was an unpleasant duty.

'Look, this is going to sound appalling. And I can't think of any way to say it that won't sound . . . Look, I want to marry you, but since I can't, I'm going to ask someone else.'

She was more flabbergasted now than she'd been all evening. The announcement was so bald and unvarnished, bringing an inelegant touch of farce to their grave and emotional conversation. What was Michael saying? How on earth could he transfer his courtship so readily? In her amazement all she could think of to say was, 'Who?'

'Tessa Hopkins,' he replied with a hint of defiance.

'Oh.'

Sarah had met Tessa a few times. She worked on Michael's beloved magazine, *Liaisons*, carrying out secretarial and editorial duties with cheerful impartiality. She was plump and blonde and around thirty. Quite pretty, but vaguely haphazard in hairstyle and dress. Sarah remembered Michael once describing her affectionately to Maggie as 'jolly efficient and a good chap to boot', and certainly she was as keen as he for the success of the magazine. On a more personal level, Tessa's plummy Kensington voice grated on Sarah, a prejudice that lingered obstinately from her childhood in the Welsh mining valleys.

'You're surprised?'

33

'Can you blame me?' It was Sarah's turn to display a touch of pique. 'And honestly it doesn't seem fair on her.'

'To be second choice?'

'Well, exactly.'

He gave a curt, though not unfriendly laugh. 'One of the things I've admired about you, Sarah, is that you've got no notion of compromise – the idea just never occurs to you.'

'What do you mean by that?' Suddenly Sarah felt tired and jaded. She thought of Ruth tucked up in her camp bed in the sloping room under the eaves.

As though he understood her weariness, Michael laid a hand across her shoulder. 'I think you see love only in terms of an irresistible force, and you reject anything else as worthless.' He spoke gently to her, as she had to him earlier. 'I don't think you'll understand that I love Tessa. It's not the same feeling I've got for you. But it's not worthless and she won't be second best.'

Sarah pondered. Michael was right. She didn't understand. His decision to marry Tessa seemed shocking to her, calculating and deliberate. But since she herself had refused him she had no right to judge. She shivered. 'I'm cold, Michael. I think we should be getting back.'

They retraced their steps along the narrow lane. The ground felt hard underfoot. Sarah took Michael's arm. 'I think there's going to be a frost tonight.'

They stopped at the gate. Michael looked down at her. She could see his face clearly now by the light of a lantern hanging in the porch, could read the concern in his expression.

'No hard feelings?' There was just a tinge of anxiety in his tone.

She shook her head, smiling. 'For you? Never.'

* * *

Upstairs Ruth was fast asleep, breathing almost soundlessly. Sarah turned back the quilt on her own narrow bed. Undressing by the dim glow of the bicycle lamp she felt a dull sense of depression, directly related to the announcement of Michael's possible marriage.

Of course, she was being a dog in the manger. Having refused to marry him herself it was mean-spirited of her to begrudge him consolation with someone else. But she liked their friendship as it was. She felt comfortable with Michael. Talking to him was as pleasurable and relaxing as wearing old clothes. The addition of Tessa's brisk personality would alter the balance between them, jangle their peace.

A tune drifted through her mind as she turned out the lamp then padded across the room and got into bed, the Billie Holiday song. Mournfully the words came back to her. 'Never be the same. Never be the same again.'

3

Dominique hurried down the Fulham Road, her red high heels tapping on the pavement, bright hair bouncing against the shoulders of her red wool sweater, her tartan skirt outlining the shape of her legs as she walked. It was the first fine day of the year. The sun was harsh and clear, highlighting the winter pallor of the passers-by. Rashly Dominique had left off her coat. In fact it was just too cold for comfort, but she didn't regret the gesture.

Under her arm she carried a cumbersome portfolio which she was beginning to wish she'd left at home. A familiar restless feeling was taking possession. Officially she was on her way to classes at the Royal College of Art. But in her heart of hearts she knew she was never going to get there. She'd been so good recently, too. On a day like this, though, the thought of being closeted with a lot of studious girls, glumly painting a goosefleshed nude, was unutterably depressing.

It might have been more fun if the classes had been mixed. When Dominique had mentioned to Sarah that drawing lessons were segregated, she had been open-mouthed. She'd stared at Dominique and declared, 'That's impossible! I just don't believe it.' Apparently, when she'd been at art school all of fifteen years ago she and the other female students had forced the administration to admit them to the men's life class. But Dominique couldn't picture her stodgy contemporaries taking part in that kind of revolution. Her father had hit the nail on the head when he decided that the atmosphere at the Royal

36

College would be more serious than that which pervaded any of its equivalents in Paris.

A group of workmen digging up the road shouted after her. 'Hallo, darling!'

'Feel like a bit?'

She smiled and waved to them. Some girls seemed offended by this kind of attention but Dominique had always found it jolly and rather amusing. In any case she felt on top of the world this morning. The previous day she'd called on Sarah who was full of the news that Michael had offered her a reviewing assignment in Paris. The magazine would pay her fare and basic expenses if she'd write a longish article on an exhibition of Surrealist photography that was due to open in a month's time. Normally Michael handled these jobs himself, but in May he'd be in Italy on his honeymoon.

Sarah was ecstatic at the opportunity, and knowing that Dominique was due to go back to France about then she'd suggested that they travel together and spend a few days in Paris. Dominique liked and admired Sarah. She'd accepted on the spot.

In fact she'd been guilty of deception. Six weeks or so ago Dominique's leaden-eyed drawing master had written to her father – with whom he was acquainted – to report that although his daughter had plenty of ability she was woefully lacking in application. She was cutting classes and failing to complete her work.

Dominique's father was a painter himself, but there was nothing bohemian about him. He was a staunch bourgeois Catholic who earned a steady living producing flattering, predictable portraits of local notables and who had always been baffled by Dominique's mysterious light-mindedness. He'd reacted by summarily ordering her home. This much Sarah knew.

Since then, however, Dominique had promised to do better and begged to be given another chance. Grudgingly her wish had been granted. She'd decided not to tell Sarah about this latest development, blindly pushing to one side the thought of any complications that might result.

Her reckless acceptance of Sarah's invitation had made Dominique feel much more like her old self. The weeks of being a model student hadn't suited her at all.

Now she was planning the day ahead. A picnic, maybe, in Hyde Park in the spring sun. Perhaps the rowing boats would be out in this weather. And afterwards? She'd always had a secret desire to go to a tea-dance and sit there eating toasted buns until asked to dance by some smooth young man. A lounge lizard, she thought delightedly. It was a phrase she'd learnt from Sarah.

Who could she persuade to come with her? Not Sarah, that was certain. She'd have taken Ruth to school by now and settled herself at her easel. There'd be no tempting her away.

Robert? At the thought of him a shadow crossed her day. He was so difficult now. Moody, and jealous of everyone she talked to. He'd come, she was sure. But then he'd start a quarrel over nothing and spoil any fun they might be having.

He hadn't always been like that. She could still picture him as he was when she first met him in a dark, panelled pub on the Charing Cross Road. She'd gone there with a girl from her drawing class who was meeting a boy called Angus. The three of them planned to go to the pictures later. Robert had been sitting with a group of students, including Angus, and he was the focus of attention. Leaning back in his chair so that only its two back legs touched the ground, and holding a pint mug of beer, he was regaling his companions with an account of an interview he'd had with one of his lecturers at the London School of Economics. She could remember him saying with a bemused, but somehow cocky smile, 'He told me I was too much of a cleverdick and I'd come unstuck one of these days.'

The others laughed. Robert had a low, flat voice and what she later learned was a south London accent. At the time she'd been intrigued by his narrow, knowing face and vaguely insolent eyes. His hair was fair and cut short, and his habitual expression was one of secret amusement.

A girl next to him had gushed, 'You *are* awful, Robbie.' He'd paid her scant attention.

It had got too late for the pictures and six or seven of them had gone for a meal at a cheap café nearby. They all had bangers and mash. Dominique had never heard the expression before and repeated it, fascinated. Robert sat next to her, teaching her more slang terms and laughing at her French pronunciation of them.

Quickly they'd become inseparable. And a week after their first meeting Dominique had gone back to his untidy room in the Caledonian Road, and they made love in his iron-framed single bed. They had to go to his digs. Dominique lodged with her father's sister, who was married to an Englishman, and was constantly having to cover her tracks.

He was her first lover. With his bold, radical views he'd boasted fashionably that sex was no more significant than drinking a glass of water when you were thirsty. Dominique was convent-educated and indoctrinated with the idea of sin. But to her surprise, losing her virginity had been easy and delightful. Paradoxically, Robert had taken it all far more seriously.

She found the experience magical, with the gas fire

glowing in the late afternoon dusk and Robert, naked and white-skinned, brewing tea for her afterwards.

She was still excited by his slim body and the hard look in his eyes when he made love. They'd had a wonderful time at first, with their irreverent attitude to life, and Robert introduced her to people who interested her, like Sarah, Maggie and Ilya. When he went off to Spain to fight she'd been proud of him, though she hadn't showed it. He was quite conceited enough without that.

When he came back, though, he seemed to change, becoming possessive and sulky when she saw other friends, belittling her in front of people if she said anything stupid or obvious, yet at the same time telling her repeatedly that he loved her madly and that she was the most attractive woman in the world.

Recently she'd begun to be secretive and had started going out with other men just to prove to herself that she was free. Robert dreaded her going back to France and talked about marriage, though it must have been obvious even to him that they'd drive each other mad within a week.

The Victoria and Albert Museum loomed in front of her against the brilliant blue of the sky. The sight of it always lowered her spirits, for it meant that college was near and it was time for her to put on a brisk and businesslike air.

Of course, there was always Clive.

He often lingered by the entrance, ostensibly to smoke a cigarette, but Dominique knew he was waiting for her. She quite liked his sulky dark looks. If he was there she'd persuade him to take the day off. It shouldn't be difficult. She imagined his diffident, pleased grin with pleasure.

4

In a spartan gallery on the boulevard Raspail in Paris the photographs were displayed – identically mounted – against a flat, silver-grey background with no hint of ornamentation to distract the eye from their content, their perverse, disturbing images. Dominique was enchanted, Sarah less so.

There were broken dolls, their limbs splayed at obscene angles. There were drab human figures topped by baleful, staring carnival masks, and female nudes, made abstract with criss-crossed or undulating shadows, or twisted and truncated. A torso, the head above it thrust so far back that it appeared to be surmounted only by the blunt, jutting bone of the chin. Toes, fingers, ears, isolated from the attached body, becoming dehumanized – mere folds and crevices fashioned in pliable putty.

'So original!' Dominique kept exclaiming.

To Sarah there was a coldness about it all, as though the fantastical images had all been observed and recorded with the same bland, detached, unblinking eye. But Michael was fascinated with Surrealism. He'd been converted by the remarkable exhibition at the Beaux-Arts the previous year. It was why he'd begged Sarah to cover this particular exhibition for *Liaisons*. Only something as compelling as his own honeymoon could have kept him away.

Some of the names were familiar to her, the American Man Ray, for instance, and Max Ernst. And the photographs themselves came as no sudden relevation. At

41

Michael's she'd often leafed through back copies of *Minotaure* and other periodicals that preached the surrealist doctrine.

'Look at these. Aren't they beautiful!' Dominique exclaimed over two studies of flowers by Dora Maar, her grey-green eyes shining as she drew Sarah into her enthusiasm. The plants were starkly, precisely photographed against a white background so that they seemed artificial, almost sculptural.

'Striking,' Sarah agreed. They were. And she had no wish to dampen Dominique's ardour. It was right that at nineteen she should fall in love with each new idea that came along. She was like a dragonfly in her red and blue patterned summer dress, settling delightedly in front of any exhibit that caught her eye.

Robert seemed forgotten, though during the boat journey she had talked compulsively about him. *'Il est tout à fait impossible,'* she had declared with a gesture of finality that almost sent her sophisticated pink gin flying. She had spoken at length about his moodiness and jealousy, both of which Sarah had witnessed at first hand. 'But I love him, really,' she said. Sarah had noticed, with a rush of sympathy, tears shining in her friend's eyes, spilling over and running down her cheeks, her mouth unsteady with emotion. She'd been sincere at the time. But now, three days later, Sarah doubted that Dominique would be much troubled in future by memories of Robert.

Later, her raptures temporarily exhausted, Dominique retired to an austere chrome and leather bench in the middle of the gallery. She waited there for Sarah who was doing the rounds with great thoroughness and making notes, ready for the article she was to write. Dominique half-closed her eyes. Through her lashes the shiny wood-

42

block floor looked like a giant skating rink, peopled with dreamy, slow-moving figures.

She was enjoying her stay in Paris. Last night she and Sarah had spent the evening with a painter friend of Michael's called Casimir Szabo – a Hungarian or something, slight and wiry with a big, black moustache. He was married to a pretty Frenchwoman called Annette, who wore her glossy dark hair in a thick fringe and sported plum-coloured lipstick. They'd eaten *moules marinières* and drunk wine in a smoky bistro, then Annette and Casimir had taken them to a Bal Musette in the rue de Lappe, a cheerful, crowded place that seemed to have rather a shady reputation. The Szabos looked quite at ease there, chatting to acquaintances at every turn. Dominique had been danced off her feet by a succession of young men, most of them wearing flat caps – which seemed to be the fashion in that *quartier* – and giving themselves tough, laconic airs. The evening had not been without a hint of danger. A girl with sharp, black eyes and kiss-curls had begun talking loudly and gesticulating towards Dominique. Casimir had leaned over and murmured, 'I think you danced with her special friend.' There had been quite a scene, but eventually it had subsided. Dominique had found the whole night perfectly wonderful. Previously she'd visited Paris only under the careful supervision of her parents.

She opened her eyes again. She felt rather tired. They'd not got to bed till the early hours. Sarah was still poring over each exhibit in turn and writing in a small notebook. She looked chic in her slim black dress. Once Dominique had asked Sarah why she wore so much black. The reply had been a negligent shrug. 'That way everything matches everything else.' Dominique couldn't imagine anything duller than to wear the same colour so often. All the same

43

she admired Sarah's style. Last night, at the Bal Musette, she'd seemed so young and pretty with her shoulder-length dark hair curling round her face, brown eyes glowing in the muted light, and her olive skin flushed with the wine.

Dominique began to take note of the other visitors to the exhibition. Some were so colourless in their pinstriped suits, their faces bland and smooth. She wondered what they made of the bizarre images in front of them.

A woman walked by with a gaunt, ravaged face that somehow managed to be beautiful. Her hair was pulled tautly back from her temples then released into a waterfall of hennaed curls. Her eyebrows were pencilled swoops above deepset sockets smudged with gunmetal grey, her lips starkly etched in scarlet. She seemed a heroic figure, Dominique thought, like a character from a Greek tragedy, and much more in keeping with the outlandish notions on display. The woman paused in front of an ambiguous nude study and gazed at it, not changing her expression.

Dominique was susceptible to looks and mentally applauded anyone with a strong style of their own. Her eyes were caught by another figure about ten paces away from her – a man this time, tall, in a corduroy jacket with a dark shirt underneath. She thought he looked like a gypsy with his swarthy skin and fiercely moulded features – prominent cheekbones and uncompromising hooked nose. His hair was black and thick, though greying slightly, and long enough to fall over the collar of his jacket behind. Dominique guessed he must be in his late thirties – old – but his appearance had a compelling quality that made age irrelevant.

She watched with interest as he browsed among the photographs, pausing occasionally to peer closer. Eventually he came to where Sarah was standing and stopped alongside her. Both stared straight ahead of them lost in contemplation of a close-up of a voracious, rouged mouth.

Engrossed, Sarah made as if to move on and almost walked into him. She started, and obviously began to excuse herself. They were some way from Dominique now, and their confrontation was in dumb show. The two of them stopped short and gazed enquiringly at one another, then exploded in abrupt cries of recognition.

'Sarah!'

The man's stronger voice carried to her across the gallery, and he bent and kissed Sarah eagerly on both cheeks. There followed an excited conversation and much gesturing. Finally Sarah pointed in Dominique's direction and the two of them walked towards her.

'Dominique!' Sarah led the way. She looked flushed, pleased, and rather dazed. 'Incredible coincidence! I've just met an old friend!'

'He's stunning!' As they sat down to lunch in a restaurant three doors from the gallery, Dominique was agog. 'Where did you know him, Sarah?'

Sarah smiled guardedly across the red-checked tablecloth. 'It was an awful long time ago,' she said, speaking carelessly in an attempt to neutralize Dominique's over-eager curiosity, and reaching automatically for the menu. She felt unusually flustered without quite knowing why but put it down to the total unexpectedness of the encounter. Guy. She hadn't thought of him in years. They'd arranged to meet later at a café and spend the evening together.

'In the turbulent twenties?' Dominique teased. To her, the previous decade with its rumoured naughtiness was something of a joke. She'd picked up the attitude from Robert.

'I'm afraid so.' Sarah scanned the listed dishes vaguely, her mind still elsewhere. Dominique never bothered with menus, making her decision only after quizzing the waiter at length.

He appeared with a measured, professional smile which displayed regular white teeth under an upturned moustache. 'Ladies?'

Sarah made her decision on the spur of the moment. '*Poulet au riz* and salad.' She hated to dither and anyway, in this kind of solid restaurant, it was all much of a muchness. But Dominique recruited the smiling waiter to help her in her choice. He leaned over her, charmed. Sarah required nothing further of a waiter than that he do his job efficiently, but Dominique craved personal contact.

She laughed now at some small witticism of his, her face coloured by the light that filtered through the stained-glass panel in the door, the amber and red mingling in her bright, unruly hair. At Dominique's age Sarah had had a failed marriage and a stillborn child to her credit. Not for the first time she envied the girl her careless youth.

'*Sole au vin blanc*,' the waiter was insisting, like an indulgent uncle.

'It's good? You're sure?' Dominique's smile was wide and flirtatious.

'I guarantee it.' He put his hand to his heart.

They ordered two Pernods while they waited. Sarah had mixed feelings about the watery aniseed flavour, but it brought back memories, and after all this was Paris.

'Pretty, eh?' Dominique held her glass up so that it caught the colours of the stained glass, then she took a hefty swig. 'But you don't escape, Sarah. You were telling me about Guy.'

'There's no story attached.'

'But he kissed you . . . like a man who dies of thirst.'

'No.'

'An old flirtation. No?'

Sarah shook her head. 'No.' But an image came to her mind. Herself as a young girl on her last night in Paris. A much younger, slightly drunken Guy bending to kiss her. Gaslight in the bare studio flat. She'd pushed him away. Gently.

'Years ago I stayed in Paris for three months with a friend. Harold. A lover if you like.' Sarah turned her glass on the chequered cloth. 'But I've told you this before. We were idealistic little art students. We got to know Guy. And Rosa, his wife. We saw them a lot. We had fun together. Then Harold and I went home.' Shrugging her shoulders. 'That's all there is to tell.'

Dominique had already downed two-thirds of her Pernod. 'No, there's more. I feel it.' Her lower lip drooped, not unattractively, whenever the tiniest drop of alcohol entered her bloodstream.

Sarah smiled. 'You can't convey an atmosphere.'

She thought back. Probably her time as a student in London and the three months in Paris were the closest she'd ever come to the kind of heedless life Dominique enjoyed. But even then she'd been vastly more serious. Her studies had always come first. In their studio flat, flooded with sunshine, she and Harold had painted obsessively and talked of nothing but their work. The evenings spent with Guy and Rosa had been almost their only relaxation. There had been a special magic to those meetings, heightened by the obvious attraction that existed between Harold and Rosa, Guy and herself. 'We

47

had such good times. Lots of silly private jokes and laughs.'

Sarah had never dreamed of taking the attraction any further. Guy was married; Rosa was her friend. And during their months in Paris she and Harold had become so close. But Harold had had no such scruples. The incredulous pain of that betrayal was burned into her memory. Harold had reacted with a self-righteous and studied negligence . . .

'*Voilà, mesdames.*' The food arrived. The waiter boned Dominique's fish with dazzling dexterity. She exclaimed at his skill and he departed with a complacent little bow.

Sarah drained her Pernod. 'Since then I've completely lost touch with Guy and Rosa.'

5

Back at the Hôtel Lutétia, Casimir Szabo, Michael's painter friend, had left a message. Could Sarah and Dominique meet him and Annette at the Café de Flore on the corner of the boulevard Saint Germain that evening at half past eight? He had mentioned this café the previous night as an interesting place, fast becoming the haunt of writers, artists and film people.

Obviously Sarah couldn't go. She'd already arranged to meet Guy – and, she assumed, Rosa – at the Closerie des Lilas. But Dominique? Sarah offered her the choice. She dithered, having been intrigued by Guy's unusual looks, but in the end she plumped for the Flore. 'I think you'll be talking about the good old days,' she explained, with a wry lift of the eyebrows. 'The scandalous twenties.' Miming a vast and heartfelt yawn. 'No, I'll go to the Flore.'

It was settled. Sarah telephoned the Szabos to let them know and asked them to keep a wary, though discreet, eye on Dominique. While they were in Paris Sarah felt responsible for her, though in London what Dominique got up to was none of her concern. Annette laughed and told her not to worry. 'We'll sit one each side of her, like stone lions guarding a monument.'

Sarah decided to walk to the Closerie des Lilas. It was a superb late May evening, an evening of powdered gold, and a scent of tobacco hung in the air, stirring vague and pleasant feelings of nostalgia. A soft, warm breeze brushed her bare arms and this evening she'd rejected her practical black in favour of an expensive white crêpe dress, bought for a party and rarely worn. It was artfully cut on the bias, the skirt fluid and flattering. Dominique had exclaimed, 'You're so elegant!' as she turned Sarah this way and that, making enthusiastic, admiring sounds.

The contrast with her usual severe style was so marked that as she crossed the boulevard du Montparnasse Sarah herself had the brief fantasy of being a butterfly released from its inert, dun-coloured chrysalis. The couples she passed exuded the well-being that warm weather brings to cold, northern climates.

Both Sarah and Dominique had noticed since their arrival a far sharper awareness of the political situation. Probably the comforting presence of the Channel gave England an unreal sense of security. Only a few days earlier Hitler and Mussolini had entered into an unholy alliance, causing new ripples of consternation throughout Europe. But this evening politics seemed remote and pleasure ruled.

The approach to the Closerie des Lilas was intensely familiar to her. It was always comforting to rediscover the place. There, sure enough, was the bellicose statue of Marshall Ney, sword drawn, alongside the café. On the two or three occasions that Sarah had revisited Paris in the last ten years, she'd always made a pilgrimage there.

She and Harold had made it their local, allowing themselves one apéritif most days after a morning of concentrated work. They'd sat on the terrace too with Guy and Rosa many times, drinking wine in the gathering dusk. No doubt Guy had remembered this when he suggested meeting there. As she neared the café Sarah felt a tension that surprised her, as though the reunion was to be in some way momentous.

She strained her eyes to see whether she could make

out Guy's long figure, his dark shock of hair, and the smaller, fragile shape of Rosa, on the terrace under the tight, bright young leaves of the chestnut trees. Intently she scanned the faces of the customers. Then her eyes met Guy's. He was alone. He raised one hand in greeting and as she approached he stood up with the relaxed air that she remembered. Again he bent and kissed her on both cheeks.

'Sarah. You're so elegant,' he said, unconsciously echoing Dominique's words.

'No Rosa?'

'No.' A shade abrupt. 'And your friend?'

'Dominique had another engagement.'

'Good.' She recalled the direct manner of his speech. He softened his reaction a little by adding, 'A nice girl, sure. But we can talk better alone.' There was an American lilt to his English. He'd learnt much of it from the US expatriates who'd thronged Montparnasse in the twenties.

With a barely perceptible movement of the head he summoned a waiter. Sarah knew the man at once. Tall and thin with a dragoon moustache. Paul, his name was; it came to her out of nowhere. He used to joke with her and Harold, teasing them about their paint-stained fingers. He hadn't been there on later visits to the café. It was a shock to see what an old man he'd become. He didn't recognize her, and Sarah thought it pointless to try and introduce herself. Again she chose Pernod, and Guy ordered two.

He sat back in his chair, studying her, composed and amiable. 'It's so good to see you again.' Then, deliberately, he added, 'But, Sarah, this morning you asked me how was Rosa. I said she was well.' He shrugged. 'She is well. But I must tell you that Rosa and I are no longer together.'

51

Sarah was unprepared for the baldness of the statement, his total lack of preamble. Simultaneously, though, it occurred to her that this very directness had been one of the aspects of Guy she'd found most endearing. She was taken aback, but on second thoughts not terribly surprised. She'd understood too late that Guy and Rosa had an open, unconventional marriage. Rosa in particular had flaunted her sexual attractiveness. Their relationship had suggested risk.

'You're divorced?' With Guy there was no need to express routine regret.

He nodded.

'You still see each other?'

'Montparnasse, Saint Germain – they're villages. I see Rosa often. We're good friends.'

'And neither of you has remarried?'

'No.' An air of finality.

The waiter brought their drinks. Guy held his glass up in a laconic toast. Behind him, singly, the streetlights came on. A breeze ruffled the dark hair across his forehead and the realization hit her like a sharp shock that she still found him overwhelmingly attractive.

'And your friend Harold?' he asked. 'You still see him?'

Sarah replied drily, 'We quarrelled over politics.'

An image came back to her. Two years ago, when she'd first known Robert, he'd taken her to a rally of Oswald Mosley's Fascist Blackshirts. It had been a despicable affair, the elegant, aristocratic Mosley mouthing increasingly overt anti-Semitic jibes, cheered on by his followers, who were in the main brutal-looking thugs. Sarah described it to Guy. She and Robert had sat quite close to the platform, and Robert had heckled recklessly, drawing a dangerous amount of attention to himself.

Sarah's eyes momentarily met those of a black-clad acolyte on the rostrum, a pale, good-looking man with a beard. With horror she had recognized Harold, whom she hadn't seen for years. She felt sick and had to leave the meeting. Robert followed her from the hall, mystified, to the accompaniment of jeers and catcalls.

Guy nodded sagely. 'That doesn't astonish me.' A silence. Then he asked in a tone that wasn't quite casual, 'You're married, Sarah? *Divorcée*? A lover?'

She smiled, awkward suddenly. 'It's a long story.'

'You must tell me.' Again, the abruptness that she liked.

She began haltingly to talk to him about her husband, Stephen, and their life together, about New Mexico and Ruth, Stephen's death and her grief. She described the career and the life she'd made for herself since. Guy listened with grave interest, an intimacy blossoming between them. Sarah told him about Holman, her first husband, and their stillborn child, an episode already behind her when she first knew Guy, but which she'd kept close and secret. Guy talked about his rift with Rosa and the bitterness between them – now resolved into a stable friendship – and about the women he'd known since. As they exchanged confidences it grew darker around them so that the terrace with its tables and chairs and absorbed couples was like an island of light. Sarah asked Guy about his painting. Apparently he'd had a good deal of success in the early and mid-thirties with his career. Now he felt jaded and sombre, even guilty.

She was startled. 'Why guilty?'

'Many reasons.' His glass was empty. Absently he picked it up in his long, brown fingers and held it at an angle so that it caught the gleam of a nearby streetlamp. 'I have a friend in Vienna. He's a sculptor and a Jew.

Three months ago he visited me. He had escaped from his country. But first he had been held by the Gestapo.' An expression of disgust crossed Guy's face. 'He had been tortured and beaten. His eyes, his nose was like this.' He indicated the swelling with his hands across his own face. 'He was bruised, blue, and marked with cigarette burns. They have accepted him in America now. He is safe, but others . . . He has friends in Dachau and other camps.' Guy spread his hands. 'With this *connerie* so close to us painting seems mere . . . *égoisme*.'

Sarah remembered her relief last autumn when the peace had been saved. 'Yes. You're right . . . But we're so powerless.'

'Now I would be for war. You can't shut your eyes for ever.'

She didn't reply. War seemed to her too terrible to contemplate. At the same time she was ashamed of her selfish instinct for self-preservation. She thought of Albrecht, the young painter who lived near her. He'd escaped in good time. But to a life that wasn't of his choosing. She and Michael sat on committees to improve the lot of such people. But they risked nothing by doing so.

Guy said, almost inconsequentially, 'Rosa's Jewish.'

She hadn't known, but in the light of their conversation, the statement took on a new significance.

Suddenly Sarah shivered.

'You're cold. I've neglected you.' On the pale table top Guy placed a large, warm hand over one of hers. Their glasses were empty, forgotten. Neither had thought to order another drink, Sarah had lost all sense of time. She glanced at her watch. More than two hours they'd been sitting there. She could hardly believe it.

'You're hungry?'

It occurred to her that she was. She nodded. 'Famished.'

'You remember Chez Brice?' It was a smallish family restaurant in a sidestreet behind the rue de Vaugirard. Unpretentious and informal, with black and white marble-topped tables.

She nodded again. 'Of course.'

'A cognac, Sarah?' Guy prepared to summon the waitress.

Sarah leaned back on the red plush banquette. 'No more of anything. I feel wonderful. Any more and I might not feel quite so good.' She was expansive, euphoric, ready for indiscretion, a state of mind she rarely allowed herself.

They had eaten a hearty, aromatic ragoût, washed down with liberal amounts of Beaujolais. Guy, too, had recovered his spirits quite remarkably. They'd talked about the cinema and film stars. Guy was fanatical about American films and saw them whenever he had the chance. It helped his English, so he claimed. He could imitate James Cagney and Humphrey Bogart rather well for a Frenchman.

From time to time Arnaud, Brice's chubby son, stopped by at their table to refill the glasses, gliding away with a sinuous Fred Astaire swoop, and looking back over his shoulder for their reaction.

There was a comfortable, family atmosphere in the old-fashioned panelled restaurant. Arnaud's mother sat knitting in a shiny wooden and glass booth containing an imposing till. From time to time she called across to Guy with snippets of gossip about mutual acquaintances. Occasionally Brice emerged from the kitchen, rumpled in a large, striped apron, and played a move or two of chess

55

with a patient friend installed at a corner table with a small carafe of red wine.

Sarah found that their shared past – however remote – formed a kind of common ground between herself and Guy, so that they were far more at ease with one another than they would ordinarily have been at a first meeting. Random memories surfaced during the course of the evening and they resurrected some of the silly private jokes they'd invented all those years ago.

After the meal they strolled down the darkened street. Guy put his arm through hers, casually, as he used to. The wheezing, sentimental strains of an accordion drifted from a lighted café, along with sounds of laughter. Handsome in the muted, artificial light, he looked down at her.

'*Tu veux danser*, Sarah?' There was a caressing tone to his voice.

'Why not?' She spoke lightly, but experienced a vivid stab of anticipation at the implied physical contact.

Inside, the dance-floor was tiny and crowded, a mere oblong-shaped space between the tables. It was smoky and the lights were red-shaded, giving the innocent café a vaguely sleazy air. Given the lack of space the couples were forced to dance close, and they bobbed up and down in – to Sarah's eyes – a comically antiquated style.

But it was fun. Both she and Guy were still full of the euphoria that had invaded them in the restaurant. They took to the floor with a will, bobbing like the rest, wryly amused with themselves. The tunes were unknown to Sarah, chirpy and jangling.

Then the accordionist slowed the tempo. The dancing was reduced to a mere token, the couples clinging and moving on the spot. Guy pulled Sarah close. She didn't resist but relaxed against him, enjoying to the full the contact with his hard body. His hands moved, caressing her back. She had a sudden sense of unreality. This morning she had been taking cool, precise notes in an art gallery. The musician played a tune she recognized – 'The Way You Look Tonight'. Guy began to sing along with some of the words in his French-American accent. She grinned up at him, feeling happy.

He bent and placed his mouth on hers, slowly and deliberately. Sarah raised one hand to the back of his neck.

Guy pulled away. 'Come home with me.' His voice had a melting huskiness.

She barely hesitated. If there was one lesson she'd learned from Harold – and she'd learned it the hard way – it was not to refuse sexual opportunity if she wanted it. She wanted it now.

She said simply, 'Yes.'

Her decision to spend the night with Guy was a luxury, like a bottle of champagne brightening a workaday life. A thing apart, to be enjoyed for as long as it lasted and then forgotten. By some odd logic of her own, Sarah felt she was owed this night. Years ago she had refused Guy out of a misplaced loyalty to Harold. But Harold had required no such sacrifice.

Since Stephen's death she had entered, eyes open, into one or two affairs. But they had been unsatisfactory. There was nowhere for them to lead. She still remembered the ecstasy, the generosity Stephen had awakened in her, and lesser emotions seemed pallid. So the affairs petered out for lack of a direction. At least with Guy that problem wouldn't arise.

And physically she was more tempted than for years. Guy's bold gypsy face, his long, strong hands and his muscular body were powerfully attractive. Already graphic sexual images were writhing through her brain, making her tense with desire.

He lived in a studio flat off the boulevard Saint Germain. One large room which served all purposes. In her present state of anticipation she took in little about it, except that it seemed to be crammed with books and photographs and canvases. She noticed the bed-quilt, woven with stylized fan shapes in shades of brown and orange.

Guy stood there, tall in the arc of the lamp, his hands on her shoulders. 'So, Sarah.' Stroking the back of her neck under the ruffled hair. 'At last.'

In this total intimacy, stupidly she felt shy and out of practice. Wanting nothing but the oblivion of making love she reached for him prematurely, impatiently. Guy, she could see, would have proceeded more slowly, but he went with her, making her clumsiness all right, becoming as urgent in his turn. They coupled without finesse on the orange quilt, silent and convulsive. His face above hers was hard and impersonal. Afterwards he lay with one leg across her body, stroking her hair.

'You have no patience.' There was only the hint of a reproach.

'I know.' She lifted her head and looked steadily at him. The lamplight was muted and warm. 'I was scared. I don't know you. Not really.'

'Are you scared now?'

The deed was done. She felt calm. 'No.'

Deliberately Guy removed the rest of her clothes, then his own, and put them over the back of the chair. He stood by the bed, naked, his skin darker than hers, the hair on his body black and wiry. She shivered. He was so desirable.

'We'll be slower this time.' He climbed into the bed

beside her. His skin against hers was electric. He began to caress her insistently, precisely, with his strong fingers.

'It was worth it, Sarah. Don't you think? To wait for all those years?' Guy lay with an elbow each side of her, teasing, possessive, his face open and intimate. The weight of his body along the length of hers was relaxed and slick with sweat.

She nodded with a lazy smile, savouring the well-being in every part of her after the prolonged, convulsive climax. Her skin was damp and soft, the images still with her of Guy's hard arousal, his eyes lost and wolf-like, the whispered words in his own language, half understood, unbearably erotic.

'Infinitely worth it.' She lifted one arm languorously, gently touched his lips.

Softly he bit her finger. 'And next time we don't have to wait so long.'

6

At just after ten in the morning Dominique knocked on Sarah's door. The green satin coverlet from the hotel bed was draped round her, sari-wise, and her eyes were heavy with sleep. But she'd brushed her red-gold hair and it hung in a frizzy, Pre-Raphaelite cloud round her shoulders. There was no reply from the room. She knocked again. Then Sarah's muffled voice called her to come in.

It was unusual for Dominique to be the first up. Usually Sarah bullied and pleaded, even physically dragged her out of bed. And never after nine, no matter how late they'd been the night before.

Now Sarah lay groaning at the light, pulling the sheet up to hide her eyes as Dominique drew the heavy, rose-coloured curtains. 'What time is it?'

'After ten,' Dominique replied, happily self-righteous.

'God.' Sarah hoisted herself up to lean against the pillow, pushing her tousled hair away from her forehead.

'What time did you get back?' Dominique was curious. She herself had returned at about half past two and she'd noticed that Sarah's key was still uncollected.

'The early hours. The late early hours.' Sarah smiled with a flash of mischief. 'How was the Flore?'

'Wonderful!' Dominique gave a broad, reminiscent grin. 'We got talking to this friend of Casimir's. He was so witty and he wants to paint me. And Jacques Prévert was there. You know, the man who wrote *Quai des Brumes*.' Dominique mentioned a film from the previous year, hailed as a masterpiece. She hadn't seen it yet, but had championed it doggedly several times in discussions with Robert and his friends.

'. . . And he wants to make a film with you,' Sarah teased. Dominique's innocent egoism amused her.

'No.' The French girl pouted. 'But I saw him looking at me – and once he smiled. It's a remarkable place. You must go there, Sarah.' Remembering her manners. 'And how was your night out?'

'Wonderful.' A brilliant smile.

Dominique was struck. 'You look like the cat with the cream. What did you do?'

'Had a drink and talked.' She smoothed the dimpled pink coverlet. 'Then a nice meal. Then Guy showed me his flat . . . Oh, he's divorced now. He lives alone . . .' Sun streamed through the window, finding chestnut lights in Sarah's dark hair. Her face was pretty and flushed with a sort of secret animation, unwarranted by her account of an unexceptional evening out. One might almost have thought . . . But Sarah was so *raisonnable*. Dominique quickly checked her sudden unworthy suspicion.

'Today,' she announced grandly, 'I look for work. A good, steady job.'

'You?' Sarah laughed, stretching and leaning back against the starched white pillow as she raised her hands behind her head. 'Pull the other one, Dominique.' She mimicked a favourite expression of Robert's.

'No.' Dominique played up to the interest she'd aroused. 'I am going to become a working girl.'

'What on earth put that idea into your head?'

'I have a plan.' Dominique settled herself on the end of Sarah's bed, adjusting her green satin wrap. She looked endearingly self-important and pleased with herself. 'You see, I've decided that Paris is my spiritual home.'

'Really?' Sarah raised an eyebrow.

'I want to stay here . . . I feel good here. London . . .'
She shrugged. 'Well, at the *collège* they want me to be
too serious.'

'It's a pity you don't enjoy it. You've got talent.'
Occasionally at the Fulham Road flat Dominique had
dabbled with Sarah's paints, producing bright, original,
impressionistic water-colours. But Sarah couldn't imagine
her ever buckling down willingly to an academic routine.

Dominique ignored the remark. 'And I don't want to
go back and rot in Évian with my parents and wait for Mr
Right.' A gamine grin. The expression, Mr Right, struck
her as irresistibly funny. 'I want to stay here in Paris. But
my parents won't allow it unless I can tell them I already
have a job and somewhere to live.'

'What kind of a job?' Sarah thought it sounded rather
a good idea. She could imagine Dominique thriving in the
enthusiastic bohemianism of Saint-Germain-des-Prés.

The French girl waved her arms vaguely. 'I can't type,
but I have three languages.' As well as French and English
she spoke remarkably correct and confident German,
learned at her strict convent school. 'I'll wear a suit and a
white blouse and pin up my hair.' She demonstrated,
holding up her bright curls with her two hands, startling
and exotic in her green sari. 'And I'll look serious.'
Summoning an expression of eagerness, humility and
willingness to learn, a look quite dazzling in its sincerity.

'I like it.' Sarah watched her, suppressing laughter.
'Well, if all else fails, Dominique, you can always go on
the stage.'

Dominique's decision to search for a job was rather
convenient from Sarah's point of view. She and Guy had
arranged to meet for lunch. At present her feelings were

in a turmoil, and she suspected that the presence of a third party would have made matters worse.

As it was, Sarah was relieved when Dominique – looking most unlike herself in a grey suit and shiny black shoes, her hair tied behind in a black bow – kissed her goodbye and strode off down the hotel corridor, a resolute light in her eye.

Sarah bathed and dressed with a deliberate lack of haste, reliving a kind of mosaic of impressions from the previous night. Isolated words, expressions, tones of voice, images, drifting at random through her brain. She was almost unaware of her physical surroundings. She felt emotional and vulnerable, like a young girl, the instability heightened by lack of sleep.

She grew impatient with herself. It was stupid. She had viewed the night as a luxury. It was nothing more. Ridiculous to get sentimental about it. She put on a black shirt and skirt, refusing to dress up or try and look alluring.

Sarah had washed her hair, leaving it to dry naturally in curls to her shoulders. Now she stood in front of the amber sunburst mirror in the hotel bedroom to brush it and catch it off her forehead with two side-combs. She was shocked by her eyes, deep, staring and intense, dwarfing her small olive face and pale lips. Their look was naked. Instinctively she half closed her lids. It was pointless to deny it; she hadn't felt like this since . . .

'Can't you stay?' His tone was direct, neither hectoring nor pleading.

'No, I can't. Ruth's expecting me.' Lying back in the dappled shade of the chestnut trees. As she spoke Sarah pictured her daughter's fair hair and grave, grey eyes with a sudden wave of longing. Close by, other children played, shrill and quarrelsome.

'Where is she?'

'She's staying with a friend. They're sleeping in a tent in the garden.'

Guy shrugged. 'So she's happy. Why can't you stay?'

Sarah shook her head. 'She's happy because she knows when I'm coming back.'

'So we have only tomorrow.' His face was closed as he screwed up the paper that had wrapped their picnic cheese and ham. Rolling it into a ball and skimming it abruptly and accurately into a nearby bin, the routine gesture invested with a kind of savagery. Turning back to her. 'You're incorruptible, you know.'

Precisely he laid the flat of his hand on the skin in the V of her shirt, his face expressionless. 'I like your black clothes. You look different. Like yourself.'

Her body reacted instantly to his touch. She tried to hide the fact with a show of negligence. 'What shall we do this afternoon?'

His look was amused and blatant, inviting her complicity. 'I know exactly what I want to do.'

Sarah sat on the rumpled wreck of Guy's bed, arms round her drawn-up knees. The orange coverlet lay in a heap on the floor. Guy had opened the window on to the balcony and rich early evening sunlight filtered through the pale curtains, which moved from time to time in a light breath of wind. A canvas stood on the easel, a city landscape, a watery, brilliant sun outlining stormy slate-blue clouds. It had the rolling, rhythmic quality she remembered of Guy's painting. Sarah had the impression that time was slowed almost to stopping. Each detail of the room presented itself, sharp and precise, to be memorized. She was torpid and satiated. The afternoon would never end.

Guy lay beside her, watching her, silent. Reaching to touch her skin, idly tracing the line of her backbone. 'Sarah.'

'Mmm?' She turned, smiling, to look at him, hair falling across her face.

'*Je t'aime, tu sais.*'

She kissed her fingers and lightly laid them against his lips.

'It's done! I'm a working girl.' There was a scraping sound as Dominique pulled out a chair for herself at the table where Sarah, Guy, and another woman were already seated. Arriving at the Hôtel Lutétia, she'd had a telephone message from Sarah to meet her at Chez Brice. Dominique was elated. Her day had been wholly successful. She still wore her smart grey suit, rather pleased with the businesslike air it conferred.

'What sort of a job?'

'I'm a travel agent.' The bureau she'd applied to had arranged three interviews for her. In fact the second job had suited her very well. She had been interviewed by a Monsieur Rambert, a small, choleric man with a florid face that overhung his stiff white collar. But he'd been visibly impressed by her earnest manner and linguistic ability, calling her *chère mademoiselle* at every opportunity and offering her a job on the spot. Dominique shrugged carelessly, laying down her handbag on the marble table top. 'It'll do till something more inspiring comes along.'

'You found a room?' Guy spoke in French.

'That too,' she beamed. 'It's a rat-hole in the rue Jacob, but it's cheap. And I've phoned my parents. They were rather miffed. But they're giving me a chance to make good.' It was a breezy understatement of the case. In fact her father – under the impression that she was still redeeming her soul in London at the Royal College – had been beside himself. But he and her mother were off on holiday to Switzerland in the morning. They'd promised retribution at a later date. Dominique was unfazed. She'd face that when she had to.

Sarah introduced the unknown woman. 'Dominique, this is Rosa.'

'*Enchantée.*' Dominique extended her hand impulsively, awkwardly, palm upward. The older woman took it, seeming amused, and shook it like that. About Sarah's age, she was darkly handsome with a long, expressive face that was attractive and lived-in both at once. She wore a flowered dress in dark reds and violets, and sombre amethyst earrings.

'Rosa's a pianist.'

Dominique was impressed. 'Concert pianist?'

'No.' Rosa gave a slow, self-mocking smile. 'Ballet classes. Choir practices. Bar mitzvahs.'

'Thursday night jazz at the Café Philo,' Guy chipped in.

'I'm versatile, if nothing else.'

'You're brilliant,' Guy reproved her. Then, addressing Dominique, 'She can play anything, any style, with her eyes shut.'

Rosa interposed mildly. 'I don't have to shut my eyes.'

Arnaud appeared at their table, stolid and unhurried, with his notebook. They ordered *coq au vin*. Over the meal they talked about the surrealist photography exhibition, which Rosa had seen as well. She and Dominique were enthusiastic but Guy and Sarah had reservations.

They were instinctively hostile to the detached quality of the photographs, their lack of warmth.

'They make me think of a lizard, looking at the world with dead eyes.' Sarah spoke French hesitantly, but rather well.

Dominique began to lose track of the conversation, mesmerized by her gradual awareness of currents passing between Sarah and Guy. It wasn't anything they said. The discussion could hardly be more neutral. But Sarah glowed with a kind of luminous animation, her eyes deep and dark. A lock of hair fell across her brow. She shook it back absentmindedly. It flopped again. Guy leaned across the table and tucked it behind her ear in a movement rich with sexual intimacy. As he did so, their eyes met, and a calm, secret smile passed between them.

Suddenly it was glaringly obvious to Dominique that the two of them had made love mere hours earlier, that her hastily suppressed suspicion of that morning had been correct. Sarah had never looked like this. There was incredulity and a sort of disapproval. They were adults. Such secrets belonged to the young. She had an unreasonable sense of betrayal, having seen Sarah as serene and wise, beyond such weakness. The conversation bowled on without her.

'Eat, Dominique.' Suddenly she realized that Rosa was addressing her. 'You're way behind the rest of us.'

7

Ruth lay in the tent on a khaki sleeping-bag. Her skinny legs, ending in gym shoes, were propped high against a precarious pole. Idly she examined the tiny blonde hairs on her legs, golden in the sunlight that filtered through the open tent flap. It was Saturday. No school. Her friend, Christine, was reading a comic and eating an apple. Ruth was bored and slightly grumpy. It had been fun sleeping in the tent, for the first couple of nights at least. But inevitably she and Christine had giggled and whispered through most of the night, so that in the daytime they felt unreal and light-headed. Sarah would be back later today. Ruth pictured her own bed with its cool sheets. It seemed the ultimate luxury.

Christine's brother, Malcolm, stuck his head through the tent flap. 'Squirrel-cheeks,' he said, conversationally, provocatively. It was an insult that had the power to pierce Christine's hide. She felt it to be true.

'Pillock!' she spat back, skimming her apple core deftly at the boy and catching him just above the ear. 'He's such a pain in the neck.' Then she returned to her comic. Surprisingly the apple core wasn't returned. Malcolm was distracted by the arrival of a friend.

Christine had three brothers. All four children bickered from morning till night. As ever, Ruth found herself envying her friend the privilege of having brothers to treat with such casual dislike. All the same she wouldn't be sorry to get back to the quiet of her own flat. It was always so noisy here.

'Don't worry! I'll rout her out.' Ruth's heart leaped. It was Sarah's voice, calling back to someone in the house. So she was home! Already.

'Mum!' She scrambled to her feet, brushing her head against the sloping canvas roof. Stepping unceremoniously over Christine she dived through the flap.

She blinked in the sunlight. There was her mother, smiling, wonderfully familiar. Ruth threw herself into Sarah's arms.

Sarah found herself in a state of heightened awareness that was almost uncomfortable. Suddenly the world seemed full of a breathless beauty. On the journey home she stayed on deck, spellbound by the silver shimmer of the sunlit sea and the tender, transparent blue of the horizon. She sat entranced in the bright, clear air, hair whipping across her face. Life seemed so spacious to her, so good.

Then there was Ruth. Her slight figure in boyish shirt and shorts. Her open-hearted grin. It came almost as a shock to recall how quick she was, how graceful, how perfect.

As they walked home her daughter rattled on about a science lesson they'd had the day before. An experiment had gone wrong. There'd been an explosion and the teacher had singed her eyebrows.

'Honestly, Mum, she looked so surprised and sort of daft, we couldn't stop ourselves laughing.' Turning to Sarah, her grey eyes dancing with the memory. Unselfconscious and so full of life. 'Weren't we mean?' Sarah's heart contracted with a tenderness that was like pain.

They bought fish and chips and ate them in the back garden out of the paper, talking non-stop and washing down the food with a bottle of dandelion and burdock.

Happy with the impromptu meal and with each other's company.

There was a kind of relief at being back in her own territory after the overwhelming, unlooked-for intensity of Paris. Sarah could breathe for a space while she made room for this new and compelling dimension to her life. In any case she'd be seeing Guy soon. He'd vowed to come over in July.

Ruth stood up, licking her fingers and wiping them on the seat of her shorts, knowing that today nothing was taboo, and taking full advantage. 'Ginger Rogers is on at the Rialto, Mum.' A calculated, ingratiating grin. 'We *are* going, aren't we?'

Michael was pleased with Sarah's article on the surrealist exhibition in spite of the fact that her opinions on the subject were diametrically opposed to his own. He'd had one or two letters recently accusing *Liaisons* of being little more than a mouthpiece for the surrealists. 'This'll put paid to all that nonsense,' he decided, flourishing her typescript like an offensive weapon.

In the weeks following her return from Paris she saw a great deal of Michael and his new wife, Tessa. Sarah was in excellent spirits, working hard, and looking forward to Guy's visit. Perhaps her own sunny mood was one of the reasons she found herself liking Tessa far more than she'd ever expected. True, there were only the most minimal opportunities for the close, quiet talks she enjoyed with Michael. But a three-sided conversation – with Tessa's commonsensical, dry comments – was increasingly an agreeable substitute.

In fact there was a great deal more to Tessa than Sarah would have guessed from her surface air of brisk efficiency. She had a wry, endearing sense of humour and a gurgling, irresistible laugh, coupled with a comical sense of despair over her own inability to keep a blouse tucked into a skirt, or her blonde hair in curl or her stocking seams straight. At the same time Tessa was sensitive to music, and poetry and paintings to the point of sentimentality. And she had contacts in all these spheres of activity, along with the uncanny ability to produce tickets at the drop of a hat for concerts and plays reputedly long since sold out.

She and Michael appeared very happy. They had an affectionate, jokey relationship that seemed built to last. Sarah knew that henceforth her dealings with Michael would be altered. She would never again see him vulnerable or at a loss. His most secret thoughts belonged to Tessa. That was as it should be. Still she couldn't deny the occasional stab of regret at the knowledge.

Their contentment was a wholesome, solid thing, but to Sarah, possessed by her new passion for Guy, it was somehow prosaic and tame. Perhaps it was just that they were adults and she had never grown up. She had read in Dominique's eyes a kind of disapproval, and Michael, months back, had accused her of having too uncompromising an attitude towards love. When she thought of Guy's gypsy face and dark body she tensed with an urgent, feral lust. The calm and caution she'd built round herself over the last years seemed utterly routed. She still wasn't sure, though, how this new turbulence was going to fit into her life.

For a week or so after her return Sarah saw nothing of Robert. Then he arrived unexpectedly one morning as she was showing a couple of prospective clients round her studio. They were art dealers, young and citified, patently prosperous. Their faces had the kind of smooth arrogance

71

calculated to bring out the worst in Robert. Sarah was secretly relieved that the business side of the meeting had already been successfully concluded.

As it was, Robert merely sat on an upright chair in one corner of the long, light room until they left, looking down at his feet and radiating an almost tangible aura of hostility.

'How can you do business with those oily bastards?' he growled, as she came back into the studio after seeing them off.

'Unfortunately I don't have the choice.' Sarah began to collect up the canvases propped here and there about the room. Robert in this mood was a pain in the neck. None the less she still preferred him to the 'oily bastards'. 'I've got the rent to pay and a daughter to clothe and feed, so I can't afford the luxury of waiting for clients with the right political credentials.' She added pointedly, 'Nor do I have a daddy and mummy to keep me supplied with ready cash.' This wasn't quite fair. Robert earned what he could and hated to take money from his parents for his studies, though they'd have made any sacrifice. They themselves were uneducated and he was their pride and joy.

To her surprise Robert made no effort to pursue his line of thought. Listless, he lounged in her worn leather armchair, smoking a cigarette with quiet concentration and gazing out of the window. He looked pale, as though the summer sun had never touched him. He moved slightly and his head came into a shaft of harsh sunlight. Sarah was shocked at the shadows under his eyes, the puffiness of his young face. He had on a grey sweater and trousers. They were crumpled as if he'd worn them for too long. She had been wondering how he'd cope with

Dominique's absence. The answer, evidently, was very badly.

She sat down on the chair opposite him. He was passive, content to sit silent as though she weren't there. Normally he was bursting with gossip and ideas, eager and opinionated.

'How are the exams going?' He was in the middle of his finals.

He looked at her absently and shrugged. A brief smile turned into a grimace. 'I can't seem to get interested.'

'But you'll pass?'

'I doubt it.' His indifference was frightening. Robert was cocky and ambitious. Her heart went out to him. Possibly this dull resignation was something of a pose. But, clearly, beneath it lay a searing hurt.

She said gently, 'It's Dominique, isn't it?' Though there was no need to ask.

He said nothing. Then, 'Yeah, it's Dominique.' And in a snarl, bleak and overloud, 'What else? Everything's Dominique.'

Sarah thought of the girl, so vivid and happy in her bright, thoughtless vanity, planning her conquest of Paris. Her vital red hair and broad smile. The contrast with Robert's grey suffering. 'It couldn't have lasted, Robert. She's not ready.' The happiness was no fault in her. She hadn't promised him anything. 'She's just restless. Adventurous.'

There was a kind of shrinking at the description, as if he found it too painful to bear. A silence. 'I won't ever get over her, you know.' He looked down at the grey-green rug beneath his feet. 'She's not like anyone else.' The words jerked out. It was clear he found them almost too personal to utter. Her heart wept for the laying low of his arrogance.

'You won't believe me, Robert. Things do pass. In time. You *will* get over it.' She'd lived the truth of her own words more than once, but to him they were conventional and without meaning. He ignored them.

Fixing her with a strangely baleful look. 'You know what? I wish the war would come. I really wish it. That way my life'd be taken out of my own hands.'

She touched his arm. 'You could well be lucky.' Hitler's claims to Danzig dominated the news with increasing insistence.

Robert lit a fresh cigarette from the stub of the old one, and began to smoke it, his face as blank and unresponsive as a sleepwalker's.

8

Dominique remembered telling Sarah that Paris was her spiritual home. At the time it had simply been a glib remark she thought sounded rather well. But as the weeks passed she became more and more convinced that unwittingly she'd spoken the truth.

There were her digs in the rue Jacob. She'd described them as a rat-hole, but they suited her perfectly. Her room was strictly functional, with a white-painted wooden bedstead – the sheets changed fortnightly – a table, two chairs, and a chest of drawers. Since she was rarely at home she'd done nothing to prettify the place, but her clothes, draped over every piece of furniture, gave it a chaotic, lived-in look.

And there was a pleasing anarchy about her fellow-residents. Dominique reflected happily that her parents would have hated every one of them.

Across the corridor lived Horvath, a punctilious young painter. For two weeks at a time he'd sit in his room from morning till night, churning out the most vapid and sentimental of landscapes, the kind of thing Dominique had been taught to despise from her earliest childhood. After a fortnight's solid work he would take a whole bundle of canvases to the *quais* opposite the Île de la Cité. Competitively priced, they sold like hot cakes. Then for a week he'd celebrate, with the clink of bottles, and singing, and an assortment of tough-looking male lovers, until his money ran out and the cycle would begin all over again.

Below her was Suzanne, a genteel prostitute who called her clients 'my gentlemen' and whose room was a positive bower of cushions and draperies and fringes and artificial flowers.

On the floor above lived Edmond, a medical student. He made a habit of knocking on her door late at night to engage her in political conversation, while his eyes flickered with a life of their own at the sight of her in a thin, white nightdress.

The job she found easy and fun. Getting up early was the worst part. But once that was over it was no hardship during the summer months to wash in cold water in the communal bathroom – she was the only resident up at this hour – put on the smart, formal clothes that rather amused her, and walk to Rambert's travel agency, just a few streets away. There she felt almost as if she were acting a part, gracious, helpful and, above all, humble. Everyone was impressed by the deft way she could switch from language to language. Dominique suspected that Monsieur Rambert had a crush on her. He seemed to treat her with special consideration, and go slightly pink when she talked to him.

But the evening was the focus of her day. She'd change into clothes that were becoming daily more outrageous as she mixed unlikely colours and barbaric jewellery bought from the flea-market. Then she'd set out, with the deliberate intention of making contacts and getting herself noticed, to some fashionable café – the Flore, the Dôme, or the Deux-Magots. She saw them as havens of light and opportunity. They represented the world she aspired to – artistic, bohemian and stylish. Here she could rub shoulders with actors and film-makers, writers and sculptors, the famous and the unknown. Dominique knew that she had nothing to offer – yet – in the way of success, but she was prepared to pay her dues with patience and persistence.

She kept her ears open for scraps of inside information about the people she knew by sight, and picked up gossip about films in the making, books being written, plays in rehearsal. She was good at this. With her native wit she turned the snippets to her advantage, dropping them into her conversation negligently, giving the impression that she was in the know.

A middle-aged painter called Raymond, with quite a solid reputation, asked her to sit for him. But it became clear when she got to his studio that his main intention was to inveigle her on to a dusty *chaise-longue* in a dark corner of the room. He tried to kiss her. His breath smelt of strong cigarettes and, oddly enough, cough lozenges.

He whispered huskily, 'You're so appetizing, Dominique. You're like a peach.'

She fended him off good-naturedly, and he became sarcastic and sulky. Dominique took the setback philosophically. It was just a hiccup in her continuing plan of campaign.

By now she was recognized as a regular at all three cafés, and at each there was a little group she could sit with as of right. Mostly they were young hopefuls like herself, trying to feel their way, some talented, some not. Dominique kept quiet about her daytime job – so, probably, did the rest of them – but she dropped hints about her painting. It was a handy prop to be going on with.

From time to time she ran into Casimir or Annette Szabo, or Guy. They passed the time of day with her, but generally speaking moved in their own circles. Occasionally, though, she had a drink and a chat with Rosa. The older woman seemed to like her and to be interested in any small success Dominique had notched up since their last meeting. She never condescended. Dominique admired Rosa's exotic clothes, her heavy brown eyes and voluptuous mouth, and imagined her to be something of a *femme fatale*. She was secretly flattered to be seen on friendly terms with such a striking creature.

Each Sunday afternoon, without fail, Dominique sat down at the table in her dowdy room to compose a long letter to her parents. She talked at length about happenings at the travel agency, and amused herself by inventing a list of worthy pastimes – concerts, plays, lectures, long walks. She picked on a female colleague, an anxious, mousy girl called Thérèse, to be her companion on these imaginary expeditions. According to her letters the two of them spent every spare minute on improving jaunts. Sometimes they even attended early morning Mass together. In this way she hoped to soothe her parents' fears and suspicions about life in the capital. It seemed the ploy was successful. Gradually they appeared to accept Dominique's new plans as a *fait accompli*, and the awful retribution threatened by her father on the telephone never came.

9

The meadow shimmered, hazy with buttercups, marguerites, clover, and pale, rosy spikes of dock. On the bank opposite, a massive thicket of dog roses trailed thin, arching branches into the water, the blossoms pink, fading to white as they became full-blown. On her way to Maggie's, Sarah had stopped her Morris and parked it by the roadside. She thought this meadow beautiful and wanted to show it to Guy. In the blue sky the few fluffy clouds were outlined with a white that shone silver. In this pastoral Hertfordshire setting Guy looked more than ever swarthy, foreign, almost forbidding.

'Very pretty.' He gazed round him. 'Very domestic.'

She was obscurely let down by his reaction, and remembered that he was from Provence, where the landscape was rugged and dramatic. Her disappointment must have showed. He took her arm. 'I like it. Really.' Spanning her wrist.

Sarah looked down at his dark hand on her smooth arm. How unreal it seemed to her, suddenly, that he now had the right to touch her, casually, in this way. Somehow she'd always found it hard to grasp that strangers came together – chose each other out of the whole world – then gradually built up a web of habits, rights and expectations. As yet, she and Guy weren't in very deep. There was passion, quick and close to the surface, but no claims.

'We're strangers.' She voiced the thought with surprise.

'Yes.' His hand slid up her body, coming to a stop over her left breast. To Sarah the gesture symbolized the contradiction. The intimacy. Their separateness. 'But it's exciting to make love to a stranger. You think so too.'

'Yes.' Picturing his hotel room yesterday. Carpeted, standardized. The modern divan bed with its beige, anonymous coverlet. Identical to the one next door, no doubt, and the one beyond that. In the anodyne surroundings the convulsions of their bodies had seemed the more animal, urgent, almost ugly. And exciting, yes.

'One day we'll be old friends.' His lips came down on hers, deliberately. She felt his tongue open her mouth. Like this he had the power to rouse her instantly. When he stood back she could read the desire in his eyes. 'One day.' He smiled slowly. 'But not yet.'

The garden was fragrant with lax, voluptuous roses, mock orange and lavender just coming into bloom. As usual Maggie was welcoming and hospitable, feeding them royally with cold meat, pâté, salads, and warm, fresh bread, and serving the chilled Muscadet that was one of the hallmarks of the home at Alder.

Ilya had hoped to be there, but he was busy at the theatre. He was working all hours recently. 'It's only a drawing-room comedy,' Maggie commented tartly. 'But from the fuss the management's making you'd think they were staging *Tamburlaine the Great*.'

The boys were at school, so it was just Maggie, looking cool and pretty in a flimsy yellow blouse and a skirt that seemed to be made out of silk scarves, her hair drawn back into a ballet dancer's chignon. She had set up the table at the edge of the lawn under an apple tree. Natasha, the Labrador, lay alongside, eyeing the three of them mournfully and meaningfully.

Guy was enchanted with Maggie's domain. After the meal he asked to be shown round the house and garden and was obviously captivated by its sprawling charm. But he was horrified by the state of the vegetable garden. 'Name of God. This is a crime.' Tough clumps of groundsel and the young, sticky fronds of goosegrass had taken over. He bent and pulled some weeds by hand. 'It looks like a forgotten graveyard.'

Maggie pulled a face. 'I know, it's awful, but Ilya's so busy and I never seem to find the time. And to be frank I really only like growing flowers, anyway.'

Guy shook his head. 'Where do you keep the . . .?' He made a hoeing motion. Maggie pointed to the shed, close by. He said decisively, 'I'll do it for you.'

'No, Guy.' Maggie was shocked. 'You're my guest.'

He stood his ground, smiling, but firm. 'I must. It hurts me to see this.' Indicating the weeds with a sweeping gesture.

He looked out the tools he needed and started straightaway. Sarah was intrigued by his air of competence. He worked with rhythmic, economical movements and obviously knew what he was doing.

She and Maggie retired to the shade of the apple tree. Watching his progress – the rangy figure bent over the hoe, the intent expressionless face – Sarah suddenly glimpsed him as a peasant, with generations of peasant blood in his veins. She could picture him working like that, steady and unhurried, in the furnace of some sunbaked Provençal landscape pictured by Van Gogh.

Abruptly she asked Maggie, 'What do you think of Guy?'

'I don't know him, do I?' Maggie met Sarah's eye frankly. 'He seems to be his own man, and that's good, I think. If you like him that's enough for me.' She patted Sarah's arm with a grin. 'I trust you to pick a good 'un.'

A silence. Then Sarah said slowly, 'You know, Maggie,

I've been knocked sideways. Nothing like this has happened to me since . . . well, Stephen. But it's a gut reaction.' Natasha pushed a cold, wet nose against her knee and was petted absently. 'He says he loves me and I say the same, and God knows I mean it. But I don't know him. I felt that very strongly this morning.' She nodded towards the vegetable garden and Guy's workmanlike figure. 'That, for instance, it's a revelation. I've only ever seen him in Montparnasse, and it's not quite the same.'

It was two hours or so before Guy was satisfied. The plot looked immaculate and organized. For good measure he'd staked the sprawling tomato plants so they stood to attention in rows like soldiers. Maggie admired his handiwork and he gave her advice in his abrupt French-American accent. He said very seriously, 'You must not neglect it like that again, Maggie. It's important to grow food. It's not a hobby.' She nodded gravely.

Maggie went into the house to make coffee before they left, and Sarah turned to Guy. 'You've surprised me.'

Guy was crouched down, making friends with Natasha. He looked up and shrugged. 'I'm a country boy.'

Ruth kept her distance. She wasn't a child to give friendship easily. When Guy was at the flat she was straight-backed, straight-faced and self-contained. Not hostile, simply holding herself in reserve.

Nor did Guy try to force his personality on her. Once in a while he'd ask her a question, casually, as though he were dealing with an adult, and Ruth would answer with a composed gravity. One night he helped her with her French homework, and afterwards, like a present, she gave him her first wholehearted smile. 'They'll wonder how I got so good so quickly.'

However, this small breakthrough wasn't followed up.

For the rest of the week Ruth was away on a school trip to Stratford-on-Avon.

'Your daughter has a terrifying dignity,' Guy remarked to Sarah out of nowhere. He was sitting on the long brown velvet sofa in the living room, leafing through the current *Picture Post*. Sun poured in at the window, lighting up the grey strands in his hair. 'I wouldn't dare insult her intelligence by treating her as a child.'

He grinned at Sarah. 'She's like you. Both of you look at the world from inside. Through a window.' Framing his eyes with his hands, as though to demonstrate. 'And you make up your own minds – without haste. It's remarkable how you're alike.' He added, as an afterthought, 'But she doesn't look like you.'

Sarah said sharply, 'She takes after Stephen.'

He looked at her, without comment, for a long, uncomfortable moment, then deliberately down again at his magazine. She was startled by her own acerbity. By now she was well used to talking about Stephen openly and without reserve. Why should she suddenly be so abrupt with Guy? It was unnerving to be wrongfooted like this by tensions she hadn't known existed.

The moment passed. They spent the day browsing round the back streets of Chelsea and Soho. Guy wasn't keen on conventional sightseeing. In the evening they drove out to a country pub and drank beer and bought pork pies with hard-boiled eggs inside. Guy ate his with relish, but thought the raw pink and yellow an execrable colour combination.

Later that night, in bed in his hotel room, he asked her gently, 'Is Stephen still alive for you?'

She was struck by the way he'd phrased the question. It was unexpected. Guy often was. She thought about it. 'No. Not at all. I've accepted his death completely.'

'Today you looked troubled when you talked of him.' His arms went round her naked body. She settled drowsily against him. With this warmth and peace she could look into herself without fear.

'I think it was talking about him to *you*.' For a second she had felt unfaithful, experiencing for the first time emotions as powerful as those she'd felt for Stephen. 'It was only for a moment.' She had no urge to look back. The present was all-absorbing.

After that Guy had three more days to stay. It was a lazy, private time. They got up late and saw no one. They didn't go out much, but talked endlessly, sitting on the bench in Sarah's back yard in the sun, or lying on her patch of grass side by side. Sarah took photographs. Guy bare-chested by the back door, eyes narrowed against the sun, his hair tousled. Guy again, in the garden of the local pub, in his shirtsleeves, holding up a very British mug of beer. By the end of the week she had largely lost her sense of their strangeness. Imperceptibly they had advanced to a closer plane of understanding.

Guy talked to her about his childhood in Provence. His father had had a smallholding. Guy was the oldest of four sons and the family had lived off the soil, selling their surplus produce for the money to buy extras. From his earliest childhood he'd helped on the land, though his parents made sure that his education wasn't neglected. His life, like Sarah's, had been disrupted by the war. For four years Guy had been the man about the house, doing a man's job, shouldering responsibilities almost too great to bear.

Afterwards, in the early twenties, when he announced his decision to go to Paris and earn his living as a painter, the family had been scandalized, though there were younger brothers eager to carry on the tradition. Even now, a generation later, when he went home, successful and bringing money, he was treated as the family wastrel.

'I don't think it would be different if I were a doctor,' Guy added with a wry smile. 'In their eyes the soil is the only living.' Sarah could see that, like most people, he still carried his childhood scars.

On his last day there was a storm. They sat in the glass lean-to and watched the rain. It was cool. The sky was a livid blue-black colour and the surrounding trees appeared lime-green by contrast. Sarah went and stood in the doorway, breathing in the smell of the moistened earth. Guy came up behind her, placing his hand on the nape of her neck. 'You know, Sarah, all week, since Maggie's, I've had this picture in my head.'

She turned and smiled. 'What's that?'

'There was this house near us when I was a child. It was beautiful. Quite large, old, and painted a gold colour, the colour of sand. And the walls had such texture.' He leaned forward and gently kissed her cheek. 'And there was land. An acre, maybe less. A vine. And cypresses. That house comes to my mind now, all the time. And I imagine living there with you.'

'That's a nice fantasy.' She looked out at her own small back yard. Her own territory. It was tempting to go along with Guy's vision, encourage him, elaborate on it, an attractive dream. But she was rooted in her own life, and the two weren't necessarily compatible. Her priority, always, had to be Ruth.

'Such things can come true,' he was teasing now, and laconic. 'It's a fantasy, but one day . . .'

'Look, a rainbow.' It was magnificent, the colours strong and glowing against the dull sky. They stood silent, consciously sharing the glory of it.

85

Then Guy spoke, suddenly earnest. 'If there's war, Sarah,' his arms tightened round her, 'and if I can't see you for a long time, I don't want you to forget me. You understand.' He placed his hands one each side of her head. 'There. You *will* remember.'

She had a feeling then of immense desolation. The rainbow was fading almost as quickly as it had come and the bleak sky remained. Few people now doubted the imminence of war, though they might cling to a blinkered hope. With Guy's presence and the sunny, lazy days, she had allowed the thought to retreat to the back of her mind. But there was no escaping. At that moment, selfishly, all she could think was that her unfledged happiness would be brought low at a stroke, not by any weakness in itself, but by forces she was powerless to control.

'You don't really think I'd forget you.' To her ears the words had a hollow, neutral ring, making it sound as if she were giving the assurance more out of duty than conviction.

But Guy seemed not to be deterred. It was as though he was voicing something he'd thought long and hard about and now had to express. 'Listen, Sarah. Probably we'll see each other again in two months.' They'd agreed to meet again in Paris in early September. 'But in case we're prevented I must say this now. In war every man has some picture in his mind of what he's fighting for. It's you, Sarah. If I have to fight, it's for you. I want you to understand that. And afterwards, if we both survive, I want us to be together.'

He was facing her now, his hands on her shoulders, speaking with a deliberate lack of emotion as if to convince her that his words were considered. It was miraculous – she sensed rather than phrased the thought

– how quickly his uncompromising features had become the norm for her, so that other faces seemed lacking, and somehow insipid. His right hand came up and touched her cheek. 'And you? What do you say?'

She nodded, and gave a shaky, reassuring smile. 'I'll be here for you afterwards, Guy, if I survive.' Reaching up to kiss him. It had the gravity of a pledge. 'I promise.'

But finally the breathless solemnity became too much for her and she pushed him away. 'This is morbid! And anyway, you never know, it might not happen!'

Part Two

10

Dominique sat glumly in the Café de Flore, alone at her table. There was no one there she knew apart from two unemployed actresses giggling and whispering at a nearby table, whom she ignored. In fact half the tables were empty, and the atmosphere was stodgy, as though the handful of customers were merely killing time until eleven when, under the new wartime regime, the cafés closed. Dominique poked distastefully at the cold dregs of her coffee with a spoon. Odd to think she'd drunk it with relish less than a quarter of an hour ago. It looked revolting. The milk had separated and congealed, forming a fatty layer on top of the rest.

At a corner table a sombre group of men in uniform huddled, pulling long faces and nodding sagely, for all the world as if France's military future rested on their care-worn shoulders alone. It was rare now to see men under forty. Paris seemed full of women, children and the elderly – in Dominique's eyes not the most stimulating of combinations.

The first few days of the war had been exciting, with people seizing on each new edition of the newspapers and the police suddenly sporting tin helmets and carrying gas masks. And there was the blackout. She and Suzanne, the prostitute from downstairs, had bought blue powder, mixed it with water and oil and painted it over the inside of their windows. It stopped the light from getting out, but also from coming in. Dominique's spartan room looked positively funereal, and Suzanne's ornate *fin-de-siècle* bower like a well-appointed mausoleum.

Cafés, too, had to put up thick blue curtains so their lights couldn't be seen in the street, and car headlamps were painted blue or purple, giving a sinister, science-fiction effect. Early on it had been a novelty to walk about the streets in near darkness, tripping over the gutters or sandbags or bumping into lamp-posts.

It had been amusing to see friends and acquaintances suddenly appear in uniform. Everyone wore it differently. Edmond, the student upstairs, had looked about sixteen in his, sheepish and over-awed. To Dominique he seemed like a drummer boy or a mascot, not a real soldier at all. He'd been rather huffy when she 'a-a-ah'd' him and told him he looked sweet.

Raymond, the lecherous painter, wore his uniform as though it were made of cardboard. His boots squeaked, and he held his head above the stiff jacket at a rigid, unnatural angle. Guy, on the other hand, instantly subdued his army gear, treating it as casually as his peacetime corduroys.

But after the excitement of the early days and the first alerts – all of which turned out to be false alarms – Paris had settled into a numb routine, as if real life were suspended until such time as the war was brought to some kind of conclusion.

Dominique toyed with the idea of going back to her room, although it was only just gone nine o'clock. But now, in November with the weather turning frosty, her cell seemed cold and bare, and, with the blackout, thoroughly depressing. She could always order another coffee but then again, now she'd given up her job, it'd be wiser to save the money.

The door of the café opened and someone walked in.

Dominique was aware of the fact, but didn't look round until a voice said, 'All alone?'

It was Rosa, in a dramatic long black coat, her cheeks glowing with the cold. She pointed to the empty chair next to Dominique. 'May I?'

'Of course.' It was always heartening to see her. Dominique perked up.

Rosa sat down, taking off her coat and hanging it over the back of her chair. Small drops of moisture beaded her curly dark fringe. She blinked. 'It's so startling to come in from total darkness to total light. It's a job to focus.'

She ordered coffee for herself and Dominique and paid for both. Nowadays you had to settle up the moment your order was brought, in case you had to leave in a hurry.

'How's the worthy Monsieur Rambert?' Rosa was the only Flore regular to whom Dominique had confided the secret of her job.

'He doesn't figure in my life any more. I've left.' She spoke with a touch of defiance. Dominique wasn't sure she'd done the right thing and didn't want her doubts made worse by a dismayed reaction from Rosa.

But the older woman merely asked, 'Why?'

'It was the mornings. So dark and cold.' Dominique smiled guiltily. 'Two days running I just couldn't drag myself out of bed. But, anyway, in wartime I can't see there's going to be much future in a travel agency.'

Rosa laughed. 'I'm sure you're right. But what are you doing for money?'

'I've saved a bit, but only a bit. Actually I went home for a week last August and my parents slipped me a little something, strictly for emergencies.' She pulled a face. 'Well, this *is* a kind of emergency.'

'Something'll turn up.' Rosa was sanguine. 'In my experience it always does when you really need it.'

93

Dominique was delighted to have her own optimistic view of life confirmed by someone older. Sarah had always been rather disapproving of her friend's lack of perseverance at anything she didn't like. It probably came of having a child to support. She warmed towards Rosa. 'Like another coffee?'

Rosa considered. 'No, I don't think so.' She looked about her. 'It's not very gay in here tonight. Why don't you come back to my place? I've got a bottle of Calvados. We could get squiffy.'

'Wonderful.' Dominique jumped at the idea. It postponed the dismal hour when she'd have to go back and face her own dreary room. It wasn't far through the pitch-black streets to Rosa's hotel in the rue Bonaparte. At one point a car drew up alongside the kerb and its unseen occupant invited them to get in. They refused him good naturedly enough, and were insulted for their pains.

Rosa's room was warm and welcoming, the complete antithesis of Dominique's own. It was on the ground floor and heated by an old-fashioned, black, pot-bellied stove. It smelt clean and cared for. The woodwork was polished to a high gloss and an array of copper pans hanging from hooks gleamed, reflecting the colours of the room. Yet there was nothing fussy or house-proud about it. The armchairs were broad and yielding and covered in a plum-coloured velvety material, and the floor was hidden by a faded carpet in a soft, warm brick colour. Here and there were odd, individual ornaments – a shell, like a huge barnacle, mottled in pink, white and palest lilac, some smooth black stones, a statuette of a bison in coppery-green porcelain, all undulating curves. And there were photographs, unframed, propped up on the mantelpiece or stuck in the frames of mirrors. One was of Guy. Dominique didn't recognize anyone else. But pride of

94

place went to an upright piano in some dark, gleaming wood and decorated with ornate, fretted curlicues.

'What a lovely room!' Dominique exclaimed. After the cold, dark streets it was like entering a spacious and eminently comfortable womb. She noticed the thick plush curtains masking the windows so that no vestige of light could escape.

Rosa seemed pleased at her enthusiasm and waved her towards one of the inviting chairs. 'Make yourself at home,' she said and disappeared into an alcove that held a couple of gas rings, a cupboard, a small table, and a sink. She bustled a little and returned with a bottle and two glasses on a tray, together with a few slices of dark rye bread and two kinds of cheese. It was all appetizingly presented. Unlikely as it seemed, the exotic Rosa was highly domesticated. Dominique felt pleasantly pampered, almost as though she were at home in Évian.

The tray was deposited on a low table between their two chairs. 'Help yourself to cheese.' Rosa poured generous measures of Calvados and handed one to Dominique.

The younger woman settled luxuriously back in her chair. 'Have you heard from Guy?'

Rosa nodded. 'Yes. He seems all right, thank God. I don't know where he is. He's not allowed to say. Hasn't had any action yet.' She smiled ruefully. 'Actually he says boredom is the worst problem.'

'There doesn't seem to be an awful lot happening here yet.' The Calvados was burning her insides agreeably, making Dominique feel open and relaxed. 'You know, one thing puzzles me. I mean, we went to war over Poland, didn't we? So why on earth didn't we do more to defend it. We don't seem to have done anything.'

'Oh.' Rosa was supremely scornful. 'That's politicians for you.' She sipped her drink with a disillusioned air.

Then, out of the blue, she said, 'Sarah's a good friend of yours, isn't she?'

'Yes.'

'Guy seems to have fallen totally in love with her. I've never seen him like it.' Rosa's tone was neutral, as if she were waiting for Dominique's response.

Dominique nodded. She felt expansive and indiscreet. 'Oh, Sarah's very popular.'

Rosa raised her eyebrows. 'Who with?'

'Well, there's Michael. He's a friend of hers in England. An art critic. I'm convinced he's in love with her, although he's just married someone else.' Dominique drained her glass. 'And there's Robert.'

'Who's he?'

'Oh, a boy I used to go out with.' Cheerfully Dominique dismissed her former lover. 'I'm sure he liked her more than a bit, although of course he was years younger. And there's Guy.'

Silently Rosa refilled Dominique's glass.

The younger woman raised it in thanks and prattled on. 'Mind you, Sarah's picky. But she was definitely keen on Guy.'

'What's she like?' Rosa topped up her own glass, and settled back in her chair, tucking her feet underneath her and resting her chin on her hand, as though inviting confidences.

Dominique looked at the ceiling, considering. 'She's nice. You can talk to her. And she doesn't beat about the bush. She'll give you her honest opinion.' She looked across at Rosa. 'But you know her, anyway.'

'Yes.' Rosa looked thoughtful. 'She always seemed to me . . . serious. About life. I don't mean solemn – she could be as silly as any of us. But serious. Much more so than me.'

'Me too.' Dominique was eager to identify herself with Rosa's confession. 'I mean I *frittered* my time away at art school, and I know Sarah disapproved. And she'd think I should have stuck my job here.' Feeling suddenly disloyal. 'It's probably because she had a hard life in so many ways – everything's been easy for me.'

Rosa leaned forward to drop a few nuggets of coal from a polished wooden box in to the stove. 'This stuff's getting short. It's not always easy to find. Still, I'll be warm while I can.' The fire wasn't flaming, but had a hot orange glow, lighting up her face with a flattering warmth.

'Guy's serious as well, you know,' she said, abruptly turning back to Dominique. 'That's why we . . . I think he liked that in her, even then. They're probably very well suited, if the war . . .' There was an odd new intensity in her tone.

Then she stopped short, and sat back with a deliberate languor. When Rosa spoke again it was in her previous careless manner. 'As I say, I've never seen him like this. He's so attractive, there've always been women around, but . . .' She shrugged, picked up her glass from the floor where she'd put it down, and took a hefty swig. The subject apparently was exhausted.

They chatted about mutual acquaintances for a while, then Rosa began to talk about a lover of hers called Pierre, a saxophonist, who in peacetime played with her at the Café Philo. She had a brisk, emancipated way with her affairs, but was specially fond of Pierre. They'd arranged a code between them and he'd been able to let her know that he was stationed in a small village in Alsace. Rosa was in the process of trying to obtain a safe-conduct pass so that she could go and see him. She was obliged to pretend that she was going to see a sick relative. Visiting the troops was not encouraged.

She was determined to go, but not relishing the prospect of the trip in wartime in November. 'I know what it's going to be like.' Her long, beautiful face took on an expression of comic resignation. 'The trains'll be full to bursting and icy and pitch-dark, and I'll have to take a freezing cold room in some country inn where they'll charge triple for beer and sauerkraut "because of the shortages".'

Dominique laughed, basking in the glow of the fire and the Calvados, appreciating them the more keenly in the light of Rosa's glum prognosis. 'I'm sure true love'll overcome all obstacles.'

Rosa growled, 'It'd better.'

All at once they were distracted by the sound of voices from the staircase outside. A ferocious quarrel sliced through their calm. A man's voice swearing, the language positively scorching. A woman replying with a torrent of hysterical self-justification. The dispute continued, full tilt, for a couple of minutes and was followed by a crescendo of heavy footsteps and the slamming of a street door.

'*Salaud!*' the female voice screamed. 'And don't come back!'

'My God!' Dominique was shaken. 'Shouldn't you do something?'

Rosa sat back, heavy-lidded and imperturbable. 'No point. They're at it like this three or four times a week. It's their little routine. It blows over.'

'Phew.'

Rosa smiled. 'Actually, it's quite useful. A bargaining point. They ignore my piano and I turn a deaf ear to their racket. Live and let live.'

Dominique said, suddenly, brightly. 'I wish you'd play.

I've never heard you.' It seemed to her all at once that this would be the perfect ending to their cosy evening.

'You don't know what you're asking. When I've had a few I'm unstoppable.'

'Go on then. I'd like it.'

Rosa got up and crossed to the piano in her stockinged feet, lifting the lid and seating herself on the stool. Her face was expressionless as her fingers touched the keys. She had trained as a classical pianist, but tonight she chose an easy jazz style. Her repertoire was more American than French. She played 'These Foolish Things' and 'Pennies From Heaven'. Dominique was impressed by the sureness of her touch, the nonchalance.

From instinct Rosa improvised at length on the basic tunes, it seemed for her own pleasure rather than Dominique's. Her face and body took on a languor that reflected the lazy, sensuous rhythms. Her playing had a warmth and flow that seemed almost sexual.

Smoothly she dovetailed into the yearning chords of 'I'll Never Be The Same'. Sarah's favourite. It recalled to Dominique that evening at Maggie's more than a year ago. Already it seemed to her a time of innocence, a golden age. Sarah had played the record to her since. The words came back to her now. She began to sing along with Rosa's playing. Emboldened by the alcohol, she gave free rein to her voice, imitating the phrasing of Billie Holiday. She began to enjoy herself, consciously playing up a certain smoky huskiness her voice had naturally.

When the song ended she grinned at Rosa, pleased with herself and self-conscious at the same time, like a child. 'That was fun.'

Rosa was studying her with interest. 'You're not bad.'

She struck up a French popular song of a couple of years back called 'Les Mensonges'. The tune and lyrics had a world-weary edge to them, obviously inspired by some of the Brecht-Weill songs of the late twenties. 'D'you know this one?'

Dominique nodded.

'Sing it. It'd suit your voice.'

The song was one that appealed to Dominique for its combination of vulnerability and cynicism. She began to sing. This time Rosa subordinated her playing to Dominique's voice, following her phrasing intuitively.

Unconsciously Dominique assumed a knowing, worldly expression to suit the lyrics, standing braced and defiant, her head slightly lifted, picturing herself in the beam of an arc-light, in black like Edith Piaf, her face starkly white, her voice filling the room. Putting the song across with pleasure and total conviction.

When she'd finished Rosa seemed impressed. 'Not bad.' Nodding slowly in emphasis. 'Not bad at all.'

For the next three-quarters of an hour they thought of songs and played and sang them, half-serious, half-playful, laughing when they couldn't remember the words, making up their own. Dominique hadn't had so much fun in all the dreary weeks since the war had begun.

The tunes were mixed, partly jazz numbers, partly French standards. Dominique clowned, and then a song would catch her imagination and she'd perform it in all seriousness, surprising herself.

There was a song Rosa had written, a tender-aggressive love poem called '*Tes Yeux*', addressed perhaps to Pierre, the saxophonist. She'd brought the single sheet of manuscript out from a drawer, looking quite uncharacteristically abashed.

'Can you read music?'

'Yes.' It was one of the many useful things Dominique

100

had learnt at her convent school. She scanned the paper briefly. 'Okay. Play.'

She sang the song and liked it, surprised and touched that the worldly-wise Rosa should have penned lyrics of such simple sincerity.

The older woman was awestruck. 'You do it so well.' Then rediscovering her tough, self-protective smile. 'It sounds almost like a real song.'

After that she closed the lid of the piano and turned to Dominique with a thoughtful look on her face. 'You wouldn't fancy having a go singing at the Philo on Thursdays, would you? We had a singer – a man. But, naturally, he's in uniform. My boss is always asking if I know anyone.' She stood up, pushing the piano stool back with her legs. 'Actually, it'd be more fun for me. The place is half-empty these days. And there'd be a bit of money in it. You could do with that, couldn't you?'

Dominique blinked. The idea was a complete novelty. Pictures flashed into her brain, mingling with the Piaf fantasy she'd had earlier.

'Give it a go,' Rosa urged. 'I think you'd be good.'

Dominique wasn't one to turn down a challenge. Already the prospect was beginning to attract her strongly. So strongly she was almost embarrassed.

She shrugged her shoulders, pretending negligence. 'Yes – why not?' Inside, a tiny bubble of excitement began to expand, shiny and iridescent.

11

They practised for a couple of weeks to get a repertoire together. Then Rosa left for her visit to Alsace. She returned with a streaming cold, but otherwise in excellent spirits. The journey had been as cold and uncomfortable as expected, and she'd been lucky to be able to rent a room little bigger than a broom cupboard. But she had managed to snatch a number of meetings with Pierre at odd times of the day and night. The landlady had looked kindly on them and turned a blind eye to his untimely comings and goings. Once she'd even got up early and lit the stove so that Rosa and Pierre could breakfast together at six in the morning, sitting just the two of them at one end of a long trestle table, bleary and dishevelled, with bowls of steaming coffee.

Rosa had caused a stir among Pierre's companions with her flamboyant clothes and showy earrings. They'd been followed by cheers and leering remarks as they retreated down side streets, much to Pierre's discomfiture. His main complaint about army life to date was that his fellow *poilus* never talked about anything but women.

The first Thursday after Rosa's return was the date they'd agreed on for Dominique to make her debut at the Café Philo. She was nervous, but in a pleasurable kind of way, never having been frightened of risking her dignity. In fact she'd always loved to show off, but had never expected to be paid for the privilege.

In the days beforehand she gave a good deal of thought to her appearance. She had a green velvet dress with long sleeves and a low V-neck that brought her compliments whenever she wore it. She tried it on in front of the tarnished waistlength mirror in her room, ducking awkwardly to get the full effect. With her hair piled up – and a small jet chain that had belonged to her grandmother round her neck for luck – Dominique could see she looked appetizing and attractive.

At the same time the fantasy she'd had while singing in Rosa's room lingered in her imagination. A plain black dress, a white face. Her red-gold hair brushed into a cloud, rich against the sombre background. It was less charming, but more dramatic. Finally she settled for this alternative. Wryly she reflected that probably she'd be singing for two middle-aged couples and a drunken soldier. Still there was no harm in going for maximum effect.

The Philo was known as a jazz café, so much of her repertoire would consist of American standards. Rosa was sure that the customers would be impressed by Dominique's cool command of English. But these songs would be imitations of records she'd heard. Her strength, they thought, lay in dramatic, even poetic French material, with less of a jazz beat. They included Rosa's song, '*Tes Yeux*', in their plans, and '*Les Mensonges*', and agreed that they'd sneak in as much of this kind of stuff as the audience – and the proprietor – would take.

Rosa's boss, Grimaud, the proprietor of the nightclub, was a small, wiry man, who looked to be in his early sixties, with a high colour and features that receded smoothly back from a jutting, predatory nose. To Dominique he looked like some canny bird of prey.

Grimaud respected Rosa for her classical training, in spite of the fact that it was perfectly irrelevant to her work at the Philo. By the same token Rosa claimed that Dominique had studied at the Conservatoire and hoped

103

to make her career in opera. 'He might up your money a bit. He's none too open-handed,' she told Dominique.

Grimaud had granted Dominique an audition but, as she sang 'Stardust' and 'Honeysuckle Rose' in a sultry, torchy style, he'd listened distractedly, chatting at the same time to a jowly man in a cream-coloured suit. After two numbers he stopped her. 'That'll do, little one, we'll give you a try.'

Dominique had been disappointed by his offhand attitude. Secretly, unrealistically, she'd hoped for raptures, admiration. But at least she'd got the job.

Thursday evening was cold and wet. Just the kind of night, Dominique thought, to keep potential customers glued to their firesides. But half an hour before she was due to go on the audience numbered more than twenty, which wasn't bad for nowadays, Rosa said. She'd already played a thirty-minute spot, and found them to be a quiet lot, apart from her own faithful regulars.

'Never mind.' Dominique grinned jauntily. 'I'll think of the money. It'll keep me going.' Inside, she felt sick, with a tense, tight pain in the pit of her stomach.

Just before she went on, Grimaud hissed at her, 'All the same, you could've worn something a bit sexier!' Indicating her plain black dress with an abrupt, irascible gesture.

But his attitude changed immediately they came into the spotlight. As they stood side by side his arm went round her shoulder in a sweeping, fatherly manner. He introduced her as a kid they were all going to love.

'Be kind,' he added, with a foxy grin at the audience. 'It's her début. The little lady's a bit nervous.' Dominique resented the assumption, and his assumed familiarity. 'But I know she's going to be fine.' He began to move away, indicating his new singer with a professional flourish. 'Ladies and gentlemen. From the Paris Conservatoire. Mademoiselle Dominique David!' There was a smattering of polite applause.

Almost blinded by the white glare, Dominique launched into 'Stardust'. On the very edge of her arc of light she could see grey tables and chairs, pale customers, like actors in a black and white film. But they seemed a long way off. Reality was herself, the music and the song. The tune had never sounded more beautiful to her, or Rosa's playing more languorous and limpid. She had learned the phrasing off pat, but now she sang the words with clarity and passion, their meaning suddenly vital to her.

In a kind of narcissistic trance Dominique performed for herself alone. On the edge of her consciousness she could hear snatches of conversation. Rosa had warned her that in a club like this people talked. But, focused inward, she didn't mind a bit. When the song finished she stood confident and poised, braced for applause. It came, slightly more enthusiastic than earlier, but still lukewarm to Dominique's ears.

With the same involvement she sang two more American songs. And now, out of the darkness, faces began to impinge. There was one man particularly, in uniform, who looked less bovine than the rest. He reminded her of Maggie's husband, Ilya, with a moustache and attractive dark eyes. Mentally she directed her singing at him and was gratified to see that after the third number, 'It Had To Be You', he clapped with a contagious warmth.

Then she sang 'Les Mensonges'. For Dominique it was a private, earth-shattering experience. It was almost as though for years she'd been wandering lost in a wood and had suddenly come across a wide, straight path, bordered with meadows. Singing felt marvellous, and the song was perfect for her. She put it across without undue drama, sensing that a lift of the eyebrows, a subtle movement of the shoulder, would be more eloquent than strident histrionics. She could imagine herself as thirty-five, bruised by life, but tough and resilient. Instinctively her body adopted a sexy, defiant stance, and her face a sulky, heavy-lidded look.

It seemed to Dominique that she performed the song brilliantly. The man with the moustache clapped rapturously, hands held high, and a broad grin on his face. She rewarded him with a special smile. The other customers applauded with rather less zeal, then went back to their drinks with every appearance of indifference.

Back in their cramped dressing room Rosa kissed her. 'Congratulations! You did well, really well.'

Dominique pouted. 'They didn't seem all that thrilled.'

'Oh, but they were. You broke through the apathy all right. Believe me.' Rosa touched her arm. 'It's only in films that everyone goes wild and you're a star overnight. In real life you have to go back and keep on working and build up a following.'

'Oh.' Dominique appeared subdued but, inside, her future glowed like a candle. Singing – applause or no applause – was more satisfying than anything, ever. A pause. Then she asked negligently, 'Did Grimaud say anything?'

Rosa imitated the boss's beady, hawk-like stare. 'The little one's not bad.' She grinned cheerfully. 'Doesn't sound like much, but I tell you, from him that's praise.'

Over the following weeks the war still seemed shadowy and insubstantial to Dominique. Such news as there was came from Finland – beleaguered by the Russians – and seemed remote and irrelevant. Her career was of far more breathless concern. Each Thursday she returned to the Café Philo with the absolute determination that she would wrest the adulation she deserved from its dull-eyed customers. By the sheer brilliance of her performance she would move the sparse and ragged wartime audiences to energy and enthusiasm. It became an obsession.

Gradually she began to win and to collect a following of her own. To start with there was an elderly publisher who frequented the cafés of Saint Germain. Once he'd happened upon her Thursday night performance, and afterwards congratulated her with a courtly, old-world charm.

After that he came back every week, specially to see her, and brought friends who applauded loudly from their table close to the dais. Sometimes Dominique would go and sit with him and his party. He was grey and gentle and unfailingly polite. Once he drew her attention to a song of Kurt Weill's, translated into French, that he thought would be right for her, writing out the lyrics on an old envelope and humming the tune. She liked it and incorporated it into her repertoire.

It was more difficult for her to keep a following among the young. Soldiers on leave would see her and admire, but by the next week they'd be back at the front. Occasionally, though, a shy young private would introduce himself, saying how much he'd enjoyed her performance, and tell her she'd been recommended by a mate returning from leave. Incidents like these were small oases of encouragement along the featureless road she could only hope was leading her to success.

The best was when she was poached. One evening in the Flore she was approached by a large woman in her fifties with dyed red hair and a mask of pink, grainy face powder. Dominique knew she was Ruby, the patronne of a cellar-bar close by, a countrywoman from the Dordogne region, whose premises happened to be in the right place to attract an intellectual clientele. Once called Chez Ruby, the bar had been re-christened Le Pessimiste at the suggestion of one of her customers. The piquancy of the new name had added greatly to its success. Dominique had been there once. It was like a damp, dark cave, though the dim lighting lent it a certain sleazy charm. She could remember watching the haze of cigarette smoke spiralling lazily in the glow of the lamps.

Ruby proposed that she should perform there on Friday and Saturday nights. The fee she offered was no higher than that paid by Grimaud. Dominique pretended to hum and ha, though inwardly she was bowled over by the honour. She made a show of haggling over pay, but Ruby was immoveable. Dominique gave in with an ostenta-tiously bad grace. Having won this point, Ruby was not disposed to be difficult about further conditions. Domi-nique insisted that she must have complete freedom as to the material she chose to perform. To her this was the vital point.

Ruby shrugged her solid, beefy shoulders. 'Sing stand-ing on your head, if that's what you want.'

Dominique was ecstatic. From then on her professional life was split down the middle. At Le Pessimiste she worked on her true image, finding unusual, experimental songs and putting them across, she hoped, with a witty, quirky negligence that was personal to her. Thursday nights at the Café Philo were like a holiday now she had this other outlet. She sang nothing but jazz standards, wore low-cut dresses, and generally performed in a style that delighted Grimaud.

'You're getting the hang of it at last, little one,' he told her with his beaky grin, and patted her complacently on the bottom.

After her act at Le Pessimiste Dominique never wasted time bowing and smiling. Such ingratiating manoeuvres had no part in the personality she was trying to project. At the end of her final song she would simply cast a slow and challenging look round the audience – she enjoyed that – before sweeping off. This unexpected tactic delayed the final applause but, Dominique suspected, doubled it in volume.

Here she was accompanied by a pianist called Serge, a skinny, taciturn person with a clipped grey beard. He was an old professional who understood exactly what she wanted in the way of background music.

One Friday night in February, about three weeks after she'd started at the club, Serge approached her after her performance. Jerking a thumb in the general direction of the main room he said tersely, 'There's a soldier out there – nice lad. He used to be a regular here. Wants to meet you.'

In general Dominique cultivated a certain aloofness, believing that it would add to her mystique. But it didn't come naturally to her, and tonight she liked the idea of a little company.

She smiled into Serge's unresponding features. 'Okay, I'll say hallo. I'll be out shortly. Tell him mine's a Scotch.'

Five minutes later he led her over to a table where three young soldiers were sitting with a blonde girl. He tapped one of the men briefly on the shoulder and introduced him. 'This is Daniel.' Serge's eyes twinkled momentarily with a kind of frosty private amusement. 'He thinks you're the most alluring woman he's ever seen.'

Dominique was taken aback by the boy's youth. Normally lads as young as this were too diffident to invite her for a drink. He was blushing furiously as he got to his feet.

'Can we go and sit somewhere else?' His companions were grinning delightedly at his discomfiture.

'Yes of course.' Dominique was rather touched by the boy's obvious embarrassment. She led him towards a small empty table by a pillar under a dim lamp that shone through red glass. Clumsily he pulled out the curve-backed chair for her to sit down.

'A Scotch was it?'

She nodded. He looked round vaguely for the waitress who happened to be passing. 'Mademoiselle, two whiskies please.' The manners of a well brought-up young man, underlaid with just a hint of conscious charm.

He turned back to her and said confidingly, 'I must admit I'm nervous.'

'Of me?' She gave her most reassuring smile. 'I'm not frightening at all.'

'You were so . . . enticing up there. So . . . mysterious and petulant and defiant and amusing. Seriously . . . I fell in love with you.' Across the table he looked her straight in the eye with an expression of the utmost earnestness, the utmost sincerity. It occurred to Dominique that his nervousness was a bit of a ploy. Genuine, perhaps, but not at all disabling. He was clumsy, but not lacking in confidence.

She laughed. 'It was successful then, my act.'

The waitress brought their drinks. Dominique could tell by the woman's manner that she thought her young companion interesting.

She examined him. He must be about her age, twenty, or even younger, with brown hair cut short, necessarily,

110

in the military style. He was of medium height and build. His most compelling features were his dark brown eyes which had an insistent, unselfconscious steadiness to them. And his mouth in repose had a kind of smile. Defensive or covertly insolent. She couldn't decide which.

'How do you like being a soldier?'

'I sleep and play cards a lot.' He shrugged. 'And I'm learning to be a wireless operator.'

'What do you do in real life?'

'I'm a poet.' He spoke without a trace of abashment.

Dominique wanted to laugh, but she thought him terribly sweet. 'Is that what it says on your passport?'

He blushed again, faintly. 'No. It says schoolboy.' Adding hastily, 'But the passport's three years old.'

She found out that Daniel, like her, was from a respectable Catholic family. His father, a doctor, lived in Lyons. Ever since Daniel was a boy he'd written verse and his family had encouraged him, but they drew the line when he told them he wanted to make it his career. For a year before the war started he'd been based in Montparnasse, living from hand to mouth, writing, and, so he told Dominique, watching and experiencing. If he needed money he'd take a casual job, and he'd had individual poems published in magazines and literary reviews. When the war broke out and he was mobilized he'd given up his room and now, on leave, depended on the hospitality of friends. As he spoke, telling her all this, Dominique noticed that he shifted his gaze from time to time. She suspected that his friends were making encouraging gestures across the room, and that Daniel was doggedly avoiding eye-contact with them.

She found that he made her feel motherly, and superior in experience and *savoir-faire*. At the same time, paradox-

111

ically, she had the urge with him to cast aside her dignity and chatter and giggle like a schoolgirl.

He ordered two more drinks for them with a man-of-the-world air. They were large ones. He downed his rapidly, and soon Dominique, too, became aware of a loose, languorous sensation in her limbs.

Daniel smiled at her across the table, beatific and flushed with alcohol. 'I feel like the rising sun,' he proclaimed.

In their present state the thought struck them as irresistibly funny. Crazy laughter bubbled between them, becoming more convulsive as they tried to control it. A pale, ascetic man at the next table stared at them askance. His pained expression added to their mirth.

When, finally, they regained their self-possession, Daniel took her hand across the table and gave her a melting look. 'I want to be alone with you.'

Dominique replied vaguely, 'Yes, why not?' Outside was deep snow. It occurred to her that it would be nice to walk in it, tipsy, with Daniel. And a buried, practical side of her thought that if they left now she could still salvage a portion of her compromised professional persona.

He asked, 'Where shall we go?'

'To my room, of course.' The answer seemed obvious to her.

With alacrity Daniel went to find his pack, which was stowed in the informal cloakroom. He took leave of his companions, who looked laughably surprised at their joint departure.

Outside, the city was in a state of chaos. A few days earlier there had been blizzards and there was no one available to sweep the streets. In places the snow had drifted several feet deep and even in the middle of the road you sank up to the ankles in brown slush. Everyone was complaining at the inconvenience, but Dominique thought the snow and the starry blackout night magnificent.

She and Daniel linked arms quite naturally and began to walk in the middle of the road. The cold was intense and already, after a few yards, their legs and feet were soaked.

Dominique pointed to the bundle he carried, slung over one shoulder. 'What's in there?'

'All my worldly possessions.' He grinned. 'That's all there is of me. What you see is what you get.'

'Like a snail. How simple. I envy you.'

He touched her red hair spilling over the shoulders of her coat from under a woolly hat. 'And you're a fox . . . with a nice warm lair, I hope.'

She pulled a face. 'Not too warm.'

Recently she had moved into a room in Rosa's hotel in the rue Bonaparte. It was small, but an improvement on her cell in the rue Jacob. Money was tight, though, and she couldn't always afford to heat it.

Suddenly, as they turned the corner into the rue Bonaparte, Dominique's feet slid from under her. She landed on her back in a snowdrift. In the pale light from the stars and the gleaming snow she could see Daniel's face grinning above her.

She lay back and waved her arms and legs in the air with mock-helplessness. 'I'm a beetle, not a fox. Look, I'm a beetle on its back!'

Laughing, he tried to pull her up, but lost his footing, and fell on top of her in the drift. Clumsily he kissed her with his cold lips. Dominique lifted a gloved hand to the back of his neck, pulled him close again, and kissed him back. She could feel his chin and cheekbones through the cold, rigid flesh of his face.

They were both frozen and drenched when they reached her room. Hastily, because of the blackout, Dominique drew the curtains. Then she switched on the light. In spite of her cautiousness with heating, the room had a cosy look. Rosa had sewn red linings into her dark curtains and Dominique had hung some of her bright watercolours on the walls.

'So this is where you live.' Daniel looked about him. 'It looks like you.'

In the full light it struck Dominique afresh how young he was, his cheeks flushed with the cold and stray snowflakes still visible in his hair. 'I bet you're not old enough for the army,' she teased. 'I'll bet you lied about your age.'

A trace of hurt flickered in his eyes. 'I'm nineteen.' The words came out, overloud, like a confession. 'Anyway, what about you? You looked much older up there on stage.'

'Twenty.' She was almost surprised. Most of the people she met were older than herself.

'See!' He was scornful. 'What's the difference?'

'Girls mature earlier.'

But there were more pressing things to think about. They were both soaked to the skin. Dominique decided that now, if ever, was the time to splurge on heating.

'We'll have to dry your clothes.' She assumed an efficient, bossy air.

He looked down ruefully at his wet uniform. 'I go back tomorrow, too. I've got to catch a train at nine o'clock.'

'Tomorrow!' Dominique was taken aback and realized that she felt a sharp regret at the prospect of losing him so soon. She hid it with a show of bustle. 'Take off those things.' She lit the gas heater. Daniel hesitated. She said

114

exasperatedly, 'Name of God, do you want to get pneumonia?'

He turned away and took off his clothes in a modest, cautious fashion. There was a towel hanging on the bedpost, which he clutched round him as he handed her his things.

Busily she put them on a hanger and anchored it on the mantelpiece. Then she turned the heater so its glow was directed, from a safe distance, on to the wet garments.

He asked, 'What about you?'

'All in good time.' For some reason Dominique clung to her bossy, fidgety persona. Turning to Daniel. 'You might as well get into bed. Or you'll freeze anyway.' She spoke with a brisk impersonality, not wanting the remark to be construed as an invitation.

Obediently he pulled back the red counterpane and slid in between the blankets. Dominique began to take off her own clothes, finding that she was abashed at doing so in front of him but not wanting to show the same kind of foolish modesty. For a moment she was naked, then she found a flannel nightgown and pulled it on over her head. It dated from her convent days. She put her clothes to dry next to his.

Now came the awkward moment. Nothing was settled between them. She stood irresolutely and turned towards Daniel. Dominique wasn't even sure of her own intentions. Did she see him as an amusing comrade or a potential lover? He seemed composed now, sitting up, bare-chested, in her bed, looking handsome with his dark, steady eyes and slight smile.

He held out his hand and said hopefully, 'There's room for two.'

She switched off the light. The gas fire illuminated the

room with a warm, flickering glow. Steam was beginning to rise gently from their wet clothes.

Daniel asked, 'Will you come to the station with me tomorrow?'

'All right,' she said, getting into bed next to him. Her feet, she noticed, were like blocks of ice. They sat awkwardly side by side, not knowing who would take the next step, or even whether a next step would be taken.

Daniel spoke. 'Dominique?' A questioning note in his voice. He looked like a boy, shy and uncomplicated. He stretched out one hand and placed it against her cheek. She found his hesitancy touching and wanted to reassure him.

Sliding down under the covers, she reached for him. 'Don't be scared.' His eager body came down, hard and ready, on top of her own.

It was a long way to the station, but they decided to walk it, not wanting to spend their last hour together in the crowded métro. Daniel left some of his belongings with her, including several exercise books full of his poems. They were 'best copies', so he told her, the titles underlined, the margins ruled, pages of his even, sloping handwriting. Dominique was pleased that he trusted her with them.

'If I'm killed,' he said, joking, but with a sharp, vulnerable look in his eyes, 'you can be my literary executor.'

He stood there, looking at her, barefoot and barechested in his uniform trousers, pretty well dry after the previous night's soaking. And she saw him then, with a fierce pity, as a helpless pawn of events that had nothing in the world to do with him.

She wanted to enfold him in a huge, protective

116

embrace. Holding him against her, half-mother, half-lover, still imbued with the scent of his body and its secret animal urgency. 'You won't be killed. Nothing's happening out there. You'll be fine.' Trying to convince herself as much as him.

Outside, the sky was heavy and slate-coloured. They trudged through the snow, holding hands, their fingers red and stiffening, Daniel carrying his bundle on one shoulder. At the station there were scores of other couples parting. A kind of nervous jocularity was in the air, giving way easily to tears. Dominique felt as though something had been torn from her as she saw Daniel disappear inside the train.

12

A small, smoky fire burned in the grate of the gloomy tea-shop, raising the temperature to a degree or two above zero. The room was long and low-ceilinged, painted white with dark, shiny beams, and almost totally deserted.

Ruth took a gulp of thin, weak tea, cupping her hands round the warm china. The drink heartened her a little. She took a deep breath. And a decision. Once she'd spoken there would be no turning back.

'Mum, I want to come home.'

There, she'd admitted it. Her months-long stoic silence was broken. She felt cowardly and brave at the same time. Fixing her eyes on Sarah's face to wait, breathlessly, for a reaction.

Her mother frowned, puzzled. 'But I thought you liked it here.'

'I hate it, Mum. I hate it. I absolutely hate it!' The chill atmosphere of the tea-room encouraged customers to talk in whispers, but Ruth felt her vehement, hissed confession was all the more shocking for that.

'Ruth! What is it?' A startled concern in Sarah's eyes. 'Has something happened?'

Ruth shook her head. 'Not really.'

'Then what is it?' Sarah's voice was sharp with anxiety. The sour waitress looked up from her knitting with a disapproving jerk of the head.

Ruth leaned forward over the table so that her pale hair curtained her face. She could feel the tears rising. Yet she'd remained dry-eyed for the six months since last

September when the school had been evacuated, in a body, to Shropshire. Against her will, a loud sob broke from her. Now that, finally, she'd spoken, her tight, self-imposed control gave way.

'Don't cry.' Stricken, Sarah got up from her place and knelt down next to her daughter's chair, cradling her. 'Don't cry, love. I'm here.'

They weren't tears of self-pity, but of relief. Relief at having admitted to weakness. They came, tight and hard. It took time to control them, but she knew she could. After a bit she pulled away and sat upright, taking a bite out of her dry scone to show that she was better.

Sarah sat down again and crossed her arms. 'Right, now.' Fixing Ruth with a searching stare. 'I want to know. What's all this about?' She paused. 'Is it the Duttons?' Naming the couple Ruth and Christine were billeted on.

'I hate them,' Ruth said forcibly. The waitress tutted. Sarah cast a baleful look at the woman. 'They're brutes. Ugly. And their house is like a morgue.' It was wonderful to spit out these heresies. She'd kept them in for so long . . .

'But you said . . .'

Now she could explain. 'Everyone told us we mustn't worry our parents. It was our duty not to upset the folks at home – our bit in the war effort.'

'So you've been pretending all this time . . .?'

'In a way.' Ruth thought about it. The silence had been her choice. 'But at first I believed all the patriotic talk, and I tried to keep a stiff upper lip, you know . . .' She shrugged. 'But then – well, there weren't any air raids, and some of the other kids started to go home – and it all seemed a bit pointless.'

Sarah asked sharply, 'Why don't you like it at the Duttons?' The room was so cold that when she talked a

119

cloud of vapour showed in the air. Her hands looked red and chapped on the starched white cloth.

Ruth made a face. There were so many reasons. Some sounded petty and unimportant. She could only try to explain. 'They think I'm posh. And if I leave a bit of food they say, "Not good enough for you, is it?"' She imitated Mrs Dutton's grating, singsong whine. 'And they read my letters. And Mrs Dutton has rages and goes berserk and smacks us and her face goes all blotchy.' Sarah was listening with a pained intentness. 'And Mr Dutton walks about in his underpants.' Ruth had come to loathe the sight of his dimpled body skimpily clad in yellow-grey interlock. 'And the house is so tidy, and they make Christine and me go to bed at seven o'clock, and now Christine's leaving . . .'

It was impossible to convey in words the total bleakness of the Dutton household. Ruth suspected that her torrent of words sounded jumbled and foolish. 'The teachers don't like the kids that go back to London.' Now the floodgates had opened there was so much to say. 'They call them waverers and make them stand up in assembly.' It had been Christine's turn yesterday. Her face had flamed as Miss Cook, the teacher in charge, had singled her out for yet another gung ho tirade. Ruth had grabbed her friend's arm and together they'd swept from the hall while the teacher spluttered and their schoolmates looked on in awed, breathless silence. Christine had left now, collected by her mother, but on Monday Ruth would face the inevitable retribution.

'I lie in bed, Mum, and think how I can get away. But I don't know how to get home . . .' She peered at Sarah from under lowered lashes. Her mother smiled. It was a smile of solidarity. Ruth understood that it was going to be all right.

* * *

Bringing Ruth home was the easiest decision Sarah had taken since the war began. It had been much harder to let her go. Right from the start she'd had misgivings at the thought of sending her daughter off into the unknown – even in the company of schoolmates and teachers. But official propaganda had it that to do otherwise was dangerous and selfish. The cities were an obvious target for air attacks. In the event the predicted German bombardment hadn't materialized. The war, so far, was drab and undramatic.

At the station Ruth had been composed, but Sarah had seen a lost look deep in her eyes. The last view of her daughter's small, upright figure was imprinted on her heart. In her grey school mac, gas mask slung diagonally across her slight body, pale hair precariously anchored with a tortoiseshell slide, she'd put Sarah in mind of some wan, though oddly dignified refugee.

Since September there had been the Saturday visits. The dismal sessions at the local fleapit or in the inhospitable tea-room. Ruth had assured her doggedly that all was well, a victim, it now seemed, like Sarah, of the inflexible official dogma.

The revelation, after nearly six months of silence, that the child had loathed her surroundings and dreamed nightly of escape, had come like a body-blow. Sarah could picture now, all too vividly, the Duttons' sly hostility and Ruth's dumb, resentful submission, as well as the stubborn pride that had kept her from complaining. The thought of it made her hot with anger.

Miss Cook, the mistress in charge of evacuees, had received Sarah's decision with barely suppressed hysteria. Her lashless eyes had held a kind of panic, like those of a drowning woman. Sarah had the impression that the whole evacuee situation was slipping out of her control.

121

Weekly the Fulham contingent dwindled, and there was nothing she could do about it apart from making life as unpleasant as possible for potential defectors.

The journey home was icy and uncomfortable through the frozen February landscape. Inside the train all blinds were drawn, the carriages lit only by the regulation pinpoint of blue light. But for Ruth and Sarah the unexpectedness of their joint return lent a jaunty, illicit glamour to the trip. The Duttons – all smiles now that their house was their own again – had filled Sarah's thermos with weak tea and wrapped up some stale jam sandwiches. In the exhilaration of being together the meagre picnic had seemed like a feast. It was past one in the morning before they reached home. Ruth was almost dead on her feet. But her eyes shone with a drowsy, dazed happiness as Sarah tucked her in under the familiar patchwork quilt.

Three months earlier Sarah had been called upon to take another major decision. This one concerned her work, and here her feelings were vastly less clear-cut.

In November, at a party in Tessa's and Michael's flat she'd run into an old acquaintance called Nicholas Baldwin. He was editor of a fortnightly news review called *Omnibus*, a reputable and serious magazine, which treated current affairs in depth and, unlike *Picture Post*, never descended to the frivolity of such topics as 'A Day in the Life of an Artist's Model'. *Omnibus* was much bought and highly regarded, but, Sarah suspected, comparatively little read.

Nicholas had borne down on her from the opposite side of the room, arms outstretched, exclaiming, 'Sarah! The very person! Why didn't I think of you before?'

He was a squat man of fifty or so, with a high colour,

rosy, wet lips, and skin that glowed permanently with a light sheen of sweat. Sarah thought his looks unprepossessing, but didn't dislike the man himself.

Almost without preamble he offered her a regular job on *Omnibus* as a kind of artist-in-residence. Her brief would be to cover different aspects of the home front, producing candid, informal sketches to which she'd write her own captions.

'You'd be a sort of unofficial war artist,' he beamed. 'I think it's a marvellous idea. And you'd be ideal, Sarah. Your paintings always go straight to the heart of the subject.' Adding, with a look of radiant sincerity from behind his thick glasses, 'I'm not flattering, you know . . . Do say yes!'

Sarah's first impulse was to reject the proposal outright. Since her time in New Mexico she'd harboured a stubborn hostility to the merest suggestion of her work being monitored or supervised in any way. And Nicholas's offer would obviously involve editorial meetings. Her sketches would be discussed and scrutinized. Sarah's heart sank at the thought.

But other considerations weighed. She had her own – and Ruth's – living to earn and in wartime the buying of paintings came pretty low down the scale of priorities. Guaranteed money wasn't to be sneezed at. And, apart from that, there was an undeniable attraction in the prospect of dipping her toe in the war effort. Painting was an isolated occupation and lately she'd had a strong sense of events passing her by. Nicholas pressed her, Sarah still demurred. He was very keen, offering her a trial period with no obligation on either side.

This bolt-hole appealed to her. She wouldn't be trapped. Sarah gave Nicholas a wary smile. 'All right, I'm game. I'll give it a go.' She offered her hand. He shook it warmly.

A group of four pilots sat at a table by the window, playing cards. All were fully kitted out in knee-length, strapped flying-boots and fur-lined jackets, ready to go. None of them could be older than twenty-two or twenty-three. As Sarah sat sketching them they were obviously self-conscious, exaggerating their movements for her benefit, slapping down the cards on the table, expostulating loudly at good and bad luck alike. One in particular, a boy with a wild-rose complexion and a blond quiff, looked about eighteen, though she knew he must be older.

'Make a good picture, do we?' He looked at her with an expression intended to be both tough and worldly.

'Wonderful.' She kissed her fingertips expressively and flashed him her most charming smile. He blushed, the pretence of coolness crumbling.

It was odd to think of the nation's defences in the hands of these overgrown schoolboys. Yet they were efficient, she was certain. A couple of hours back she'd witnessed their response to a mock alarm. They'd been in the cockpits of their planes and ready to go in well under a minute. And men like these had already disposed of a goodish number of German bombers.

A slightly older man addressed her. 'We don't spend all of our time skiving like this, you know.'

A dark-faced boy chipped in dryly. 'Most of it, Bill. Let's face it. Most of it.'

She could see that they spent vast acres of time just waiting for alerts that rarely came. In the Dispersal Hut others read or played ping-pong, or just dozed in front of the fire. For Britain, so far, war simply hadn't happened.

From a purely selfish point of view, it made Sarah's job easier. Wherever she went she was welcomed with open arms. The various services, both military and civilian, were delighted to be interviewed, sketched, written up. It gave them a kind of belief in themselves and bolstered them up through the months of inactivity. The ARP services, in particular, were known as the Darts Club and ridiculed. The lack of incident – and the heavyweight reputation of *Omnibus* – ensured that Sarah was treated with courtesy and co-operation wherever she went.

She was finding it fascinating to do the rounds – of fire stations, first-aid posts, ambulance depots and such military installations as were not on the classified list. She was meeting people daily, all of whom were absorbed by a single idea, that of making ready to defend their country. However diverse their personalities and occupations, they were organizing themselves into units, some efficient, some less so, learning new skills, working alongside new people. Sarah's days in the field were full and engrossing. Ruth was agog each evening to hear what she'd been doing and proud to see Sarah's name above the double – even triple – page spread of reproduced sketches and captions.

As she'd feared, though, her relations with the editorial staff of *Omnibus* were less enjoyable. It had transpired that Nicholas Baldwin's idea of candid sketches was radically different from her own. Sarah favoured drawings like the one she was engaged on, showing the human side of the war. Real people relaxing or concentrating, joking or working. Ordinary human beings caught up in a conflict and coping.

Baldwin praised the quality of her work, but wanted technology featured, or equipment, with the figures as extras or cyphers, made unimportant. At one meeting feelings had run very high. Baldwin had told her forcibly that she had a *Picture Post* mentality, to him the ultimate insult. In return she had accused him of terminal high-mindedness. Neither would budge an inch.

But over the months an uneasy truce had developed. Sarah included a percentage of meticulous drawings of manned ambulances, bombers, wireless equipment. And he allowed her two – sometimes three – sketches of human interest. The situation was unsatisfactory to both. Sarah saw her future on *Omnibus* as strictly temporary.

'Sorry, Jimmy-boy. Better luck next time.' The oldest of the pilots collected and pocketed a small pile of silver coins from the table top, grinning wolfishly across at the scowling blond youth.

'I'll get you, you bugger,' the lad replied, with a furtive sideways glance at Sarah.

From outside they heard the rattle of a tea-trolley, another small focal point in the featureless waste of their day.

126

13

Sarah tried not to think about Guy. There was simply no point, no way she could hope to see him in the foreseeable future. The post from France was intermittent and unreliable. When letters did arrive they were heavily censored. Any concrete information was blanked out. She was comforted by the thought that France seemed to be in the same situation of stalemate as England, so presumably he was in no immediate danger. Always, though, he renewed the pledge to find her when hostilities ceased, and urged her not to lose faith. But who was to know when that would be? The war stretched ahead, an unknowable landscape. Better not to think.

She was grateful that her life at present was full and absorbing. There was little time for regret. By the end of the day all she wanted to do was cook something quick for herself and Ruth and read perhaps, before falling easily into sleep.

But inevitably there were spare hours and days less busy than the rest. And then in spite of herself, disconnected images of his eyes, his face, his body would drift into her brain. Fragments of conversation in his voice. Memories of their times together. And then – she couldn't stop them – other pictures would come to her. His face and body transposed on to some photograph of death and carnage seen in a newsreel or paper, the flesh eaten away, limbs trampled into the mud.

One day Ruth said casually, 'I quite liked that Guy. I hope he doesn't get killed.'

The chance remark chilled her. Hearing his death spoken of like that by someone else made it seem a possibility. Not the unthinkable spectre locked away in the back of her brain, but something commonplace.

One day as she looked through her window at the Fulham Road under a hard-packed layer of dirty snow, she allowed herself to picture the house in Provence that Guy had talked about, with the vine and the sand-coloured walls under a hot blue sky. Imagining the warm air and sun that relaxed the body instead of clenching it like the cutting wind outside. Seeing herself and Guy walking in the garden and laughing. Stooping casually to pick herbs. Kissing. She closed her eyes. The glass against her forehead was hard and ice-cold.

Nowadays they visited Maggie by train. People were discouraged from using precious petrol for frivolous journeys. As ever, her house was a haven of laughter, comfort and, even under the new rationing, good food. She had a knack of making tasty meals out of unpromising ingredients, which nowadays stood her in good stead. She'd started to keep chickens and she and Ilya had dug up a good large square of the lawn to supplement the existing vegetable plot.

'This year,' Maggie vowed, 'I'm going to make a vegetable garden even Guy would be proud of.' She'd already planted broad beans, onions and early potatoes.

With the coming of spring, the war seemed to be hotting up. Hitler's troops had just invaded Denmark and Norway and it was rumoured that British forces would soon be making landings. But in the garden blooming with prim-roses, violets and daffodils these happenings still seemed distant. After the icy winter April was bright and beauti-ful. Ruth's school in London had been forced to re-open.

More than half of its evacuees had returned. Sitting in the garden again, over coffee with Ilya and Maggie, Sarah thought that life still seemed almost normal.

Unusually, Ilya was home. Behind his moustache the quick, shy smile was the same as ever, but he seemed restive. He was still occupied in the theatre, but impatient with the work, knowing that sooner or later his call-up must come. Sarah had noticed that Michael, too, was fidgety and uninterested in his beloved magazine, as though this kind of job belonged suddenly to a time made obsolete. Meanwhile, as he remarked, conscription progressed with all the speed of a constipated tortoise.

Ilya asked, 'Have you seen Robert?'

Sarah had. Men in Robert's age group had been called up as soon as war was declared. He was training somewhere in Hampshire, but he'd been able to spend a weekend in London recently. She thought he looked alert and healthy in his uniform, without the puffy, listless air he'd worn last summer. He was expecting to be posted soon, but didn't know where. He'd talked politics, seeming less idealistic than formerly. He'd been devastated by the Russian alliance with the Nazis.

'Is he still pining after Dominique?' Maggie asked.

Sarah thought about it. 'Dominique's like a scar. If you touch it, it hurts. If you don't . . . He's functioning okay. But he wouldn't talk about her, even mention her.'

'There was always something so sure, and sort of audacious about him.' Maggie's eyes were dark with sympathy. 'I'd never have thought . . .' She looked pale after the ghastly winter they'd had. Everyone did. And the piercing spring sunshine emphasized the fact.

Ruth came out into the garden with Sacha and Stephen. She had a handkerchief tied round her head like a nurse. Happily, dramatically, the boys flung themselves down on the grass, arms outflung, in the guise of wounded men, while Ruth practised the bandaging she'd learnt at first-aid classes. She tickled Sacha while she tied his arm in a sling made out of an old net curtain. He gurgled appreciatively.

Sarah watched them. With their unselfconscious scuffling the three children reminded her of young animals. Unbidden, contrasting memories of Ruth's evacuation came to mind.

Maggie seemed to have the same thought. 'Different from at the Duttons', eh?'

'It wasn't that they were wilfully cruel.' Sarah leaned forward in her deck chair, resting her chin on her arms. 'It was just so arid there. No love or silliness or fun.'

Maggie leaned across and touched her arm. 'You know, if the bombing *does* come, I'd have Ruth. Ilya and I have talked about it. She'd be so welcome.' She fixed Sarah with an earnest gaze. A lock of dark hair blew across her white face. She brushed it back. 'Really. I really mean it.' Last autumn she'd housed two boy evacuees from Bethnal Green, but in January they'd joined the drift back to the city.

Maggie's suggestion burst like sunshine into Sarah's mind. If the air raids ever came it would solve so much, putting Ruth in a place of safety while she, Sarah, could carry on earning their living. Sarah hoped, everyone hoped, that it wouldn't be necessary, but if it was . . . 'Thanks Maggie.' Her smile mirrored her profound gratitude and relief. 'I'll take you up on that. It's a brilliant solution.' She raised her cup in a heartfelt salute. 'You know, everyone ought to have a friend like you.'

In May, Hitler's troops surged into mainland Europe with tanks and bombers. Blitzkrieg it was called. Neutral

130

Holland and Belgium crumbled in a matter of days and France's defences were brutally broached. Finally the war was close enough to seem real to the British public, and the reality was fearful.

The newspapers carried pictures of towns and villages bombed to rubble, parents searching for their children among the ruins. There were places people knew from holidays and trips abroad. Now familiar roads were choked with columns of refugees carrying pathetic parcels of belongings, bombed or machine-gunned by the Nazis in their flight, ordinary citizens crouching in ditches or behind trees.

The British troops were driven ignominiously to the sea and rescued by a hastily assembled and motley armada of ships. An attempt was made by the press to present this piecemeal evacuation as glorious. Certainly it was impressive, but made necessary by the enemy's conclusive out-manoeuvring.

Now Sarah's imagination ran riot. After news bulletins she would picture Guy's charred corpse in some fire-razed village or see him lying in a peaceful field, hands clasped over sticky, suppurating guts that teemed with black flies, above him the translucent blue of a perfect summer. She imagined endlessly, but knew nothing, had no conceivable way of finding out. With the enemy on French soil, even the sporadic letters would now come no more. Her fears could not be laid to rest.

During the day her rounds of home-front installations began to pall. The work she was doing began to seem vapid and useless. There was a new urgency in the air. People had less time for her and gave the impression that they now had bigger fish to fry. She was invaded by the lurking desire to be doing something else, something practical, as though by doing so she could somehow establish a kind of link with Guy, the feeling that they were both cogs in the same huge struggle. To join the forces was unthinkable with Ruth dependent on her, but there was Civil Defence . . . Everywhere vacancies were advertised.

On 13 June the Germans entered Paris. Sarah was devastated. Little more than a year ago she'd walked there with Guy in the golden evenings with the warm scent of tobacco in the air. She pictured them at the table in the Closerie des Lilas, with the long, leisurely night ahead. Time to renew their friendship, drink, eat, flirt, make love. And she thought of Dominique, careless and vital in her bright dresses, with her broad, life-loving grin. What of her? Paris was a city of peace and small pleasures. Now rumbling tanks and long, dark, disciplined columns of men filled its streets.

The young factory girl looked over Sarah's shoulder, confronting her own image on the sketch-pad.

'It's smashing.'

Sarah smiled up at her. 'Glad you like it.'

'Brilliant.' Her smile was entranced.

The girl was perfectly, classically beautiful. A madonna of the munitions factory. She had pale skin, a rounded, oval face, and hair like corn silk, parted in the middle and caught up under her cap, so that she resembled some modest Victorian parlour-maid. But the drawing showed her managing heavy, complicated, greased machinery, coolly, her face blank with concentration. It was a study in contrasts – the girl's elegant white arms and the metallic, geometrical shapes of the equipment. Amid the horrendous din of the factory, her expression remained serene, almost spiritual. Mentally Sarah purred like a cat. She was critical of her own work, but this drawing pleased her profoundly. And she'd rendered the machinery with painstaking precision, so Nicholas should be satisfied too.

'It's going to be in a magazine, you said?'

'Yes.' Sarah nodded. '*Omnibus*.'

The girl pulled a face. 'That always looks so dull and clever. Still, if I'm in it . . .'

'If you like I'll put your name under the picture. What is it?'

She looked pleased. 'Anne – with an "e" – Paxton.'

'All right. I promise.'

Under her flawless skin the girl flushed with pleasure.

Nicholas was late for the next editorial meeting.

'Long lunch,' his secretary remarked succinctly. She was a thin, dry woman who served Baldwin with a unique mixture of casual efficiency and thinly veiled contempt. In front of her lay shorthand notebooks, files, and a row of sharpened pencils. She tapped long, sinewy fingers expressively on the polished table top.

The others sat and waited. The rest of Baldwin's lieutenants were, to Sarah's mind, a pedantic and bloodless lot. Bit by bit conscription had made off with the younger, more robust talent. There was a listless air to the room, which was situated somewhere behind Chancery Lane. It overlooked a sunless courtyard and a lone tree embedded in concrete.

It was clear that her presence here discomforted the majority of her colleagues. She had the impression – rare now she was in her mid-thirties – that they saw her as a girlish upstart, too young and wayward to be taken seriously. If she hadn't been there, Sarah guessed, they'd have been exchanging learned puns, and huffing with creaky laughter. As it was, conversation was desultory, and every so often Thomas Fields, the deputy editor, would clear his throat and remark, 'Nicholas is a touch tardy this afternoon.'

He finally arrived thirty minutes late, his face shining with the inevitable patina of perspiration, his colour higher than usual. The small room was bombarded with the blast of beer fumes. But the alcohol and associated conviviality didn't seem to have improved his temper. There was no apology as Nicholas took his place at the head of the table, growling, 'Well, gentlemen, let's get down to business.' It seemed his aim was to get through the meeting as quickly as possible. He adopted a brisk, rather grand manner. Certain articles were accepted and others rejected simply on his say-so. Thomas Fields and the rest of them today accepted his word without demur. Possibly they had worked together for so long that all of them thought alike. Or perhaps they, too, merely wanted a speedy end to the meeting. It was Friday afternoon and the weekend beckoned.

Eventually the time came to discuss Sarah's contribution. She submitted a pile of drawings for general consideration. Separate sheets of paper held her captions, numbered to correspond with the drawings.

'It's the munitions factory, as we agreed. I've spent the best part of a week there.'

Omnibus had received a fair number of letters praising her work. Thomas Fields had commented on the fact with a mildly disparaging air, as though the courting of popularity was not their function.

Nicholas took the drawings, leafing through them, blank-faced, and without passing them on. He piled four of the more technical sketches to one side. 'These'll be fine.' Then he held up the picture of Anne Paxton at her machine and remarked to Sarah, 'More of your popularist tendencies.' His smile was intended to be indulgent, but succeeded only in making him look irritated.

Sarah had tried to school herself to think of her work on *Omnibus* as lucrative and steady, and not to get personally involved. Nonetheless she felt herself flush with indignation. Making a determined effort not to sound heated, she said, 'That's by miles the best drawing in that batch. I really think it should be used.'

Under normal circumstances Nicholas would probably have offered a grudging truce and used the picture, since it was important to her. But today, with his inexplicably sour humour, he was in no mood to back down. He replied imperturbably, 'No, we'll use these four and . . .' pulling out an unremarkable drawing of a girl filling shell-cases, 'this one.'

'I promised the girl in the other picture she'd be in the magazine.' Sarah spoke quietly, but found she was hot with anger at Baldwin's cavalier dismissal of her rights. 'It never occurred to me that you wouldn't use it. It's got a tension that the other one completely lacks. It's an immeasurably better drawing.'

Nicholas gave a strained and mirthless grin. 'Our aim on *Omnibus* is to inform the public, not to pander to your artistic vanity, Sarah dear.'

She tensed. She had always loathed the combination of endearment and sarcasm. Sharply she answered, 'Have you ever heard of photography? You might find it answers your needs far better than I can.' His secretary, she noticed, looked slyly amused at her remark.

Nicholas smiled blandly. Their sparring seemed to have raised his spirits a little. 'You may well be right,' he conceded, after a moment of thought.

Thomas Fields and his colleagues gazed silently at the two of them. Sarah fought with the desire to laugh. More than anything they reminded her of a row of greying garden gnomes.

135

14

Dominique sat by the side of the road, her head between her knees. Her face and lips were ashen. Moments earlier she had vomited copiously into a hedge. It had been a relief. Now she was beginning to feel almost human again. Monsieur Rambert, her boss from the travel agency, massaged her back sympathetically, while an endless stream of slow-moving cars passed by, heading south, bursting with occupants and piled high with suitcases, pots and pans, blankets. There were bicycles, too, and exhausted-looking people on foot, many of them trailing children, some pushing prams or hand-carts full of belongings. All fleeing the German advance on Paris.

'A little better now, Mademoiselle David?' Monsieur Rambert's voice was tenderly solicitous.

She nodded weakly, tasting the bile in her mouth.

'Ready to get back in the car?' His Renault stood parked by the side of the congested road. Inside were his son, a neat and tidy eleven-year-old, and his wife. Madame Rambert was still munching expressionlessly on a stick of garlic sausage. The smell of it, combined with the cloying mixture of sweat, facepowder and petrol, had defeated Dominique. The thought of getting back into the hot, stuffy vehicle was horrible. Madame Rambert beckoned impatiently. Shakily Dominique got to her feet. She couldn't delay them. Monsieur Rambert grasped her elbow unnecessarily, as she made her way back to the car.

Opening the door, she was assaulted once more by the smell of the sausage. It was incredible to think that yesterday she'd been eating the very same thing with enjoyment and gusto. Apparently it didn't occur to Madame Rambert that her snack was at the root of Dominique's trouble. Either that or she didn't care. Dominique could cheerfully have snatched it from her hand and thrown it under the wheels of the passing cars. But she was obliged to the Ramberts for her lift and couldn't antagonize them.

'Better?' Madame Rambert inquired, with a brisk air, indicating that she had no patience with Dominique's vapours. She was a small, hardfaced woman, who wore a smart navy suit and a hat, as though she were merely out for a Sunday afternoon spin. Her husband held the door as Dominique seated herself. He patted her leg, as if to settle her comfortably. Since she'd accepted his offer of a lift out of Paris he'd assumed the right to pat and prod her. At the agency he'd always kept a respectful distance.

It was not easy to pull back into the stream of traffic. The refugees were too intent on their own flight for any thoughts of courtesy. Madame Rambert remarked several times acidly on the inconvenience of Dominique's attack of travel-sickness, while her husband soothed her in an absent-minded fashion. Eventually a car stalled or ran out of petrol a few yards up the road, giving him the opportunity to nip out and join the procession. Tempers ran high. People honked and gestured furiously as they overtook the stranded vehicle.

'Oh God, look at that poor woman!' Dominique stared helplessly as they passed by. An elderly woman, her face a deathly yellow colour, lay by the side of the road, eyes closed, still clutching a small bundle of belongings. It was impossible to tell whether she was dead or merely exhausted. The pedestrians streamed by, their Samaritan instincts dulled by danger. All were only too aware that columns like these had been machine-gunned from the air by German troops.

'Papa, I need a pee.' Jean-François, the Rambert's pale son spoke up. Dominique thought him studious-looking and rather sweet. Monsieur Rambert was less patient with him than he'd been with Dominique.

'You'll have to hang on. You're not a baby any more. Why didn't you think of that when we stopped back there?'

The boy bit his lip and relapsed into silence.

To Dominique's relief Madame Rambert finished eating. But now she got out a small mirror and began to repair her make-up, dabbing a powerful scent called Bois de Rose behind her ears, repowdering her face and applying a fresh layer of lipstick. In the claustrophobic heat of the car Dominique soon felt queasy again. The cocktail of perfumes was overpowering. Madame Rambert wouldn't have the windows down because of the dust. Dominique closed her eyes and prayed that her stomach would hold out.

Suddenly, one by one, the cars in front of them pulled up short. Monsieur Rambert braked.

'Now what?' Madame Rambert craned her neck like a curious chicken.

People were getting out of their vehicles, the pedestrians milling about.

Seizing the opportunity, Dominique wound down her window. In any case it was half blocked by an upright suitcase. 'What's up?' She took a deep, thankful breath of fresh air.

'Alert!' A bearded man in front of them was shooing some young children into the field that flanked the road. In his arms he carried a plump, staring toddler. Other people began to make for the meadowland.

'Alert!' From further down the road an official-sounding voice, amplified by a megaphone.

'Oh, my God!' Madame Rambert's exclamation rasped like a sob. The four of them scrambled from the car and stumbled through the ditch that bordered the road, jostling and jockeying for position. Like the other refugees they flung themselves face downward on the parched grass. Dominique was vividly aware of its rough, strawlike texture as she lay with her hands clasped over the back of her neck. She noticed the sun, wonderfully warm, the air fresh and sweet.

Almost immediately she heard the engine-roar of aeroplanes, approaching rapidly, getting louder, becoming deafening. She pressed herself against the earth, monstrously exposed and vulnerable, her back and legs tingling with expectation. All life was suspended. The noise was unbearable, brutal, and then – was she imagining it? – began to recede. She summoned the courage to turn her head sideways. Yes, the planes were retreating, must be a mile away. Was it over?

Gingerly she lifted her head from the ground. Next to her lay Jean-François, his face still pressed into the stubbly grass. How young he was, with his skinny boy's body. She passed an arm across his back to comfort him, feeling his spine and narrow shoulder-blades. How fragile. How easily he could have been ripped apart by gunfire.

'You all right, Jean-François?'

Cautiously he turned and looked at her, pale as death, with a smudge of earth down one side of his cheek, wisps of dry grass caught in his hair. His face was blank with shock, his eyes wide.

'They've gone.' She sat up slowly, and patted his shoulder. 'They've gone.'

Around them people began to get up, looking warily at

the sky and, absurdly, adjusting their clothing, brushing off the grass. Jean-François pulled himself into a sitting position.

'Chéri!' Madame Rambert knelt, throwing her arms round her only child, rocking him, holding his head against her breast.

'Bastards!' Monsieur Rambert's small face was contorted with a heroic hatred. He looked excited, even elated. Dominique registered a similar reaction in herself. 'The bloody Boches!' Even under these admittedly unusual circumstances, she was surprised by his language. He was always so correct.

'Thank God it wasn't worse.' But even as she spoke her ears caught a rumbling, low and insistent. She understood at once. They were coming back. 'Get down!' she yelled, but Madame Rambert had already flung herself across her son's slight frame.

Dominique found herself, once again, flattened against the ground. Pinned, rather. Monsieur Rambert had thrown himself full-length on top of her. His wiry muscles were pressing her down. She could smell his sweat. Her head was to one side. This time she watched, transfixed, as six planes approached, swallowing up the distance, with the same hideous, lacerating roar. She closed her eyes, shut them out. They were so low. The rattle of gunfire must come, now, any second. Her whole being tensed, braced towards it. Now.

But, incredibly, once more the deafening vibration was retreating, as though the Germans were making sport, scaring them for amusement, with no further end in view. They'd been known to machine-gun cattle for the same reason. Could they really be safe?

She became aware in the ensuing quiet, of her eyes screwed tight, fist jammed against her mouth, which was

140

stretched in a rictus of fear. Also of Monsieur Rambert's erection hard against her buttocks. It seemed unsurprising to her, even comforting. Warily she relaxed her features and lay passive, luxuriating in the temporary absence from fear. Rambert lay still against her. It was a moment almost of peace. Then she moved. 'Get off. They're gone.' He did so at once, sitting up, his face showing no sign of his body's arousal.

People were slow, this time, to trust their luck, but lay huddled for some minutes, looking anxiously in the direction of the vanished planes. Eventually, though, they began to get up and drift back to the road.

'Shall we get going?' Dominique nodded towards the car. 'It seems safe for a bit.'

Madame Rambert retrieved her hat from the ground and began to dust it off. She was quiet. As Jean-François stood up Dominique noticed a dark patch round the fly of his grey trousers. With the planes he'd wet himself, poor kid.

Madame Rambert had a sister called Estelle who rented a couple of rooms in a village near Angers. Angers itself was choked with refugees. There was no accommodation left. People simply squatted among their possessions, guarding them, while others foraged for beds or food.

Estelle's flat was tiny and as stuffy as the Ramberts' car. Her husband was away in the army and she had two prim, shrill little girls. She looked askance at the arrival even of her own relatives. Dominique she regarded with blatant distaste. Monsieur Rambert took his sister-in-law into the adjoining room, and their voices could be heard, hissing vehemently. He could be quite a martinet, as Dominique knew from her days at the agency, and somehow he convinced Estelle that this strange female

141

should be allowed to stay. The following week was sheer hell. Estelle and Madame Rambert made it plain at every turn, with pinched lips and raised eyebrows, that Dominique's presence was an imposition. She slept in the lounge on two armchairs pushed together, sharing the room with Jean-François and the two little girls, who whispered together for most of the night, relating with a strange complacency the supposed atrocities of the German troops – the ripping-off of gold earrings, the severing of hands and, the hushed word, rape.

Estelle and Madame Rambert shared the double bed and Monsieur Rambert slept on an inadequate sofa. This brought on a recurrence of the back trouble that had kept him out of the army and he looked grey, pained and grouchy. But on the rare occasions when he was alone with Dominique, he was solicitous and ingratiating, patting her arms and thighs with a timid lustfulness. Dominique was evasive, but nice to him. In this environment he was her only ally.

There was nothing to do but wait, listen to the news bulletins, bargain with the local farmers for food, the prices suddenly sky-high, speculate on the 'delaying tactics' of the French forces, and repeat variations on the atrocity stories that were doing the rounds. Dominique felt like screaming, but held her tongue. Better to be here, she supposed, than back in Paris with the raping, hand-hacking Germans.

Then, one lunchtime several days after their arrival, the fatherly voice of Marshal Pétain came on the radio to announce an armistice. France had surrendered. TheRamberts and Estelle sat round the dining-table and listened, suitably hushed, while the remains of an orange-yellow lentil soup crusted their bowls. Dominique stood by the window, looking out disconsolately at the deserted village. Estelle's little girls began to sniffle.

Afterwards Monsieur Rambert flicked off the wireless, pronouncing piously, 'It's the best we can hope for under the circumstances.' His womenfolk nodded stoic agreement.

'I'll wash those,' Dominique offered. It had become a game. Neither Estelle nor Madame Rambert would let her lift a finger, thus implacably preserving her status as an intruder.

'No, no.' Estelle whisked away the pile of crockery, face averted. Crossing the room, her small figure tight and hostile. 'Suzanne, you can help with the drying.' Sharply she summoned her elder daughter.

Dominique stretched and yawned, looking round the cramped living room. A pink and smirking print of Saint Catherine was the target of her particular dislike. With pillows and a hot water bottle at his back, Monsieur Rambert sat awkwardly in an armchair, one of the two that formed her bed at night. He'd taken up a dog-eared detective novel and was reading it, po-faced. The younger of Estelle's girls was arranging the hair of the long-suffering Jean-François, teasing it into kiss-curls over his forehead and temples. The momentous public announcement seemed already forgotten.

'I think I'll go for a walk.' Dominique wandered a lot recently. It was a way of killing time and escaping from the claustrophobic boredom of Estelle's flat.

Monsieur Rambert looked up from his book. 'Don't go far, Mademoiselle. The Germans'll be on our little village any day now. Be careful.' His left forefinger marked his place half-way down the right-hand page. He smiled at Dominique, then grimaced at a sudden twinge of pain.

Outside, her sense of boredom persisted. The dusty

143

village street was empty, the sun shining down on it with a jaundiced, sultry light. It was as though the village was in mourning for France's downfall. Languidly Dominique wandered towards the surrounding countryside. She tried to think about Pétain's broadcast. What did she feel about the new truce? Relief, she supposed, but it hardly seemed real. Reality was her suffocating days and nights with the Ramberts and Estelle.

The high road stretched ahead of her, leading north, flanked by tall, thin poplar trees that fluttered desultorily against a blue-white sky. Dominique had the irrational urge to set out along it, simply walk, and leave her two-roomed hidey-hole far behind. How straight the road was. She shaded her eyes, squinted ahead, then looked again. Surely something was moving on the horizon. Crawling. Something unfamiliar and large.

As she stood and stared, realization came with a gut-wrenching lurch. There, bearing down on her, relentless, along the dusty line of the road, was a sizeable contingent of German soldiers. She knew immediately that they were German for no reason she could have put into words. As yet they must be a mile or so off, but every moment they came closer, looked bigger, and she was alone.

Her first impulse was to run. Retreat to the safety of Estelle's flat. But then that would be to nip any possibility of adventure in the bud. Her curiosity was sharpened. The Germans were like mythical beasts. She had to see them with her own eyes.

She slipped into the field that bordered the road. A small herd of cattle was grazing. The animals stopped munching for a second, raised their heads and stared at her with bland eyes. Twenty yards or so away stood a small stone outhouse. The ground close to it was bald and still quaggy in spite of the dry weather. No matter.

144

Dominique made for the shelter and crouched down behind it, peering cautiously along the rough, mossy sidewall, pressing the side of her face into it in an attempt to feel smaller and less visible.

She could hear them coming minutes away. A rhythmic stamping, foolishly putting her in mind of a mass tap-dancing sequence she'd once seen in a Busby Berkeley film. At the time she'd thought the noise oddly threatening. At present the oncoming crescendo of sound was terrifying. Too late, though, now to change her mind and run. She pushed her head and body even closer into the pitted wall.

And then they were there, marching in step and looking straight ahead, seeming grim, tall, powerful. The rigid helmets shading their eyes hid expression, made them in some way machine-like, dehumanized. It took a long time for the column to pass. Dominique watched, transfixed, her attention riveted from first to last. The men were followed by horses, trucks, tanks, guns, field-kitchens, the whole paraphernalia of war. So this was what it was like. She was deeply impressed.

Even when they retreated again on their progress, in the direction of the village, Dominique did not at once relax. But gradually she became aware of her own body again, of the roughness of the wall, the muddiness of the ground below her. Still she clung to the side of the building, her knuckles white, as though, if she let go, she would collapse in a heap on to the rutted, boggy earth. She was stiff, and unwound slowly and painfully from her crouching position, noticing that her bare arm was pock-marked with the gritty surface of the stone hut, her shoes caked in dark brown mud and God knows what else, with all these cows about.

She wiped them on the long grass of the meadow, still

145

bemused, her brain full of the passing of the soldiers. She stumbled across the field to a stream she'd discovered a day or two earlier, and sat down beside it, numb and drained as though from an intense emotional encounter. She lay back on the grass and closed her eyes. The sun was beautifully warm.

More than an hour later she realized with a shock that she'd been sleeping. It surprised her, though goodness knows she got little enough sleep at Estelle's. It was a miracle how the children coped after their restless, whispering nights. Dominique stretched her limbs luxuriously, feeling calm and rested, then remembered the Germans. She'd be wary returning to the village, though with the armistice presumably they wouldn't be cutting off hands. In any case Dominique had always been sceptical of the villagers' gloating horror stories.

The high road was deserted again. Dominique approached with apprehension. She couldn't imagine how a victorious army behaved in a conquered land. In the distance a lone figure approached. Civilian, she could tell. As it came closer she recognized a village lad, a boy of about fourteen.

As he drew level, she addressed him. 'You've come from back there?'

'Yes.' He jerked a finger over his shoulder. 'The Boches are making themselves at home.' With his breaking voice, the words had a direct and graceless rasp. His thin face had a scowling immaturity that Dominique found touching.

'What are they like?'

'All smiles.' He spat dourly on to the dusty road.

A reasonably sized detachment of the troops had stayed behind in the village. The high street was bustling now. The two cafés particularly were doing a roaring trade.

146

Grey-clad Germans lounged outside on the terraces and the pavements with beer or wine, seeming good-natured, but not rowdy. The dull street had never seemed so lively. Dominique thought, with a twinge of guilt, that it was a definite improvement.

'Hey, redhead.'

As she passed the second café a soldier called to her in French. Not loud and jeering, but simple and friendly. He had a nice deep voice and curly hair. He raised his glass to her with an impish grin.

Her overwhelming impulse was to smile back. He was a young man like any other. Just in time she remembered that these were their enemies and turned her head away.

'I can leave.'

That night, as she lay scrunched on the two armchairs her mind repeated the words again and again. The euphoria that came with them made her night more sleepless than ever. The word in the village was that these Boches were nice, polite lads, who paid for what they bought. And, with the new armistice, surely she'd be safe now to travel alone.

In theory she had two choices. Go north again, back to Paris, or try and get home to Évian. In reality there was no contest. The thought of sitting out the war under the stifling regime of her parents was too depressing. Paris beckoned, chancy but exciting. Perhaps it would even be possible to carry on with her singing jobs. In any case she was leaving first thing. Now the decision was made she couldn't wait.

Exhilaration made her charming and chatty as she took leave of the Ramberts and Estelle. She thanked them heartily for their hospitality and momentarily she meant it. They'd had no need to take her, though admittedly she'd more than paid her way financially. The women responded with tight, unwilling smiles. Monsieur Rambert made sheep's eyes as he jokily kissed her hand – his wife's presence precluded anything more intimate – and wished her all the luck in the world.

Outside it was a marvellous blue morning. Dominique swung down the street with her bundle, revelling in the sense of release, but with no real notion as to how she was going to get to Paris. She had the idea of inquiring at the little filling-station at the end of the road, though she knew they'd had no petrol for days. She was in luck. The proprietor was in the middle of changing a tyre on a smart black Renault. He told her it belonged to a chemist who was heading for Le Mans, and who had the petrol to get there. When he arrived, the owner, an earnest little man who resembled a hamster, agreed to take her, waving away her offer of payment.

The roads crawled with traffic. The surrounding countryside seemed peaceful enough under the bright morning sun, but in one village they passed a row of devastated buildings, and in many places burned-out vehicles stood beside the highway, some overturned, or protruding starkly from the flanking ditches.

Le Mans was choked with German troops and stranded vehicles full of refugees trying to make their way home, hoping vainly for an official issue of petrol. People were being encouraged now to return to their own towns, but some claimed to have been waiting here for days. Rather than join this disgruntled crew, Dominique began to trudge along the Paris road in the hope that someone who still had fuel would stop and offer her a lift. In spite of the difficulties, she still felt elated. Even this confused coming and going was preferable to the eternal waiting of the last week or so.

She fell in step with a smart young woman who was tottering along on red high heels, her hair and make-up worthy of the cosmetics counter of some big store. There seemed no room in any of the passing cars. Her new acquaintance was becoming discouraged.

'I can't walk to Paris in these shoes.' She was further encumbered by a largish suitcase secured with a leather strap. The highway gleamed before them, endless, dusty and daunting.

'Something'll turn up,' Dominique assured her serenely.

Almost as she spoke they heard the clatter of a truck behind them, and turned sharply. It was German. But as it passed them it was slowing and it came to a majestic halt thirty yards or so down the road. From the open back civilians hailed and hallooed and gestured to them to climb aboard.

'Paris! Paris!' Two young German soldiers were sitting with the French refugees. They shouted and waved their arms at Dominique and her companion.

Paris! The two women broke into a run. They were hoisted aboard by the two Germans who were grinning broadly and seemed hugely tickled by the situation. With exaggerated courtesy they stowed the women's luggage and indicated a pile of tarpaulins for them to sit on, bowing and murmuring, 'Please.'

Dominique and the other girl took their places. A beery, bearded Frenchman called out, 'All aboard the cattle truck!' There was a picnic atmosphere in the air and the young Germans seemed a part of it.

As the truck pulled away one of them, a well-built blond boy of about Dominique's age, offered cigarettes. Her companion took one, smiling at the soldier, blatantly flirtatious. Dominique was about to turn away, but changed her mind. What would be gained by this small gesture of unfriendliness? The soldier lit her cigarette, cupping his hand round hers to protect the flame.

He reminded her, fleetingly, of a German boy she'd known in her home town three or four years back, who used to call on her – brushed and scrubbed and bringing flowers for her mother – and try and seduce her in the summer-house down the end of the garden. The remembrance stirred a pleasant ripple of retrospective desire.

'*Voilà.*' The soldier released her hand, and Dominique drew on the cigarette. It was fine. She nodded and smiled at him in confirmation.

It was a lovely hot afternoon, and they'd be back in Paris by nightfall. A warm wind stirred her tousled hair and bright floral dress. Dominique crossed her legs and leaned back against the side of the truck, turning her face to the sun with an undeniable sense of wellbeing.

15

Throughout her adventures on the road Dominique had carried Daniel's notebooks with her in a yellow oilskin bag and kept them safe. His remarks about her being his literary executor had been a joke, and yet she'd sensed an underlying earnestness. Instinctively she had responded to his appeal and she took her role seriously. She'd read the neatly transcribed verses to herself time and time again, and thought them brilliant, direct and passionate. He'd written to her from the front, too, enclosing further poems, which she'd dutifully copied into his exercise books. Some of them were about herself and made her cry.

Since the Germans had invaded she'd had no news of Daniel. She could only hope that he was alive, a prisoner of war, perhaps. But if so, under the terms of the armistice, there seemed no immediate hope of his release.

She could still remember the urgent and surprising anguish she had experienced as he disappeared inside the train after their one night together. But through the intervening months the memory had become just that. A moment trapped, as though in amber. Nothing she could feel. Out of sight, out of mind. Dominique had lived the truth of the words at other times in her life, and joked about her own shallowness.

But now she wanted not to forget. She had his letters, open and confiding, and a blurred photograph, and the knowledge of her parting anguish. There must have been a reason for it. She longed for Daniel to come back, stand there in the flesh and, with a kiss, like the prince in *Sleeping Beauty*, re-awaken the raw feelings that his absence had dulled.

The Parisians had got used to seeing the German uniforms everywhere and, if Dominique was honest, she thought they livened the place up. For the next month or so, she and Rosa existed in a kind of limbo, with no work, and eked out their money while they waited for things to settle down, and life to return to some kind of normality.

The night Dominique arrived home Rosa had been quietly reading by the reddish light of a fringed standard lamp. She'd looked up from her book with an ironic, pleased smile, for all the world as if Dominique were back from an afternoon's shopping. She herself had refused to take part in the panic-stricken exodus from Paris. 'The Germans'll be everywhere soon enough,' she'd claimed, with an elegant shrug. 'I may as well wait for them in comfort.' With hindsight Dominique thought she had a point.

With her usual warm hospitality Rosa had made her a tasty soup out of some rather tired-looking vegetables – food wasn't easy to come by – and they'd talked far into the night, making reckless inroads into her bottle of Calvados. Curled up in one of Rosa's soft armchairs Dominique had recounted her wanderings with the Ramberts – in retrospect it seemed a superbly eccentric episode – and Rosa had laughed, looking pretty, flushed and slightly tipsy. Her black hair was longer than usual and hung down over the red blouse she was wearing, and gold hoops glinted in her ears.

But suddenly her mood darkened. There was a silence between them. She looked across at Dominique and said,

'I'm scared.' Her smile was almost apologetic, as if she were embarrassed at dropping the carefree mask that was a part of her, but there were demons behind her eyes.

Dominique was shocked and startled, and didn't understand. 'Scared,' she repeated. 'What of?'

Rosa said slowly, 'I'm Jewish, you know.' Her smile remained, strained and mirthless, as though she'd forgotten to wipe it off. 'The Germans don't like them.'

It took Dominique a second or two to extract the meaning from this understatement. She knew, of course, that the Nazis persecuted the Jews. Sarah had shown her some pictures in a magazine once, even before the war, and had been very upset. Dominique had agreed that it was awful, but surely it couldn't happen in France . . .

'They wouldn't dare do anything here,' she proclaimed confidently. 'Honestly, Rosa, all the Germans I've met seem all right. They seem to want to be friends.' Earnestly she tried to restore her friend's equilibrium. Rosa wasn't a Jew like in the propaganda pictures, in Sarah's magazine. And she was French. There were rumours from Poland but they'd never do anything like that in this country. She had a blind faith in France's privileged position in the world.

Dominique didn't want to believe that Rosa was endangered. It opened up a chasm between them and made her uncomfortable. 'Anyway, there's your name.' Rosa had kept her married name of Doinel. 'No one'd ever guess. I'm sure you've got nothing to be frightened of.' She spoke with an almost hectoring conviction.

'I wish I had your confidence.' Rosa emptied her glass at one swallow, as though the alcohol might give her the required faith. By tacit mutual consent they dropped the subject. She never mentioned her fears after that and Dominique assumed they'd receded.

Parisians in general came warily to terms with the occupying troops. By most they were heartily resented but, perforce, tolerated. There were some, though, who openly admired their discipline and single-mindedness, and declared forcibly that France could do with an injection of the same. Shopkeepers and restaurateurs relished the extra business they brought. The Germans spent lavishly in the early days on luxuries they couldn't get at home.

Grimaud, at the Café Philo, had an eye to the main chance. Business was brisk and, so he told Dominique with a canny wink, he was changing the labels on some of his wine bottles, and selling inferior vintages to his German clientele at inflated prices.

'A little patriotic revenge,' he commented, giving his sly, cocky grin. 'And why not?' Adding with a scorching contempt, 'They'd drink dog-piss and never know the difference.' He thought it wouldn't be long before he could offer Dominique her old job back. 'Things are settling down nicely, and with your looks you'd go down a treat with the Boches.'

Ruby, at Le Pessimiste, wasn't so sure. She hated the conquerors with a blind ferocity, and made them so unwelcome that they seldom came back a second time. Many of her regulars were prisoners of war, so she couldn't even count on their intermittent presence, and she struggled on from hand to mouth. Still she promised, dourly but faithfully, to contact Dominique if things got better.

As she walked back from Ruby's across the Place Saint Germain, boldly striped in the late afternoon sunshine with the long shadows of trees and buildings, Dominique felt unusually glum. She was relieved, from a financial point of view, that Grimaud had as good as promised her work, and she had an inkling that she could push him up a little on pay. But her job at Le Pessimiste was her passion. The one in which she tried to express herself and try out odd new songs and develop her style into something of her own. And this, it now seemed, was closed to her.

With her buoyant vanity Dominique had the firm conviction that she deserved to succeed as a singer, and for the first time she vehemently cursed the war. Until then she'd thought of it merely as a bore, a necessary and inevitable evil that everyone had to share. Now her resentment became intense and selfish, as though some high-up potentate had singled her out as a target for his spite and she was powerless to do anything but submit to his malice.

As she opened the heavy black door of the house in the rue Bonaparte, she was thoroughly disgruntled. A dull evening stretched ahead. Rosa was out, but even if she hadn't been, the two of them were so short of cash that they hesitated even to spend the price of a couple of cups of coffee at the Flore. Dominique stumped up the stairs, weary and irritable. Normally she took them two at a time.

Her room was at the top of the house. She always hid the key in a crack in the wall behind a rickety cupboard that stood in the corridor, seemingly belonging to no one. But when she slid her hand into the familiar cranny she found it empty. That was odd. Only Rosa knew of the key's whereabouts, and she was supposed to be in Clichy today, visiting her sister.

With a touch of apprehension Dominique pushed the door. It was open. She stepped into the room.

A man's voice came softly, 'It's me. Don't jump out of your skin.'

She was confronted by Daniel's brown eyes and ambiguous grin. He was thin and filthy and looked totally exhausted.

16

Sarah brought her ambulance to a halt opposite the burning tenements. No problem with visibility here. The sky was red and bright with the collective glare of a dozen or so fires in the vicinity. You could have read a newspaper by the light, as people kept saying to each other, wonderingly, when the bombing first started. The buildings were silhouetted, tall, black and precarious against the shivering sky. Flames leaped behind the façade and licked with a fearful vigour from the empty windows. Three jets of water arched, criss-crossing, into the fires. From high up on a crane a fireman directed another jet downward into the inferno. Even in the horror of the moment Sarah registered the scene as one of savage beauty.

As she engaged the handbrake something in the sky caught her attention. 'Look up there. Those birds.'

Above the fires, in the red glare, a flock of pigeons circled endlessly, restlessly, their wings looking pale in the lurid light.

'Poor things.' The soft, little girl's voice of Sarah's attendant, Joan Lewis. 'It's so bright, they must think it's dawn.'

'They look like doves. Birds of peace.'

Joan gave a short, breathy laugh. 'That's a joke.'

Hastily they climbed from the ambulance, ready for the next consignment of casualties.

A voice called, 'Over here, girls!'

There was a huddle of figures to the left, twenty yards

or so in front of them. The women picked their way through coils of hose and strewn bricks. As they drew closer Sarah recognized Bill, the leader of the rescue squad, a small, wiry man with a thin, lined face under his tin hat, and a chipped front tooth.

'Passengers for you. Hospital jobs.'

On the ground lay four stretchers. A dark-haired man, one of the stretcher party, was kneeling by a prone figure whose face, emerging from a blanket, was covered with a lint mask. Thin, anguished sounds came from behind it. The voice sounded female. The dull desperation of her moans crawled on Sarah's skin like spiders. The man talked soothingly to her, his voice low and almost hypnotic.

One of his companions pulled a face and shook his head, signalling the extent of the woman's injuries. 'Burns. Bad.' He had lowered his voice so that the patient wouldn't hear, and the hubbub beyond made his words barely audible.

He jerked his thumb at two of the other stretcher cases, a boy of about fourteen and a woman, lying pale and stoic under their blankets. The woman had smiled as Sarah arrived.

'Fractures. Lucky really. Jumped before the fire took hold.'

A fourth figure was completely covered by a long rust-coloured curtain. Blankets were running short. 'Dead,' the man said briefly. In the red glow you could see that the material in the region of the head was saturated with blood. It was almost the same colour as the makeshift shroud.

Sarah nodded. 'Right, load them up. Quicker the better. It's going to be a slow job getting them there.

Nothing stays still. I get to a street I know and it's not there any more, just piles of rubble.'

The stretcher party loaded the injured into the back of the ambulance. Joan got into the back with the patients. They were in pain and the journey would probably be neither comfortable nor safe. With her soft voice Joan had the knack of calming the overwrought. And the scrubbed youthfulness of her face below the official tin hat had a way of shaming frightened adults into silent bravery.

'Good luck, love.' The dark stretcher man gave Sarah a reassuring grin.

'We'll be okay,' Sarah said, as much to convince herself as him.

The first bit of the journey was all right, but then, down a sidestreet, she found her way blocked by fallen rafters, beyond which she could see flame and swirling smoke. She turned back, taking a longer, but clearer route. She was near her own part of London tonight, and was unlikely to get lost. When she entered the Fulham Road Sarah thought she was home and dry. The hospital was a couple of miles or so up on the left. Here the sky was darker and you couldn't see much through the slits of light from the headlamps. She'd done the run twice before that night. The second time, in a backstreet, a building a mere thirty yards in front of her had swelled up, for all the world like a spoof effect in a Disney cartoon, before exploding in a storm of flying debris. Sometimes she had to get out and clear away chairs, tables and beds which had been blasted from bombed-out houses. Earlier that night she'd driven the route with shrapnel rattling on the roof like showers of pebbles.

Suddenly, ahead, the sky turned bright as day. A cluster of flares hung in the void, dropped by a plane, showing up the black buildings as if in a dazzle of lightning. Experienced as she now was, after a couple of months of raids, Sarah knew it meant that bombs would be coming down any moment. Doggedly she told herself that the odds were hugely against being hit, and resisted the temptation to put her foot down and drive hell for leather. A jolting like that was the last thing the patients in the back needed. And speed, she knew, would make her less careful, less alert for possible obstacles.

She drove on with determined care, body tense, hands rigid on the steering-wheel, hearing the intermittent thuds of explosions on her left. It seemed – thank God – that the bombs were a mile or more away. The rattle of anti-aircraft guns was a comfort, though Michael claimed that they were hopelessly inaccurate. At last the solid black shape of the hospital loomed ahead against a sky clearing to grey with the hint of dawn.

As the ambulance pulled away again from the hospital gates they heard the wailing of the all clear.

Her attendant, Joan, mimed cringing relief, fanning herself with white, tapered hands and making 'phew' noises. 'Another night gone. And Hitler hasn't bagged us yet.'

She was a skinny girl of twenty, slightly gawky, with pink skin, freckles and sandy hair permed into small curls. When she smiled she looked about sixteen, and her voice had a childish, breathy, wondering quality. Before joining the Ambulance Service she'd worked in a shoe shop and, in spite of everything, she still maintained that the change had been for the better.

Sarah was grateful that Joan didn't think it necessary to don a bossy, blustering persona with her uniform, as some of the other women did. Yet for all her fragility she was rock-steady. Nightly for weeks now she'd faced fires, explosions, showering shrapnel. And worse. The pain and distress of bomb-victims, their often hideous injuries. Both she and Sarah were hardened a little to the shock of encountering in the rubble disembodied sections of human anatomy – an arm, a boot with a sock and tendons protruding from the top, even a torso. In the early days they'd been made physically sick by the sheer horror. Now they felt – cautiously – that they could take it. Perhaps it was true that you could get used to anything. They were a team. That helped.

'How long can this go on?' Sarah voiced the question asked each morning with increasing incredulity by Londoners as the capital awoke to fresh, unthinkable devastation.

She didn't require an answer. Joan shrugged, then shivered in the damp early November dawn. 'I could do with a cup of tea, I can tell you.' Another great cliché of the Blitz.

As they drove back down the Fulham Road a lethargic cloud of grey smoke hung in the air to their right. It was silvered at the edges with the tentative light of the rising sun. The sight was majestic. Sarah felt half guilty each day at the beauty she saw in the fearful destruction.

At the scene of the bombing a ragged group of people had collected in the bleary dawn, back from their night spent in some underground station or public shelter. Warily they confronted the ruins of their home. It was to be expected, yet somehow you never thought it would happen to you. The fires were largely damped now, but smoke still rose from the hot rubble. There was the familiar, raw, penetrating smell. Brick dust, soot, gas, smoke, sewers. It filled the throat. A fine rain drizzled.

A WVS van was dispensing hot drinks. Joan climbed wearily from the ambulance and made towards it.

'Get me a cup,' Sarah called. 'I won't be a minute.'

She joined a huddle of civilians standing with Bill of the rescue squad. He had his arm round a middle-aged woman in a brown coat and a paisley headscarf covering tight rows of iron curlers. She was weeping steadily, easily, and looked to be in shock. Her gloved hands gripped a brown paper carrier bag.

'What's the dog's name, love?' Bill was asking. The woman took a breath, as though to reply, but broke down again.

'Sammy,' someone ventured helpfully from the crowd.

'Could you call him?' Bill tightened his arm round the woman's shoulders. She wept harder, passing a hand across her face.

'I'll call him,' a small boy piped up. He was pale, with a straight-cut fringe, glasses, and a navy gaberdine mac. 'He's my dog.'

'That's the boy.'

The child and Bill approached what had been a two-storey house to the left of the burnt-out tenement shell. This building had escaped the fire, but falling chunks of masonry from the larger building had demolished the roof and the front half of the house. Bricks, rafters, broken glass were piled high. Behind them a section of concrete leaned in a V formed by the collapsed roof.

Bill and the boy stood on a pile of loose bricks and stared downward into the debris.

'Okay, lad, call him now.'

The boy bent, as though to direct his voice low into the ruins.

'Sammy! Sammy!'

There was an expectant hush. He called again and squatted down, listening intently. There was a quiet but unmistakable scrabbling sound, and a faint whining from deep within the rubble.

'And you say the dog would've been sleeping on your sister's bed?'

The pallid child nodded.

'Evelyn!' Abruptly the woman called out. A rough, raucous cry. 'Evelyn!' The anguish in her voice chilled the blood.

Sarah moved towards her and put a hand on her shoulder. 'They'll get your daughter out. If it's humanly possible, they'll get her out.'

The woman turned her head. Her face in the cold dawn was naked-looking, without defences, and swollen with tears. There was a kind of pleading in her eyes. 'She got fed up with the shelter. Said she'd stay at home and get a decent night's sleep. Well, she's eighteen nearly. You can't force them at that age.' Her voice held a desperate note of self-justification.

'Where would she have been sleeping?'

'Under the stairs, like I told him.' She jerked her head towards Bill. 'I made sure of that. Safer there. I made a bed up for her myself.' Again the desire to convince this official stranger that she'd not been negligent. Tears welling afresh.

'I've known lots of cases where that's saved people.' Sarah longed to give warmer reassurance, but didn't want to raise the woman's hopes unrealistically. In any case she seemed a touch calmer now as she watched Bill examining in detail the layout of the ruins of her home.

Sarah went over to him. 'What do you think? Any chance that she's alive?'

Bill looked up. 'There's a good chance.' His expression

was neutral as if to warn against any premature jubilation. 'If only someone could get to her.'

He bent and pointed to where a narrow opening could be seen in the rubble, forming a kind of shaft. A couple of thick beams supported a section of brickwork that had remained sound instead of collapsing into a pile of dust and loose debris. 'See that. I reckon that goes through to where she was sleeping. But it's too small for me and the other lads. Safe, though, as far as I can tell.' He pulled and prodded at the section of wall, which stayed firm. 'It'll take a hell of a lot of time to make that opening big enough for a man. And if the kid's dead . . .'

'The effort would be wasted.' Soberly Sarah finished his sentence for him. Time was precious. There were so many other cases like this one.

Still Bill tested and pushed at the wall. 'Solid, see. I'd stake my life on it . . . well, almost.' He pulled a wry face. 'It'd make sense to send the boy in. He'd get through. But . . .' He shrugged. 'And, anyway . . . well, you don't know what he's going to find at the other end.'

A brief silence lent tacit emphasis to his words. Sarah understood. Some of the things she and Joan had seen . . .

Sarah looked at the narrow opening. And wondered. What if she . . . The frenzied activity of the last weeks had taken its toll. Always small-boned, never plump, she was at present thinner than she'd ever been, though she was only vaguely aware of the fact. There was never time to think about yourself. But only the other day one of the women at the Depot had remarked, with shock in her voice, 'Sarah, you'll waste away if this goes on much longer. You're skinny as a kid.'

'Do you think . . . ?' she began impulsively. Unconsciously she narrowed her shoulders. 'Maybe I could . . .'

She glanced across at the girl's mother, still standing in shock with her carrier bag. Neighbours rallied round. The woman hardly seemed to notice them. Sarah had the pressing desire to bring news, to put an end, one way or another to the mother's anguished wait. To offer the ecstasy of relief or, at the very least, knowledge, certainty.

Bill grasped her by the upper arm, as if to test her skinniness for himself. 'There's nothing of you. I wonder . . .' Attempting to be cautious, he already sounded half convinced.

'Let me try.' Her urgency was overwhelming.

His face was a mask of conflicting emotions. Her suggestion was unethical, but it could solve so much. If the girl was alive he could give the go-ahead to the rescue workers to enlarge the shaft and get her out, in the knowledge that he was wasting neither time nor manpower. If dead, well there were a hundred more urgent jobs . . .

'Seriously,' Sarah urged.

Abruptly he decided. 'Okay, love. You try. I'll take responsibility.'

Sarah took off her uniform jacket. She was wearing trousers and a shirt. Bill handed her a torch. The drizzle had increased now to a steady rain which soaked gradually into the rubble, turning it to a vile, gritty paste. As she advanced her feet into the opening, Sarah was aware that a hush had fallen over the crowd of huddled observers. She felt for footholds, testing them gingerly before advancing further into the rough shaft. It was a tight squeeze but, to her relief, with a twist and a wriggle she was able to fit her shoulders into the gap. It was necessary, though, to position one higher than the other. Her arms, too, she held one low, one above her head. It gave her a kind of purchase on the rough surfaces to either side of her. In a brief instant of detachment, Sarah saw herself as a Victorian climbing boy. Her face scraped against the jagged brick, grazing her skin, and tipping her tin hat askew. Bill had insisted she wear it, 'or the whole thing's off. It's about the only precaution you can take.'

As she inched herself down the shaft, Sarah stirred little falls of brick-dust. With each one she waited, her heart in her mouth, to see whether the disturbance would dislodge something larger. Odd slates from the roof had slipped into the shaft and some of these became detached from their loose moorings. One clattered from above on to her tin hat, but by and large it was the ones beneath her that came adrift and rattled harmlessly to the ground below.

Far worse was her sense of claustrophobia. In the tight shaft, with the loose debris, she had graphic visions of being buried alive, choking on the dust, being crushed by beams, bricks. She breathed deeply, willed herself to be calm. Bill had said it was safe . . .

Her feet encountered solid floor. Thank God. And here there was a bit more room. The stairs were relatively unharmed, and harboured below them a long, narrow space. But Sarah hesitated to go forward, aware of the precarious weight of brick, wood, slates, glass above her. It was dark. She switched on her torch and shone it in front of her. The passage was strewn with shoes, a couple of hand-brushes, an iron bucket, all the paraphernalia that the family kept under the stairs. Cautiously Sarah took a couple of steps, still directing the beam of the torch on the ground ahead.

The pale light revealed the dull, submissive eyes of a dog, lying silent, ears slicked against its head. The animal made no sound nor movement to greet her, though earlier, outside, she'd heard it whining. Moving the torch

165

beam she found that it was trapped under the heavy, metallic weight of a fire-basket, which straddled its back and pinned it to the floor. No doubt another of the items the family kept stacked there. Sarah suspected that the dog's back was broken, or almost. Its eyes followed her, but otherwise it showed no sign of life.

Her torch encountered the legs of a bed. She let the beam travel upward, revealing a green tartan rug. The pallid light passed along the blanket and discovered a white arm attached to a torso. The blue flannelette of the girl's nightdress was saturated with blood. The brutal weight of a massive iron girder had collapsed across the bed, pinioning the neck of its occupant.

With horrified reluctance Sarah shone the torch higher to find a dark, soaked pillow and, precariously balanced on its outer edge – at a crazy sideways angle – a head, pale-skinned and sightless, its mousy hair matted with blood. Sarah started violently. The movement was enough to dislodge the head. It rolled to the floor and lay there, white and unreal. An unthinkable hallucination. A gruesome prop for some gory Jacobean tragedy.

Abruptly Sarah was sick – on herself at first, with the suddenness of the reaction, and then, doubled over and convulsed, into an open wooden box of shoe-cleaning materials. There was a kind of relief in the involuntary spasms of her body. Even after her stomach was empty she retched, tasting thin bile in her mouth, until finally her throat was raw and there was nothing more to come. She stood then, eyes closed, braced against the wall on one arm, caked in dust and spattered with her own vomit. At that moment – in the dim ruins of someone's family home and in the company of a headless corpse – the trappings of normal life, of frivolity and careless good cheer, which even a few weeks ago she'd taken blandly for granted, seemed as remote to her as some imagined Shangri-la.

She turned to retrace her steps. There was the dog. She bent and heaved the heavy fire-bucket, releasing the animal. It lay, showing no sign of life, its spine distressingly caved. The eyes had stopped moving. Sarah made for the shaft and began to grope her way out.

The damp air was cool and fresh. She could breathe it even before her head emerged from the hole. Bill reached down and gripped her arm, hoisting her out. It was a job to stand. Her legs were as loose as a puppet's.

'You look like death.' He rubbed the brick-dust from her face with the side of his thumb. 'Well, what's the news?'

She shook her head, the expression on her face answering him even before she added tersely, 'Dead.'

At half past ten that morning, back at the Ambulance Depot, Sarah finally had the cup of tea she'd craved since dawn. She and Joan had done two more hospital runs before returning to the disused repair garage that served as their base.

The tea was strong and sugared. Sarah gulped it down like a badly needed drug, luxuriating in the warmth and sweetness it spread through her insides. She took a half-hearted bite out of a doorstep of bread with cheese. As usual the night's events had left her with little appetite.

'The East End had another basinful last night,' Ivy, one of the other drivers, observed with relish. 'Two-hundred-and-fifty-pounders. It's a wonder there's anything left standing over that way.' She was a busybody who thrived on misfortune. Now, with the damp stub of a cigarette drooping from the corner of her mouth, she was pink with animation, her eyes avid. Any talk of disaster revived her energy quite wonderfully, even after the grimmest and busiest of nights.

Joan poured herself another cup. The tea looked dark and stewed now. 'That means a whole lot more poor devils with no homes to go to.' Contingency arrangements in the East End were scandalously inadequate. The subversive, whispered joke was that the government would have preferred a higher death toll. Corpses were easier to dispose of than the living.

Jenny, Ivy's attendant, a pretty, blonde, ex-hairdresser, was doing her nails. The varnish had been chipped with her night's exertions. 'My Auntie Jo's still living in that house of hers, with no gas, no windows . . .' Jenny's auntie was an almost mythical figure, who embodied all the misfortunes of the East Enders. But the women had seen for themselves. Their ambulances had been called to the district several times when the desperate emergency services could no longer cope.

'That's going to be bloody good when the real cold weather comes.' Even with her boundless energy Ivy's eyes looked tired, pouched and bloodshot. 'Old Churchill says we can take it, but it's not bloody him that's taking it.' She stubbed out her cigarette, picked up her cup and saucer, and clattered over to the cold water tap to swill them out.

The Depot's living quarters consisted of a roughly furnished wooden hut. The inside walls were distempered a lacklustre yellow. Pus yellow, Joan called it. A small baize-topped card table stood in one corner with four kitchen chairs, and on the brown linoleum floor eight mattresses were laid, close-packed in two rows of four. The arrangement was adequate. Indeed, compared to some of the Depots, it was luxurious.

'You're quiet.' Joan turned to Sarah.

Sarah gave an unsuccessful smile. With Joan there was no need for explanation. The death of the teenaged girl preyed on her mind. It had been so stupid and so unnecessary. The girder that had severed her neck hadn't even been part of the structure of the house. Just some piece of scrap that one of the family had kept in case it came in useful. Probably it had been there for so long, propped against the wall in the dark, that they'd forgotten its existence.

'You're thinking about that kid,' Joan said accusingly.

'Mmm.' Sarah nodded. Whenever she encountered death or injury in a young girl, bleakly she imagined Ruth . . . For the thousandth time she thanked God that her daughter was safe in Hertfordshire, and blessed Maggie.

'Stop brooding. You'll drive yourself barmy.' Joan spoke with sturdy good humour, cradling her chipped, white cup which contained the tepid dregs of her tea. There were brown shadows below her eyes which, perversely, made her look younger than ever.

'Barmy. Never let it be said.' Sarah roused herself to assume the air of breezy resilience which – real or fake – saw all of them through the job. 'I'm fine. I'll manage.'

Joan grinned. 'Bloody right.'

They could cope, both of them were sure of that now. With the grim and gruelling vortex of danger, destruction and death. With the days and nights that gave no time to draw breath, no peace or privacy to restore a balance. There were times when she and Joan went whole days together without a chance to change out of their grimed and blood-stained uniforms.

They could put up with the lack of sustained sleep, with the necessity of being constantly on standby. They could cope because this, now, was their life. In the thick of it they could hardly remember any other. They went along

169

with it, meeting each demand as it arose. There were no guidelines or professional ethics. There had never been a situation like this before.

But sometimes Sarah wondered. What would happen now if the bombing stopped suddenly? If life came back as before, humdrum and trivial? A life in which charm and humour and smalltalk were at a premium. She had schooled herself to deal with the focused horror of the Blitz. But the other? Sometimes she felt it had become totally beyond her.

'Ready for a bit of shuteye, girls?' Ivy drew the streaked and dusty blackout curtains. Another colleague, Ann McBride, was on duty by the telephone in the adjoining room. Sarah wondered how long they'd be allowed to sleep before a yellow alert jerked them back into consciousness.

17

Ruth heard the click of the telephone receiver being replaced. She stuck her head round the kitchen door. 'Well?'

Maggie was crossing the living room towards her, a broad grin on her face. 'Yes.' Raising her arms in a kind of boxer's salute. 'It's almost certain. She'll be here first thing – and she can stay the night if no one calls her back.'

'Fantastic!'

It was only then that Ruth allowed herself to realize how terribly disappointed she'd have been if Sarah had been prevented from spending at least part of Christmas with them. It had been weeks since she'd seen her. Ruth understood why, but . . .

'How's that stuffing coming along?' Immediately Maggie was back to practicalities. The kitchen was beautifully warm and had a bright, expectant Christmas Eve air. A hand-glued, hand-coloured paper-chain made by Stephen hung in a double loop along one wall, a rosy mask of Santa dominated the mantelpiece, and mince pies cooled on a wire rack.

Ruth showed the bowl in which she'd mixed sausage-meat, onions and herbs. There was enough to stuff two chickens. Large ones. Maggie had steeled herself to kill them yesterday while Ruth took the boys and Natasha for a long walk. When they got home the birds had been drawn and plucked and the mess cleared away, and Maggie, looking a touch pale, was drinking tea in the kitchen.

'Well', she'd commented warily to Ruth, 'at least I know now that I can if I have to.'

Now Maggie picked out a tiny piece of stuffing and tasted it. 'Mmm, it's good.' She gave Ruth a quick hug. 'I'm so glad Sarah can make it. We must make it really nice for her. Give her a rest. She's had such an awful time recently.' She put on a striped apron and began to stuff one of the pallid chickens with Ruth's mixture.

'I'll make up the bed if you like.'

'Thanks.' Maggie looked up and nodded. 'And while you're up there, could you make sure the boys clean their teeth. And calm them down if you can. They're so excited, they're never going to sleep.'

'All right.' Ruth nodded carelessly, but her heart swelled with a quiet pride, as it always did when Maggie casually offered her responsibility. She loved to fuss over the boys, boss them and read to them. Maggie said she was good with them, and Stephen called her his big sister.

Passing through the living room, she stopped to admire the Christmas tree. Ilya had dug it up out of the garden at the weekend, and Ruth and the boys had decorated it with lights and glass droplets from a dismantled chandelier that Maggie had rescued from a house in London years ago. Sacha called them diamonds. The room was dark apart from the bright radiance of the tree.

Suddenly she became aware that she wasn't alone. Alan West, an evacuee of about her own age, was sitting on a divan in the corner, silent and still.

'Gosh, you gave me a shock.'

'Sorry.' A flat irony.

Ruth couldn't see the expression on his face, but guessed that he'd be wearing his normal, restive, scowling look. Maggie had tried to involve him in the festive preparations, and for fifteen minutes or so he'd split kindling wood, filling a cardboard box for her. But then, as usual, he'd drifted away to be on his own.

Ruth shrugged and walked on. Alan made her feel uncomfortable. She was sorry for him but hid the fact. He'd been here a month or so, arriving in the village with a group of evacuees from Dagenham who'd been bombed out. He'd had a fresh-looking scar alongside one eye where he'd been cut by flying glass. His mother, like Sarah, had stayed on in London to carry on with her war work. His father was in the army somewhere. The boy was a constant brooding presence in the house, withdrawn and apart.

In her attic-room Ruth made up the camp bed for Sarah with soft, flannelette sheets, tucking in the red blanket that normally lay folded. Usually it was Ruth who slept in the canvas bed, but since her evacuation she'd laid claim to the more permanent divan. For some reason she felt the need to demonstrate to Sarah that it was she, Ruth, who belonged here now.

Sacha and Stephen were ludicrously excited. It was only by promising to read to them from their comics that she was able to get them to clean their teeth. Maggie wouldn't read aloud from comics. She couldn't be bothered with deciphering the balloons. But Ruth loved to act out *Film Fun* for the boys, all of it, with a different voice for each of the characters. With her rapt, captive audience she got carried away and flattered herself that she was rather good. Sacha and Stephen listened, open-mouthed, and they'd got over their silliness by the time she finished.

Ruth checked that their stockings were hanging safely from the mantelpiece and tucked them in. They settled down like angels.

As she bent over Sacha he asked sleepily, 'Who would you rather be, Ruth, Laurel or Hardy?'

'Laurel. He's sweeter.'

'Me too.' His eyelids were closing. Stephen looked to be asleep already.

Downstairs in the living room Ilya had arrived home and was setting a match to the pile of kindling and logs in the hearth. 'So everything's all right, and Sarah's coming.' He looked up from his manoeuvres with the poker.

Ruth always thought how nice he looked with his moustache and shy smile. He was in ENSA, a government-sponsored organization devoted to entertaining the troops and war-workers. He had mixed feelings. It seemed a rather unheroic way of spending the war. But he enjoyed the challenge of setting up impromptu scenery and props in shelters and factories. He was performing too, and liking it, much to his own surprise. He'd always considered himself 'quiet'.

Maggie came in with some mince pies and a bottle and glasses on a tray. 'Time we tested the pies.' She put the tray down on a small table, looking pretty in the coral firelight, her long hair loose round her face. 'Now the kids are in bed we grown-ups can have a proper drink. 'There's some port . . . Ruth, would you like a drop?'

Ruth nodded, loving the cosiness of the fireside, the flattery of being included among the adults. Maggie poured her a small glass.

'Alan?' She spoke in the same light tone, but there was a kind of tension in the air before he replied.

'I don't like it.' The answer was terse and factual.

'There's beer.'

'Okay.' Alan nodded shortly. His fringe of brown hair reached his eyebrows, giving him an untidy, secretive look. Even when he was supposedly relaxing by the fire his hands remained clenched in his pockets.

'I think I'll have a beer too.' Tentatively Ilya proffered the sullen-eyed boy a touch of solidarity.

The next morning Ruth brushed her pale, shoulder-length hair in the mirror above her chest of drawers, the one Maggie had painted with sturdy, Picassoesque nursery-rhyme characters for the boys when they were toddlers. Humpty Dumpty, particularly, had a calm, restful immobility. You couldn't imagine that he was about to come to grief.

She looked with surprise at her reflection, in the dark red dress Maggie had sewed for her. It was flattering with a square neckline – not low exactly, but showing her collarbone and two or three inches of white skin – and sleeves that puffed over the shoulders and tapered into tight cuffs above the elbows. Her shoes had small heels. She'd never looked so grown-up before and she hoped Sarah would see the change in her and be impressed.

Ruth looked at her watch. Nearly eight. The boys had woken her before six to show off some cap-guns they'd found in their stockings, though Maggie had had the foresight to hide the caps until a more suitable time of day. Once awake, Ruth had investigated her own stocking. There'd been sweets, a couple of books, some pink nail varnish. After that she'd been too excited at the thought of Sarah's arrival to go back to sleep, and the time had dragged.

Lovingly she touched a parcel wrapped in blue paper, standing on a chair near the chest. It was her present to Sarah. A pot she'd thrown herself, painted, and fired in Maggie's kiln. The most successful thing she'd ever made. She couldn't wait to see Sarah's wondering smile when she unwrapped it.

In the kitchen she helped herself and the boys to toast

and some milk. Just before nine Maggie came down, in a white, high-necked blouse, black skirt, and high heels, her hair piled on top of her head.

'You're smart,' Ruth commented.

'God knows why I bother to get dolled up just to buzz about the kitchen all morning like a blue-tailed fly.'

'I'll help.'

'The hours must be going so slowly for you.' Maggie eyed her sympathetically. 'Sarah said she'd be here really early. I'm sure she won't be long now.' She began to peel muddy potatoes, looking flighty and incongruous in her festive clothes, her hands elegant and tapered, but roughened with work.

Ruth and Ilya brought in coal and logs. Ruth laid the fire carefully, grateful for any chore that would pass a few minutes.

At five to ten Sarah drew up in the Morris, beeping triumphantly as she turned into the drive.

'It's Mum!' Ruth dropped the shovel and ran to greet her.

Sarah got out of the car. 'Hallo, love. Happy Christmas.' She looked wonderfully familiar, but different too. Thinner and with heavy shadows round her eyes. Her dark hair was scraped back and looked in need of a wash. She wore black trousers and a sweater with a kind of gallant, haggard chic. In her new dress, with her smooth, shining hair, Ruth felt privileged and self-conscious.

Her mother kissed her, holding her close – Ruth could feel the intensity in Sarah's thin frame – then she studied her daughter at arm's length. 'You look so nice. So smart and grown-up.' Ruth noticed, as she rarely did, Sarah's Welsh intonation. To her surprise, her mother looked as if she might cry.

Ilya came and joined them in the cold, bright air, with

his corduroys and his nice smile. 'So Goering's given you a day off.' He hugged Sarah with a special warmth.

'It's so good to be here.' Her smile was almost a grimace, with the effort of holding back some kind of strong emotion.

'But *why* can't I come home?'

Ruth paused at the top of the stairs. It was Alan's voice she could hear from the hall, vehement, exasperated. It must be his Christmas phone call from his mother. She was a nursing auxiliary, and hadn't been able to get away. Ruth stood still, hesitating, shy of making her presence known during such a personal exchange.

There was a pause, then Alan's tones came again. 'I don't care, I don't care. I could live with Nan.'

Another silence. Ruth decided to wait until the phone call was done. It seemed the simplest.

'Please, Mum. *Please.*'

It was a shock to hear such naked pleading from the sullen, contained boy. And her heart went out to him, remembering her own isolation during her months at the Duttons' last year, the overwhelming sense of aloneness. She felt like an eavesdropper now, but was frightened of being heard if she crept away.

'Please.'

There followed a prolonged pause, as though, at the other end of the line, old explanations were being aired. Once or twice Alan put in a hollow word or two of acknowledgement. Then he said, 'Bye,' in a subdued, toneless voice and hung up.

He must have been sitting on the bottom step, round the corner, must still be there. Ruth heard no sound of movement. She couldn't stay here forever. She began to walk down the stairs noisily, breezily, to give him warning, hoping he wouldn't notice how close she'd been.

If he did know it didn't seem to bother him. He was sunk in his own thoughts, chin in hand. He moved slightly to let her pass, but didn't look up.

The lunch was perfect. It didn't seem like wartime, what with the plentiful meat and white wine from Ilya's diminishing hoard. With the one glass she was allowed, Ruth began to feel oddly detached, seeing the faces around her as if through a lens. Sarah, it seemed to her, looked tired and sort of dazed. Like a foreigner surrounded by people joking in a strange language, mechanically echoing their laughter without ever quite grasping the point. Occasionally, too, she'd go quiet and distant, as though her own thoughts were more compelling than the world about her.

But then the impression would pass. After lunch Sarah chatted placidly with Maggie and Ilya about old friends. She'd had a letter from Robert who was serving in North Africa under General O'Connor. He seemed ebullient and exhilarated at his first taste of action. Michael had been posted at last, to some hush-hush establishment in Buckinghamshire, doing work so vital he'd not been released for the holiday, and Tessa, who was Air-Raid Warden for their street, was spending her Christmas trying to cheer up the homeless in a Wandsworth rest centre. As she talked Sarah seemed to relax, but was quieter and more serious than usual.

Sacha and Stephen were clamouring for their presents so they all gathered round the tree. And it was the boys' present that eclipsed all others. A wooden train-set, made by Ilya through the year in odd, stolen moments, and painted, wittily, by Maggie. A station with two engines and lots of carriages, passengers, trees, fences, signals.

The children were dazzled, the grown-ups smiling and benevolent.

But Ruth's concern was for her own offering. The vase she'd made for her mother. She was half afraid that, with her present other-worldliness, Sarah would merely smile vaguely and place it with the rest of her gifts. Ruth craved a strong reaction. She watched Sarah avidly, silently, as she removed the blue wrapping paper, the layers of tissue, and drew out the vase. It was white, wide and rounded at the bottom, narrowing in the neck, the shape Sarah said was best for flowers. Ruth had painted it with a pattern of red geraniums and green ivy leaves, clean and simple. She admired it anew as her mother held it up.

'It's so lovely.' Sarah's voice was warm and wondering. 'It's beautiful. I can't tell you . . .' She kissed her daughter. 'Thank you so much, love.' Through the brilliant smile, her eyes had the bright, crying look.

'Glad you like it.' Ruth shrugged off her mother's emotion, but in her heart she was well satisfied.

They did have twenty minutes or so alone together. Sarah offered to take Natasha for a run across the fields, and asked if Ruth wanted to come with her.

It was a clear, cold day. In the bright air the tree trunks shone grey and bone-like, with a patina of bright mossy green. Frost still gleamed in the shady places under hedges and walls.

Sarah threw a stick for Natasha who raced for it with a crazy, bounding enthusiasm. She laughed. 'Look at that mad animal. All that energy for a paltry little twig.' The cold air had brought colour to her cheeks, and for a moment Ruth thought she looked like her old self.

'I can't get over how grown-up and independent you seem.' Sarah put an arm across Ruth's shoulders and gave

179

her a quick squeeze. 'I'm so glad you're happy here.' Her tone was warm, but held an almost imperceptible breath of sadness.

'What about you, Mum?' Ruth posed a question that lurked behind her mind like a stealthy, caged animal. 'What's it like for you? Sometimes we can see the flames and everything from here. It looks awful . . . I get frightened about you, but Maggie says the chances you could be injured are millions to one . . .' Her voice carried a muted, but urgent note of appeal.

'She's right. I'm not in any danger.' Sarah spoke with a matter-of-fact air that seemed a kind of withdrawing. 'You mustn't worry about me.'

That evening, before she got in to bed, Ruth opened her small bedroom window high in the roof. It was freezing and the stars were very clear. She leaned out to breathe in the cold air, feeling obscurely dissatisfied and dejected. She could remember this same sensation on Christmas night ever since she'd been old enough to be aware of it. It was as if the day itself could never quite justify the weeks of excitement and anticipation it aroused.

But tonight there was more to it. Impressions of the past hours flickered in her mind, crystallizing her vague sense of depression. She pictured Alan, sitting hunched at the bottom of the stairs, tight, prickly, alone among strangers however well-meaning they were. She wished she could reach out to him, show him that she knew how he was feeling, but he wore his sullenness like armour and seemed unreachable.

And there was Sarah. Ruth felt somehow cheated, thinking that after weeks of not seeing her their meeting should have been more memorable. It had been as if they'd said goodbye only a day or two before. And she'd looked distant some of the time and sort of haunted. And she'd changed the subject when anyone mentioned the bombing . . . Ruth shivered. Her toes were like ice on the cold lino. She closed the window and made for bed. Her feet touched the warm, smelly rubber of her hot-water bottle.

So much for Christmas. But at least Sarah had loved the vase . . .

It was a beautiful morning as Sarah drove back to London. The sun pierced brightly through a slight haze. The fields were silver-grey with frost, the bare trees a veiled misty blue. Idyllic. But as the Morris headed steadily homeward Sarah was disconcerted by the relief she felt at going back to the exhaustion, confusion and sheer grind of her current life. It was as if this, now, was her natural element.

She couldn't deny that yesterday had been a strain. She'd found herself estranged from Maggie, with her placid, charmed life. Jumbled images of the bombing and the injured, had kept filling her head. The sunny domesticity had seemed unreal. Oddly she'd felt a closer affinity with Alan, the sombre young evacuee, than with her own daughter.

Ruth had evoked in her a helpless love, but that, it seemed, was all Sarah had to offer. She'd had a longing to hold the child to her in a wordless embrace, but hadn't been able to respond to her enthusiastic tales about her new life at Alder. She'd failed. Ruth had looked different to her. Feminine and self-possessed, not the familiar tomboy of Sarah's imagination. No longer flesh of her flesh, but someone with a new and separate identity.

All the same, regrets were selfish. Maggie had offered Ruth a home in which she could thrive, safe from the devastation of London, and for that Sarah was profoundly in her debt.

Driving through London, she passed areas of total destruction. Buildings with whole walls ripped away, like cross-section diagrams, revealing the pathetic and intimate remains of the lives they'd housed. Three-little-pigs wallpaper, a large, dog-eared pin-up of Marlene Dietrich hanging by one corner, torn and soiled net curtains stirring slightly in the breeze, a large celluloid doll, legs splayed, face crumpled, the mouth still an unchanging pink rosebud. Sarah drove through it all, almost indifferent. In the last three months she'd been surfeited with scenes of this sort.

In the backstreets there were bomb-damaged houses, still inhabited. Some displayed small Union Jacks, jammed in a window or a drainpipe. It showed patriotism of a sort, Sarah thought, but perhaps more simply a kind of defiance, the determination to survive. She felt hopeful now. They'd come this far and people still joked and cleared up the mess and got to work on time.

There'd been moments in the beginning when all had seemed chaos. And as she drove past blackened, flame-filled buildings with her maimed cargo, she'd felt like one of the howling, harried victims in a huge and lurid Bruegel painting she'd once seen called *The Triumph of Death*. But, months later, she was still here, and so were lots of other people, and the breakdown of social order, so grimly prophesied, had simply never happened.

Ahead, on her right, a young woman in curlers, with bare feet in pink, fluffy slippers, ran down the front pathway of her house. It was on the end of a row of homes in varying states of collapse. The roof was patched with a large, dirty sheet of tarpaulin. In the street she caught rough hold of the arm of a small boy with a blond fringe and a parrot-tuft of hair on the crown of his head.

'I'll teach you to play out in those trousers, you little toe-rag,' she yelled, bringing her free hand smartly across to smack his skinny, grey-flannelled bottom. The child began to cry in a mechanical snuffling fashion.

Sarah grinned to herself. Life went on.

18

Peter Borchert pulled out a chair, inclining his long body slightly in a sort of symbolic bow. Smiling, Dominique took a seat.

'A drop of champagne?'

The question was almost rhetorical, a ritual between them. The tall German was already reaching towards a shiny ice-bucket for the dark bottle beaded with chill moisture. The Teutonic accent lent his French a pleasing formality.

'Just what I need. My throat's as dry as a bone.' She felt worldly sitting here in a red satin dress with this sophisticated older man. The first time Dominique had agreed to join him at his table, at the invitation of Grimaud, she'd felt tense and vaguely shame-faced. He was, after all, a member of the occupying forces. But he'd been tactful and made it clear that he understood her scruples. In time she learned to relax. He was nice and seemed sensitive, and she knew that their relationship would never go further than a casual drink. Peter's companions were a blonde society-type Frenchwoman, whom she knew by sight, and an unknown man in black SS uniform. He introduced them. 'Dominique, this is Irène.' He didn't elaborate further. The woman bestowed a cold, careful smile. 'And Wolf, an old friend who's got a few days' leave. He's stagnating in Le Mans, poor fellow.'

'Bad luck.' Dominique grinned broadly and took a slug of her champagne. She liked Peter's complicity, the way he assumed that her reaction to Le Mans would be the same as his.

His friend was overweight, blond and, to Dominique's eyes, rather coarse-looking. He said smarmily, 'I congratulate you on your performance, Mademoiselle. The true French *joie de vivre*.'

What did he know about it, this fat German? But she smiled with a good grace, looking at him over the rim of her glass. Where and how Grimaud got his champagne was a mystery to her. At the Flore there was ersatz beer or coffee and that was that.

Nowadays at the Philo, Dominique was forced to sing horrible, sentimental-roguish songs about mimosas in bloom and strolling in the moonlight with the one she loved. They were what the German clientele expected – the Nazi party despised jazz as sleazy and decadent. She performed the songs with a tongue-in-cheek verve that had the occupying forces rolling in the aisles, even singing along on occasion. Her popularity was such that she'd been able to prevail upon Grimaud to double her salary. At the time he'd been sullen as a cornered mongrel, but he'd had no alternative. The German customers were his life-blood.

'I liked that new song about the lilacs by the Seine.' Peter's eyes held a malicious gleam. He knew her feelings about the material she was obliged to sing and it amused him. Dominique was cheered to think that at least one patron of the Philo was on her wavelength.

'Adorable, isn't it?' Her own eyes flashed a teasing reciprocal message.

She was flattered by Peter's friendship. She admired him. There was about him an unbreachable aura of *savoir-faire*. For reasons she'd never stopped to analyse he wore civilian clothes – well-cut suits, laundered shirts, sober ties – and cut an elegant figure. Yet the man inside the clothes had a down-to-earth ruggedness. A muscular body. A long face, slightly pock-marked. Red-brown hair, thinning a little perhaps, but in no way detracting from his air of contained competence. And he accepted Dominique as she chose to be, making it clear in his matter-of-fact way that he'd like to sleep with her if she were willing, but if not . . . well, they were too mature to let a thing like that stand between them.

In fact they only ever met at the Café Philo, for the odd half hour or so after her performance. Over the months they'd talked about art, books, music. He listened to her opinions – and remembered them. Once or twice he'd given her postcards of paintings she'd said she liked, and once a gramophone recording of the *Dies Irae* from Mozart's *Requiem*, one of her favourite pieces of music. Thoughtful tokens, but nothing expensive to place her under an obligation. And he'd showed her photographs of his wife, an attractive, angular blonde, and their two daughters, girls of about ten and twelve, their light hair pulled back so tightly and austerely that their faces appeared vacant of all expression.

Grimaud beamed paternally on his singer's civilized friendship with the distinguished German. He thought it good for business. Arrogantly, unreasonably, he detested the tarts, as he called them, who flocked round the German troops, though they made up a large proportion of his clientele.

Dominique smiled inwardly as she watched Wolf's lumbering attempts to impress the glacial Irène. He had obviously labelled her as classy, and had dredged his memory for cultural nuggets to lay before her. His face hung, red and sweaty, above the table as he prattled of

186

French novelists, with a pop-eyed, slightly desperate expression.

'Balzac. Now there's a talent. So vigorous and . . .'

'Robust.' Irène gave a small, judicious nod.

'But perhaps a touch . . . coarse. Now if I had to choose between him and Stendhal . . .'

'A real psychologist.' Just a shade of amused irony.

'Absolutely.' Wolf laid a large, warm, pink hand briefly on her slim wrist. 'The human heart. He dissected . . . turned it inside out.'

A covert struggle was under way between the two Germans for Irène's favour. But while Wolf plodded like a persistent rhino, Peter remained affably detached, and Irène, with her immaculate blonde hair and pencilled eyebrows, serene and passive, though she signalled her preference for Peter in small, subtle ways.

Wolf ploughed on. 'The seduction scene. What's the woman's name now? In *Le Rouge et le Noir.*'

'Madame de Rênal.' Irène's precise, crystalline tones.

Dominique had seen her in the Café Philo many times and always with one or more German officers in tow. She'd become something of a legend. Grimaud had raved about her aristocratic looks until it dawned on him that she was no better than the tarts he so despised.

To her surprise Dominique discovered that she, too, disapproved of Irène. It was a gut reaction. She herself would chat to the Germans, treat them as human. Why not, since they were there? A fact of life. But to go with them, sleep with them. The enemy. It seemed ignoble.

Abandoning his increasingly lame struggle with culture, Wolf asked Irène to dance. There was a decorous three-piece band – all men in middle-age – whom Grimaud hired for next to nothing. Irène rose, a politely resigned expression on her face. Wolf clasped her thankfully to his beer-belly, obviously feeling himself to be on firmer ground. Her figure, in powder-blue silk, remained obstinately straight-backed and unyielding.

As they circled the small floor, Irène's face was visible over Wolf's left shoulder. She wore a fixed, well-bred but slightly pained smile. Dominique caught Peter's eye and grinned irrepressibly.

'Poor old Wolf. He's always been a trier.' Peter's stiff German accent made the remark irresistibly comic. Dominique giggled, enjoying the moment of half-guilty complicity.

Le Pessimiste, in the summer of '42, was like home. Its regulars were a family. No German ever set foot inside it. The odd few who tried, over the months, had been chilled by the atmosphere of overt, watchful hostility, and hadn't returned. In any case its damp, sweating walls and cavernous gloom held little charm for any but the initiated.

Early in the previous year Ruby had sent for Dominique, having decided that the time was ripe to re-employ her former singer. Under the Occupation Paris had settled back into a kind of makeshift normality, and Le Pessimiste had gradually regained at least a proportion of its old clientele. Young in the main – or young at heart – many with aspirations as poets, actors, musicians and the like, they had in common a simmering hostility towards the occupying forces.

Dominique had been summoned to Ruby's office one dreary morning in February. If anything, the club looked even more squalid in the daytime. Ruby's peasant bulk had been enveloped in a large man's dressing-gown and she'd shuffled around in grey socks and backless felt slippers. Without her mask of peachy face powder she seemed less alarming. But before Dominique had a chance to speak Ruby had stated flatly, 'Two nights a week and I'll pay you the same as before. Take it or leave it . . . and what you do on stage is your own affair.' Shrewdly she'd understood that money was less important to Dominique than a free hand.

With the vivid and challenging stage personality she cultivated, and the unexpected, uncompromising, unsentimental material that she searched out, Dominique was a natural in the self-consciously avant-garde atmosphere of Ruby's nightclub. Serge, the taciturn pianist, was re-engaged to accompany her. She was passionate about her work here. She believed in it, would stake her reputation on it. She was assiduous in finding new songs, in making sure that her act remained fresh and surprising. Since the majority of her audience were regulars, this was a real challenge. But now, nearly eighteen months after her debut, she was queen of the close, incestuous world of Le Pessimiste.

Her search for new material went on all the time. She became resourceful, translating American and English songs herself if she thought they'd suit her style, discovering poems and setting them to her own melodies, appropriating a number of Kurt Weill's bitter-sweet ballads. Daniel let her borrow a couple of his verses and they made up tunes between them, enlisting Rosa and her piano. Rosa was amused at the casual way Dominique compiled her repertoire. 'Haven't you ever heard of the law of copyright?' she demanded. 'One day when you're famous, mark my words, you'll have a thousand lawsuits on your hands.' Dominique merely shrugged at Rosa's misgivings. No one at Le Pessimiste cared two hoots.

She could read and write music and scribbled out her ideas on envelopes and paper bags, even on the fly leaves of books, much to Serge's exasperation. But, in his poker-faced fashion, he was sympathetic to Dominique's fancies and learned to put up with her disorganized demands.

Ever since his surprise appearance in the rue Bonaparte almost two years ago now, Dominique and Daniel had lived together in cheerful chaos in her room at the top of the house.

To begin with he'd been in hiding. He'd deserted rather than offer himself up as a prisoner-of-war, and was liable for arrest and worse.

Dominique was the first to admit that his abrupt arrival had given a huge fillip to her life. She was bored and disgruntled at the time, with little money, only the vaguest of job prospects, and few friends in the partially deserted city.

Then suddenly there was Daniel, bringing with him an exciting aura of lawlessness, and lending an immediate purpose to her days. She found it fascinating to hide him, find him food and clothes. And, by dint of patient enquiry, dull, fruitless waits in strange cafés, long treks to distant *quartiers* like Neuilly and Clichy, and furtive evening visits to anonymous apartments, she finally managed to obtain for him the forged papers that would regularize his presence in Paris.

Since he'd come on the scene her life had got better and better. Quite soon afterwards Grimaud had contacted her about a job. And she loved singing at the Café Philo – in spite of the awful songs – wearing bright, sexy dresses and acting a bold, breezy role that wasn't really false, but just one aspect of the person she was. It occurred to her that it was just as well that her twin worlds remained totally separate. Most of the regulars of Le Pessimiste would have disapproved of the Philo's clientele. Mentally Dominique shrugged off their imagined reproof. Her conscience was clear. She held no brief for the enemy, but she liked being liked, seeing the starchy Germans in their stiff uniforms relax and become human.

And then Ruby's offer had come, and with it the total fascination of fashioning an act and a personality that was personal to her and quite unique. In the joy and absorption of her days she scarcely noticed the restrictions and shortages that loomed on all sides. She was consciously happy and occupied Paris was her stage.

Alongside all this there was Daniel. He was careless, like her, and light-hearted. Their room at the top of the house in the rue Bonaparte was messy and chaotic and neither of them minded. They were always hard up. Daniel had odd jobs. He helped out in a local bookshop and worked intermittently as waiter, cook and general bottle-washer in a nearby café. Between times he scribbled poetry, reworking one verse a dozen times, or disappeared to spend hours over one cup of coffee with friends – making silly intellectual jokes or discussing abstruse, unimportant philosophical questions, Dominique supposed. Such pastimes bored her, but she liked the fact that he felt not the smallest twinge of guilt over his idle hours.

In some way, she thought, they were more like brother and sister than lovers, laughing and squabbling with none of the possessive anxiety that Robert had brought with him. Except that their physical attraction was ever-present. Daniel's body seemed in a constant state of readiness. They slept late, cuddled like puppies, made love among the discarded clothes and piles of books, with the sun shining in at the window and workaday street sounds in their ears, then argued over whose turn it was to make the coffee.

She loved him like breathing, without having to think

191

or talk about it. His brown eyes and ambiguous smile were a part of her life. His poems, though, made it clear that his feelings for her were deeper and more complex than his easygoing exterior suggested.

Daniel nourished a scalding contempt for every aspect of France's collaborationist policy. He hated Marshal Pétain and Pierre Laval with a sustained, personal intensity, as the two most visible figureheads of the Vichy regime. Of the two, his loathing for Pétain was the stronger. Laval, he maintained, was an out-and-out bastard in anyone's book, but Pétain's projection of himself as an elder statesman and patriotic old soldier sickened him. In their room he'd pinned up a full-page magazine cutting of the man and defaced it with insults and anti-Vichy slogans. Alongside it was a copy of de Gaulle's rallying call to the French from exile in London.

To be honest, it had never occurred to Dominique to hate either of them. To her Pétain was just someone who'd done the necessary in the aftermath of defeat. But by dint of living alongside Daniel she got used to mentioning his name with the obligatory curl of the lip.

They'd argued over her working at the Café Philo. Daniel hated the idea of her singing to the enemy. But Dominique pointed out that it was just a job. The Germans were everywhere. Daniel himself was forced to serve them in the restaurant and the bookshop where he worked. What was the difference? Reluctantly he accepted her logic.

At Le Pessimiste Daniel found plenty of like-minded souls, whom he brought back to the rue Bonaparte for clandestine meetings. Though Dominique loved the camaraderie of these occasions and had many good friends among the regulars she secretly thought their attempts at resistance well-meaning but half-baked. Not that she'd have said as much. What, realistically, could they do? Their sole act of defiance seemed to be the founding of an underground arts review.

The Germans made great play of encouraging the arts, but everything had to pass through the fine sieve of their censorship. The *habitués* of Le Pessimiste scorned to submit their work to official scrutiny. They took matters into their own hands. André Delarue, a quiet, intense young lithographer, with deep black eyes, suggested the title of *Métro*, because of the subterranean nature of their publication. The idea was greeted rapturously. Dominique was pleased and rather surprised that it had been André's suggestion. Usually he was withdrawn and easily overlooked.

The review contained poetry, short stories, woodcuts, lithographs, all by regulars of Le Pessimiste. The tone was irreverent and anti-German. André, in particular, had submitted some grotesque cartoons of Nazi soldiers.

'They're superb,' Daniel had exclaimed delightedly, but the committee had got cold feet and dithered. Daniel had been so scathing about their cowardice that finally they'd gone ahead and published out of sheer bravado. Personally Dominique couldn't see that they risked much. What had the Germans got to fear from their childish lampoons?

A printer called Thomas, a stick-thin individual with a stubbly beard who reminded her of Van Gogh, printed their copies of *Métro* in his workshop at night. 'Lovely job,' he'd comment complacently as he handed over the anonymous pigskin suitcase that held the latest issue.

The nice thing about the review was that it formed a bond between them all, and cheered them up during the drab days of the Occupation. And Dominique found it a useful source of material. There were always poems in it she could use, either set to music or simply recited in a defiant fashion, her slim figure picked out from the surrounding darkness by a single white spotlight, while in the audience you could have heard a pin drop. To please her public, Dominique made sure that a proportion of the poems and songs she performed were covertly anti-German. You never stated your views openly – there could be informers among the audience – but wrapped them in metaphors and symbols so that only those in the know would understand and enjoy the rebellious little secret.

Otherwise the main Resistance activity among the male regulars consisted of growing their hair long in pointed contrast to the shaved necks of the Nazis. Both sexes participated in after-dark forays to paint V-signs and crosses of Lorraine on posters, walls and German-owned cars. Dominique occasionally joined these expeditions. For her their forbidden naughtiness was on a par with playing knock-down-ginger when she was a child.

19

In the long beam of the single spotlight Dominique could see cigarette smoke drifting in slow curls. It had a herbal smell. True tobacco was almost impossible to find. Her audience were black silhouettes, some recognizable. To her right she could see Daniel's shaggy curls and Rosa's shoulder-length bob. But individuals were unimportant. She sensed a general warmth, a waiting hush for the climax of tonight's performance.

She'd discovered something different. A fable by the sixteenth-century poet La Fontaine. It was called *The Wolves and The Sheep* and pointed out the foolishness of 'making peace with villains'. She was thrilled by the aptness of the allegory, and knew that the patrons of Le Pessimiste could be relied upon to draw their own conclusions. It was the sort of thing they loved.

The silence was electric. She stood there, in black shirt and trousers, her face white with make-up and the artificial light, red hair frizzed to shoulder level. Then she began to recite, clear and unhurried. As the fable proceeded she experienced again, forcibly, its relevance to the French predicament, forgetting, in the intensity and conviction of her speaking, the general lukewarm attitude she had towards the resistance activities of her friends. There was a kind of narcissistic rapture in hearing her own voice, so young and earnest, filling the hushed cellar. She was totally convinced by the fervour of her own performance. The poem was potent in its utter simplicity, the plain, archaic language rising slowly to its climax, the artless, almost childlike declaration, 'Tis an evil, never-theless, when enemies are faithless'.

The ingenuous final words were followed by a stunned silence, then, as the listeners came to themselves, the darkness erupted with tumultuous applause. It went on and on, a release, it seemed, a brief escape from the humiliation of their daily existence.

Dominique stood still and passive. To acknowledge the cheers in any conventional way would have been to admit to the artifice, the theatricality of the moment. She found that her cheeks were wet with tears. She wished almost that she could split herself in two, and be a part of the audience, to witness a performance of such simple power. Gravely she inclined her head, then turned and quit the stage.

Ten minutes later when she came to join her friends her emotion had subsided. Her route to Daniel's table was punctuated with greetings and congratulations, eager hands touching her arms, friendly eyes smiling. Some belonged to people she knew well, others to near-strangers. But she was used to that now she was, in however small a way, a personality.

Her stage persona spilled over into her real life. Nowa-days she wore her theatrical black nearly all the time. With her red hair it was a kind of trade mark, making her instantly recognizable at the Flore, the Dôme, in the streets of Saint Germain. Sarah would have been proud of her, she thought with a wry, inward smile. She'd dyed nearly everything. It was hard to come by new clothes nowadays, and, like almost everyone, she wore shoes with wooden soles. But she half regretted her renunciation of colour and enjoyed the bright dresses she wore for her bread-and-butter job at the Philo.

In an alcove by the rough wall Daniel was at a table with Rosa, Guy and a boyfriend of Rosa's called Luc. They looked vaguely conspiratorial, Dominique thought, with their heads almost touching and illuminated by the faint, reddish lights with which Ruby veiled the shabbiness of her establishment.

She was surprised to see Guy. He didn't often come to Le Pessimiste. But Daniel would be pleased. He had a great admiration for the older man.

Dominique greeted him with a bright smile. 'Hallo, stranger.' She was a little in awe of Guy.

'Hallo.' He kissed the cheek she offered. Adding, after an almost imperceptible pause, 'A very moving performance, Dominique. A positive *tour de force*.'

'Thank you.' She always had the uncomfortable feeling that Guy read her like a book, and found her insincere. Well, that was up to him. She hadn't *felt* insincere up there on stage. 'I couldn't believe it when I came across that poem. It's so absolutely appropriate. And written all that time ago. Amazing! I just had to use it.' He always had the effect of making her prattle wildly to cover up for his air of reserve.

'Absolutely.' She wasn't sure whether she detected a note of irony in his voice. Dimly she recalled a conversation she'd had with him months ago. She'd had the impression that he was subtly sounding her out as to her attitude towards Resistance activity. She'd been vague, evasive, not at all keen. Presumably he remembered too.

She rattled on. 'I wasn't sure whether it wouldn't be a mistake to end on a recitation. I've never done it before, though I've used . . . I'm a singer after all.'

Guy gestured at the people around them. 'How can you doubt yourself? You were a *succès fou*.' Again she wondered if she didn't deduce just a trace of mockery, as

197

if he saw both her own performance and the audience's raptures as twin aspects of the same hollow theatricality. But she told herself she was being over-sensitive. And anyway, what did it matter what he thought?

At the time of France's surrender, Guy had been lying wounded in the leg in a military hospital near Paris. In this way he'd escaped the fate of thousands of his compatriots who'd been rounded up and deported to Germany as prisoners-of-war. So, unlike Daniel's, his presence in Paris was wholly legal.

'Luc's got some whisky,' Daniel whispered.

Dominique mimed surprise and delight. 'I don't believe it!' It was a relief to break off from her conversation with Guy. 'You must have shady friends, Luc,' she declared flirtatiously. It wasn't really a joke. Luc dabbled openly on the black market. He gave a pleased little smirk.

Dominique wasn't sure about him. He taught music at a local *lycée*, but longed to be known as a composer. So far, though, his works had been performed only by his pupils, the sole captive musicians he could command. She was intrigued by his fly, freebooting side. It seemed so out of character.

'We've been putting it in our beer.' Surreptitiously he raised an anonymous medicine bottle a couple of inches above the rim of Rosa's bag.

'Lovely stuff.' She enthused to be polite. Actually she had no great use for spirits of any kind.

He was younger than Rosa, round about thirty, and not bad looking. Slim and dark with cleanly chiselled features, hair cut *en brosse* and gold-rimmed glasses. Rosa maintained that he was kind and caring and forgave him his moments of social clumsiness. She had been seeing him for about six months. Her saxophonist, Pierre, was a prisoner in Germany and seemed likely to stay there for the duration of the war. Dominique suspected that Luc was a touch intimidated by the Pessimiste regulars. He was sensitive about his steady job and used his privateering skills to add colour to his personality.

She ordered a beer and Rosa had one too. Dominique had the impression that she'd already had several. Once Rosa had tippled sociably, light-heartedly, but recently, when she got the opportunity, there seemed almost a kind of desperation to her drinking. When the beers arrived Luc tipped into each a generous measure of the whisky, handling the bottle furtively. He'd wrapped it in a check handkerchief. Dominique thought his secrecy a little overdone, but found his self-important airs rather appealing.

The composition of the beer currently served at Le Pessimiste was a mystery. It tasted distinctly odd and its effects were negligible. The whisky made it taste even stranger, but at least lent it a certain potency.

'Wonderful.' Dominique gave a sigh of satisfaction as she downed the first gulp, largely to humour Luc. 'I can feel it racing round every vein in my body. Not like the usual dishwater.'

'Plenty more.' Luc tapped Rosa's handbag with a complacent air.

Rosa was quiet. Usually her natural gaiety, or a pretence of it, held sway. But there were increasingly times when she seemed preoccupied by her own thoughts. She'd given up her music and taken a job in the office of a local bookshop, as though her only security lay in making herself as inconspicuous as possible.

Dominique tried to distract her. 'How was Odette?' She knew Rosa had been to visit her sister in the suburbs. Speaking softly, to make the conversation a personal one, between the two of them.

Rosa appeared pale and strained. She'd already half finished her drink, as if she were too restless to leave it standing in front of her. She looked haunted tonight, Dominique thought, and beautiful, in a grey dress. Her sombre state of mind seemed to be reflected in her clothing. Hanging pewter earrings showed against her dark hair.

She grimaced. 'They were wearing the star. All the family.'

Dominique placed her hands over Rosa's. There was nothing she could say. The Germans had made a new ruling a fortnight or so earlier. All Jews were to wear a yellow star 'sewn firmly to their clothing' to declare themselves. Though Rosa had ignored the edict.

She went on, 'Odette told me the kids have been bullied at school, called filthy names. And the teachers just turn a blind eye . . .' Her voice broke on the last words, and again she reached for her glass.

'It's unbelievable.' Dominique was shocked at what she'd said about the teachers. 'The bastards!' She could show the correct indignation, but could offer no reassurance. She remembered the evening, two summers ago, when Rosa had first mentioned her fears. How glibly she'd been able to dismiss them. But now . . . You heard stories of arrests, internments, though perhaps there was more to them than met the eye . . .

She'd mentioned the matter to Peter one evening, when they'd been talking quietly. He'd spread his hands. 'I don't like it any more than you, Dominique . . .' Then he'd changed the subject, seeming uncharacteristically subdued.

The others were listening now, her conversation with Rosa no longer private.

Suddenly, without preamble, Luc appealed to them in

general. 'You know, Rosa refuses to wear the star. I think she's wrong. It's sheer stubbornness.' He turned to Guy, as if to an authority figure. 'Don't you agree, the important thing is to keep your nose clean, obey all their little regulations? If you do that, you'll be okay. They'll leave you alone.'

'Shut up, Luc. It's none of your business.' Rosa's interjection was overloud, just a shade slurred. Dominique realized suddenly that her friend was drunker than she'd thought. Rosa moved her arm, abruptly, awkwardly, and sent her glass flying. The remains of her drink splattered Dominique's trousers. Spilled, the liquid seemed to increase in volume. The front of her right leg was soaked.

Rosa was mortified and dabbed clumsily at the material with Luc's check handkerchief.

'It's all right.' Dominique wished she wouldn't. It would dry out soon enough. 'It doesn't matter.' She was upset by Rosa's confusion. It wasn't like her. But at least the fuss might enable them to change the subject, since she could do nothing for Rosa but bleed for her.

A waitress passed. With a large gesture Luc ordered fresh beers all round. Dominique felt exasperated. Surely he could see that Rosa had had more than enough. And no doubt he'd be splashing his wretched whisky about.

Daniel produced some cigarettes and offered them around. 'Acorn and dried parsley, anyone?' Dominique was grateful for his imperturbable good humour.

'Not acorns, surely.' She grinned at him. He looked so young and sure of himself, his face above the dark sweater slightly flushed in the reddish light. 'Don't the acorns go into coffee? I mean there wouldn't be enough to go round.' She took a cigarette, glad of the diversion, though

201

she hated these herbal monstrosities and knew the smoke would make her tonsils feel raw.

'I wonder what the squirrels live on nowadays.' Rosa sounded more like herself, smiling, but fragile.

Guy fanned the air as Daniel and Dominique lit up. 'Smells more like shredded cabbage leaves.'

'Then it's good for you as well.' Dominique inhaled deeply, as though drawing in a blast of fresh spring air. The smoke rasped the back of her throat and made her cough. The others laughed. The mood had lightened. The beers arrived. Once again Luc wielded his medicine bottle.

Rosa put a hand over her glass. 'Not for me.'

Luc urged her. 'Come on. It'll cheer you up.' Silently Dominique cursed him. Rosa allowed herself to be convinced.

As soon as they were settled with the drinks Luc blundered back to the fray. 'Seriously, Guy, what do you think about this question?' Dominique was exasperated at his total lack of tact. He seemed braced for a full-scale confrontation.

'What question?' Guy spoke with a bland detachment that hinted at hostility, but Luc seemed utterly impervious to atmosphere. Either that or he was so determined to have his say that he didn't care.

'The star, you know, and Rosa.'

Guy took a long swallow of his beer. There was a reflective silence. His swarthy face seemed deliberately drained of expression. 'I think Rosa's a big girl. She can make her own decisions.'

'If I obeyed all their rules and regulations I wouldn't be here now,' Rosa pointed out, stumbling a little over the words. She appeared overwrought again. They all knew she shouldn't be at Le Pessimiste. Jews weren't supposed to leave their homes now after eight o'clock at night. Rosa had consistently flouted this ruling as well.

Luc ignored her, concentrating on Guy. Behind the metal-rimmed glasses his eyes were earnest and intense. 'So you have no point of view, Guy.' His clean-cut features had a self-righteous look.

Dominique was aware that she and Guy and Daniel shared, at that moment, an unspoken, but palpable irritation with the man. Unfairly probably. To them he seemed an insensitive, self-important Johnny-Come-Lately, who was trying to organize Rosa and enlist the help of friends who'd known her far longer. He was fond of her, obviously, but no more than they.

Guy shook his head. He said slowly, 'You're wrong, Luc. I've got two points of view.'

Dominique thought he looked tired and greyer than she remembered him.

Deliberately Guy raised his right forefinger. 'One. Yes, I think Rosa should wear the star. It's what the Nazis want, and they're the bosses . . . Two.' He raised the finger alongside it. 'Two. No, I don't think she should wear the star. It makes her less identifiable, and it's quite possible that she'll avoid certain sorts of trouble that way.' He shrugged. 'I don't know which point of view's the better one. So don't try and get me to tell Rosa what to do.' His words, forcibly expressed, were followed by a silence.

Dominique glanced at Rosa and was shocked. She was still and deathly white, like a Medusa, her eyes fixed and empty. Tears rolled down her cheeks, easily, silently, seemingly with no effort of will on her part. She saw Dominique looking and placed a deprecating hand in front of her eyes. It's the bloody whisky, Dominique thought. Luc should have had more sense.

20

Alan West reached up with a long stick and pulled at a high, branching cane of blackberries. They gleamed, plump and dark, in the sun. 'There's loads on this one.' He caught hold of the branch gingerly with finger and thumb. 'Grab them, Ruth, quick.'

Deftly she stripped the prickly cane while he held it down. 'Don't let go suddenly. I'm scratched enough as it is.' Several handfuls went into the large basket standing on the ground beside them. Already it was brimming. Another stood by ready to be filled.

The lane was a mile or so from the village and not much frequented. Ruth had come across it one day out on a solitary walk. One side of its narrow length was completely flanked by blackberry thickets.

Alan released the branch and reached up for another. 'No one else'll have a beat like this.' He squinted into the sunlight, selecting another likely bough.

'We're bound to get the most again. We've got to. Won't old Ma Gifford be choked.' Ruth was scathingly triumphant. With his scowling diffidence and London accent, Alan was looked at askance by some of the village worthies. But none could deny his patriotism. They were forced to admit that he outclassed the local lads by miles in his exertions for the war effort.

He and Ruth were beadily ambitious salvage collectors. Whether it was paper, scrap-metal, bones, or herbs and rosehips, almost unfailingly they turned in the largest hoard. They did so with a modest air which belied their foxy triumph. They liked to prove the superiority of the Londoners. It was a kind of pact between them.

Their success wasn't popular. Villages, Ruth had discovered, were riddled with underground seams of rivalry. The congratulations they earned were sometimes thin-lipped. But the worst anyone could say of them openly was that they were 'pushy'.

'We'll eat in ten minutes, okay?' Ruth gave him plenty of warning. Alan was apt to get so engrossed in the task in hand that he couldn't be bothered.

It was a perfect day in early October, the air clear and warm after a morning mist. They were surrounded by mellow, tawny colours – the dried grass, bracken beginning to show brown, rich red haws gleaming from the hedgerows, the yellowing brambles. They picked steadily. After almost quarter of an hour the second basket was half full.

Alan gloated over the contents. 'We'll take these home later, then come back for more.' The WVS was standing by, with extra sugar allotted by the Government, for a marathon of jam-making. The local children had been given Friday off school for the essential task of picking.

'I'm famished.' Ruth sat down on the opposite bank in the sun and began to rifle their bag of provisions. Her legs protruded, long and lanky, from her khaki shorts. Her pale hair fell wispily across her face.

Alan stood by, waiting for her to hand him his packet of sandwiches. He said suddenly, 'You look like Veronica Lake.' His tone was merely factual.

Ruth felt herself blush, as though he'd read her thoughts. They'd seen a film of hers at the village hall last week and since then, in whatever she was doing, Ruth had imagined herself as the silky-haired film star.

She gave a cocky grin to hide her embarrassment.

205

'Well, I *am* a bit of an actress, don't you know?' Recently her evenings had been taken up with rehearsals for the school's production of *Twelfth Night*, in aid of the ever-present war effort. Ruth was playing Maria. The experience was delightful. A twin daydream wove itself through her Veronica Lake fantasies – that of being a Serious Actress.

'Big 'ead.' Alan's rejoinder was without malice. 'Give us my sarnis.'

She threw the packet at him none too gently. He sat down and began to unwrap them. Ruth uncorked a flask of weak tea. Tea was always weak nowadays, the leaves used repeatedly till there was barely colour or flavour left in them. She poured the pale liquid into a plastic cup.

'Oh God! She's done it!' A cry from Alan, disgusted and amused all at once.

'What on earth . . . ?'

'Look!' He waved a sandwich under her nose, and lifted the corner of the top slice of bread. 'She's done it! Look what's in here.'

She peered, then understood and laughed abruptly. 'Oh no! Nasturtium leaves. I never thought she would.'

They'd often teased Maggie for poring over the Ministry of Food Bulletins and mocked the sometimes outlandish suggestions given therein for ensuring proper family nutrition. Nasturtium leaf sandwiches had been a particular target of their wit, and Maggie had used them as a threat on many occasions.

Ruth grinned. 'I thought she had a funny smile on her face when she handed them over.'

Alan examined the contents of his sandwich. 'At least she's washed off the black fly.'

'Awful waste of good protein.'

She was aware of feeling happy, sitting here companionably with Alan in the autumn sun. When they were alone, like now, with a common aim in view, they relaxed. At school, out of a self-protective instinct, they more or less ignored one another. They had no desire to be bracketed together and teased. Even at home they communicated more with Stephen and Sacha, or Maggie, than with each other.

Their friendship dated back just over a year. It had happened, in the last summer holidays, that they'd been left alone together for almost a whole day. Maggie had taken the boys to Cambridge to try and buy them some school shoes. Alan and Ruth had started a game of Monopoly. With only the two of them the game had been less than thrilling, and they began to cheat outrageously to liven it up. It ended with Ruth sweeping his ship and her top hat from the board, and throwing money and cards at him. Alan lay on the floor, laughing, his hair in his eyes, weakly throwing back handfuls of the paper.

His high spirits had surprised her suddenly. Yet she realized then that they weren't at all at odds with his manner over recent months. And she understood how much he'd changed since the previous Christmas.

She said, in a tone of discovery, 'You're okay here now, aren't you? You quite like it.'

For a split second he seemed to consider the question. Then he answered, quite seriously, 'Yes, it's all right.'

Ruth had confessed then something she thought of as a half-guilty secret. 'I heard you telephoning once. To your mum. Asking her to take you home. I was listening. I couldn't help it.'

He gave a worldly-wise grin. 'I know. Don't worry. I didn't care.'

'Oh.' Momentarily the wind was taken out of her sails.

They'd talked then, heart to heart, in the deserted

house, about their homes, their mothers, the village, the war. He was in the same boat as she was. They understood one another. Then the others arrived home and Ruth and Alan took refuge in their customary separateness.

They'd made contact again. Ruth hadn't expected to at first. In many ways Alan was still the prickly boy he'd been before. Then gradually she understood that he liked their moments of closeness too. Relied on them, expected them. They were a shared secret.

'These sarnis aren't that bad.' He chewed up his last mouthful and reached for the flask.

'You know what I'd really like?' Ruth lounged luxuriously on the grass, screwing her eyes against the sun.

'What's that?'

'Sandwiches with a great big thick slab of cheese. Three weeks' rations at one go, with pickles and tomatoes.' Staring beatifically skywards as though they might appear, like a celestial vision.

They heard vague rustlings and turned their heads. Two figures had appeared in the lane, and were approaching. Two boys, they saw. Ruth stared as they came closer, but didn't recognize them. Must be from the next village. They looked about eleven.

One was conventionally dressed in grey shirt and shorts. The other was startling. A strikingly handsome child with blond hair and regular features, full lips, a wild-rose bloom on his cheeks. He wore a red shirt and dark trousers tucked into socks, a heavy strap round his waist. With a jolt Ruth saw that four dead rabbits hung from the belt, swinging loosely. The boy had an air of surly arrogance. He seemed to her suddenly primitive, a kind of pagan vision.

He came up to them. 'Seen any rabbits round this way?' She had the impression that the child would have addressed the King of England with the same bold lack of ingratiation.

She shook her head and grinned. 'Just molehills.'

He gave her a brief, contemptuous glance.

Alan stepped forward. 'How much do you want for one of those rabbits?' He jingled coins in his pockets. Last weekend his mother had visited.

'Four bob.' A note of aggression. The child's grey eyes hard in the bright sun.

'Give us one.'

The transaction was conducted without further ado and the boys went on their way.

'Lucky, eh?' Alan turned for her approval. His smile was open, enthusiastic. He was hugely proud, she realized, of his contribution towards keeping the household fed. 'I'll skin it when we get home. I'm getting good at that sort of thing. Maggie'll be pleased.'

21

The clock sounded overloud in the silence. A slab of heavy black slate, it crouched on the mantelpiece in the dim room, the dry, rhythmic ticking lending it a kind of life. Next to it, a stump of candle flickered, throwing a pale, warm light, giving the room a softness. Like a de la Tour painting, Sarah thought.

'Better now?' She spoke quietly to Tessa Mason, who sat in the opposite chair. She was in the early stages of labour. She looked awkward and uncomfortable, cushions at her back, her ballooning stomach and heavy legs giving a stolid, earthbound set to her body.

Tessa nodded, breathing deeply. 'Yes. It's passed over for a bit.' Cradling her belly with her hands, as if it were fragile.

'D'you want anything? A drink?'

Tessa shook her head. The blonde hair was bunched in rats' tails where she'd run her hands through it when the pain came. 'No, nothing. Just talk to me. About anything. It helps. Tell me about Ruth.'

Sarah smiled in the dimness. 'She's fine, blooming. It's as if she'd always lived down there.'

'Wouldn't you like to have her here with you?' Tessa's voice was sympathetic.

'I dream of it. Literally.' Sarah pulled her cardigan round her, suddenly defensive. 'But it's not practical. She's happy there. It's a community. A Grand Place for Kids.' She spoke as if in quotes. 'And if I brought her back here, who knows? The bombing could start again. I can't keep moving her about.'

There was a sharp intake of breath. Tessa tensed her body, arching her back, grimacing with the shooting pain. Sarah knelt by the chair and took her hand. Tessa gripped it. Sarah braced her arm as if she could literally support the other woman against the contraction. Tessa rode it, eyes narrowed, her whole being focused on her body's convulsion. Eventually she relaxed again and brushed the lank hair off her forehead. 'Ugh!' She grinned shakily. 'It's like having a stout piece of elastic inside from neck to groin . . . then someone comes along suddenly and stretches it as hard as they can.'

It was funny, Sarah thought, how the plummy voice that had once so grated on her now seemed an irrelevancy. Likeable even. Just part and parcel of the woman herself.

For the last three weeks of her pregnancy Tessa had moved into the Fulham Road flat. It was agreed that Sarah would drive her into hospital. She'd hoarded some precious petrol for the purpose. Afterwards Tessa would live here for a while with the baby. Michael could come home so rarely from the austere de-coding establishment at Bletchley Park.

With her pregnancy Tessa had had to resign her post as Air-Raid Warden. Time had hung heavy after that. Now she breathed a quiet excitement. Unbelievably the grand finale had arrived.

'Tell me about the play Ruth was in.' Relentlessly she returned to the conversation that would occupy her until the next contraction.

Sarah thought back. 'It was one of those worthy evenings. Somehow it made me think of a temperance meeting. The school hall was cold and draughty.' She

211

smiled reminiscently. 'We were sitting on those hard wooden chairs that are just too small for an adult bottom.'

Tessa grinned. 'Only right you should suffer for the war effort. I trust the acting was good and stolid too.'

She grimaced. 'Like suet pudding . . . that is until Ruth came on.'

'Then you swelled with maternal pride.'

'Well, yes, that's what I thought, at first. Then it dawned on me that Ruth really was much better than the others . . . Honestly, she sort of shone . . .' Sarah could visualize it clearly. Ruth was wearing a white dress that Maggie had made. Her daughter's acting was naïve, without technique, but she'd brought to the role of Maria an airborne quality, a wide-eyed rapture that Sarah knew from real life. Whenever she appeared the stage was lit up with her bright conviction, her sense of fun.

'It wasn't just me who felt it.' Sarah experienced an urgent desire to make Tessa understand the revelation of that evening. 'Each time she finished a scene the audience applauded, but warmly, enthusiastically, not just that kind of polite, automatic clapping that doesn't mean anything . . .'

Afterwards each of the leading actors took an individual curtain call. At fourteen Ruth had been the youngest of them. Her smile was playful and self-possessed. Saucily she blew a kiss before gathering up her skirts and tripping off.

Sarah was interrupted by a discreet knock at the door. 'Can I come in?' It was Maud, Sarah's neighbour from upstairs.

'Yes, come on.'

Maud was stopped in her tracks. 'Oooh, you're sitting in the dark.' Her voice went up and down the scale, wonderingly.

212

'We found a bit of candle, and thought it'd be nice. Restful. Tessa's started labour, but it's early days yet.'

'Has she!' Ruth always swore that Maud hit top C in her moments of enthusiasm. 'Oh, Tessa love, how's it going?' Her rosy features radiated concern.

'I'm surviving – I think.' Painfully Tessa pulled herself upright. 'Ouch. I can't get comfortable. That's the worst thing.' She stood by the chair, body braced, one hand in the small of her back.

'Never mind. The first two days are the worst.' Maud winked hugely to show she was joking. Discreetly she poised her large body for an early departure.

'Oh! Silly me.' Suddenly she remembered the reason for her visit, tutting in mock-exasperation at her own forgetfulness. 'Put your radio on, Sarah. There's an announcement. At midnight. Good news, so they say.' Again she made as if to go.

Sarah touched her arm. 'Stay and listen with us. Jim's out tonight, isn't he?' Sometimes Maud's bus-driver husband combined the late shift with his early-morning workers' run. Then he stayed over at the garage.

'Well, if you're sure . . .' Maud gave a doubtful look at Tessa.

'Don't mind me. It all helps to pass the time.'

Maud settled herself, stretching out her large legs in lisle stockings and check slippers. Sarah switched on the radio and went to make the inevitable tea. Lacklustre music was still playing when she returned. Tessa had plonked herself heavily back into her chair.

'Lovely.' Maud poured her tea into her saucer and began to sip it with contented aahs of satisfaction.

The slate clock chimed midnight. It was a touch fast. A minute later the music stopped and was replaced by the voice of Bruce Belfrage. Jubilantly he announced an important British victory at El Alamein in North Africa.

'Good old Monty,' Maud put in in a stage-whisper.

'The Germans are in full retreat,' the announcer continued with relish.

'Oh, marvellous.' Tessa's Kensington tones were at their most fulsome.

As she listened with the others by the wavering candlelight, Sarah was vividly conscious of being one of millions. All over Britain there were rooms like this and people like them, drinking in relief, hope, a new courage with the announcement. Though she didn't consider herself a die-hard patriot Sarah was hugely moved at the pictured solidarity. Her throat choked up, tears pricked. She blinked them back.

Maud had no such scruples. Her eyes were frankly streaming. She wiped at them with the sleeve of her jumper. 'What an old fool I am.' Tessa, too, wept quietly, forgetting for a moment her own personal adventure, the increasingly urgent demands of her body.

Sarah pictured Robert's sharp, watchful face and prayed that he was all right.

It was the best news they'd had for months, and once they'd got over what Maud called their fit of the grizzles, Sarah found that she was quite remarkably cheered by it.

They *needed* something like this. For ages now the bulletins had been dispiriting, and it required a constant exertion to flog oneself into the old enthusiasm for the war effort. A victory like this gave a point to all the fuel-saving, salvage-collecting, rationing, shortages, the general drabness of everything.

It was odd how, only eighteen months later, the Blitz was looked back on with something like nostalgia. Stupid, really. And yet in those days they'd had a certainty, a sense of urgency, even a kind of exhilaration. You knew what you were doing. You were fighting for survival, and that was that.

The lack of a clear-cut goal showed down at the Ambulance Depot as much as anywhere. There were constant directives from above, reminding them that their work was essential, that they mustn't let their standards slip. Ambulances must be kept in tiptop condition; manoeuvres, exercises and first-aid drill diligently practised.

But at the same time they were laying people off. There were only two full-time teams left – herself and Joan, Ivy and Jenny. The others were part-timers now. And the work they did was useful, but hardly a matter of life or death. Ferrying pregnant women and kids to and from hospital, and toddlers to day-nurseries and back . . .

Still, it was a living – just – and the way she'd chosen to do her bit. Sarah was temperamentally incapable of opting out.

She remembered an argument she'd had with Dominique, when she'd reproached her once for cutting anatomy classes.

The French girl had shrugged elegantly and declared with her own irrefutable logic, 'But if I'm not *passionnée* about something, then I don't do it.'

There were times when Sarah envied Dominique her simple hedonism, but she'd long since come to terms with the fact that she was made differently. Sometimes she did think about giving up the ambulance work and going back to her painting, but it was just idle speculation. The reality remained. She'd taken on a task and would see it through.

Apart from anything else, there were Joan, Ivy and the

215

others to think of. They were friends now, comrades-in-arms. Impossible to turn her back on them and return to her old life. Not yet, anyway. Not until the job was done.

Between contractions Tessa dozed. The clock ticked on implacably. It was nearly half past one. Sarah watched in the womb-like dimness of the room, at peace, barely sleepy.

Tessa jerked awake. 'Oh . . . God.'

'What's the matter?'

'It's the waters. I'm leaking.'

Sarah stood up. 'Then you're getting close, I reckon. Time we got you to hospital.'

While Tessa fetched her personal effects, Sarah went outside to start the car. The street was deserted, wet and blustery, the dead leaves blowing in fitful bursts from the stumpy trees, spinning desultorily in the damp air. The car's slitted headlamps were reflected in the black puddles bordering the road. Sarah could never make the journey to the hospital without being reminded of the Blitz winter, all the times she'd made the run with shrapnel rattling on the ambulance roof, the night sky bright as day.

Out of the blue, as they drove along, Tessa asked, 'Do you think about Guy much now?'

'What on earth made you ask that?' Momentarily Sarah shifted her eyes sideways from the road.

'I was thinking of Michael, and that made me wonder about you and Guy.' Her voice held an oddly bleak tone.

Sarah thought for a moment or two, then said, 'I suppose he's become an idea, rather than a living person. He's always there somewhere at the back of my mind. It's as if I've filed him away until the war's over . . . I mean, Tessa, I don't even know if he's alive.' It hadn't always been like this. In the first year she'd been able to conjure up a living presence, even hear the tone of his voice . . .

Out of the darkness next to her Tessa probed again, quiet but persistent. 'You say an idea. Is the idea real to you?' Her question hadn't been idle, Sarah realized. For reasons of her own Tessa really wanted to know.

'It's really difficult to answer that.' Sarah shook her head. 'What I *do* know is that the last time I saw him I wanted terribly to be with him, stay with him. And I felt such anger because the war would keep us apart . . .' The memory of it came alive for her as she spoke. 'I've got two photographs of him, you know. And looking at them's like looking at a stranger I once knew. Class of '39, something like that.' Her words brought a sense of desolation.

'Do you still expect to be together?'

'I don't know. If we hadn't made a pact I expect I'd have put the whole relationship behind me.' She smiled. 'Just part of my chequered past . . . But you know me. A promise is a promise. I'll keep my side of it. That's how I am. I'll be there after the war. I wish I had boundless faith, but I've just got hope. That when . . . if I see him again it'll be like before.'

'Yes.' Tessa's voice had a dying fall. 'That's more or less how I feel about Michael.'

The corridor was long and totally deserted. It was painted a harsh, institutional yellow and lit by a single, naked light bulb. Tessa had been hustled away by the experts, leaving Sarah sitting alone on a slatted wooden bench, hands sunk deep in the pockets of her coat. It was chilly and the sleeplessness of the night was beginning to catch up with her.

In a glass-panelled door next to her she caught sight of

217

her own reflection. She was thin now in a way she'd never been before the war, cheekbones standing out against the dark hair that spilled over the shoulders of her black coat. She looked washed-out and by no stretch of the imagination younger than her thirty-nine years. It seemed to her that everyone round her had the same shop-worn look – Maggie, Tessa, Joan.

She thought of Michael, her mind nudged by Tessa's remark. He'd been home on leave recently. He'd seemed altered too, but in a different way. Not drab like the civilians she knew. On the contrary, he'd looked polished and impressive in his well-cut uniform, his hair neat and close-cut. But he'd seemed less open somehow. Not the Michael she knew. There'd been an elusive air of reticence, as though the secretive nature of his work had begun to pervade his off-duty personality.

Sarah guessed that Tessa felt it too. She sensed a bewilderment in her. But Tessa had highly developed notions of loyalty. Her words in the car had been the first overt hint of misgivings on her part.

On his last leave Michael and Sarah had spent an evening alone together. Tessa had to keep a longstanding engagement. Sarah had been pleased at the thought of having Michael to herself. It'd be like old times.

It had been a lovely evening. Rashly she'd lit a fire, though it was still only October, and coal was none too plentiful. Michael had been given a half bottle of whisky by an old friend he'd run into, and it had washed down their leathery dried-egg omelettes a treat.

Sitting across from her in the firelight, nicely relaxed from the Scotch, he seemed more like himself. She could visualize him now, in shirtsleeves, sandy hair ruffled slightly, his long body draped across the chair, one leg crossed high over the other. Times like this were rare

218

now. Everyone was so busy, so conscious of work to be done. She herself had swapped night duties with Ivy so as to be free for Michael.

They reminisced about the old days on *Liaisons*, about various clients of Sarah's and other mutual acquaintances. Sarah talked about her visual images of the Blitz. There were stark, horrifying, majestic visions in her head. They obsessed her and one day she was going to produce a series of paintings that would be as strong and passionate as her New Mexico work. Michael was fascinated and encouraging. She'd never talked to anyone else about this project, and it was good to put her half-formed ideas into words.

He asked after Ruth, and Sarah had confided her regrets about their separation. His sympathy had a certain vehemence about it, a hint of fellow-feeling. It was clear that his own experience, in some unsuspected way, paralleled her own.

He said, 'If there's one thing this war does it's separate people. You move around. You make new connections. And that's not always so good for the old ones . . .' He spoke with a dour emphasis, as if articulating a hard-earned lesson.

A little later he offered to refill her glass. She leaned towards him, and as he poured the whisky he said, with a crooked, diffident smile, 'I'm having an affair, Sarah. With a colleague at Bletchley Park.'

Sarah held up her hand to indicate that he'd filled her glass enough, and settled back into her chair. She was shocked, she realized. And surprised. Not that Michael had ever been short of girlfriends. But never in her wildest dreams had she seen him as other than a faithful husband. And devoted father, she supposed – he was almost that.

'I'm amazed.' Without stopping to think she spoke her thoughts aloud.

'Why?' He was mildly stung.

'I suppose I saw you as more of a true blue.'

He smiled ironically. 'Yes. That's always been my role in life. Typecasting. And this is out of character.'

'Does Tessa know?'

He replied shortly. 'No, she doesn't.'

Sarah was conscious of trying to speak in measured civilized tones. 'How important is this woman to you?' She sounded pompous, she thought.

A small fragment of hot coal spluttered from the fire on to the red hearth-rug. Michael seized the tongs and deftly returned it to the grate. There was only the faintest smell of singed wool.

Sarah smiled. 'Neatly done.'

'Thank you.' His grin was mischievous, familiar, with just a hint of conciliation.

He thought for a moment. 'It's hard to say how important. She's very unlike Tessa. Sharper. Not so nice, really. She interests me.'

There was a moment of silence between them. Then Michael said, 'If I were acting in character I'd say I regretted it. I regretted the lapse. I'd say I was going to finish it.'

'But you're not.'

'No.'

Outside, footsteps clipped on the pavement, getting louder then dying away.

Sarah asked, 'Why did you tell me this?'

'I thought you'd understand.'

There was a feeling between them of mutual disappointment. It curled in the air like thin smoke. She was disappointed in Michael for not living up to her view of

220

him; he in her for the unmistakable – though unspoken – hostility of her reaction.

Later, when he kissed her goodbye, he said, 'Look after Tessa for me, won't you?'

'Of course I will.' She met his eyes. 'You didn't have to ask. I would've anyway. She's a friend.'

As dawn approached Sarah went to stretch her legs in the hospital grounds. It was bleary and damp. In no time her hair was beaded with fine drizzle. The grey bulk of the surrounding buildings was veiled in thin mist. A few nurses and auxiliary workers passed, pallid faces ducked against the cold and damp. Inside, a child struggled to be born. It was a dreary day to start a life, Sarah thought. Babies should draw their first breath on bright, hopeful days of snow or sunshine.

She went back indoors. Just before eight a sturdy, red-haired nurse approached Sarah's lone bench in the yellow corridor.

'Mrs Mason's asking for you. She's had the baby.'

Eagerly Sarah stood up. 'Boy or girl?'

'Boy. Hefty little thing.'

'And he's all right?'

The nurse nodded.

Tessa had been cleaned and tidied, but she was still an anomaly against the shiny, starched whiteness of the hospital sheets. Rosy, blooming, beaming, her fair hair sticking out in exuberant spikes in spite of the nurses' efforts to make it lie down. She grinned broadly as Sarah approached across the gleaming expanse of parquet flooring, as though relieved to see a fellow being from the dirty, noisome outside world.

'You did it!' Sarah bent to kiss her. 'And you look wonderful.'

221

'I feel it.' In the aftermath of the birth, she was euphoric. Cooing with her sinuous Sloane Street vowels, 'He's so-o-o adorable. Look!' Pointing to a crib at the foot of the bed. 'Go on, look!'

Obediently Sarah went to peer. She saw some wispy mid-brown hair, the outline of a pale cheek, a tiny closed eyelid, a snowy cotton blanket. She didn't need to see more. It was a kind of shorthand, reminding her of Ruth new-born – of all babies.

'He's lovely. Truly.'

'Thanks, Sarah. For everything. You've been a pal.' The clipped diffidence of the words underlined their sincerity. There was a flicker of a shadow in Tessa's blue eyes as she added, 'You'll ring and leave a message with Michael, won't you?'

22

Dominique awoke suddenly, with a sense of desolation. Alien forces – not German necessarily – had overrun the town where she lived and were rounding up survivors. She'd escaped down a blind alley, but was being followed by a black car. There was nowhere to run, and as the vehicle approached, she caught the driver's eye and understood that he wasn't going to spare her. Now, semi-conscious, she knew it was a dream, but the feeling of disorder and hopelessness remained.

Daniel was sleeping soundly. A glimmer of early morning light shone in at the window. She could dimly make out his features – black eyelashes, lips full with sleep, half-smiling. She prodded him, indignant at his imperturbable sloth. His dazed reflex was to reach clumsily and pull her in to his warm, naked body. 'Go to sleep, Dominique.'

She poked him, this time with her right foot. 'I need comforting. I've just been run over.'

He patted her absently on the hip and buried his head under the sheet. He was the most difficult person in the world to wake up.

'Slug,' she hissed.

He murmured vaguely into her shoulder, 'We'll talk about it when I'm awake.'

She might as well give up. Rosa's bed was supremely comfortable. And the momentary anguish left by her dream was ebbing away. Dominique snuggled into Daniel's warmth. No need to wake for ages yet . . .

* * *

She struggled to regain consciousness, gradually becoming aware that the knocking was real. Not a dream this time. There was no ignoring it. The rapping was loud and insistent and importunate. Dominique rolled sideways and out of the bed, searching blearily for some garment to cover her nakedness. There was a check shirt of Daniel's. She slipped it on.

Gliding half-awake through the living room, she yelled crossly, 'All right, I'm on my way!' But the knocking persisted.

She struggled with Rosa's door catch. She still wasn't used to it. Some time ago they'd swapped apartments temporarily. Dominique's room at the top of the house was a bolt-hole where Rosa felt safer.

Dominique opened the door, leaving the chain engaged. She peered out and came face to face with a uniformed gendarme. He had a fussy, bossy look on his face, which was blotchy with annoyance. It seemed he wasn't used to being kept waiting.

'Open up! Open up!' he blustered, making sharp, irritable gestures with one hand. Dominique released the chain and he entered with unnecessary force.

To her bemusement and alarm he was followed by a German soldier, a young man with sharply chiselled features. Her first thought was that he'd come to claim Daniel for conscription into some forced-labour unit, though his forged papers included a medical exemption . . .

A smaller man in civilian clothes came next. He was pudgy and insignificant. A bureaucrat, Dominique thought. He flashed a silver disc, which she remembered someone telling her was a Gestapo warrant, but she was still too bleary to assess the implications.

It was the civilian who spoke. 'You are Rosa Doinel.'

There was a bark to his voice, as if he were trying to convince himself as much as her of his authority. He looked what he was, a petty official, wearing a drab, long raincoat, his face in the dawn light still puffy from sleep.

'No, I'm not.' She spoke with a subtly insolent drawl, designed to demonstrate her lack of awe. 'My name's Dominique David.' But she reflected belatedly that insolence was out of place. The man had power, however nondescript he might appear. And it dawned on her, with a cold lurch of fear, that this was the call that Rosa had dreaded since the huge round-ups of last summer, the reason why she now chose to tuck herself away in Dominique's cramped attic.

The man looked put out. He reddened and consulted a typed list. 'This is the address we were given. Flat One.' His tone was pettish. 'Where is Madame Doinel?' He was absurd, self-important, but he had the might of Nazi bureaucracy behind him.

She answered more politely. 'I believe she did live here before us. But I'm afraid I've no idea where she is now.'

Daniel entered the room, bare-chested, his hair tousled, sleepily buttoning a pair of grey trousers. To her relief, Dominique read in his eyes an immediate understanding of the situation.

'What about you?' The bureaucrat pounced. 'Can you throw some light on Rosa Doinel's whereabouts?' Patently hoping that his clumsy surprise tactics would elicit some more concrete information.

Daniel continued to look dazed. 'Who?'

'Rosa Doinel.'

'Who's she?'

'You know, *chéri*, she lived here before we moved in.' Agilely Dominique repeated her story for Daniel's benefit.

225

'Oh.' He blinked. She thought he was rather over-doing the stupor. He shrugged, blank-faced. 'We didn't know her.'

There was a long moment of conscious stalemate. Dominique held her breath. She half expected to be slapped, for Daniel to be held and punched like in the gangster films. The cold-eyed young soldier looked capable of it. The scowling gendarme, too, for that matter. Was she being melodramatic?

In any case, it didn't happen. They had other fish to fry, it seemed. The bureaucrat retreated behind a bland officiousness, instructing the gendarme to examine their papers. Covertly she watched as he read them over. Daniel's were forgeries. Good ones – they'd passed muster before – but . . .

With an ill-tempered nod the policeman handed them back. 'We'll call again. There may be questions . . .' It was hard to tell whether the intention was genuine or mere bluster.

As she closed the door behind the ill-assorted trio Dominique's first impulse was to laugh. She was light-headed with relief. They'd simply gone, without the smallest attempt at a search. Like Rosa she'd expected jackboots on the stairs, the slamming of doors, the clank of rifles, barked orders, anything but the bumbling face of petty officialdom.

She turned and grinned incredulously at Daniel. 'Did you see him blush when he found out his little list was wrong?'

If they could be fobbed off as easily as that then surely Rosa could continue with her cautious existence until such time as the enemy was defeated. Given the recent hopeful signs internationally – and their ears were constantly

226

pressed to the forbidden BBC broadcasts – Dominique was in no doubt as to the final outcome of the war.

She lay cold and numb on Rosa's bed. There was no emotion left, just the bleak knowledge and an icy fear. No more tears, though hours back she'd sobbed till her eyes swelled almost to closing. Daniel had come and lain alongside her, covering her body, pressing her down, as if by doing so he could annihilate the pain.

She felt as if she'd woken out of a dream-world. In spite of everything she'd heard, Dominique realized she'd never truly believed that anything could happen to Rosa. It had been totally illogical. She'd accepted Rosa's fear, the necessity for caution, without ever having come to terms with the reason for them. She could remember saying that nothing like this could ever happen in France, and in a sense, somewhere inside, the belief had survived.

It had been Luc who'd broken the news to them, arriving not ten minutes after the absurd German bureaucrat had left. She and Daniel had been brewing a cup of ersatz coffee to take to Rosa, to wake her up and tell her gently what had happened. But she wouldn't have been there. According to Luc she'd been arrested the day before out in Clichy, with her sister and her sister's children. He'd looked pale but composed. He was holding a piece of paper. Dominique had seized it. It was a note from Rosa that she'd managed to slip to one of her sister's neighbours.

Behind his wire-rimmed glasses Luc's eyes had been dazed and defenceless. But he had plans. 'I know this bloke. A financier of sorts. He's really in with the Boches. He owes me a favour . . .' They listened, clutching at straws. Neither of them had anything better to offer.

* * *

Rosa was at Drancy, north of Paris, in a makeshift concentration camp rigged up by the Germans from an unfinished housing project. They heard the news, not via Luc's friend, who was reluctant to get involved, but through an acquaintance of Guy's, a wholesale-meat merchant called Mario, who had some kind of an understanding with two of the Drancy guards. They had a racket going, so he claimed complacently. Guy didn't trust him, but thought he was their only chance. Mario wanted money. Five hundred thousand francs, and cheap at the price, he claimed. Guy believed him. He'd heard of people being asked at least four times that.

He contacted a dealer and offered him a set of paintings that he'd sworn to himself never to sell. Luc pitched in with his considerable black-market profits. Dominique sold jewellery that had belonged to her grandmother. They managed to raise close to the price demanded. There was an air of fatalism about their fund-raising, as though, at the end of it all, they expected to be gypped.

As a token of good faith, they had a note from Rosa. It was strangely neutral, asking for clean clothes and some soap. She'd added nothing personal, but beyond a shadow of a doubt the handwriting was hers.

A couple of days later Mario reported that a large consignment of Jews had been deported to Germany, but he'd arranged for Rosa to be left behind. Guy and Dominique made a trip out to Drancy. The camp was almost deserted and they were able to walk right up to the perimeter wire. Some way off, in the inner enclosure, a huddle of prisoners stood talking. Guy had some field-glasses and they were able to make out the black and red dress Dominique had packed for Rosa a day or so earlier. They yelled and waved. Eventually she saw them and waved back, wordlessly – probably it was too risky to call out. The image of her was engraved on Dominique's retina, like a frame from a silent film.

Rosa's head was shaved. Illogically, this fact horrified Dominique almost more than anything. But at least Mario had been speaking the truth. She was still there.

After that, though, he became more evasive. Guy put pressure on him to make clear exactly what Rosa's future was to be. Mario blustered inconclusively. Then he didn't come to a meeting Guy had arranged with him at Chez Brice. They made enquiries and discovered through the grapevine that Mario himself had been arrested by the Gestapo.

'We've got to face the fact,' Guy said gently to Dominique, 'that there's nothing more we can do.' As he spoke she thought how strained he looked, his eyes shadowed, skin earth-coloured. She found it loathsome to accept his words. She wanted to scream, hammer on the walls, attack someone, anything rather than this dull-eyed resignation.

'There must be something!' she protested, her face contorted with a helpless indignation. 'There's got to be.'

He put a hand on her shoulder. 'There's nothing left. You can hope. That's all.'

While Guy negotiated with Mario, Dominique felt unpleasantly helpless. All she could do was wait, while Guy busied himself with meetings, phone calls, bargaining. She found the enforced idleness profoundly frustrating. Wanting to act, she felt herself reduced to a passive role.

Now she thought back to a conversation she'd had with Guy more than a year ago, when he'd questioned her discreetly about her attitude to resistance. She'd had no interest and had answered him vaguely, evasively. The remembrance brought on a fluttering of regret. She'd turned away and opted for a blind, blithe involvement in her own career.

Dominique had never tried to find out about Guy's Resistance activities. She'd always assumed somehow that they were adult and organized and went far beyond the graffiti and juvenile lampooning of the Pessimiste set. Then she heard that Thomas – the beanpole of a man who printed the secret copies of Métro – had been picked up by the Nazis. She was dumbfounded. Patronizingly she'd assumed that the Germans would turn a blind eye to her friends' juvenile spleen.

It seemed not so. Thomas was held and questioned roughly enough that he named shy André Delarue as author of the mocking cartoons of Nazi grotesques. André was arrested in his turn.

'But André wouldn't hurt a fly,' Dominique harangued Daniel. 'What do they want with him? What possible good can he do them?'

Daniel looked up from the book he was reading and gave her an old-fashioned look. 'You're a bit of an innocent, Dominique,' he remarked not altogether kindly.

Was she? For the first time Dominique began to have self-doubts. She'd been blinkered and self-absorbed, she realized, but wasn't sure whether she could learn to be any different.

During the period of uncertainty over Rosa's future, Dominique had felt herself incapable of working. Then one day she heard from Guy that Rosa had been deported along with a later exodus of prisoners from Drancy. So he'd been right and there was nothing more they could do. From now on she must pick up the thread of her everyday life as though Rosa had never been.

Grimaud had been cantankerous when she returned to the Philo, his canny hawk's face taking on an uncharacter-istically sulky, parrotty look. 'Don't imagine you're irre-placeable.' He'd tried briefly to hector her. 'I've kept your place for old times' sake, but there's been no shortage of offers . . .'

She'd stared at him with sincere incredulity. Rosa was powerless, imprisoned, and he talked of his own conven-ience. He'd backed away, defeated, from her righteous indignation.

Ruby had been more sympathetic, though Dominique was under no illusion. Her money-conscious peasant soul had deplored the temporary absence of her star attraction. It was simply that she liked Rosa and hated the invaders with a cold, abiding fury.

Her first night back had been at the Philo. After the pressure of recent weeks the experience had been unreal. In her red dress and make-up she felt like a painted clown posturing for an audience of wolves and jackals. The spectators seemed not to notice and she was rewarded with the usual whistles and rowdy applause. She responded with a smile like that of a death's head, though the watching Germans appeared oblivious.

Afterwards she joined Peter Borchert at his table. In spite of everything she still saw him as a friend. He was sitting with Irène – the aristocratic trollop, as Grimaud had dubbed her. It was whispered among regulars of the Philo that she and Peter had a regular-as-clockwork, once-a-week sexual liaison. Tactfully Irène left to chat with friends at a neighbouring table as Dominique sat down.

'I've missed you.' Peter squeezed her arm with discreet

affection. 'You look awful tonight. Upset and bewildered and sort of dazed.'

'Does it show that much?'

'Only to me.' His eyes held friendship, sincerity. She warmed to him, and despite herself a dormant vanity reasserted itself. She was flattered by his interest. He was impressive, powerful, a man of the world. Solicitously he poured her a drink. Their table seemed a small island of peace among the swirling, laughing couples.

It seemed natural to her to tell him about Rosa. After all the harm was done. She remembered too that he'd once expressed his own dislike of this particular aspect of Nazi policy. He listened with grave interest as she poured out the tale.

When she'd finished he commented tersely, 'I wish you'd told me all this earlier.' Leaning across to refill her glass. 'It's just possible I might have been able to help you.'

This afternoon on the Champs Élysées the air was warm and soft as thistledown on her bare arms. There were flower-sellers offering lilies-of-the-valley, just as though it were peacetime. Dominique bought some and held them up, admiring the modest little bells with their disproportionately powerful scent. The fragrance was deeply nostalgic, recalling, she supposed, her childhood. It was a scent she'd known forever. In a canvas shopping bag she carried a new black cotton dress. The shops were so uninspiring nowadays that she couldn't believe her luck in finding such an attractive garment.

The terrace of the Colisée was packed with pretty women and a fair number of young men. Dominique noticed an exotic, dark-eyed, olive-skinned girl in a red tartan skirt. She was laughing caressingly at something

232

her companion had said, then she sipped at a drink, throat curved, head thrown back, looking serene and pleased with the day and her own part in it. Even the ubiquitous grey German uniforms didn't jar today. They were just one aspect of the general pageant.

Dominique thought, I feel happy. Almost. Life did go on, it seemed. There was a flicker of shame in the realization. But the sun shone and made everything painless. Or bearable at the very least.

'*Mais ça alors!*' An elderly gentleman in front of her exclaimed and examined the sky, shading his eyes with a gnarled hand.

Dominique looked up too, and so, in no time, did everyone else. There was a buzz of wondering comment. Some way ahead at roof level a plane hovered. At the same height it flew the length of the boulevard. The passers-by pointed and exclaimed with frank delight, all except the sprinkling of uniformed Germans, whose faces were a gratifying mixture of anger and embarrassment. It was an RAF aircraft, and when it reached the Arc de Triomphe it rose again for altitude, simultaneously releasing something into the air. Dominique watched incredulously as a huge French flag unfurled lazily in the sky above them, its movement appearing suspended as if in some surrealist dream-sequence. The flag seemed to hang against the blue of the sky for an uncanny length of time before fluttering down and disappearing into a jumble of buildings.

No one who saw it could miss the powerful symbolic message of hope and good cheer. Dominique saw a couple in front of her embracing spontaneously, their little girl jumping round them in her white socks and shoes.

'Magnificent, wasn't it, mademoiselle?' A bent old woman in black touched her arm. In the wrinkled face her eyes were radiant and childlike. Impulsively Dominique bent and kissed her.

23

'I'll just drop by and say hallo to the baby.' In the raw, harsh, early-morning June sunshine Joan looked weary, but still no older than sixteen. She was engaged now, to a fireman. They were saving to get married, and both of them put by a little each week. Sarah marvelled at such steady resolve.

She smiled. 'Fine. Come on, then. Tessa'll be glad to see you.' On sunny days it was glorious to walk home after night duty, along pavements striped with sunshine and shadow, past trees fresh with young leaves, and here and there a rose bush blooming valiantly among the stone and concrete.

The few weeks Tessa had intended to stay with Sarah had extended to months. And now they both accepted that she would remain until further notice. They enjoyed the companionship, and the baby – named Monty after the hero of El Alamein – was a joy to have around. He was spoiled rotten according to Tessa, what with the doting attention of Sarah, Maud and Joan, as well as that of his mother.

'He's so cute.' Joan broke into a fond smile at the mere thought of him. Sarah could see that babies were beginning to hold a fascination for her, now that the prospect of children of her own loomed on the horizon of her life. She turned to Sarah. 'What are you going to be doing with your twenty-four hours?' It was that long before they needed to report for duty again.

'Dig for victory, probably.'

Sarah had amazed herself by discovering a lively enthusiasm for vegetable-growing. Out of duty rather than inclination she had converted the small plot behind the house into a kitchen garden, but now she derived a keen pleasure from digging and manuring it and hoeing between the tidy rows of burgeoning radishes, peas, lettuces, and tomato plants.

Back at the Fulham Road flat Tessa was welcoming, but harassed. She was about to leave to spend a couple of snatched days in Buckinghamshire with Michael, and she was busy gathering together the hundred and one small items she'd need for the baby during that time. Joan offered to give Monty his bottle, leaving Tessa free to rush about like a blue-tailed fly.

'You're an angel.' She handed him over gratefully. His plump little legs hung down in tight, white leggings.

Joan was a tired-eyed Madonna, sitting on an upright, slat-backed chair in one of the long rectangles of light reflected on to the red kitchen tiles. Monty was eight months now, weaned, and quite absurdly healthy and happy. His whole being was centred on the rubber teat through which he sucked warm milk as though his life depended on it. His eyes were fixed on the bottle with a ferocity incredible to see in the round baby face.

Sarah made tea and toast and sat down opposite Joan and the baby, luxuriating in the warmth of the sun filtered through the long window pane. There were moments of contentment in the endless desert of the war. She wouldn't go to bed, she decided. It was too nice a day. She'd managed to snatch a few hours last night in an armchair next to the phone. Not that they'd had a night call for ages. But like fire-watchers they must always be on the alert. Official propaganda drummed in relentlessly that disaster could strike at any time.

As Monty finished his bottle a knock came at the door. 'That'll be my lift.'

Miraculously Tessa was ready. A large green canvas holdall stood ready in the hall. The woman who delivered the milk had offered to drive her to the station on her horse and cart. While Tessa changed Monty's nappy and Joan rinsed out his bottle, Sarah stowed the pushchair and the bag on to the trap. Then Tessa clambered up and settled herself on the passenger seat next to the vinegary milk-lady with her whip. Joan handed Monty up to her and she settled him on her lap. He stared about him with an expression of wide-eyed curiosity.

'Best of British luck.' Sarah laughed at Tessa's refugee appearance. 'Rather you than me, girl.'

Tessa gave a crooked grin. Increasingly, setting off to see Michael, she looked like someone cheerlessly fulfilling a family obligation. It hurt Sarah to see her like it and she wished she hadn't mentioned luck.

There wasn't really an awful lot to do on the vegetable patch, she tended it so often. But a sprinkling of robust groundsel plants had sprung up – they grew as quickly as mushrooms – and she hoed them out with smooth, even movements, leaving them to wither in the bright sun.

Sarah was barefoot. She liked the feel of the dry, warm earth under her feet. She'd changed into a cotton skirt and a loose blouse and tied her hair back in a handkerchief. In a bit she'd sit in the sun for a while and brown her legs. She tanned easily.

It was odd to be alone in the house, but nice for a change. She could please herself and not be bound by things like regular meals and the exigencies of Monty's routine. She stood back, leaning on her hoe, to admire the rows of young vegetables, so orderly and geometrical.

The human will imposed on the chaos of nature – how strange that she should take such pleasure in it. The pea plants with their twiggy supports, the baby lettuces, shone in the sun with a fresh tender green. Later on they'd be taller, fill out, and the green would darken.

There was a knocking at the front door. Lazily she decided to ignore it. Maud would answer. Sarah rather hoped that it was no one for her. She was enjoying her unusual solitude.

She bent down to pull out a small clump of weeds growing root-to-root with the lettuces, too close to get at with the hoe, then laid them down on the friable earth, where the sun would shrivel them to nothing. It was time she thinned the lettuces out a little. She could use the young leaves in sandwiches later on. She pulled out a few here and there, widening the spaces between the remaining plants.

Standing up, she realized with a start that she was being watched. Someone was standing in the doorway of the glass lean-to. The figure was male, in uniform. Her eyes scanned his face. It was thin and deeply tanned, the hair fair and close-cut. She was disorientated.

The man spoke. 'Struth. Not a flicker. Don't you know me?' The voice was flat with a shadow of a London accent.

'Good God, Robert!'

She could hardly believe it. It must be well over two years since she'd seen him. The features in front of her began to make sense, but still he looked different. So much older than her mental picture of him, the sharp cynicism of his expression biting deeper, not lightly marked as she remembered it. 'It's wonderful to see you! When did you get back?'

'About two weeks ago. I've been at home. Relaxing.

Don't get up till midday usually.' His smile was brief and didn't reach his eyes. 'Feel as if I've got years of sleep to make up. Haven't been anywhere much and today I thought, Sarah, that's who I want to see.'

'You're lucky I'm off-duty.' There was something about him that was discordant. A kind of weariness in his voice.

He roused himself. 'You look wonderful.'

'Do I?' An ironic gleam.

'Like Mother Courage.'

'God.' She laughed. 'Sweet talk or what?'

He shrugged. 'I mean it.'

There was a moment of silence, then Sarah said quietly, 'So. You're a conquering hero.'

'Yeah.'

'Do you feel like one?'

He grimaced. 'Sometimes.'

His grey eyes seemed very clear in the harsh sunlight. There was a tension between them. An unfamiliarity, due to their long separation. At the same time Sarah felt she knew him very well.

'Was it awful?'

He shook his head. 'No. Not while it was happening.'

Robert took a slug of his pint, then put his glass down on the table, making a wry face. 'The beer's gone bloody watery since I was here last.'

'You're lucky to get any at all. You can't always.'

Chairs and tables had been set up in the garden of Sarah's local, an official sign that summer had come. The thought crossed her mind that she'd sat at this very table with Guy. She could feel no emotion and vaguely regretted the fact. She tried her own beer. Robert was right. It was even worse than usual.

The end section of the garden had been fenced off and

laid down to vegetables. The everlasting grow-your-own drive. She couldn't resist going to cast an eye over the fence to make comparisons. Rejoining Robert, she remarked with satisfaction, 'Not a patch on mine.'

He smiled an impish, unbelieving smile. It was the most spontaneous expression that had crossed his face since he arrived. 'The nation's in the grip of some sinister garden-fever. My dad's the same and he never knew one end of a spade from the other in the old days.'

'It's life and death to us on the home front, laddie.' She turned her face to the sun, closing her eyes, to bask.

'You know what really makes me laugh?'

She opened one eye. 'What's that?'

'It's those adverts for things you can't get. You know the sort of thing. Won't it be nice when Chivers jellies are available again? And we're sorry you can't get your usual supplies of Velvex toilet paper, but it *is* the very best, soft, strong, hygienic . . .'

Sarah grinned. 'I suppose it *is* funny when you put it like that. We're so used to it we've stopped even noticing. D'you know I had to go to ten different shops the other week before I could get a new toothbrush . . .'

'Deprivation indeed.' The sarcastic note she remembered in him from years earlier.

She was mildly stung. There'd been hugely grimmer matters she could have mentioned. Sarah had noticed before that there existed a covert, abiding, impersonal hostility between those who'd seen action and those who hadn't, both sides feeling their hardships were undervalued. He was unfair, though. She'd tried to talk to him about his experiences in North Africa, but he'd been unwilling and evasive.

'I wonder what Dominique's doing.' After three pints Robert was more expansive, less brittle. All the same

239

Sarah was surprised to hear him mention the French girl. It was a conversational subject that implied a certain intimacy, a confidentiality, and it was this that Robert had seemed determined to avoid.

'She's a survivor.' Sarah pushed away the remains of a strange, almost meatless shepherd's pie. 'If anyone comes through, I'd expect her to.'

'I'd really like to know.' Robert was slightly flushed. He drank a lot since he'd been on leave, he told her. It wasn't like him. In the old days he'd rarely run to more than the odd pint, a glass or two of wine.

She asked softly, 'Do you still think about her?'

'Yes.' He looked levelly across the table at her. 'But I'm not eating my heart out if that's what you mean.'

'Is there anyone else?'

'No one important.' He grinned at her in mock reproach. 'Give us a chance. I've been busy for the last couple of years.' A pause. 'There was a girl in Cairo for a while, a nurse, but . . .' He shrugged.

He'd taken off his jacket and rolled up the sleeves of his khaki shirt. His arms were as dark brown as his face. Sarah noticed that the girl who cleared the glasses from their table gave him a look of more than routine interest, and that he cast her a brief, evaluating glance. There was a new hardness about him, reflecting the exclusively male world he'd been inhabiting.

She had no thought of pressing him further about his love life, but Robert himself blurted spontaneously, 'It was a bloody good thing, you know, that Dominique chucked me.' He smiled, with a trace of sheepishness. 'Not that I thought so at the time. But I was obsessed with her. It hurt, God . . . All the time. I had no freedom. You can't live like that . . .' He sounded momentarily overwrought, as if the memory of it still had the power to

240

disturb him. Adding with a flash of boyish self-justification, 'I've never been like it with anyone else.'

The pub's cat, a ruffianly tabby with scruffy spiky fur disappeared under the table and began to rub against Robert's legs.

'A sucker for uniform.' Sarah smiled.

Absently Robert bent and stroked the animal under its chin. He seemed to be launched on a talking jag. Sarah was pleased. He sounded more like his old self, fluent and opinionated.

'When the war's over – we're going to win, no doubt of that – I'm going to get into politics. I can't wait. There's going to be big changes. Churchill'll be out. People won't stand for the old boy brigade. Not after all this.' The cat had leaped on to his knee. Absorbed by what he was saying, Robert ignored it. 'There'll be no going back. This war's opened people's eyes. Apart from anything else, there's a quite different attitude towards the Soviets . . .'

Sarah felt old. She'd heard similar confident predictions of change as a girl after the previous war. But Robert wouldn't remember that.

He darted back to the subject of women. 'Anyway, *if* I ever marry it'll be to someone who wants to change things, like me. Dominique was like a butterfly . . . gorgeous, but totally apolitical . . .' To Sarah's eyes his dismissive smile didn't ring quite true.

After lunch they strolled aimlessly through the sunlit London streets. The activity was an end in itself, highlighting their unwonted leisure and freedom. It was as if the two of them had stepped outside their lives and back to a time when pleasures like this were commonplace.

There was an optimism in the air that hadn't been present earlier in the war. On walls and hoardings the

241

scrawled legend, 'Second Front Now', appeared with insistent and energetic frequency.

They ended up in Hyde Park. Sarah flopped down on the grass. 'I'm not moving from this spot for half an hour at the very least.'

She lay back and looked upwards. The sky sparkled between a dappled screen of chestnut leaves. 'That's how you ought to paint trees. From underneath. It's *the* viewpoint.'

'If you say so.' He lay down beside her. 'You're the expert.'

A little way off from them a group of GIs were getting to know some English girls. It had been the previous year when the Americans first swept into England. Confident, optimistic, well-fed, monied, they were a heartening contrast to the bedraggled, war-torn British. To the chagrin of their men, the female population was dazzled. Overpaid, oversexed and over here was the cliché that had been spawned by their arrival. It had such currency that, watching the group, it was impossible to stop the words from springing to mind. Only five minutes earlier Sarah and Robert had been passed by a truck full of Tommies, bearing the glum message, 'Don't cheer, girls, we're British.'

Boosted by the presence of their fellows, the Yanks sported knowing, foxy grins. The women greeted their every witticism with gusts of laughter. One boy put his arm round a girl with a turned-up nose and a pink jumper and she raised no objection.

Sarah saw Robert watching. 'Bloody Yanks, eh?' she teased.

'Nah. Good luck to them.' He turned towards her with a grin. 'I don't feel my masculinity under fire.' His eyes were narrowed against the brightness of the sun. To her

242

surprise she had the impression that his smile was subtly flirtatious.

She thought then that the distancing effect of his absence had been emotional as well as physical. So that she saw him now as someone unfamiliar, not the jagged, prickly boy she'd always taken for granted. And she realized – for the first time consciously – that she found him physically attractive. Quite strongly so.

He turned on to his stomach and looked across at her, chin cradled on his arms. 'You know this is the first day since I've been home that I've felt human.' One of the GIs in the nearby group made a mock attempt to snatch the shoes of one of the girls, who let out a sudden piercing screech of laughter. 'Silly cow,' Robert remarked conversationally.

They dined off spam and new potatoes, which Sarah dug recklessly and prematurely from the garden, the lettuce thinnings, and the remains of a bottle of horrible sweet sherry that someone had given Tessa ages ago. They drank the last glass out in the garden with the wood-pigeons still cooing, finding a spot that the long evening shadows hadn't yet invaded.

Then they went inside and played records in her studio. Michael had entrusted his collection to Sarah's safe-keeping for the duration – Tessa wasn't interested in jazz – but she rarely had time to get them out. They browsed among them on the floor, sorting out songs with nostalgic connections for them both.

Sarah put on a Bessie Smith record. The timeless voice spiralled from the busily revolving disc with a strident beauty. Nobody knows you when you're down and out. A harsh yearning in the rise and fall of the melody. The voice stirred a gut response. Guy had loved this song. In

243

the instant she could picture him with great clarity. The fierce cheekbones, steady eyes, the heavy black hair. She could conjure up his aura, the calm, the slow smile that lit into spontaneity, the abrupt, direct speech. She was stunned by the sudden vividness of the image. It had been so long since she'd been able to picture him at all.

Robert sat on the floor smoking, leaning back impassively against one of the leather armchairs by the window. He seemed withdrawn into himself again, his sharp profile outlined against the darkening sky.

Later he crossed to the gramophone and put on Tessa's record of 'Moonlight Serenade'. The music surged, syrupy and sentimental, quite beautiful.

He approached Sarah. 'Dance?' There was a self-mocking light in his eye. A defence against her finding him absurd.

She glanced up at him, surprised, then smiled. 'Why not?'

Their bodies interlocked easily. They'd danced together before, but never ever when they'd been alone. Robert held her close but not tightly.

It was an unfamiliar sensation. There was entertainment enough in wartime, yet she hadn't danced for ages. There were hops laid on for servicemen of all nationalities. Joan had pressed her several times to come along, adding – tactfully or otherwise, Sarah hadn't decided – 'You look loads younger than you really are.' Laughingly she'd refused. Such gatherings, with their bright promiscuity, weren't aimed at her generation.

When she'd danced with Robert before it had been conventional, a glide round the floor, a laugh among friends, with no sense of physicality. Now she was acutely conscious of the long muscles of his back under her hands,

244

the wiry solidity of his frame. Almost against her will she could picture his body, tanned, lean and smooth. The music awakened a kind of drowsy lust. You could drown in it.

When the record ended he didn't release her. They stood for a moment entwined. The room was dark apart from the glow of a single lamp in the corner, and his face was a pale blur. Robert lowered his head and placed his lips on hers. They were smooth and cool. The kiss was controlled, deliberate. She savoured it, then thought that perhaps she should have pulled away, gently, that accepting it signified a certain acquiescence. So be it. When he moved his lips away she reached for him again and kissed him back.

Afterwards he re-started the record, came back and took her in his arms again. 'The music's an excuse to carry on holding you.' There was a shyness in his manner but his movements were sensual. As they danced it came to her how much she'd missed the touch of another body. You got by without it, without the comfort and the animal warmth. Then someone held you and you understood the deprivation.

His voice came out of the darkness. 'All evening I've been trying to pluck up courage.'

She looked at him questioningly.

'Asking you this may be the clumsiest . . . But I'll say it anyway.' They'd stopped moving. He touched her cheek. 'Would you . . . Sarah, I want to come to bed with you.'

She knew then that she'd expected the question, wanted it from hours back. But passively. Robert was younger. It was up to him to make the first move.

She smiled at him in the dim light. Delicately running her right hand up his abdomen and chest to caress the

245

curve of his neck. 'I want you to as well.' Her voice was a murmur in the still of the room. On the edge of her consciousness she noticed that the music had stopped, leaving the needle to grind on relentlessly in the record's central groove.

The blackout curtains falsified light, but Sarah had developed an instinct. It must be around five. In an hour she'd brace herself to leave the ease of the bed, get dressed and go on duty.

Robert slept now, his head on her shoulder. She could only dimly make out the lines of his face. It was odd to witness his sharp, mobile features expressionless with sleep. She'd known him so long and never seen him like it. The past hours had had a kind of heightened unreality. The two of them had been aware of an almost hypnotic compulsion to turn to one another again and again, drive their bodies to the limit, to satiation point and further. A kind of wordless acknowledgement, perhaps, that the night was unique, unlikely to be repeated, something outside the norm of their lives, with its own singular magic.

They'd been in darkness. There'd been the new intimacy of their voices, touch, sensation. Nothing visual. She learned his body like a blind woman. They'd reached for each other in the black void instinctively, trustingly, like animals seeking a kind of mutual comfort.

Robert stirred and opened his eyes to the shadowy dawn light. He looked at her for a moment in the blank aftermath of waking. He said drowsily, 'Is it really you?' Then fell asleep again, instantly, like a child.

24

Ruth butted into the adults' earnest conversation. 'I'll be off then, Mr Whelpton.' She spoke rather loudly. They were beginning to get heated, and she'd been standing like a lemon on the edge of the group for ages.

Whelpton turned round, bemused, as though he'd forgotten her existence. 'Goodbye, my lovely.' He rested one hand briefly on her shoulder. He had a dewy-eyed look sometimes when he spoke to her, as if he were smiling through sentimental tears. He seemed able to summon up the expression at will. 'Friday, remember. Next rehearsal. Half past seven . . . And practise being precocious and winsome at home.'

He gave the order with total conviction. Ruth nodded gravely, wishing there was someone of her own age present to share her inward snigger. She grinned faintly. 'Goodbye then.'

There was a chorus of farewells from the assembled grown-ups, a circle of ingratiating smiles. Only Norman, who played Jack Worthington, kept a normal expression on his face. He fancies himself though, she thought uncharitably.

Before leaving she cast a look round the familiar village hall. Bare boards, chairs stacked at one end of the room, a makeshift stage at the other, specks of dust dancing in the rays of evening light that slanted through the high windows. In spite of her youthfully harsh views on her fellow actors, rehearsals were bliss.

She was quietly aware of the honour of having been

chosen by the Alder Drama Group to play Cecily in their summer production of *The Importance of Being Earnest*. Her fame as an actress had spread. She was only fifteen and the rest of the cast were ancient. Of course she unbalanced the play a bit – the actress who played Gwendolen was in her early thirties – but such details were unimportant when she was on stage. Then she believed in herself and the others. She became the precious, precocious Cecily with every fibre of her being. And the others were transmogrified from middle-aged denizens of the home counties to Wildean sophisticates, swapping arch paradoxes and witty sidelong glances.

Outside, the evening was still, golden and balmy. Nine o'clock. Alan should be just about finishing at Gifford's smallholding. She decided to walk down and meet him. She took the route that led out of the village, walking in the road – there was so little traffic about nowadays. The grass verge was ethereal with lacy clouds of cow parsley, patches of blue speedwell flowers, and here and there a bold splash of red poppies.

In a lot of ways Alder felt like home to her now. She was under no illusion, though. Fundamentally she would always be an alien. There was a stratum, like an underground seam of rock, that she could never hope to breach. However long they lived here, whatever good they did, people like Maggie and Ilya would always be excluded. You'd have to inter-marry, Ruth thought, and live here for about a hundred years before some people would even give you a smile.

Gifford – whose potatoes Alan was even now digging – was a case in point. His fleshy, pink face was closed to all but his fellow natives. The same with his wife, Ma Gifford, as she was called by friends and foes alike. Behind owlish glasses lurked a hard, rigid mask. Yet, incredulously, Ruth had seen her, with women she considered to be of her own kind, giggling girlishly and indulging in lumbering sexual innuendo. But her face would freeze over again when she addressed an outsider, by which she understood fifty per cent of the village.

Two other lads were helping with the week-long after-school blitz on Gifford's early potatoes. They were twins, Tom and Sid Tyler, whose family had lived for two centuries in their square, gloomy cottage at the other end of the village. He'd taken them on because he drank with their father. But Alan was employed on merit. Everyone knew he'd shift more potatoes in an hour than most of the village boys could during a whole evening.

The ramshackle gate to Gifford's smallholding became visible further along the road to her right. Ruth hoped Alan hadn't already left. He expected to finish the job tonight and get paid. He enjoyed having money in his pocket, and he usually had. Odd jobs of all kinds came his way, and he loved to buy sweets for Sacha and Stephen with the proceeds, or slightly shifty under-the-counter groceries for Maggie.

She saw the gate open. A figure emerged. It was Alan in a grey shirt and trousers, sleeves rolled up, trailing a jacket over one shoulder. His brown hair, as ever, hung in his eyes. He was followed by the squat, blunt figure of Gifford, whose bald head and thick neck protruded from his patched tweed jacket like a sore pink thumb, so Alan said. The villager was gesturing angrily. She heard him call Alan a money-grabbing little bugger and saw him glower. The boy shrugged and turned away with a provoking nonchalance.

As he came towards Ruth he pulled a face. Gifford stumped back up his drive. Ruth found it oddly painful to see how Alan covered his hurt with a wry, tough smile.

249

She wanted to hug him, to show solidarity, but contented herself with a grin and a casual nod in the direction of Gifford's retreating figure. 'What was all that about?'

He grimaced. 'Miserable old bastard.' Under the mask of indifference he was rattled, flushed, his mouth not quite under control. She saw he was trembling.

They fell into step. 'Looks like you've been upsetting the natives.'

He gave her a self-mocking sideways glance. 'I had my reasons.'

'Aren't you going to tell me?'

'It was when he came to paying us. You'll never guess what he did.' His crooked grin prepared her for the shock value of what he was about to say.

'Well?'

'You know the God-awful sour crab-apple drink Ma Gifford's been pushing at us to keep us going.'

'With the soggy potato pasties.'

'And the stale carrot sarnis.'

'What about them?'

'When he came to pay us the old bastard kept back ten bob for refreshments.' He related the information with a modest air, allowing the enormity of it to speak for itself.

'I don't believe it!' Her eyes were wide with an incredulity that bordered on delight. 'The bloody old scrooge!'

'That's what I thought.'

'Ten bob for that lot.' She shook her head. 'You told him, I hope.'

An ironic gleam. 'That's why we've fallen out.' He mimicked Gifford's pinched Hertfordshire accent. 'My wife don't feed the likes of you for the love of it.'

'But you didn't have any say in the matter.'

Again Gifford's dour tones. 'You'll find it's practice hereabouts.'

'Rubbish!' She glanced up at him. 'What did the others say? Tom and Sid.'

'Nothing.' Alan paused. 'They're a creepy couple. They were fed up all right. They just looked at each other like . . . meaningfully, I suppose.'

'I can imagine that.'

The Tylers were taciturn, handsome boys. Ruth thought them vaguely menacing. There was something stony and timeless about them. She could visualize them in medieval dress, by candlelight, with the same watchful faces.

She and Alan turned towards Copse Hill and Maggie's home. Ruth gave him a reassuring pat on the back. 'Well, if nothing else you're a sadder and wiser man. You won't be giving the benefit of your brawny muscles to those old miseries again.'

There was a letter from her mother when she got home. Ruth took it upstairs to her attic room. It was getting dark now, the angles of the ceiling blurring into the walls. She pulled the rush-seated chair across to the window, where there was still light enough to read by. Sarah's letters were a luxury, and she never allowed herself to split open the envelope until she was quite ready. It wasn't that they were vastly significant – usually gossip about Tessa, the baby and Maud – but they sounded like Sarah talking and, as she read, she could visualize her mother's sudden brilliant smile, picture the affection in her dark eyes.

In some ways these were the best times. Though her mother visited as often as her war work would allow, in one another's company there seemed always a grain of tension between them. Ruth felt herself flighty and selfish if she had to go out or see friends when Sarah was there. It wasn't that her mother tried to make it so. There was

251

no hint of moral blackmail. Yet Ruth fancied she could read hurt and disappointment in Sarah's eyes at such times. She wasn't sure whether it was real or imagined.

On her last visit they'd been sitting on the lawn after tea and Ruth had described some fancy-dress costumes Maggie had rigged up for Sacha and Stephen for some school do or other. They'd gone as Potato Pete and Doctor Carrot, two characters dreamed up to enliven the official Digging for Victory bulletins.

'How does she find the time?' Sarah had marvelled, glancing down the garden to where, in trousers and wellingtons, Maggie toiled over her vegetables, while Natasha, in a fit of puppyish high spirits, chased her own tail.

'Oh, Maggie's always got time,' Ruth had replied airily. 'Not like you. You always had your paintings to do.' In her mind she'd meant no criticism, but this time the wounded look on her mother's face was patently not her imagination.

'It was our living,' Sarah said quietly. Nothing more. But inwardly Ruth had shrivelled with guilt. And yet the impression she'd given was false. She was proud of Sarah's talent and of her success. As a young child she'd resented at times the attention her mother paid to her work, but she'd long since accepted the necessity.

And, when she acted, in her mind it was Sarah's approbation she sought. Other people's praise counted for far less. Acting was a revelation. It was something she could do, balancing her mother's painting skill, offering her a way of making Sarah proud of her.

The policeman's voice rumbled on and on. It was impossible to catch the words. Maggie had ushered him into Ilya's study, asked Alan to join them and closed the door.

From the living room Ruth could hear the rise and fall of their exchange, but nothing more. She couldn't imagine what was going on. Sometimes Alan butted in, sounding het up and defensive. Constable Eliot's voice remained an even growl, like far-off thunder. Maggie's tones were composed and somehow conciliatory.

It seemed ominous to Ruth that Alan had been summoned. Yet she couldn't imagine that he'd done anything too awful. Generally speaking he wasn't popular with the adults in the village. They thought him sullen. He didn't address his elders and betters with the necessary open-hearted smile. But the worst thing she'd ever known him do was to scrump an apple or two. And he had that crime in common with pretty well all the kids from hereabouts.

She started as the study door burst open and someone flung out. It was Alan, she saw, as he passed the open doorway of the living room. His face was stricken, contorted with some powerful emotion. The brief apparition was shocking.

She called out, 'Hey, what's up?' But he was gone. She heard the front door slam. She jumped up, went out, and stood in the driveway, staring up and down the road, but Alan had vanished.

Turning to go back inside, she came face to face with Maggie, who was showing the policeman out.

'I'll be looking in again, Mrs Denisov,' he was saying. 'There's a whole lot I don't understand.' His manner was acceptably polite, but he allowed himself just a hint of jeering sarcasm.

Maggie's eyes looked large and dark in her white face. She reminded Ruth of an old cartoon in her history books showing Brave Little Belgium confronting the German Bully. 'This is totally unfair.' There was a repressed violence in her tone. 'It's got nothing whatsoever to do with Alan.'

Vic Eliot had been Alder's local bobby for a long time. He had glossy, greased, black hair, red cheeks and a tolerant professional smile, which he tried to summon up now. 'You've taken the lad in, Mrs Denisov. All credit to you. I can see the temptation to believe the best of him . . . We all know Alan's a bit of a rough diamond.' The insincerity of his grin transformed it into a ghastly grimace. 'In all conscience, you can't rule out the possibility . . .'

'Perhaps you'd better come back when you've got some proper evidence.' Abruptly Maggie turned away and went back into the house. Ruth followed and shut the door behind her.

Maggie exploded, 'The pompous idiot!'

'What did he want?'

'Up at Gifford's. There's been some malicious damage. Someone's ripped up a whole bed of onion plants and some cabbages and thrown them around. Alan had words with old Gifford yesterday so they've decided it was him.' She was shaking with anger. 'Eliot can't accuse him, not in so many words, but you can see he's closed his mind. He's just not looking any further.'

'It's what they've known all along. An evacuee. An East Ender.' Ruth mimicked Vic Eliot's false bonhomie. 'A bit of a rough diamond.'

The closed faces of the Tyler boys had flashed into her mind. They had as much of a motive . . . But she didn't voice the thought.

'What did he want, Mum?' Sacha and Stephen came out into the hall, large-eyed with the enormity of a visit from the police.

Maggie gave them a reassuring smile. 'He says Alan's a

254

wrong'un.' She bent and brushed the dark hair back from Sacha's forehead. 'But we know he's not, don't we?'

Ruth took it into her head that he'd be in the lane. Their lane where the blackberries grew. There was an oak set back from the path with undulating roots like snakes that twisted along the ground. As they merged with the earth they formed hollows you could sit in. They'd walked there a few times after supper this summer and stayed talking till dusk.

She could picture him sitting there with the blank, brooding look he wore when he was upset. She'd never mistaken it for sullenness. It was just that he felt a compulsion to keep from other people the knowledge that they could hurt him.

'I'm going to look for Alan,' she told Maggie.

'Are you sure? You don't think he'd rather be left on his own?'

Ruth shrugged and smiled. 'Well, if he would, he can always tell me to clear off.'

At six in the evening the village was relatively deserted. It was teatime for most people. A few village boys hung around the corner of the High Street.

'Where you off to, Ruth?' one of them called across to her. She liked the nosiness of village life.

But she grinned perversely. 'Nowhere.' Tonight she didn't feel like telling them.

She noticed Tom and Sid loafing in the angle of a wall. Impassive, both of them, scowling at their boots, hands sunk deep into their pockets. Her suspicions came back to her. She could almost fancy they were watching her furtively from under lowered lashes. But with them it was easy to imagine things.

She crossed the road and dodged down a sidestreet that

petered out into an unmade road. She hurried, almost running at times, picturing Alan's desolation and wanting him to know that he wasn't alone. Skirting a field of rough wheat, she found an opening in the hedgerow and entered a path that was cool with the young green of overhanging beech leaves. Underfoot the soil was slightly damp with the shade. Their lane led off to the right.

She wouldn't see him until she was close. The base of the tree was hidden by bramble thickets. You had to push through a gap to get to it. She ran now to find the opening; she'd set her heart on his being there. Fighting her way through, she caught her skirt and hair on the thorns and had to stop to unhook herself.

'Alan!' She was close enough to call him. She listened. There was no reply.

The undergrowth cleared to coarse grass, but her view was hidden by a spreading elder tree.

She called again. 'Are you there?'

Simultaneously she saw him, pale in the shade, watching her, legs drawn up and circled by his arms, chin resting on his knees.

'Why don't you answer?' She came close, looked down, and saw at once that he'd been crying. His eyes were swollen, lashes spiked. She was awed. He never cried.

'I hate this place,' he said passionately.

Simultaneously she blurted, 'We don't believe it. You do know that, don't you? Maggie and me and the boys.'

In that instant she was terribly aware of what a family they'd become, understanding how the war forced new alliances that grew stronger with time. Wondering, with one corner of her mind, whether her bond with Sarah was correspondingly weakened. But she had no leisure to pursue that thought.

She answered Alan. 'Don't hate it. There's good things here too. Lots.'

Alan declared soberly, 'It wasn't me.' As if justifying their faith in him.

'We know.' She knelt down so as to be on his level. 'I'm the only one that's seen you crying. Don't let those miserable . . . They don't have to know they've upset you.' She grasped his hand. 'You've got to treat them with the contempt they deserve.' His face, white and vulnerable, was close to hers. His mouth looked mobile and warm like a puppy's. On an impulse she leaned across and placed a kiss on his lips, softly.

25

The bureaucrat came again to Rosa's flat, and this time
he didn't seem remotely laughable. He arrived at dawn
on a gunmetal-grey February morning, flanked by two
storm troopers. They trailed an aura of the freezing,
foggy, empty streets.

'What do you want?' Dominique backed away from
them with the hazy intention of blocking the doorway to
the bedroom. As she faced them it occurred to her
vaguely, irrelevantly, that one of the soldiers looked like
the hero of *All Quiet on the Western Front*. Smooth-faced
and wholesome. He moved her aside without anger or
haste, grasping her upper arms, not looking at her.

With the same indifference they dragged Daniel from
bed, wrenching one arm up behind his back. He was still
half-asleep, and the bewilderment in his eyes was almost
comic.

Why Daniel? 'Stop!' She threw herself at the same
soldier. This time he flung her sideways to the floor, with
a negligent brutality that was truly shocking. She lay
sprawled, dazed, plucking at her dressing gown to hide
her breasts.

'You bastard!' Daniel leapt towards him, naked, squar-
ing up, beside himself, breathing hard and shallow like a
boy spoiling for a fight. He landed a clumsy punch before
being seized from behind by the second storm trooper
and held while the wholesome, handsome one struck him
across the face with a calm ferocity. Daniel reeled.

Instantaneously a bright, sticky trail of blood appeared from his nose, streaming down his chin, body, and on to Rosa's carpet.

Dominique watched with a cold disbelief. It was like the worst kind of nightmare. This thuggery on their own home ground, the official standing by, pudgy and dough-faced, lending a kind of respectability to the crudest of violence. He gave laconic instructions, and the two men began to search the flat, scattering the contents of drawers, rifling cupboards, strewing clothes, working methodically as if they took no pleasure in the mayhem.

'There's nothing.' Daniel spoke low, almost confidentially. As if he knew why they were there, Dominique thought. His naked body, blood-spattered, looked achingly defenceless. Next to the Germans in their boots and stiff uniforms, their protective carapace, he resembled a peeled prawn.

'What are they looking for?' She was totally baffled. Neither Daniel nor the soldiers replied. She knew there was nothing. They'd long since destroyed their copies of Métro, the insulting poster of Pétain, things she'd once considered to be so trivial as to be beneath the Germans' notice.

The handsome storm trooper began to examine their books, bending them backwards in his strong hands to crack the spines, then pulling them apart, peering blank-faced at the pieces. He made Dominique think of a psychopathic child, impassively tearing the wings and legs off a series of insects. Daniel's notebooks of poetry were subjected to the same brutal, indifferent treatment. Dominique felt physical pain as she watched. She wanted to cry out, but knew better now.

His colleague, who was older, his rough-cut hair showing short, coarse streaks of grey, had discovered some

259

packets of pasta and beans Dominique had managed to get hold of. He broke each one open and tipped its contents slowly and carefully on to the bed, on the rumpled blankets and the clothes they'd piled there.

Dominique sat on the floor, shivering in her thin dressing gown, watching Daniel, who was white with the cold, watching the soldiers upend the furniture and slit the upholstery, pulling out springs and horsehair stuffing. She had no sense of time. Her brain alternated between her own panic-stricken conjecture and the grotesque charade being played out in front of her eyes.

Eventually the bureaucrat looked up from a pile of papers he was studying, shook his head and said casually, 'That's enough. There's nothing here. We'll just take the boy.' She understood the muttered German, and her stomach lurched. She retched and clapped a hand to her mouth, feeling her gorge rise.

They allowed Daniel, then, to put some clothes on. He searched among the wreckage for the necessary garments. Dominique saw a warm, brown sweater of his lying close to her on the floor. She picked it up and handed it to him wordlessly. His eyes looked deep into hers, but told her nothing.

Finally he was ready, seeming small, pale and unshaven in the wintry light. And scared. A man and nothing more. The smooth young soldier who towered over him as he fitted the handcuffs was different, Dominique thought. Dehumanized. His personality was suspended behind the uniform and the duties he carried out.

'Daniel . . .' She'd never felt so helpless. They could do this. They could take him away.

Again his eyes met hers. '*Au revoir, Dominique.*' He gave her a small, apologetic smile. He seemed resigned, like a schoolboy wryly making the best of a prospective beating. His departure was quiet and unremarkable. She could hardly believe he wouldn't be home by nightfall.

'Best you don't know. Then you won't be involved.' Guy was unbending. He shook his head. There was a dour set to his mouth.

She glared at him through tears that she ignored. 'If you know *anything*, tell me!'

A pause. He didn't react.

'Christ, they've taken him! Don't you understand?'

Still he stared, steadily, as if weighing her up. She'd never budge him if he didn't want to talk. His room was icy. Over trousers and sweater he wore a heavy black cardigan. Still he looked pinched and grey. Hungry and cold, like everyone.

She gestured imploringly. 'I don't know anything.'

Guy shrugged. 'He wasn't supposed to tell you.'

She was incensed by his imperturbable conviction that she had no rights in the matter. On top of this morning's raid, her terror for Daniel. Her mind snapped. He had knowledge, and the arrogance to withhold it. She shrieked, 'Tell me, you . . .' Half-blinded by tears, she rushed at him, hand raised to strike, anywhere, anyhow.

He caught her wrist. 'What good are you doing?' Pushing her backwards, holding her for a moment at arm's length, then releasing her.

She was defeated and began to cry in earnest. 'He couldn't talk in front of them. He couldn't explain.' Her desolation was total, sincere. A tiny corner of her mind wondered if Guy could be susceptible . . .

There was no warmth in his voice. 'I'll tell you the minimum. But not here. I can't stay here now.'

* * *

It was as though she'd spent her recent life in a comfortable half-light, and Guy had come with a powerful torch and shone its crude beam into the dim, ignored corners of her existence, revealing gibbering wraiths and unsuspected demons. Her open, easy-going life with Daniel had been a lie. For a year and a half now he'd been deeply involved in Resistance activities, using his army training as a wireless operator.

He had two contacts, apparent collaborators who passed him information – Guy was no more specific than that. Often, when he claimed to be seeing friends, talking philosophy and drinking coffee, Daniel had been risking his life in secret meetings or perilously transmitting the knowledge received to the de Gaulle organization in London.

Guy told her this over a weak black coffee in an anonymous café in the rue Cardinal Lemoine. Dominique warmed her hands on the cup, but made no attempt to drink its contents. As Guy spoke his breath turned to vapour with the cold. He'd put some belongings in a bag and planned to move in with some acquaintances for a time. She could contact him through a mutual friend at the Flore.

'I've got to face the fact that Daniel could give me away.' He gazed at her warily, levelly, to gauge whether she'd appreciated the implication of his words.

'So he'll be tortured.' She addressed herself to the thought. It had lain, deliberately neglected, in a corner of her mind, like a dirty, irksome task. But sooner or later it had to be confronted.

'Very probably.' She'd wanted the truth. 'There's a place in the rue Lauriston . . .'

Dominique closed her eyes. The image of his body, naked and defenceless, was still imprinted on her brain.

Now she saw it surrounded by shadowy, slow-moving figures, each of whom had total power over him. She screwed her eyes tighter, but couldn't black out the nightmare tableau.

'Oh, Christ.' She was hardly aware of having spoken.

Simultaneously another thought crystallized. The possibility of help.

'Dominique!' Peter Borchert sounded genuinely pleased to hear from her. Some months back he'd given her a number where he could be reached during the day, but she'd never made use of it.

'Peter, I really need to see you tonight.' She injected the words with all the intensity of which she was capable. If he turned her down she was lost.

A note of concern. 'Yes, of course.' He caught the urgency in her voice and responded without hesitation. Now he mused aloud. 'Wednesday. My night with Irène – I'll cancel. And there's a function . . . That I can't avoid. Look, I'll pick you up outside the Philo at ten o'clock sharp. We'll go for a meal.' He sounded thoroughly organized, decisive, energetic.

She allowed herself a glimmer of hope.

'You're looking stunning.'

Dominique smiled graciously. She'd spent the afternoon in the icy wreckage of Rosa's flat trying to make herself so. Brushing broken pasta off a black velvet dress, washing her hair in cold water with soap that didn't lather.

Peter cocked his head to one side, examining her with critical affection. 'But a little pale.'

'It's the time of year.'

It was gloriously warm here in Maxim's. The high-

263

ceilinged room seemed permeated with a luxury she'd forgotten, if she ever knew it. Deep carpets, discreet lighting, white damask, silver, crystal, wine, the rich perfume of cigars, bland, sweet music.

The recurring image flashed into her mind in stark counterpoint. Daniel, alone, helpless, frozen . . . Under the tablecloth Dominique clawed at her own wrist. She mustn't think of that.

A French flunkey brought them huge, printed menus. She nodded coolly and tried to concentrate on the listed goodies. It was like being in a lions' den here, with all these German uniforms, but she mustn't lose her nerve.

Peter had picked her up in a black Mercedes bang on the appointed hour. He was driving himself. Dominique had expected a shaven-necked chauffeur. He'd laughed when she said as much. 'Never when I'm off-duty, *Schätzchen.*' The endearment had grated. It didn't sound like him.

He'd been in uniform in the wake of some official function – immaculate black, with riding-breeches and boots. His appearance had frozen her. The uniform changed him, aligned him more obviously with the persecutors. Dominique preferred him in mufti, illogically. She'd long since understood that the plain clothes marked him out as a member of the secret police, the dreaded Gestapo.

He'd made it clear that they wouldn't talk about her problems until they'd been properly served with food and wine. Both of them decided on *canard en daube*. It had been years since she'd eaten anything so rich. Under normal circumstances Dominique would have revelled in the luxury. As it was, she was terrified that she'd be unable to manage a single bite.

They had their traditional champagne. Dominique

drank it grimly, like medicine, hoping it would give her courage and take away the despair that threatened to engulf the smiling, seductive persona she wanted to present. Seductive, because she knew Peter Borchert wanted her and if that was what it took . . . She could've done with a stiff brandy.

He was different tonight in some way. Coarser, probably, though the signs were subtle. Like calling her *Schätzchen* when he'd never before offered her the smallest endearment, beyond a stiff and formal 'my dear Dominique'. Interrupting her once with unnecessary briskness, while she consulted with the waiter over a choice of liqueur. Allowing the dialogue between himself and her to lapse for a second or two, while he treated her to an insolent and heavy-lidded stare. But when he carried on talking it was in his normal, urbane manner, so that she could almost fancy it had been her imagination.

She'd always thought his looks pleasantly robust, the pock-marked complexion a not unpleasing contrast to the elegance of his dress. Tonight Dominique thought his face, flushed with alcohol, showed at times an elusive, thuggish quality. But she was overwrought. Probably it was a trick of her mind.

She didn't allow these observations to influence her own behaviour. She was smiling and graceful. Grave, as she talked to him about Daniel, looking up into his eyes with a trustful sincerity. Emphasizing that Daniel was small-fry. Flashing a smile of flirtatious complicity, as if she were discussing a headstrong child. Taking a sip of wine and glancing at him over the rim of her glass, each movement designed to attract, elegantly, subtly, without vulgarity. When the meal was finished Peter suggested that they might discuss the problem further back at his hotel.

She inclined her head. 'By all means.' Then wondered if she hadn't rather overdone the graciousness. After all, she was the beggar, and he held all the cards.

The Germans had appropriated many of the better hotels and town houses as living quarters for their high-ranking officers. Peter's room, overlooking the boulevard Haussman, had a gloomy magnificence – flock wallpaper striped in a dull moss green, heavy furniture gleaming sombrely, button-backed chairs upholstered in blue-grey velvet, which echoed the colour and texture of the floor-length curtains, mirrors supported by repulsive gilt cupids, a huge, immaculate, canopied bed. The heavy opulence of the place made Dominique feel cold and scared again. She'd been getting into her stride at Maxim's. She shivered now, as Peter took her coat, standing momentarily disarmed in her black strapless dress on the expanse of thick, slate-coloured carpet.

To her chagrin he caught her mood. 'You look like Gretel entering the lair of the wicked witch.' He was amused and at his ease. It seemed unthinkable that she'd be having sex in a while with this uniformed stranger in that high, formal bed.

She gestured at her surroundings. 'You certainly do yourselves proud.' A flash of malice, helping to restore her spirits.

He stowed her coat carelessly across the back of a chair, then came and stood in front of her, close, looking down, studying her face. She couldn't read his expression. After a moment he said, 'I'll do what I can to help your friend, Dominique. That's understood, *hein*?'

'Thank you.' Something came to life inside her like spring after winter. She smiled at him brilliantly. 'Thank you, Peter, so much.'

He bent and kissed her, coolly, discouraging in some way the warmth of her gratitude. Kissing her again in a detached, clinical manner that forced her to comply with it. Running his hands experimentally over the skin of her shoulders and arms. Touching his lips to her neck as if he were trying a new experience to see whether he would like it. Under his speculative caresses she stood passive.

Fleetingly she caught sight of their two figures in a full-length gilt mirror on the wall across the room. In the sombre light they made a striking picture. Peter powerful and long-legged in boots and black uniform. Herself, white-skinned, red-haired in her dark velvet dress. I look like a Toulouse-Lautrec prostitute, she thought interestedly, able to be flippant now that Peter had committed himself to helping her.

He pulled her closer now with the stirrings of a new urgency. His eyes were narrowed, his expression inward and intent, excluding her.

'*Liebchen.*' The word was like a feverish growl.

She felt a pressure on her shoulders, pushing her down. She understood and slid to her knees. He unbuttoned his fly. He'd turned slightly, so that the mirror was obliquely behind him. Dominique could see her white face, bright hair falling forward, then she closed her eyes.

There was a profound silence between them. She lay back on the velvet coverlet, the canopy above her merging into shadow. There were curtains you could draw, and he'd done so, leaving on one side of the bed a gap just the width of a doorway, through which a pale light shone. It was claustrophobic and enclosed, like being in some luxurious tent. As she lay spreadeagled on the velvet he caressed her with a calculated skill, stirring deepening waves of pleasure.

Making love with Daniel was a mutual activity, a sensual friendship, warm and happy and sweaty, with cuddling and laughter afterwards, and talking far into the night, or in the morning drinking coffee and eating whatever food they could find for breakfast.

With Peter there was distance, a deliberation. You did things to each other. With hardly a word, without a smile, even with a kind of hostility. Making her think of a clinical operation or once – but she exorcized the thought with all the force of her will – of the imagined vision of Daniel's naked body, the ministrations of the torturers.

His face above hers was blank with concentration. The sensations were becoming stronger, deeper. An exhalation like a sob. She could feel herself let go, letting the climax come in waves, and along with it the self-hatred at finding pleasure with one of the bastards who had Daniel, and the knowledge that self-hatred made the pleasure stronger. He made a sound of appreciation deep in his throat and entered her with a sudden thrust. Her arms went up to pull him close.

Peter had said he'd send word as soon as there was any news, but that it would be at least a couple of days before she'd hear anything. In the cold, grey morning she re-entered the wreckage of Rosa's flat, vague with lack of sleep, bleary with the after-effects of alcohol. But hopeful. Peter had seemed confident, like a man with the power to effect change.

She had somehow to fill the endless hours between now and then. Desultorily she picked up a blouse, shook it free of the clinging grains of rice. Clearing all this up would take time, and it had to be done, though it seemed a mammoth task like a labour of Hercules.

Doggedly she began to collect what was salvageable of

the dried food. Rations were so scarce you couldn't afford to let it go to waste. She sorted it roughly into categories, even found the packets and returned their contents to them.

She brushed down the clothes and hung them up, sorted out the contents of the drawers and put them back tidily. There were the books. She repaired the spines with brown sticky tape. It was the best she could do. Among them were the scattered pages of Daniel's notebooks, which she collected together.

She had started the job in a state of numbed bemusement, but as it went on she warmed to the task, equating it with Daniel's impending return, wanting to make it all look nice for him, welcoming after his ordeal. She did things she'd laughed at Rosa for doing, like polishing floors and washing windows. Attempting to patch up the ruined chairs, stuffing their insides back into place and sewing up the tears where possible. Covering a couple she couldn't mend with neatly folded blankets. Daniel would be amazed. He'd left the place in such a state.

She copied out his poems again into new notebooks. Happy almost, with an anticipation that she hugged to herself like secret gold.

After two days the place looked marvellous and time hung heavy. She dared not go out for fear of missing Peter's messenger. He might even come himself, he'd said, to give her the good news. She stared out of the window, flicked through books. It was possible Peter wouldn't bother with a messenger of course, but simply send Daniel to announce himself.

'Tell him it's Irène de Courcel, please.' She had attempted to phone Peter three times now. Each time she'd been informed that he was busy, engaged, elsewhere. Clickings and whirrings at the other end told her that something was happening. She hung on, coldly suspicious.

Eventually she heard Peter's voice. 'Irène?'

She cleared her throat, but still sounded hoarse as she announced flatly. 'It's Dominique.'

There was a hesitation, a palpable drawing back. Then he said, 'What can I do for you?' The tone of his voice radiated bad faith.

'What d'you think?' It was a snarl, semi-hysterical. She'd promised herself to remain neutral, polite. All might not be lost.

'You're telephoning about your friend, I suppose.' Taking refuge in a spurious innocence, as if he didn't know that Daniel was the one, the only thing on her mind. He was safe with the distance between them, the bureaucratic organization around him. His chill official-dom terrified her. If he had anything positive to say he wouldn't sound like that. She was tempted to put the receiver down, creep away, retain a grain of hope.

'Dominique?'

She realized that she hadn't replied. A paralysis of fear had come between her and outward reality, her mind silently screaming. She said with an effort, 'Yes, it's about Daniel.'

A silence, which seemed endless. She closed her eyes. He said, 'Please understand, Dominique, I did what I could . . .' His tone was insincere, like that of a politician putting across an unpalatable truth. 'It just wasn't possible . . .'

'What's happened to him?'

'You see, I don't think you quite understood the situation. Your friend's activities were really quite serious . . .'

What he seemed to be saying was unthinkable, yet he

270

hadn't really told her anything. She felt violently sick, her stomach lurching downwards. She screamed into the receiver, 'What's happened to him?'

'Dominique, please . . .' Now she was behaving hysterically he sounded more confident. Disapproving.

'Tell me, you lying bastard!'

'He's dead.' She heard the click of his receiver.

'Are you all right?' Her concierge appeared outside the café down the road where she'd made the phone call. Anxious-looking at the best of times, she seemed aghast as she gazed at Dominique, who made a deprecating gesture. She was incapable of speech. The woman watched as she passed, as though mesmerized.

Dominique was in trousers and sweater. No coat. She'd just slipped out to phone. Now she walked like an automaton without knowing where, her legs moving independently of her will, through yellowish drifts of early-evening fog. Her surroundings seemed to have the distant unreality of things viewed under water. Passers-by appeared slow-moving, dream-like. She crossed to the rue St-Benoît.

'Hey, Dominique!'

It was dark-eyed André Delarue, finally released from custody a week or so earlier. It seemed the Gestapo had at last decided that his cartoons posed no great threat to the Third Reich. He called gaily, but as she drew near, his face changed, reflecting the lost, distracted look she was wearing. She passed him by. She couldn't speak. There were no tears. Tears implied warmth, emotion. She was frozen. She hadn't known anything could hurt so much.

The sky was a doom-laden yellow-grey, the streets hard and bleak. They suited her mood. The passers-by walked,

271

white, cold, disgruntled. A woman stood laughing with a friend, her mouth red and avid. Dominique stared, glazed and fascinated. How could she laugh? How could anyone? Hating the strident life-force. Daniel was stiff and dead.

She found herself outside the Flore. Perhaps Guy would be inside, the one person she wanted to see. Abruptly she entered the smoky warmth, oblivious of covert stares.

He was there, at a table with Rosa's friend Luc. As she approached Guy stood up. 'Christ, you look awful.'

Without ceremony she pulled a chair from under a nearby table and sat down. Guy asked, 'What news?' He gestured. 'You can talk in front of Luc.'

'He's dead.' Luc was staring at her. She must look strange. She smiled vaguely to reassure him and knew she seemed mad, was mad. No matter. 'I want to join you.'

26

Although Daniel was gone Dominique still kept to her side of the bed, lying curled in a ball to keep warm, eyes open, but blank and passive. The clock on the bedside table had stopped. It felt like afternoon. Some watery sunshine filtered through the brick-coloured plush curtains, a dull shaft of light striped the faded carpet.

She pictured Daniel pulling her close as he woke, imperious like a spoiled, sensual child, the tousled hair, sleepy grin . . .

There was a clatter from outside as the concierge plied bucket and mop, sluicing the stairs, calling to one of her children to bring a cloth down, then repeating the order more sharply.

Dominique tried to recapture the vision of Daniel. It had been so real, bringing a flash of painful gladness. But it was no good. The pictures came of themselves, creeping up on her, or not at all. She pulled the blankets closer round her. She felt cold all the time, her toes white and lifeless. It was impossible to chafe any warmth into them. Sharing the bed with Daniel, she'd never been cold.

'Dominique, hold on to me,' he'd whispered. She saw him lying beside her after Rosa was taken, pressing his body down on hers. 'You've got me.' If she closed her eyes she could almost feel the solidity of his flesh, his ribcage, thigh muscles, arms . . .

This must be what insanity was like, this obsession. Living inside your head, and only occasionally, incidentally, bumping up against reality. All day and night her

273

mind was filled with pictures, conversations, fragments, more compelling than life.

'Acorns and dried parsley anyone?' Daniel leaning across the table at Le Pessimiste, holding out a box of hideous herbal cigarettes. His good-natured smile always with an edge of private amusement, the easy-going exterior which hid something more complex . . .

But there were other images. She saw him leaving the flat, reduced and frightened, flanked by soldiers. Their last moment together, bewildered, inconsequential, neither of them understanding its significance.

And the pictures of suffering and death, imagined from hearsay. His face raw and bloody, eyes and mouth swollen and pulped. She'd heard tales of prisoners gouging handprints into the walls in their agony . . . Daniel being tortured by near-drowning, lying like a corpse below the water, hair floating like weed, anonymous figures holding him down . . . His body on the floor of a cell, the smiling boy reduced to a husk, just so much detritus. Someone she'd loved, but he'd died alone, without a shred of human comfort. She let the pictures come, bright and violent, not allowing herself to blot them out or turn away. She owed him that. Watching them with a fascinated horror like some grisly film show.

Her other obsession was Peter Borchert. He was a focus of her anger, hatred, grief. She'd trusted him, the bastard, and waited like a fool, obedient and hopeful, for him to be as good as his word. He'd given the impression that securing Daniel's release was a thing of no consequence. And he'd failed and been too cowardly to tell her.

Sometimes as she pictured Daniel, beaten, tormented, humiliated, she substituted Peter Borchert for the shad-

274

owy figure of the torturer. She did it quite deliberately, to fuel her cold hatred.

'I'll do what I can to help your friend.' She could visualize him now, looking down at her, with eyes that were steady as rocks. She'd always seen an honesty in him. But he'd lied, either offering a help which he'd no intention of giving or exaggerating the extent of his influence in high places, so that she'd sleep with him like some poor, self-deluding actress on the casting-couch. And she'd been grateful, so grateful that she'd responded to his body with eagerness and pleasure. A cold sweat broke out at the memory.

Towards evening on Wednesday she got up and made herself a cup of coffee, then she put on a sweater, trousers and a dark jacket, tying back her hair and making up her face. Trying to make herself look neat and tidy to hide her madness. She was meeting Guy and Luc, Rosa's lover. They mistrusted her, she knew. They were attracted to her plan, but thought it the product of a fevered imagination. It was up to her to prove otherwise.

Tonight was only a trial run. They'd arranged to meet at Chez Brice. Dominique still didn't know where Guy was living. She was early, the first of them to arrive. As she sat down on a red banquette in the corner and ordered a coffee she felt conspicuous, as though her outward appearance must reflect what was on her mind. She forced herself to sit without jiggling a foot or drumming her fingers, though it was hard. She'd found an old packet of Daniel's cigarettes and she smoked one while she waited. It helped her to feel calm. The only other customer was an old man, a friend of Brice's, who with his chessboard and watery beer was a permanent fixture.

Luc was the first to arrive, wearing a long, grey, belted raincoat, taking off his glasses and polishing them to get rid of the spattered drizzle. He was wary of Dominique when he was alone with her, and especially now when he knew her to be distressed. They talked desultorily, but both were relieved when Guy appeared, interposing his reassuring maturity between them.

They decided to eat before investigating the lie of the land. In any case it was too early yet. Brice served them with dishes of lentils and a very little sliced sausage. It was the best he could manage. He plonked the plates down in front of them with a lugubrious air. With the shortage of food and fuel he was struggling to keep going, and he looked shrunken and older. His son, Arnaud, had been a prisoner in Germany for more than three years now, and it was gradually taking the heart out of him. But his wife, enthroned in her booth behind the till, was as curled and immaculate as ever.

Dominique took a few mouthfuls, then pushed her plate aside. 'I'm not hungry.' She'd barely eaten for days and couldn't imagine wanting to ever again. The lentils seemed dry and grainy, like eating mud. And anyway she was too strung up.

'No problem.' Eagerly the two men shared her left-overs. Like almost everyone nowadays, they were hungry all the time.

They chatted until about half past nine, then paid Brice and went out into the damp, dark street. It was a fair step to the rue Briard, where Irène de Courcel had her flat.

'It's usually deserted. There's a dress factory and ware-house on the corner, and they're empty at night.' Dominique told them as they walked. 'Ideal, really. You hardly ever get patrols . . . and there's a courtyard entrance

276

pretty well opposite.' Trying to impress on them that she'd thought everything out in detail.

Guy and Luc were quietly sceptical, reserving judgement. She'd broached her plan immediately after hearing the news of Daniel's death, and she'd been off her head, not to put too fine a point on it. Even now her impulse was to harangue them for their qualms. This was something worth doing, direct action, better than all the underground newspapers in Paris. But she held her tongue. Hysterics would be counter-productive. After all, they'd agreed to come, and that was what mattered.

The rue Briard was more of an alley than a road. As Dominique had anticipated, it was deserted. There were stunted trees, a walled gateway opposite for cover. Her main fear had been the problem of how they could wait and observe without arousing suspicion. But in the event there was no difficulty. With the blackout they were hardly noticeable, and the only passer-by was an old man walking a dog who averted his face as he hurried past. It was as if circumstances had conspired to justify her predictions, boosting her own confidence in the plan. It was all working out so well. And she guessed that Guy and Luc must be secretly impressed.

At about twenty past ten they heard footsteps approaching from the right. A tall figure strode along the opposite side of the road, a man wearing a long black leather trenchcoat. He must have left his car in an adjoining street. Dominique was ecstatic. Everything was going as it should.

'That's him,' she hissed.

They were silent, watching him from behind the wall, pressing close into the brickwork. Peter Borchert turned into the gateway opposite and disappeared. After he'd gone they stood for a time looking at the gloomy arched entrance.

'It's every Wednesday, see.' She began to whisper. 'We could wait inside the gateway opposite. He wouldn't notice us till we were on top of him. We could do it and be home before curfew.'

There would be reprisals of course. Alone in the flat Dominique turned this thought over and over in her mind. She had more trouble with it than either Guy or Luc, who had long since worked out their position on that score. Dominique could remember Guy and Daniel discussing the question endlessly. Odd that it should be she, finally, who turned it from theory into a real-life dilemma.

She could remember Daniel saying once, 'For every five or six of ours they shoot down, fifty or sixty volunteer for the Resistance. It's by far the best incentive . . .' In the end she clung to that thought and closed her mind to the rest.

In between her meetings with Guy and Luc, Dominique stayed alone. Hardly eating, she felt weightless, pure spirit, exalted by the plan they were hatching. Much of the time she stayed in bed, warming herself at the fireside of her visions of Daniel before they faded and died, and simultaneously fuelling her hatred of Peter Borchert, aware of nothing external beyond the time and date of her next meeting with the two men.

She was secretly amazed to have enlisted them in her plan. At times it seemed sheer lunacy, a collective folly. They were just three ordinary, rather ill-assorted acquaintances. She'd vaguely supposed that active resistants were a race apart, with skills and daring unknown to the rest. But probably most were nobodies like themselves, amateurs seizing fearfully, ineptly on some offered opportunity. She couldn't put herself inside their heads or understand what motivated them. Patriotism? It was a sentiment too abstract for her to grasp. Mentally she shrugged. Her own motive was simple: revenge first and last.

They heard footsteps on the other side of the wall. It must be him. Dominique felt like fainting. The moment had actually come. Up till then it had seemed in some way as if they were telling themselves a fantastic story. Now it came to her with a frozen clarity that this was truth. They'd made it so.

The moon shed a cold, clear light. She glanced fleetingly at the other two. Luc stood by a skeletal shrub. As the best shot, he was poised with the gun, an English Enfield revolver Guy had obtained from some contact of his. From her angle Luc was in profile, pale, body braced, arm at precisely the right angle, like an illustration from some handgun training manual. Guy stood poised behind him, his face hawk-like between collar-length wings of hair, ready to step in if any part of their plan misfired.

The footsteps passed through the gate. The figure turned, unmistakable, tall and bulky in the long, leather coat.

She said, 'Yes.' They'd agreed that she would identify him. A mistake was the last thing they wanted.

Immediately Luc fired. She saw a brief flash at the gun's muzzle. Peter reeled violently, but to her horror remained upright. He raised an exploratory hand to his left shoulder. His heavy face, pallid in the moonlight, reflected, so it seemed to her, astonishment rather than pain. Almost at once his expression sharpened. The hand shot down towards his pocket. She registered in the brief movement that it was sticky with black blood.

Luc fired again, missed completely, and in a moment of cold premonition she saw a small, dark gun in Peter's hand. Another flash. Luc staggered backwards and fell.

Dominique understood immediately that Peter had killed him. She said, almost reflectively, '*Salaud.*'

He swung towards her, noticing her for the first time. 'Dominique.' A mild, conventional tone of surprise, as though he'd run into her unexpectedly while strolling on the Champs Élysées. The disorientation suspended his reaction briefly, giving Guy the chance to seize and fire the Enfield. This time the bullet grazed Peter's left hand. In reflex his right dropped the Mauser with a clatter.

Darting like a striking snake, Dominique dived for it and backed away. Peter swayed towards her with a terrifying air of deliberation. Mesmerized, she stared into his eyes. They held a vague sense of purpose, as though he had something of interest to say if only she'd stand still for long enough.

'*Hure.*' Whore. The insult held an almost caressing quality.

She panicked. He lurched towards her like a zombie, like Rasputin, some creature you couldn't kill. She held out the Mauser in front of her. It was smooth in her hand. She wasn't sure what you did. Some lever you should cock? Of itself her finger pressed the trigger and to her amazement it fired, like it should, like in a gangster film. Fascinated, she fired again, once, twice. The gun recoiled heavily with each shot. The bullets caught him full in the chest, and at last he keeled over. She had the unreal impression that she'd shot an elephant.

She bent over him. He looked up at her. '*Hure,*' he repeated mildly. Almost immediately all expression left his eyes.

27

Monty toddled towards the spot where his mother sat on the small patch of grass in Sarah's backyard. His gait was rolling and unsteady. With a corner of her mind Sarah admired his sturdy, fleshy little legs, the minuscule toes and toenails.

'Want juice,' he declared forcibly to Tessa, his voice startlingly deep for the tiny frame. Absently she pulled him towards her, offering a curved, teated bottle with some remnants of orange. He stood in the circle of her arms.

Tessa stared ahead of her, broodingly, the sun shining in her wispy blonde hair. 'Divorce, I suppose.' She added realistically, 'I don't imagine we'll be the only ones when this war's over and done with.'

'And that's what you want?' Sarah looked at her searchingly. A creeping sadness under the hard, late-July sun. Two people she liked, loved. And so much in tune it had seemed. If they couldn't find happiness, who could?

'No, of course not. It's not what I want at all.' An edge of impatience in Tessa's voice. Her mouth drooping a little, not quite under control. She pulled Monty astride her lap. As she talked he patted and prodded her face and neck with his dimpled fingers. 'I want us back as we were. In the early days, working on the magazine. Those were the best times I ever had. But I don't see how we can get back to anything approaching . . .'

She'd suspected for a long time that Michael was having an affair, without ever mentioning her fears to Sarah.

Tessa was stoic and immensely loyal. Last weekend she'd tackled him and he'd admitted it. They'd come to no conclusion. She broached the matter with Sarah now for the first time. Still Sarah kept her own knowledge a secret.

'I'll stick it out. Be the little woman at home for now. What with Monty and the war and Michael being away, there's not much else I *can* do.' Covering her pain with a kind of practical energy. She shrugged. 'But afterwards . . .'

'So you've decided?'

Tessa pulled a face. 'Look, Sarah, if Michael showed an interest in rebuilding what we had . . . making the effort, I'd give it a go.' Gently detaching Monty's hands from her hair, which he was pulling vigorously. 'Or not what we had, even – we've both changed – but we've always . . . Well, I still think we could make something worthwhile . . .' She turned to Sarah, her eyes vulnerable and honest in the determined composure of her expression. 'But I'm not giving him any kind of an ultimatum. He's got to want it himself . . .'

They were interrupted by a sound from the sky, the harsh cough and splutter of an engine.

'Oh, God!'

They looked up and saw the familiar simple cruciform shape, and watched breathlessly and listened. Already the engine sound had cut out. That was when you got scared. Too late to run for cover. You waited and hoped. A few seconds, but seeming infinitely extended, the tension killing.

'It's okay.'

It became obvious the bomb would fall elsewhere. There was a flash, a burst of fire, smoke, and only afterwards the sound of the explosion. Hitler's latest weapon, the V1s. Doodlebugs, as they'd been christened with nervous bravado.

'Two miles at least, I'd say.' Sarah had become an expert. After nearly two nerve-wracking months everyone was. She stood up. 'I'd better get back to the Depot.'

Monty held his hands out in the direction of the explosion. 'Doo Bug,' he exclaimed brightly. Even he recognized the sight and sound, they were so much a fact of his young life.

The past six months or so had been vastly busier for Sarah and her colleagues at the Ambulance Depot. They'd begun to feel needed again, appreciated. The tired jokes about knitting and doing their nails had petered out. Their stock rose in the community, along with that of the other Civil Defence workers. Shopkeepers offered them under-the-counter oranges and eggs. Complete strangers came up to them in the street and told them they were doing a grand job.

One such – an unctuous, patronizing woman who worked at the local Citizens' Advice Bureau – made the mistake of accosting the forthright Ivy one evening, as she puffed on the dog-end of a cigarette outside the Depot before going on duty. Ivy had a beady dislike of her kind. She'd removed the fag stolidly from between pursed magenta lips before replying rudely, 'Look, missis, we've been here every bloody night for four years while you've been tucked up in your bed. And it's only when the bombs drop that anyone takes a blind bit of notice. We don't need you to tell us what kind of a job we're doing.' With that she'd dropped the butt of her cigarette and ground it out viciously with her foot. The woman had beaten a bridling retreat.

During the winter it had been the Little Blitz. Similar

in kind to the first, but on a smaller scale – too many of Germany's resources were deployed on the Russian Front. Still, each incident was grim enough in itself, with the same monstrous devastation, dazed survivors, the killings and maimings. This time Sarah and Joan felt like old campaigners, practical and compassionate, but totally unshockable. All the Civil Defence services had learned from the past and this time were efficient and well-prepared.

In early June the long-awaited Second Front had been launched with the landings in Normandy. There was general jubilation at what was seen as the final phase of the war, a clean sweep, almost a formality.

'It's going to be the best Christmas ever.' Joan was married now to her steady, blue-eyed fireman, and couldn't wait to get started on her proper, peacetime wedded bliss.

A few days later the rejoicing had been chilled as Hitler launched the secret weapon he'd threatened for so long it had become a joke. The pilotless doodlebugs were a complete surprise to unsuspecting Londoners. At first people took them for crashed aircraft until they saw the havoc they could cause, and they soon became familiar with the suspended seconds of eerie silence that preceded an explosion.

What was more, the V1s came at any time of the day or night. There was no safe period. You were on perpetual alert. Since it was impossible to shelter all the time, people ignored them as far as possible and went about their business.

But the general attitude towards the bombing had changed. There was little left of the ebullient, defiant Blitz spirit. People were bone-weary of the war, never-ending as it seemed, and of the eternal shortages. They were irritable and grumbled, and now there was the nagging fear of being killed pointlessly, just when the end was in sight.

The bombardment at this late stage was a huge blow and yet, guiltily, Sarah almost welcomed the renewed activity it brought. She too was heartily sick of the inconclusive conflict that dragged on and on. There was the tantalizing, twinkling prospect of peace – in three months' time, six months, a year. Always receding. She thirsted now to resume her own life, be free to put her own concerns first again. The thought of it was almost too wonderful to imagine. Meanwhile the renewed importance of their war work gave her and the other women a much-needed sense of purpose.

But there was something else on her mind. A worry that nagged with the power to depress her at any time, to spread a dull, aching gloom when it chose even over her rare moments of pleasure. It concerned Ruth and her anxiety over their growing estrangement.

It wasn't that she worried about Ruth herself. On the contrary. She was pleased by her daughter's passion for acting, and touched by the transparent intensity of her calf-love for Alan West, her fellow evacuee. But with the exhilaration of her life Ruth needed her mother less. Well-intentioned advice, even interest, was greeted with an ill-disguised impatience, which turned rapidly into outright aggression. Sarah could see that her daughter felt wise and self-sufficient and beyond adult guidance. Their areas of common interest were dwindling, and Sarah had the secret fear that when, at long last, all this was over and Ruth returned to London, the two of them would come together as total strangers.

Arriving at the Depot, she pushed the thought to the

back of her mind. Officially she was off duty, but they'd agreed among themselves that if there was any danger of a crisis the opposite team would look in. With the present fraught situation they were understaffed.

'Any word?'

Ivy had rolled up the sleeves of her navy uniform and was cleaning the windscreen of her ambulance with robust energy. She looked up. 'Nothing yet. No casualties maybe.'

Right on cue, the telephone rang from the office. She pulled a wry face, nodding in the direction of the chimes. 'Oh-oh. Should've kept my big mouth shut.'

Michael was almost her oldest friend, but Sarah felt small affection for him as they sat side by side on an upright highly polished bench-seat in what was laughingly called the snug at his local. There was a stilted, uncomfortable air to their proximity.

The meeting had been difficult to arrange, and two projected dates had fallen through. Both of them found it hard to get away, and it was even more complicated to ensure that their free time coincided. But Sarah had persisted. She'd set her heart on seeing him. And, realizing this, Michael had co-operated to the best of his ability. Thus, their meeting had taken on in advance a portentous quality that she regretted.

Now Michael looked at her, sideways on because of the seating arrangements, and asked, 'What's all this about?' But he must have a shrewd idea, Sarah thought irritably. She didn't like him in uniform. It changed him. Smoothed the rough corners, hardened the gangling amiability. Or was it her imagination? His face seemed fleshier, heavier than it used to be. The short haircut wasn't flattering to him.

'I've taken a liberty.' She began apologetically, disliking herself for it. But she was intruding – there was no getting away from that. 'I've come because you're an old friend, and we've always been able to talk to each other. Tessa doesn't know . . .'

'You look terribly stern.' The remark irritated her. The old Michael wouldn't have said it, or not in that way. It was fatuous, subtly hostile.

She smiled broadly in sarcastic exaggeration. 'Better?' They weren't off to a good start.

He grinned. 'Yes, I like it.' At the same time raising his glass to a barmaid he obviously knew, who'd just come on duty. Sarah glanced across the room at the smiling woman. She was about fifty with platinum blonde hair piled in a pompadour. Engagingly she raised a cup of tea she was drinking in return.

'Tessa's been talking to me . . .' Sarah felt as though she were clawing his attention back.

'Oh.' He replaced his beer mug on the table with more force than was strictly necessary. There was a hint of truculence in the gesture. 'Well, that's not surprising. We did some talking ourselves last weekend. Endlessly.'

'Without reaching any conclusion.'

'Precisely.' A mild antagonism, as though he didn't intend to make the impending conversation easy for her.

Sarah scanned the snug with its solid Victorian chairs – the shine on them had a kind of depth to it, as if they'd been polished daily for generations – and clean, tiled floor. At seven thirty in the evening the only other occupants were an elderly couple doing a crossword together out loud, occasionally enlisting the help of the barmaid. She heard the man say enigmatically, 'Mousy creatures hide in county town . . .'

Michael spoke again with an almost reflective air. 'I

287

know you disapprove of me . . . and Dinah. But you're judging from a rigid standpoint. You don't know what it's like here. The claustrophobia, the concentration, the same people all the time . . . It's not a natural life. I've changed, I think. I'm not such a gentleman if you like. I don't know . . . there's a kind of ruthlessness here.'

Despite their awkward sideways-on position, he turned to look her levelly in the eye. 'You know, I find it hard to feel much for Monty. I can see he's adorable, but he seems nothing to do with me.' A plaintive note in the words, which she could see he hadn't intended. 'I mean, you know him a thousand times better than I do . . .'

'Yes,' she conceded.

He shrugged. 'Not excuses – explanations. There's an emotional emptiness about my life here, and it helps having Dinah. If Tessa had found someone . . . Well, I'd have understood.'

'Tessa wouldn't, though.'

'No.'

She began to feel better disposed towards him. He'd relaxed a little and dropped the brittle attitude with which he'd greeted her. She touched his arm. 'I don't want you to think I came up here to tell you what a cad you are. It isn't that.' She'd almost finished her beer. Absently she examined the complicated optical patterns in the dimpled glass of the tankard. 'I was shocked when you first told me about Dinah, I admit. It cut across my view of you. Now . . . well, I'm not so quick to judge.'

'When you're in earnest you sound so Welsh.' A deep, quiet affection in his voice.

For some reason the remark reminded her of how far back their friendship went, what a rock Michael had been to her when she'd first come back to England. She must never forget that. She said warily, 'This is none of my

288

business, I know, but . . . I'm just very fond of you both. And I've always thought you suited each other so well, and I'd hate you to come unstuck out of sheer . . . misunderstanding.'

'How do you mean?'

'Well, Tessa's thinking of a divorce when the war's over . . .' She glanced at him to see how he reacted to the word. His eyes held a steady, determined emptiness. Whatever he felt was going to remain hidden from her. '*I'm* telling you because I don't think Tessa will. She doesn't want to put pressure on you. She wants any effort to come from you – of your own free will . . .'

The door to the snug opened and a group of three people came in. Two men and a woman, all in uniform. To Sarah the men appeared middle-aged and featureless. The woman was different. Lithe and hard-looking, her hair centrally parted and worn in a glossy chignon. Like the Duchess of Windsor, Sarah thought. They greeted Michael breezily. The woman examined Sarah with a discreet, but more than casual interest. Michael smiled, amicable but detached, as though warning the newcomers not to join them. Sarah thought she detected a shadow of embarrassment in his eyes, and abruptly the truth dawned.

'That's her, isn't it?' The group had crossed to the bar and were chatting to the barmaid.

'Yes.' He nodded, unable to suppress a faint flush.

Sarah watched the woman curiously. Even in uniform she was very smart. For some reason her legs and feet caught Sarah's attention particularly. Her feet small and shapely in expensive-looking, well-polished shoes, legs slim and finely muscled, stocking seams admirably straight. She reminded Sarah of a taut and elongated fashion plate in the manner of Erté. A contrasting image

289

rose up in her mind. That of Tessa, sturdy and rosy, pure Renoir.

She heard the woman say to one of the men, 'Oh, Charles, you're such a glutton for punishment.' Her voice was low and amused. She had style, Sarah conceded, though she thought her affected. 'Interesting.' She smiled at Michael with a flash of malice.

He said drily, 'Glad you think so.'

The round, wood-framed clock on the wall above the bar struck eight, reminding Sarah that her time was limited. 'I'll have to go soon. Ivy's holding the fort. I've got to catch the five to nine.' She grinned. 'Awful long way to come for less than an hour's conversation.'

'Yes.' He didn't attempt to contradict her.

'What it boils down to is this. If you don't do something, make an effort, you'll lose Tessa. There's no doubt about that. I just want you to know. The rest's up to you.'

He nodded, but made no reply. Sarah had the queer, quick impression that they were in a film, the camera moving in on Michael to provide the grave and thoughtful close-up that ended the scene.

28

Ruth and Alan crouched breathlessly beneath a tall, spreading sycamore in a grove of bedraggled shrubs. Ruth could feel the dry leaf-mould, laced with small, brittle twigs, beneath her hands and knees. Strictly speaking, the land was out of bounds, but the question of ownership had become blurred over the years. It had once been the woodland garden of a county bigwig, but had fallen into decay and disuse. The local children trespassed freely and in early summer, when it became a wonderland of pink, mauve and apricot rhododendrons, even comparatively responsible citizens walked there, trying to imagine what it would be like to own all this, and thinking that the nobs did all right for themselves.

Ruth peered through the network of leaves, watching Sacha pass by with cautious, creeping steps, eyes narrowed, searching, all his faculties visibly tensed. But he didn't see them and carried on, with the same alert and wary air. She and Alan exchanged smiles, as they gazed at his skinny, retreating figure. White shirt and grey flannel shorts. The familiar tuft of hair sticking up on the crown of his dark head.

'Told you it was a good hiding place,' Alan whispered. His arms went round her, slowly skirting her left breast. He leaned across and kissed her gently, his tongue softly entering her mouth. French kissing. Ruth savoured it sinfully. She still hadn't got used to the enormity of their physical contact. They'd lived side by side for so long with no such thought.

But she remained alive to their responsibilities. 'We can't stay here long. The boys'll get bored if they don't find us.' They'd offered to look after Stephen and Sacha for the day while Maggie and Ilya went for a romantic lunch in town. Ilya had just got back after a protracted tour with ENSA in Italy and North Africa.

'They'll be okay for a while yet.' Alan was reckless, tempting her, pulling her down. Always it fell to Ruth to maintain the proprieties.

Gently she pushed him away. 'I'm going to find them and tell them it's their turn to hide.'

'Spoilsport.' But he was good-natured as he followed her out of the bushes.

They held hands as they walked through the trees in search of the boys. It was cool and shady here. Outside the wood the sun had a humid, jaundiced quality.

He said out of the blue, 'I wonder what Dad's doing right now.' He was hugely, quietly proud of the fact that his father was with the Second Front in France. To his delight he'd had a postcard. A daft one with two very pink pigs in sunglasses and the legend *on rentre bientôt*. An incongruous holiday message. He'd told Ruth earnestly that he was going to keep the card as a souvenir for the rest of his life. She'd been touched.

'He's probably riding in a jeep through some grateful liberated town and having flowers thrown at him by lovely ladies.'

He smiled at her and her heart went out to him, so familiar and handsome. She said, 'I love you.' He assumed the tough, worldly-wise grin – his gangster grin she called it – that he used when he was pleased by something, but too shy to show it.

There was movement in the trees ahead of them. She called, 'Hey, Sacha! Stephen!'

* * *

Stephen accepted the cup of tea Ruth offered. 'Brandy, sir? I don't mind if I do.' He spoke in the thick, booze-sodden tones of Colonel Chinstrap from ITMA, the nation's favourite radio programme.

Pouring a cup for Sacha, she quavered, 'Can I do you now, sir?' Mrs Mopp, the cockney char. Sacha giggled appreciatively. All of them loved the programme and never missed a show if they could help it. With her talent for mimicry Ruth's imitations were spot-on, and sent the boys into ecstasies.

Stephen and Sacha had had their turn at hiding and had been found, after much head-scratching and feigned bafflement. Now, in a sunlit clearing, the four of them picnicked on sardine sandwiches and the dry cake, made without eggs or fat, that Maggie produced when rations were low. Its sawdust sweetness had become so familiar that Ruth had developed a kind of masochistic taste for it.

The dappled shade of the clearing dimmed the sultry glare of the sun, its sickly brightness filtered through cool leaves. Patches of the grass were splashed with light, but the tree trunks had damp, yellowish moss at their roots. Streamers of wild honeysuckle twined through a young oak and wafted intermittent waves of fragrance.

Alan flicked a green acorn at Stephen, whose eyes brightened at the prospect of a scuffle. He picked the acorn up and buzzed it back. It hit Alan on the forehead and he pretended to be mortally wounded, rolling around on the grass and moss with his hands to his head, groaning like a maddened elephant. Sacha and Stephen loved to combine against Alan. They picked up handfuls of grass and pelted him provokingly.

They hero-worshipped him like an older brother, proud of his height and strength and the bad-boy aura that clung about him. They assumed a stake in his father's exploits in France, and boasted to the children at school. Much as they loved Ilya, Ruth was certain they'd secretly have preferred him to be a fighting man.

Now Alan stood up, grabbing Stephen and stowing him over one shoulder.

'Aeroplane-spin!' The boy screamed with a fearful delight.

Ruth lay back on a patch of sunlit grass, turning her face to the sun. The masculine rough-housing didn't interest her. In the woodland setting the boys' voices, shouting and laughing, had an unreal, floating sound.

All the years she'd been at Maggie's had been good, but this latest had been the best. There was a low, singing happiness about her life now, unconscious as breathing, but there, reliably, whenever she took time to think about it. She and Alan had a shared confidence, a sense of being enviable, and it was clear that other people shared their view of themselves.

The affair of the sabotaged onions had been sorted out, but only after bitter and messy accusations and recriminations. Eventually one of the boys at school had ratted on the Tyler twins. The villagers had responded with a heartening indignation, and at last taken poor, wronged Alan to their bosoms. Now even he felt at home here, liked and respected for the hard physical work he combined with his studies. The money he earned was considered well-deserved, a proof of his entrepreneurial skill.

'He'll go far, that one,' people remarked sagely. It was his tag. They'd classified him. His sullen look was now seen as commendable seriousness.

Ruth had her label as well. She was the actress. It was agreed that she showed up the other stalwarts of the

Alder Drama Group with a lightness of touch that was unique. But there was no conceit there, people added. She was a nice kid – no side to her.

After her appearance in *The Importance of Being Earnest*, Maggie had reported with her amused grin, 'You were a *succès fou*. The woman in front of me kept saying, "Is that the little refugee girl? Well I never – she's *good*."'

At Christmas she'd been Dick Whittington in the Christmas Panto, and at Easter the Drama Group had mounted an ambitious Passion play. The war seemed to have stimulated their output rather than otherwise – there were so many good causes to support. Ruth had been cast as Mary Magdalen. She'd enjoyed that, playing the part with a brassy verve, surprising herself. It became clear to her, via people's comments, that she had quite a following in the village and outlying areas. Folk who didn't normally bother came to the shows because she was always entertaining and good value for money.

Against the contentment of her family life at Maggie's were now set two passions. Acting and Alan: the twin ingredients that made for the magic in her life. Acting was simply the most enjoyable, most absorbing thing she'd ever done, and, although she made no hard-and-fast career plans, Ruth fantasized hopefully that it would last for all her life, a kind of escape route, rescuing her from everything that was dull and prosaic.

And there was Alan. Her raw love for him was woven into the fabric of her days. His features, his expressions, the shape of him from every angle, formed a kind of kaleidoscope of pleasure. She knew him so well, yet now a new dimension was added to the knowledge, an intensity, a constant freshness.

They were discreet, but people accepted them as a pair, and they found the idea unfamiliar and delightful.

Recently Ruth had seen the other girls looking at him – though she didn't think he knew it. He was desirable, admired, and she was painfully proud that he was seen as hers.

Alan was shy and unused to expressing emotions, but he'd said hesitantly a couple of days ago, 'Sometimes I see you as if it's someone else, not me, looking at you. When you're across the road, or down the garden, or up there on stage. And I get choked up, and I can't believe that it's me that's going out with you . . .'

Ruth lived nowadays on the edge of emotion. Her feelings for Alan made her open and easily touched by other things – like a surprise goodnight kiss from one of the boys, a smile of Maggie's, a rainbow in the dark, grey sky over the garden. Magic. There seemed wonder and pleasure and mystery at every turn.

Only one black spot clouded the horizon. Sarah. Recently it seemed they couldn't meet without quarrelling, without Ruth being ungracious and cruel, shocking herself even as she harangued her mother with a cold hostility. She wasn't like it with anyone else.

Both Maggie and Sarah had, at different times, talked to her earnestly, kindly on the subject of her friendship with Alan. Both emphasizing their approval and liking for him, both warning her against the perils of what the girls at school called 'going too far'. She couldn't remember how they themselves had put it.

They seemed more concerned for each other than anything else, Ruth thought, Maggie pointing out that Sarah had enough worries in her present life . . . Sarah stressing that Maggie's task as a substitute mother was hard enough without . . .

An unwanted pregnancy, they called it in the magazines. But neither she nor Alan had come anywhere close

. . . She shrank from the adult sense of responsibility which turned a harsh torch-beam on the unpractised, instinctive exploration, making it commonplace, a matter for public debate.

Still, she'd listened to Maggie politely. She could hardly do otherwise. Not only did she like her, love her, but always there was the consciousness of how much she owed . . . With Sarah, on the other hand, she'd been aggressive, hateful, shouting about bloody nosiness and moral black-mail, screaming at her to mind her own business, destruc-tive resentments welling inside her that had to be got out.

Not that the anger was necessarily directed at Sarah personally. It was just that her mother was in the line of fire. She was conscious, intermittently, of a hysterical frustration – buried and denied – at living with strangers, for all you loved them, feeling obliged to show your best side. Never to be rude or lazy or bloody-minded as you could at home and still be forgiven.

It seemed a pattern had been set. Ruth greeted Sarah now with a kind of irritation that spilled easily into outright animosity. Afterwards she'd regret it, reproach herself, vow not to let it happen again. Once she'd dreamed that Sarah was injured – lying in the street with blood on her forehead and in her eyes – and woken next morning in a black depression.

The boys fished hopefully with lengths of red twine tied round their fingers and spindly, cruel-looking hooks baited with the mangled remains of their sardine sand-wiches. A small fish – a perch or something – nosed curiously at Stephen's bait, then swam casually on.

'Bugger!' Stephen said daringly, knowing Ruth and Alan would only laugh. But he wasn't really disappointed.

The fishing was an end in itself. Neither boy honestly expected to catch anything.

Ruth and Alan lay side by side in the bleached meadow grass. She had the drifting fantasy that Sacha and Stephen were their children, and they a young married couple come from some dreary district of London for a day's picnicking.

Alan lay on his back, arms folded behind his head, profile presented to the whitish sky. She could see the dotted, stubbly hairs on his chin, like small dashes, the pores of his skin, a mauve-yellow bruise on one cheekbone, brown hair, soft and lank, in need of a trim. The details seemed vivid to her and significant. He'd unbuttoned his rough grey shirt to sunbathe. His chest was already slightly tanned. Individual sparse hairs gleamed in the hazy sunshine. Watching him, she was acutely conscious of skin, muscle, bone, heart and pulsebeat, and had the urge to extend herself along the length of his body to feel the life in it. But she lay still. The boys were there.

He must have felt her gaze on him. He turned his head sideways so their eyes were just inches from each other. His irises were brown, shading outwards to grey-green. His face filled her world.

'I was just thinking about you.' No smile. His expression was blank, as if he'd woken from sleep. 'I couldn't stand it if you loved someone else, you know.' A pause. 'I'd be so jealous it'd kill me.'

'What made you think of that?' She spoke gently, with a note of wonderment.

An almost imperceptible shake of the head. 'Don't know.'

'Why ever would I love someone else?' The thought of

298

not loving him one day, some day, was too cold and sad to be entertained.

'Well – don't.' His face loomed over her, blotting out the sun. 'Please.' Brushing her lips with his. No more. The two of them keenly conscious of the boys' presence.

A squeal from Sacha. 'Ohh! Got one!' They sat up. He was manoeuvring his line, pulling it in with a steady pressure, winding it round his hand. An impression of resistance, surprisingly strong, though easy enough for the boy to counter. He was a picture of concentration, eyes fixed on his line, tongue protruding a little from between his teeth, wiry little arms flexed.

There was a writhing flash of silver as he landed a fish about six inches long. It flailed and somersaulted in the dry grass with a terrifying sinuous energy, the hook tearing its mouth.

Sacha screamed at the creature's distress, trying to push the coils of line from his hand. Ruth and Alan ran to help him. From somewhere Ruth had a confidence with wriggling things. If you only held them firmly, calmly, they'd subside. She grasped the strong, slippery body of the fish, and after a lunge or two it lay passive between her hands. She held it out to Alan. With patience and delicacy he extricated the hook from the fragile, wounded mouth. Their hands touched as they ministered to the creature. She had a vision of herself and Alan as wise and adult.

Sacha watched, his face shocked and fascinated, tears standing in his eyes. 'Throw it back, Ruth,' he pleaded.

'Diss iss Funf speaking.' To cheer Sacha up on the way home Ruth had gone back to ITMA. She grasped the back of the boy's thin neck menacingly. 'Tell uss all you know.'

Sacha giggled and hunched his shoulders. She was

299

pleased. He'd been so shaken at the incident with the fish – at its flailing and suffering and his own panic. She and Alan had tried to talk him out of it, telling him that fish didn't feel pain like humans, though neither was sure whether or not this was true. Certainly Sacha hadn't been convinced. Laughter was proving a more effective pacifier.

Ruth held her hands like claws each side of his skinny ribcage, then tickled him energetically. 'We haff ways of making you talk.' He laughed now outright, tipping back his taut, bony jawline, squirming his narrow body. She and Alan exchanged wise smiles.

'D'you think Mum and Dad'll be home yet?' Stephen asked.

'Yeah, probably,' said Alan. 'Full of rissoles and apple pie.'

It was the nicest part of the day, the early evening sun mellow rather than sultry. Ruth luxuriated in the feel of it on her shoulders. As they walked through the High Street people they knew smiled indulgently and said things like, 'Quite a little family party.' She experienced a glow at the thought, the ambivalence she'd discovered recently about her life here simplified for the moment into pure pleasure.

On their way up Copse Hill they recognized the squat figure of Old Gifford approaching, his bald head hidden under a flat check cap. He was pushing a wheelbarrow full of logs. As he passed them, eyes averted, his face seemed carved in pink granite.

As soon as he was behind them they giggled audibly, enjoying their irreverent solidarity.

'Free logs, I'll bet,' Alan remarked *sotto voce*.

'Yeah, scrounged from somewhere.' Stephen parrotted ill-natured, overheard adult mutterings.

'They *are* home,' Sacha shouted and began to run. Ruth saw Maggie standing in the house doorway. 'Did you have a nice romantic time?' she called.

Maggie didn't answer or smile. She stood silent as they approached down the path. Ruth realized that she looked white and impressively serious. When they got close she spoke. 'Alan, come into the kitchen. I'm afraid I've got some bad news for you.'

29

The enormity of Alan's loss hung, still and heavy, over the household. Ruth's heart bled for him, the sense of the words vivid to her for the first time. She visualized drops of blood like red tears. He'd been so passionately proud of his father.

Sacha and Stephen were quiet and shocked. Alan's dad had been their hero too. It was the first time a death had touched them personally. Maggie and Ilya had the helpless desire to hold Alan, protect him from the pain, as if he were one of their own.

He'd left for London the following day to be with his mother, go to a small family memorial service, help with the sorting out.

Ruth had seen him off at the station. He'd seemed dazed and washed-out, his eyes heavy and shadowed. He was dressed with unusual formality in a navy-blue jacket and trousers and carried a change of clothes in a brown carpet-bag borrowed from Maggie. His hair was smoothed back with brilliantine, so that for once it didn't hang in his eyes.

Standing face to face with him on the platform, she'd felt that she was the one person in the world who could give him comfort. She held his free hand firmly, almost vehemently, as if by doing so she could transmit to him her support and strength. The moment seemed dourly significant, yet they'd found nothing of importance to say.

'You'll write?'

He nodded seriously. 'Every day.'

'Will your mum be meeting you?'

'No. I'll make my own way.'

She hadn't wanted the train to come. When it appeared, small in the distance, she felt a kind of despair. They clung to each other recklessly, in a way they'd never done in public.

'Love you,' he muttered. He didn't say it often.

'Don't wave,' she said. 'I'll only cry.'

He got into the train, slamming the compartment door behind him. Immediately she turned and left the platform.

They all got surprises ready for when Alan came back. The boys made a big 'Welcome Home' notice the day after he'd left, colouring the poster-sized piece of paper with an unhurried patience that astounded Ruth. As soon as it was finished they tacked it to his bedroom door to await arrival. None of them knew for sure how long he was going to be away.

Maggie began to knit him a sweater, turning her back on the bright Fair Isles she personally favoured, making it in sensible black yarn that wouldn't embarrass Alan.

To his glee Ilya managed to get hold of an autographed photograph of Joyce Redman, a young actress Alan had seen once in London, and carried a torch for ever since.

Ruth found some old Victorian books on farming and animal husbandry in a second-hand shop in St Albans. They were the sort of thing Alan loved to pore over. She was quietly elated at the find, and piled the books casually on his bedside table for him to discover for himself.

The present time seemed almost not to exist for them, so much of their energy went into planning for his return. They longed to make the loss as easy as possible for him, demonstrate how much they loved him, console and cosset. Twenty times a day one of them would say heavily,

'I wonder how Alan's getting on.' The remark was rhetorical. They couldn't know.

Ruth had two letters early on, telling her that his mum was taking the situation very badly, that he'd have to stay longer than expected, that he missed her all the time. After that no more letters came. She couldn't understand it. She wrote every day and would have sworn that he'd do the same.

Alan wasn't on the phone at home so she couldn't contact him. She swung between worry for him, and an anxious gloom on her own account. She couldn't settle to anything. The sunlit days of the summer holiday began to seem endless, shapeless.

She lay on the lawn with a copy of *Gone with the Wind* beside her. She'd been trying to re-read it, remembering how it had gripped her last time – for all that the politics in it were deplorable. She, Maggie and the boys, and even Alan, had cried buckets at the film, too. But this afternoon, with her restlessness, the 'fiddle-dee-dees' and 'why Miss Scarlett's' just seemed contrived, and of no possible interest.

Maggie and the boys were out. Earlier she'd spent time brushing her straight fair hair and trying different styles, evaluating the effects critically in a mirror, holding up some earrings of Maggie's, imagining herself as Cressida – she'd just read the play and loved it – picturing a white spotlight and complicated draperies, reciting speeches in her head.

Then she'd picked up a photo of Alan, idly, and stared at the quizzically smiling boy. But she'd looked at it too many times, and by doing so sucked all the life and spontaneity from his expression, leaving a dead, frozen image. She could no longer imagine that the photograph pictured a moment that had ever existed.

Now she watched a ladybird making its laborious way through the grass as though fighting through a jungle landscape. Natasha lay close by with her head resting on her paws, her eyes becoming liquid and alert each time Ruth moved.

With the unfocused inactivity Ruth was in a savage and destructive mood. She had the perverse urge to throw stones at the smug row of earthenware pots full of geraniums, lined up on the rickety bench under the kitchen window, to pick them off one by one, leaving a rubble of shards and spilled earth on the flagstones below.

Instead she grabbed a thickish twig and jiggled it in front of Natasha to rouse her interest. Then she threw it with all her might down the long garden. The gathered force of the throw had a soothing effect, and so had the sight of Natasha's frenzied scamper to retrieve the stick.

The telephone rang inside the house, bringing a dart of hope. It could be Alan. To reassure her that things weren't too awful at home, that there was a letter in the post, that he missed her, loved her. Perhaps by just picking up the receiver she'd hear his flat, familiar voice. She turned away before Natasha came lolloping back in triumph with the stick between her teeth.

She rushed through the kitchen, living room, into the hall. Whoever it was mustn't ring off. Stubbing her bare toe on a toy car one of the boys had left lying. Seizing the phone and clamping it to her ear. 'Yes?' She was breathless.

There was a moment's silence before a female voice said, with an odd gentility, 'Is that Mrs Denisov's residence?'

'Yes.' Her soaring hopes nosedived.

'Is Mrs Denisov there?'

305

'No. She's out till late this afternoon.'

'Oh.' A hesitation. 'Perhaps I should ring back.'

'Who's speaking, please?' Ruth dredged up her telephone manner. 'Perhaps I could give a message.' Rubbing her injured toe against the back of the opposite ankle.

Another silence, presumably while the speaker considered this suggestion. Then she said in the same slightly pretentious tone, 'My name's Mrs Forester. I'm a neighbour of Mrs West's. You know, Alan's mother . . .'

'Oh?' Ruth's interest revived at a stroke. Now she was determined that the woman shouldn't ring off. 'You could certainly give me a message. It's Ruth Law. I live here and I'm a close friend of Alan's.'

The voice wavered. 'Well . . . I don't know.'

'Seriously, Mrs Denisov is often out and she relies on me to take messages . . . She'd want you to.' Attempting persuasive efficiency, Ruth succeeded in sounding hectoring.

It worked, though. 'In that case . . .' The woman's irresolution spiralled vaguely into compliance. 'Listen, dear. I'm ringing on behalf of Mrs West. She's too upset . . .'

'Oh?' A chill of fear.

'I'm afraid I've got to break some very bad news.' A pause. Ruth restrained herself with difficulty from screaming at the woman to get on with it. 'Four days ago a flying-bomb landed in our street . . . There was a lot of damage . . .'

Ruth demanded sharply, 'Alan's all right?' A monstrous suspicion, which must be cleared up at once.

'Well, no, that's it. Why I'm ringing. He was killed. His mother was out at the time – on night duty. Honestly, dear, it might've been better if she hadn't been. She's in a dreadful state, but she asked me to ring . . . You see,

306

there's a funeral service on Thursday. Ten o'clock. For all the victims. And we thought one of you might like to . . .'

The voice prattled on with a new confidentiality. Ruth stood numbed, a black hole inside her mind. A blankness. Things like that happened to other people, not . . .

The woman must have noticed suddenly her lack of response. She said in an anxious tone. 'Are you still there?'

Opening her mouth to reply, unable to make a sound, Ruth nodded slowly.

'Are you there?'

Ruth replaced the receiver clumsily, heavily on the hook. Its dry click was the only sound in the empty house.

She walked very slowly out into the garden. Natasha stood there foolishly with the stick in her mouth. Automatically Ruth took it from her and petted her ears. She sank down on to the grass, pulling the animal towards her and laying her head against its neck, instinctively, for comfort, as a child reaches for a teddy bear. She was stunned, passive. She cuddled Natasha, her mind still blank, gazing abstractedly at the stubby grass, its green mottled with a pale, dry straw-colour, at the depleted vegetable patch, the worn coral brickwork of the garden wall.

How awful, she thought, I feel nothing. Nothing at all. Natasha squirmed a little and Ruth released her. The dog crouched down beside her and she laid one arm across the animal's dark, glossy back, not wanting to lose the living warmth.

Alan wasn't in the world any more. She would never see him again. Telling herself the facts almost sternly, like a no-nonsense schoolmistress. Looking them in the eye coldly. She *was* cold, her bare feet white and marble-cool, in spite of the sultriness of the day.

And then, in a kind of swirling dizziness, a vision of Alan caught her off-guard. She saw him digging, glancing up from his spade, bare-chested, grinning, a terrier look with the long, floppy fringe. The unbidden image brought with it a wave of pain more intense than anything she could have imagined. It swept across her, a physical sensation, taking her breath away.

You'll never see him again. A moment ago the words had meant nothing. Now they horrified her with their blinding truth. Never. He was simply wiped away. The rest of her life would be lived without him. It was like looking into a chasm, a giddy emptiness. She closed her eyes.

After a while she went inside, wanting the narrow confines of her own room, like a wounded animal needing quiet, dark. Passing down the corridor to the flight of stairs that led to her attic, she was confronted by the optimistic poster the boys had made to welcome Alan home. They'd drawn grinning faces round the message. Cruel, mocking masks. She tore it down, throwing the crumpled paper into his room and closing the door in a kind of panic.

Her room was silence, solitude. She lay down on the bed, on the cool coverlet, and hid her eyes. Now there was no distraction from her suffering. She was nothing. Everything was inside, in her head and her body. The pictures, the pain. She wrestled with a writhing agony, and knew that it was only the beginning.

After some time – she had no idea how long – Ruth came downstairs again. Still nobody in the house. Her movements were dogged and full of effort, as though she had some handicap to overcome. One thought was in her head, fixed, isolated, the only one to emerge from the turmoil.

The house was still and dim. On the stairs a slanting evening light shone through a stained-glass panel, throwing rich pools of colour on to the opposite wall.

Downstairs in the hall Ruth reached blindly for the telephone and dialled a number that she knew by heart. She heard the ringing tone and waited, breathless. Please let her be in. It rang for a time, then someone picked up the receiver.

'Hallo?' Sarah's voice, untroubled and familiar.

'It's me.'

'Ruth!' A note of wonderment. A doubt. 'Is that you?'

'Mum!' The word degenerated into a harsh sob. She was forced to draw breath several times before she could add, 'I want to come home.'

30

She leaned against the wrought-iron balcony rail. Below, the rue de Vaugirard seethed with a holiday liveliness.

'Smile!' someone urged from inside the French windows.

The order was superfluous. How could she do otherwise? Dominique brandished Guy's Schmeisser sub-machine gun – looted from a German corpse during the days of street-fighting – and grinned broadly, head flung back, the sun glinting in her long, tangled red hair, a breeze blowing it across her face. She wore shorts and a loose blouse and, like everyone else in the room, an armband with the letters FFI to show she belonged to the freedom fighters. Out there on the shabby balcony, with its peeling turquoise paint, she was aware of a happiness so intense it threatened to burst her ribcage, like a strong, green plant in spring after the cold deadness of winter, exuberantly cracking the pot it grows in, a happiness that was both painful and ecstatic.

The click of a shutter. Michel Carré, a friend of Guy's lowered his camera and gave a dark, lugubrious smile. 'Such a gallant little *résistante*.' A caressing, disconcerting sarcasm. She didn't mind. She loved him. He and his wife, Odile, had sheltered her, a stranger, for almost six months. They'd risked their lives . . .

Now, in late August, the danger was past. Almost. Yesterday Paris had been liberated. From early morning Leclerc's tanks had rumbled through the streets, greeted with flowers and rapturous kisses. The fighting wasn't quite finished. There were still strongholds of defiance, Germans who still had ammunition. There was sniper fire from a variety of sources. Strictly speaking it wasn't safe to go out on the streets. But people did. You couldn't be prudent, stay at home. And in some way the awareness of danger heightened the days of sunshine and hysterical joy.

'At last it's time. The hour has come!' Odile imitated a trumpet fanfare. She was a bony, angular woman who wore her hair in a plaited coronet. She'd saved a large bottle of champagne all through the last four years against this moment. They all knew it. Now she carried the dark bottle into the room, cradling it triumphantly. The rest of them ooh'd admiringly.

Guy prised at the cork with his thumbs. It eased its way up the neck of the bottle, exploding out of the top with a satisfying pop, and sending up a spectacular umbrella of spray.

The recent days of hope and street-fighting had transformed Guy. The grey, worn look had vanished. He was tanned, handsome, optimistic, his body wiry in a khaki shirt and cord trousers, the dark, greying hair falling strongly over his collar. His cheekbones were sharper with their sparse diet, but his eyes had their old vitality. Dominique watched him with pleasure. Without his supportive presence she'd never have made it through the past months.

'What a waste!' Gaily Odile tried to catch the gush of precious champagne in a glass. Guy poured out the rest while she handed the tumblers around, flushed and animated as a young girl.

André Delarue and skinny Thomas from Le Pessimiste were there in the Carrés' shabby, homely flat. Earlier in the war they'd both been imprisoned for their work on the underground review *Métro*. Now they were fresh from the barricades which had sprung up all over Paris to hinder the progress of the departing Germans. In the summer heat they looked romantic and picturesque, like revolutionaries from a painting by Delacroix, with loose open shirts, bandannas, the ubiquitous armband denoting their emergency military status. With them were two young girls, regulars from Le Pessimiste, who'd been acting as messengers between the various barricades. None of them had slept for several nights and their faces were grimy and peaked, but sharp and alive with happiness. All of them were famished. Food was more difficult than ever to find. But in the delirium of their days, eating seemed almost an irrelevancy.

With their empty bellies, the champagne went straight to their heads. Now they kissed, and clinked glasses and hugged one another, toasting everything and everyone who'd contributed to the routing of the Germans. A smell of sweat, oil, dust and cigarettes filtered in with the sunlight through the open windows. As Dominique held up her champagne the sun sparkled through the pale, clear bubbles and ricocheted off the glass with a rainbow brilliance. Again she was conscious of a bright exhilaration which she welcomed like a long-lost friend.

'*Au bonheur.*' She spoke softly, almost without being aware of it, but the others took up her toast and drank fervently, greedily, to happiness.

After Borchert's killing back in March there had been no question of Dominique's returning to her own flat. Guy had taken her, almost forcibly, to the Carrés' apartment where he was in hiding. When they got there she'd been off her head, babbling senselessly, laughing and crying, with the fixed idea that everything she said was immensely important, and that Guy, Michel and Odile were dense, dull and unreceptive. She got angry at first, furious, then bitterly hostile and withdrawn. Weeks later it had occurred to her that it was a wonder they'd taken her in at all, let alone with such open-hearted warmth.

Odile had made her up a mattress on the floor in a tiny boxroom cluttered with piles of papers, a broken typewriter, a heap of suitcases. It had been as comfortable as she could make it, but cold, like everywhere else in Paris. After the others had gone to bed Dominique had lain stiff and frozen – and terrified, as the enormity of what she'd done dawned on her again and again in a series of sickening, dizzying lurches.

Michel and Odile were both lecturers and belonged to a Communist Resistance group. They were out for most of the day, and for weeks – until it was deemed that the Germans' attention was likely to be engaged elsewhere – Dominique and Guy were not permitted to leave the flat at all, for fear of arousing the neighbours' suspicions. Inside they had to talk and move softly, flush the toilet only when Michel and Odile were home, and listen to the radio with one ear pressed up against it. That at least was nothing new. They'd been listening to the BBC like that for years as it was.

They heard from the Carrés, who had it via acquaintances at Le Pessimiste, that the Gestapo had arrived at Dominique's flat at dawn a mere two days after Borchert's death and knocked up everyone else in the house. They'd questioned known associates of hers. In fact there was genuine ignorance about her movements and whereabouts. She'd seen no one, told no one of her plan. In time the brouhaha died down. Still Guy and the Carrés were adamant that she must remain in hiding.

She hadn't the vitality to argue with them, though the

sequestered days were hell for her, the silence, the caution. She felt crushed and imprisoned with her visions of Daniel, her remembrance of the killing.

The Carrés were rapturous about this act of slaughter. Dominique could see that they envied her, admired her for it. They themselves might have lacked the nerve, the opportunity, to do it, but afterwards their consciences would not have troubled them one jot or tittle. For them the murder would have been the ultimate expression of their beliefs. Not so for Dominique. For her the idea of resistance was just an idea. She couldn't comfort herself with moral certainties.

Again and again she saw Peter's bulky figure swaying towards her, his face pale, greenish almost, in the moonlight. '*Hure.*' A whisper, now it seemed like the dry rustling of a snake.

She dreamed the scene night after night, and awoke shivering, tense and horrified, lying with open eyes in the chill of her boxroom.

She'd killed him for revenge, and yet she'd hardly known what part he had in Daniel's death. Maybe he'd tried to save him, keep his side of the bargain. She would never be sure. Only someone had to pay. She couldn't just cravenly accept. Borchert had died for the faceless, anonymous Nazi torturers.

Or maybe in part – she could barely admit it even to herself – she'd thought to wipe out the knowledge of the pleasure he'd given her. It was one thing to sleep with the enemy coldly, for your own ends, but to be frankly, recklessly aroused . . . She closed her eyes. Had there been a wish to punish him for the truth of her own sexual response? Their transaction had died with him. No one else would ever know.

'I'm crazy. Crazy.'

314

The thoughts whirled round in her head, wouldn't be still. And she was trapped here in the stuffy, homely apartment with no distraction from her obsessions. The days were almost worse than the nights. Long, cold and drab. In her present frame of mind bland pursuits like reading, tidying, cooking seemed more unreal than the vividly experienced urge to open the windows and scream to some passing German patrol to come and take her away.

Guy had a closed self-sufficiency. The Carrés got him paints, paper, even hardboard and canvas occasionally. He read and painted and hid any restlessness he might feel. He was distant. She'd always had the feeling he thought her futile and flighty.

One day she suggested, with a hollow attempt at her former teasing carelessness, 'Why don't you paint me?'

He shrugged, indifferent. 'If you like.'

In the event the portrait was a large one, on precious canvas, which took time. Once she'd have thought sitting unbearably tedious. Now she looked forward to their sessions as the only punctuation in the dizzying emptiness of her days.

Little by little they began to converse freely, though silence was easy, since their reason for being together was the painting. Above all Dominique talked about Daniel, haphazardly, as the thoughts came to her, significant or trivial, in no kind of order. She found it calming. There were times when she felt almost happy recalling Daniel to someone who had liked and valued him.

After one of their talks he remarked in passing, 'You two were good for each other.'

She was surprised and took him up on it. 'In what way?' Such a thought had never occurred to her. She'd taken their belonging for granted.

He looked up from the canvas and across at her. She saw again how tired he seemed. There was something stony about him with his winter pallor, the black and grey clothing.

He said, 'I've rarely seen two people who loved one another with such simplicity. Such naturalness and ease. It was very touching to see.' There was a kind of dignity in his directness.

She was silent while his words sounded in the dusty living room with its dark wood shelves untidily crammed with books, the blue-grey worn carpet. She'd always thought Guy so aloof and contained and sort of superior. Yet he'd noticed their relationship and appreciated its uniqueness. She thought about his comment and it seemed to her to be true. Dominique nodded. The words were suddenly precious to her. She'd remember them as a sort of obituary to her time with Daniel, placing it in perspective. In the anguish of her loss, there was a sense of comfort.

He wouldn't talk about Rosa. If Dominique tried to he'd clam up. 'Conjecture's pointless,' he said to her one day. 'Until I know what's happened to Rosa I won't play guessing-games.' She could see the subject was painful to him, as if he held himself ready for the truth to be terrible.

Once she asked, cautiously, 'Do you expect to see Sarah when all this is over?' She was still a bit in awe of Guy.

To her surprise he answered her frankly. From him she always expected a brush-off, a vision of her father flashing into her mind, and the annoying, indulgent grin he wore when fobbing her off with answers that were just beside the point.

He replied crisply at first. 'I'm hoping.' And then he seemed to think further, about her question and his answer. He said more slowly, 'How do I know? She could be dead . . . Or madly in love with some Tommy.' The glint of a frosty smile.

'Do *you* still love *her*?' Inwardly Dominique gasped at her own boldness. He'd never, ever, talked to her about his feelings for Sarah.

But again Guy was unfazed. 'I don't know.' He shrugged. 'After all these years she's become an idea to me. Abstract.' A self-mocking expression. 'A kind of holy grail.' He paused. 'But I remember . . . when I was with her, I had the impression that she was the woman for my life.'

Unusually, Dominique was abashed by his openness and couldn't reply. A silence. Then Guy repeated. 'I'm hoping.'

She watched the portrait developing day by day. It surprised her. No one had ever painted her before, though Sarah had offered to once, but the prospect had petered out with Dominique's resistance to the idea of tying herself down to a time.

Guy's painting was bold and austere, strikingly simplified. Dominique realized that in every photograph that had ever been taken of her she'd worn a prepared, appropriate smile, whether playful, sardonic, or bright and open. It was slightly disconcerting to encounter a picture of herself without this protective mask.

She thought Guy had made her look positively plain. True, since she'd been in hiding she'd tied her hair back tightly, from indifference, for convenience. After all there was no one here to impress or charm. The Carrés and Guy she took for granted. And they were old, anyway.

And yet there was something that pleased her about the white face that gazed back at her from the canvas, above the overlarge, grey lambswool sweater of Michel's that she wore all the time for warmth. Though the girl lacked glamour and charm, she had a basic, forceful sensuality that depended on neither. And, beyond that, she radiated a vaguely defiant self-possession and a brave air of durability. Dominique was secretly flattered that Guy had seen in her such impressive and uncompromising strengths, her vanity reviving in a brief, interested flash.

Contemplating this version of herself, the conviction grew in her mind, slowly and instinctively, that she had a future. There would be a time when her anguished nightmares about the shooting would fade, and the raw wound of her grieving for Daniel be cauterized.

After the portrait was finished Dominique's days dragged even more. Spring began to shine in, bright and hopeful, through the dusty windows. She longed to go out, to walk, simply to the corner and back, and feel the soft, moving air on her skin, but the Carrés were adamant. No one, and specially not the neighbours, must know she was here. It would be sheer selfishness to compromise them for just a moment's freedom.

'It's not just your own life you want to risk!' Odile harangued her, strident, intense, affectionate, her bony face and deep-set, dark-ringed eyes alive with conviction. 'It's ours too. And we rather like being alive!'

Dominique glowered, recognizing the truth of her words but hating to admit it. 'Have it your own way, damn it,' she growled, knowing full well that she should give in more gracefully, unwillingly conscious of just how much she owed the Carrés. Screaming inwardly at the prospect of yet more suffocating days between the same four dingy, cream-painted walls.

'Be patient, dear.' Odile bent and placed her chapped,

unmade-up lips awkwardly against Dominique's cheek, half-exasperated, half-apologetic. 'It's not forever.'

Dominique replied darkly, 'I'm not so sure.'

At least since Guy had painted her he seemed less aloof, although during the long daylight hours he kept himself busy with a dull determination. But he stopped for lunch and – when electricity supplies allowed it – they cooked for themselves whatever meagre rations Odile and Michel had managed to procure. In any case they ate together at the table with the orange-patterned oilcloth that had once been smart and modern.

Their enforced tête-à-tête produced tensions. Sometimes while they talked Dominique would find herself focusing sharply on some disembodied physical aspect of Guy, the dark hairs on his forearm, the motion of his lips as he spoke. And then, although he was old – possibly almost a decade older than even Borchert had been – she would begin to speculate on how it would be to spend the endless afternoons making love with him, spreadeagled below the hard body, kissed by his well-shaped mouth, breaking through the adult self-possession, seeing him out of control, disarmed. The idea grew on her, insidiously exciting. And it would certainly help pass the time.

Willy-nilly, Guy read the speculation in her eyes. Over the days an awareness grew between them of the possibilities, drowning out the desultory conversation between them, hovering like a predatory bird.

But he made no move towards her. Dominique was disappointed. Now she'd imagined something entertaining enough to allay her boredom she was doubly frustrated by the lack of it. Surely Guy desired her. She thought of the portrait with its unequivocal sexuality. Obviously he did.

One lunch hour, as they ate bread and a flavourless

potato salad, she had a sudden vision of herself laying one hand across his arm and staring into his eyes with a steady, provoking, challenging look. Having imagined it, quite deliberately she brought the image to life. His forearm below her hand was warm and hard, live muscle and flesh. His eyes met hers, comprehending, unsurprised. For a long, unresolved moment they gazed at one another.

Then slowly he placed his free hand on hers and shook his head. 'No, Dominique . . .' Removing her hand gently from his arm. 'You're immensely attractive, but . . .'

She was seriously taken aback by this unexpected turn in her imagined scenario. 'But you want to,' she blurted, sounding to herself like an aggrieved child, inwardly cursing the petulant note to her voice.

A quick, involuntary smile crossed his face, affectionate, indulgent, recalling her father's, diminishing her further in years. He had the presence of mind to suppress it almost instantly and said, 'Look, at this moment, the idea of walking into the next room, undressing, getting into bed with you is almost unbearably tempting . . .' A soothing tone, again fatherly somehow, in spite of the content of his words.

'Well, that's all that matters.' She was breezy, but unsure.

He shook his head. 'It's instant gratification. Which is fine sometimes. But not in this case.'

'Why ever not? Look, Guy, we're here and we're horribly bored. I'd have thought now was the time if ever . . .' What an unreal situation, she thought, cold-bloodedly trying to argue this . . . adult . . . into bed. And surely, by rights, the boot should be on the other foot.

Guy looked at her ruefully. 'Dominique, I'm nearly forty-five. Old enough to reject the moment for something

320

I want badly in the future.' He laid his two hands heavily on the table. 'You're what . . . twenty-four, twenty-five? You mightn't understand. You see, I want Sarah. I want to find her, and be with her, if that's what we both decide. And I'm not going to jeopardize that possibility by making love to her friend.'

Dominique was flabbergasted. 'Sarah!' Of all the reasons that had crossed her mind for Guy's reluctance this one had never occurred to her. Sarah. In England. Worlds away, as good as. Even dead, possibly. 'Good God!'

Their eyes met with a kind of hostile honesty. When he spoke again his voice was colder. 'She *was* your friend, don't forget. According to Rosa you were very fond of her.'

Dominique said vaguely, 'Yes, she was . . .'

She hadn't thought of Sarah on her own account for ages, only in relation to Guy. Suddenly, clearly she recalled her sitting up in bed in the Hôtel Lutétia – five years ago it must be – the morning after her first night with Guy. Flushed and dishevelled, laughing at Dominique, interested in her plans, teasing her for her vanity, curly hair tousled, a secret smile on her face. Yes, she'd been a good friend, and fun. Dominique had forgotten. And surely it wouldn't be *all* that long before the world opened up again and people could travel. In that moment she actively looked forward to seeing her again.

Still, the idea of seducing Guy had been attractive. In the last days she'd almost come to rely on the prospect to alleviate the staleness of this lost time. Now nothing would be changed. But it was obviously beneath her dignity to persist. She picked up her plate, ignoring his, and began to swill it under the tap.

* * *

321

Soon enough, though, there were events dramatic enough to distract them from the tensions of their seemingly endless incarceration. One morning in early June, as all four of them were sitting round the table in the kitchen, drinking acorn coffee before the Carrés left for their day's work, they heard on the wireless the long-awaited news of the Anglo-American landings in Normandy. As one they whooped with spontaneous joy, forgetting for a moment their self-imposed rules of silence and circumspection.

Dominique was clasped by the normally sedate and sombre Michel. He kissed her soundly. He hadn't shaved yet, and the black bristles on his chin scratched her cheek. His lips were full and dry and she could smell herbal tobacco on his breath. The details of that moment stayed in her mind, even years later.

Guy had lifted Odile up bodily in her long, green quilted dressing gown. Her broad, bony face wore an expression of comic dismay, like that of a Disney-cartoon character, as she pummelled feebly at his shoulders and squealed in an uncharacteristically girlish fashion.

Then Dominique found herself weeping in tense, uncontrollable shudders. Michel was shocked. He laid an arm across her shoulders and murmured soothing words against her cheek.

'It's all right.' She waved away his concern with a small, tight gesture. 'It's all right. I'm fine. I'm happy.'

But it was still a long haul. The fortunes of the Allies were mixed as they fought their way towards Paris. To Dominique the wait seemed endless. Michel, with his stern and melancholy brown eyes, constantly warned her to take nothing for granted, and speculated grimly that even if the Germans *did* retreat from Paris, they'd be sure to blow it sky-high. But not even these gloomy forebodings could quench the marvellous new air of optimism that mingled with the golden summer sunshine.

One Saturday afternoon in late June the Carrés came back to the flat from shopping in the boulevard Saint Michel, bursting with the news of an extraordinary sight they'd witnessed from the terrace of a café where they'd stopped to drink a beer in the cool shade of the trees.

'All the time we were sitting there,' Odile was still flushed and animated at the memory, 'there were two lines of traffic passing one another in opposite directions. Tanks going west towards the Normandy Front, with the soldiers standing up in them, all grim and impressive, with radio-receivers clamped over their ears . . .' She was tanned from the good weather, her slim brown arms contrasting with the pale yellow of her shirt – Dominique and Guy were still winter-white. '. . . And passing them the other way – just as slow and stately – was this long, long convoy of ambulances bringing back the wounded . . .'

'It was quite surreal,' Michel cut in. For once there was wonderment on his face, undimmed by his habitual lugubrious scepticism. 'We just sat there on the terrace, sipping our drinks, blandly watching, as if we were an audience and the war was being staged just for us.'

Like prisoners Guy and Dominique were avid for every crumb of information offered them from the sunny, mysterious outside world.

As weeks passed the flat became hot and well-nigh unbearable, and at night there was the brightness, the dull, explosive thudding of the Allied bombardment of railways and industrial areas round Paris. Then the answering crackle of the German anti-aircraft fire, leaving them wakeful and restless.

Often, unable to sleep, Guy and Dominique would stand silently at the window in the Carrés' dark living room, with one corner of the thick curtain pulled aside, staring out – feeling that at this dead hour it was permissible for them to do so – watching the blackish coral night sky, lit by sudden flares and criss-crossed by white searchlight beams.

Then, heavy and drowsy, they'd make up for the rest they'd lost during the day. They were frustratedly aware of huge events taking place outside their four walls, but still the Carrés insisted it wasn't safe for them to leave. In spite of the rising tide of the invasion the Gestapo were still arresting people hand over fist. If anything, the Allied threat had made the Germans panicky and more repressive than ever. There were rumours from all over of mass-hangings of uncooperative civilians, and at the end of June a letter was circulated secretly from hand to hand, telling of a monstrous, unthinkable atrocity at Oradour-sur-Glane, where thirteen hundred people, mainly women and children, had been herded into their homes and a nearby church and burned alive. Reports like these made them long with an intense, almost physical urgency for the Allies to make a clean sweep across France and the surrounding countries like some righteous, biblical instrument of vengeance.

It wasn't until August, though, that Parisians were able to take an active part in their own deliverance. Then the railway workers went on strike, drastically cutting German lines of communications even at the risk of isolating and starving Paris itself. The police joined the ranks of the resistants, rejecting German authority and putting their weapons at the disposal of the partisans. There was an overwhelming feeling that when the Allied troops finally arrived they must find the population of Paris already in control of its own destiny.

'I'm giving you notice,' Guy told Michel one Saturday morning in mid-August. 'It's the parting of the ways, my friend.'

There was a half-smile on his face, but a note of total conviction in his voice. His intention was to contact members of his own resistance group and play his part in the uprising. This time Michel made no attempt to dissuade him. In any case, he was busily involved with Communist colleagues in plans of his own.

Guy advised Dominique to come and stay with him. It still wasn't safe for her to return to her own flat. The two of them left immediately after breakfast. They had little to pack. Sentiment was kept to a minimum. There would be time for that later, but as she left Dominique enfolded both Odile and Michel at once in a silent, vehement, heartfelt embrace.

Downstairs she paused for an instant on the threshold, postponing the moment when, after more than five months, she would emerge into the bright unfamiliarity of the outside world. Setting foot on the pavement for the first time she reeled slightly, as though drunk, her feet unused to the hardness of stone, her eyes to sunlight, colour and movement.

'You all right?' Guy grasped her arm.

She glanced up at him, squinting in the brightness of the sun. He looked hazy to her, his skin transparent and bluish in the early-morning light. She smiled almost fearfully. 'I feel as if I've just been born.'

She threw back her head. The city was in a state of siege, almost without gas, electricity, food. But life went on. Sharp shadows striped the sunlit pavements. Leaves shook and rustled on the trees. She'd forgotten the

325

softness of warm air on her arms, the elusive fragrance of tobacco. On the rue de Vaugirard women walked in bright dresses, strident and confident. Voices seemed to float, unreal and muffled. Dominique felt that her movements were fitful, without rhythm, like a marionette's. She pictured her limbs long and unsteady as a colt's.

She turned to Guy again. 'I feel as if I'm walking through a dream landscape. It's wonderful, but . . .'

His attention was focused beyond her, his eyes narrowed. 'Look!'

She peered in the direction of his pointing finger. 'My God!'

Two large, lumbering horse-drawn waggons rumbled towards them down the broad prospect of the boulevard Raspail. Haloed with a bright, hazy light, they appeared to Dominique mysterious, medieval, sinister somehow. She gazed transfixed as they approached. The animals harnessed to the vehicles were sturdy cobs with heavy-set shoulders and short, strong legs. Their shoes rang smartly on the asphalt.

As they came close she saw that inside the waggons were German soldiers, swaying with the motion, squeezed in among trunks and boxes, sour-faced in the main at this humiliating public retreat, nondescript, unimpressive men in sweaty grey uniforms, a far cry from the handsome heroes Dominique had first seen four years ago, marching into the dull, dusty French village, livening it up with their good-natured swaggering.

'They're buggering off,' Guy murmured as if to himself.

She saw a dark, ferrety man, who must have been forty if he was a day, mutter something to two of his companions. She didn't catch what he said, but the men laughed in a sneering, defeated fashion, and one of them spat over the side of the waggon. At the other end of the scale was

326

a baby-faced boy with pink, fleshy eyelids and non-existent eyebrows. She wouldn't have put him at more than sixteen, though his mouth had a hard, adult set to it. He saw her watching him and blushed.

The vehicles were decorated with bedraggled boughs stripped from some tree.

'What's the greenery for?' In her odd, alienated frame of mind thoughts of unknown occult rites drifted into her head.

'Camouflage, idiot. They're sitting targets for enemy planes.'

The passers-by stared with the furtive dumb insolence you saw everywhere now that the Germans were on the defensive. Three skinny urchins yelled insults as the waggons rumbled away. A few weeks earlier they wouldn't have dared. Now the retreating men were far too occupied with their own escape to exact the price for such boldness.

But one hollow-faced soldier at the back of the second waggon leaned over and gestured at the boys, raising his fist and arm sharply upwards with an aggressive leer. He shouted something in German as he pulled away from them.

'What did he say?' Guy asked Dominique.

She grimaced ruefully. 'He says not to get too pleased with ourselves. That they'll be back again before Christmas.'

31

To Dominique the next ten days or so were like a bright, dangerous, but highly entertaining carnival. In her head she recognized the seriousness of the events going on all around her, saw the wounded, even the dead, but, perhaps because of her months of enforced isolation, none of these kaleidoscopic impressions seemed quite real.

She felt like an actress in a film, swaggering about in a khaki shirt and rolled up shorts of Guy's, her red hair, which had grown even longer during the months in hiding, wild and tangled on her shoulders. Seeing her in this guise Guy had given her an amused, ironic glance. 'Well, you *look* the part, anyway,' he'd commented drily, resurrecting the sardonic attitude that had always made her feel vaguely uncomfortable with him.

Still, he must have put in a good word for her credibility with the top brass. Because of the incident with Borchert, Dominique could only suppose, she was accorded a gratifying respect. In this situation it suited her down to the ground. She tired frequently of filling sandbags for use as barricades, or peeling scabby potatoes for the soup-kitchen. And then she felt arrogantly justified in taking a breather, accepting a cigarette, lounging against a wall, laughing and chatting with acquaintances. Countering black looks with the unruffled, unspoken implication that she'd already done far more for the cause than most of these Johnny-Come-Latelies.

Out of the woodwork they came now, the resistants,

male and female, young and old, the vast majority of them people who had kept a low profile during the days of Occupation. Some were even outright collaborators, who'd decided that the wind was blowing in the direction of the Allies and had changed sides during the present confusion and chaos.

One evening Guy had returned from some campaign meeting and laughed to Dominique, 'All I could smell was mothballs. All those uniforms fished out from the backs of wardrobes.'

As the days passed she saw little of him. He was in the thick of the fighting. From one of the dead he'd acquired a German sub-machine gun. He came back to the flat occasionally to wash and change his clothes then he'd set out again, commenting with a grin that it was like reporting for a nine-to-five job.

Dominique witnessed skirmishes locally, protracted gunfire, sniper bullets. A couple of boys she knew were hurt, one badly. Still she couldn't shake off the unworthy feeling that this was theatre, though she kept such thoughts to herself.

She saw a small group of Germans surrendering near the Palais de Justice. They wore blank, indifferent expressions, as if it didn't matter to them one way or the other.

The young partisans taking them into custody used brusque, unpractised gestures – possibly aped from their former conquerors – reminding Dominique of kids playing cops and robbers.

André Delarue from Le Pessimiste was one of them. He noticed Dominique and gave her a sheepish grin, as if he too was conscious of playing a role. Passing her by, he muttered absurdly, '*Ça va?*' as if this were any mundane, chance encounter.

'*Ça va.*' She nodded, wanting to giggle, but managing

329

to frame her features into an expression of earnest approval. 'Good work, André.'

Then one day the news came that the Allies had arrived. During the night a small detachment had penetrated right to the Hôtel de Ville, the headquarters of the Resistance. The next morning they'd been followed by the rest of Leclerc's divisions, rumbling with tanks and jeeps through the city, greeted with nothing less than rapture by the populace.

Dominique had rushed to the rue St Jacques, which was jam-packed. Tricolors hung from every window. Somehow she managed to dodge and insinuate her way to the front of the mêlée. The tanks had halted momentarily. They were manned by grinning troops, filthy, burned black by the sun, their teeth showing white and flashing. Young girls had surged forward and been hoisted on to the tanks, where they embraced their liberators and pressed flowers on them. Smilingly, pleadingly, Dominique waved her arms in the air, and was immediately pulled aboard.

'Welcome!' She threw her arms round the first man she encountered. He was small and dark and moustached, reminding her, even in the confusion of the moment, of Van Gogh's portrait of a Zouave. He kissed her in a muted, courteous fashion like an uncle she hadn't seen for some time.

'So pleased to make your acquaintance.' His eyes were serious among the jostling jollity all round him. At once he was seized on by a busty, blonde girl, laughing wildly, who planted a smacking kiss on his cheek, leaving behind on his leathery skin the imprint of a magenta cupid's bow.

Exultantly, indiscriminately, Dominique embraced and was embraced by more soldiers, each moment a kaleidoscope of grins, sweat, sunshine, brown arms, warm lips, hard ribs.

'Hey, redhead,' one of them murmured in the brief second of their contact, and her mind flashed back to the first German troops she'd ever seen, the boy who'd greeted her with the same words. It seemed a lifetime ago.

In the joyful, sweating hubbub she lost the dry sense of detachment that had clung to her in recent days. Now she was living vibrantly, unequivocally in the present. A direct, childlike joy surged through her, as though she were waking to a bright morning from dull and fitful sleep.

A small group within the crowd began to sing 'The Marseillaise'. The ragged sound spread, becoming full-bodied as the song was taken up by more and more voices. Dominique found tears streaming down her cheeks as she sang fervently words that up to this very minute had been meaningless to her. A tall, lanky soldier put his arm round her shoulder and squeezed it, stooping to say something that she couldn't catch. Her arm circled his waist and they sang together, total strangers, made comrades by the rapture of the day.

Only a block away the silent silhouettes of tanks flanked the German stronghold in the Luxembourg Gardens.

Though bitter fighting was still going on in the Place de la Concorde, round the Place de la République, and in the Jardins du Luxembourg, some people lost no time in settling old scores. Collaborators were winkled out from their hiding-places and many of them viciously beaten before being thrown into cells, which, under the circumstances, took on the aspect of a refuge.

With a girl called Jeanne, a small, black-haired girl-

331

friend of André's, Dominique roamed the flag-bedecked streets, revelling in the crowds, the once-in-a-lifetime happiness. But on the boulevard Saint Germain their attention was caught by a commotion a few yards up the road, raised voices, angry and strident, slicing through the euphoria of the day. They went to see what was going on.

Across from them a fat woman in a starched, apple-green dress, was cackling, '*Putains*! *Salopes*!' Retracting her chin self-righteously into her fleshy neck with each parrot squawk.

'Sluts!' She was joined by a stout man in a straw hat whom they took to be her husband. He was smiling, as though the hurling of insults was a natural part of the day's entertainment.

Curiously, Dominique and Jeanne pushed their way to where the couple were standing on the edge of the pavement.

Along the roadway two women were being frog-marched by a group of men, all sporting that badge of credibility, the FFI armband. Both women were barefoot and shaven-headed. They walked with their eyes down-cast, occasionally stumbling, as one or other of their captors chivvied them along with a kick or a hefty nudge. Their progress was accompanied by the taunts and insults of a large proportion of the bystanders.

Repelled but fascinated, Dominique and Jeanne stopped to watch. One of the women had had the sleeve of her blouse ripped, so that it hung down her arm, leaving one shoulder bare. Both had swastikas painted on their faces.

'Where are your boyfriends now, eh girls?' the fat woman jeered. Dominique eyed her with distaste. Harpy, she thought contemptuously. She can't be all that snow-white herself, if she's as chubby as that in Paris nowadays.

Then, with a sudden shock of realization, she recognized one of the two victims as Irène de Courcel, her patrician features strangely altered by the stubby, brutally shorn haircut.

With a start she turned to Jeanne. 'I know that woman.' She stared, feeling a hot embarrassment at coming across the composed, queenly Irène brought to such public disgrace. Dominique had always been shocked at Irène's blatant courtship of high-ranking German officers, but she found the avid, prurient crowd equally sickening.

As she ran the gauntlet of their hatred Irène had a wry, resigned air. She wore an elegant, flowered silk dress which contrasted disturbingly with her shaven head and bare feet. It was as though she'd set out with the same happy expectations of the day as everyone else.

Drawing towards them, Irène glanced sideways and Dominique saw recognition enter her eyes. The woman shook her head, a small, deprecating, social gesture, as though apologizing for the awkward circumstances of their meeting. If she realized that it was Dominique who'd killed her lover she gave no sign. They were close, less than a metre apart. Then, unexpectedly, Irène raised her head and addressed Dominique with a brittle, strained smile. Because of the competing hubbub Dominique caught only the tail-end of her remark.

'. . . I'd have been just as happy to sleep with the Americans . . .' An embarrassing air of drawling sophistication like an actress in an arch comedy of manners. It seemed to Dominique grotesquely misplaced, and she could think of no reply.

One thought obsessed her now. It was pressing and secret, a compulsion.

She left Jeanne drinking weak beer with friends on the

terrace of a café, with the excuse that she was off to call on her old concierge to try and get her former room back. She retraced her steps down the boulevard Saint Germain in the direction of the rue Bonaparte.

It occurred to her as she walked that in fact it *would* be nice to have a place of her own again, and she suspected that, now he could be certain of her safety, Guy would be none too heartbroken to see the back of her.

The house door was open. It seemed deserted. Rosa's ground-floor flat was locked. There was no way of knowing whether it was inhabited or not.

Stealthily Dominique set off up the stairs, deliberately silencing her footsteps. She had no desire to meet anyone for the moment. The house was very quiet and Dominique imagined, hoped, that all the inhabitants were out roistering in the streets.

There was the familiar damp smell on the dark staircase. Madame Simonnot, the concierge, sluiced it down continuously, enjoying the little gossips that were the by-product of all this cleanliness. Often the stairs had barely had time to dry before they received their next dousing.

So far so good. But Dominique could hear the sound of voices from the concierge's rooms. Perhaps she could sneak by. Probably she could.

Round the next corner she almost tripped over Madame Simonnot's pale nine-year-old daughter, who was sprawled across the dim staircase with a doll in each hand, moving her lips, mouthing silent dialogue for the two shabby puppets. The child raised her large eyes. A gobbet of dried snot caked one nostril. At the sight of Dominique she started as though she'd seen a ghost, and yelled, '*Maman! Maman!*' in her sharp, self-righteous little girl's voice.

Dominique said quietly, ingratiatingly, 'Don't be

334

scared. It's only me.' Hoping even now that Madame Simonnot might not have heard.

No such luck. 'What is it, *chouchou*?' The concierge's careworn features showed through the slit of her doorway.

'Mademoiselle David is back,' the child announced smugly, oddly phlegmatic now that she'd got over her initial shock at Dominique's abrupt appearance. Reluctantly Dominique emerged from the shadows where she was skulking and walked up to the landing so that Madame Simonnot could see her.

'Good God!' The concierge clutched theatrically at her heart. 'Oh, Mademoiselle David, you scared me. It's like seeing someone back from the dead.'

'I'm flesh and blood, Madame Simonnot.' Dominique smiled brightly, cursing the futile chitchat which would inevitably follow on her arrival.

'Oh dear, I've let the downstairs flat. It was empty so long. The Germans came, you know, and made an awful mess. It took me days to clean it up . . . But the top room's vacant if you're interested . . .'

Dominique had always thought, unkindly, that Madame Simonnot looked like an anxious rabbit, but today there was something different about her – a pinkness to her cheeks, an expansiveness to her gestures. Then she understood. Of course. Madame Simonnot had been celebrating. She was tipsy. It suited her.

'The top room's just waiting for you, dear. I've kept it dusted and aired and your nice red blanket's on the bed, and there's your books, and your clothes in a suitcase . . .'

Dominique nodded, but was unmoved by the concierge's honeyed speech. Her husband was a calculating, fishy-eyed individual and she was certain he'd have let the room like a shot given half a chance.

'Marie!' A male voice from inside the flat.

The woman glanced hastily over her shoulder. 'I'm coming!'

'Surely you can take time off today of all days!' A head came round the door. A face she didn't know. Younger and thinner than Monsieur Simonnot. Dominique was intrigued.

'I'm coming, *chéri*. It's just an old *locataire*.' Flustered she turned back to Dominique. 'I'll give you the key right now. If I can't trust you . . .'

'Wonderful!' Whoever this new man was she was grateful to him for hustling his Marie and sparing all of them the inevitable long drawn-out explanations. Dominique was impatient to continue on up the stairs. Madame Simonnot brought the key, apologizing pinkly for her haste, and disappeared back inside the flat.

Dominique climbed the remaining two flights. To her relief the familiar, rickety old cupboard still stood where it always had on the landing outside her former room. Her heart was in her mouth as she pulled open the left-hand door. The lower section of the cupboard was flanked by a board rising six inches or so above the base, hiding the floor of the bottom shelf. It was too dark to see inside. Fearfully Dominique felt with her right hand. What if it was gone? But, miraculously, after all these months, her hand encountered the smoothness of paper. Thankfully, she drew out the fat exercise book which held all of Daniel's poems.

32

Grimaud embraced her ostentatiously. 'We've missed you, little one!'

'Of course you have.' She grinned and kissed him on both cheeks, experiencing a rush of sentimental, euphoric affection for the canny entrepreneur. What an opportunist he was. In the current climate his friendship with Dominique could stand him in good stead.

The popularity of the Philo with the occupying forces made his present position rather touchy. Not that Dominique suspected him of collaborating in any concrete way. And he'd always kept a foot in both camps, belittling the Boches behind their backs, selling them cheap wine at inflated prices, quietly vilifying Irène and her like for their indiscriminate fraternization. Nonetheless he'd been on good terms with his German regulars, joked with them and clapped them on the back. Even drunk with the most favoured.

Dominique, on the other hand, was well in with Resistance stalwarts like Guy, Michel, Odile, André, however much, in her heart of hearts, she thought her own credentials questionable and ambiguous.

Grimaud gestured to a passing minion, and muttered with a show of discretion, 'Three bottles of the Moët. No charge.'

He turned back to the table where Dominique was sitting with the Carrés, Guy, André from Le Pessimiste and his girlfriend Jeanne, declaring with a broad sweep of the arm, 'Tonight you're all my guests. My comrades. *Amusez-vous bien!*' Shortly afterwards he moved on prudently, a bland smile on his predatory features, not wanting, at this stage, to push his luck any further.

'He's shitting bricks, your friend,' André remarked crudely.

Dominique shrugged. 'He's all right. Never harmed anyone.' She leaned forward with her elbows on the table and gave a beatific smile. 'What a superb day it's been!'

She thought back. That morning there'd been Odile's hoarded champagne, the ecstatic sensation of freedom and friendship. Then during the afternoon, from an office window high above the Champs Élysées, they'd watched de Gaulle and Leclerc head a triumphant Liberation parade. Even then there'd been bursts of sniper fire and casualties but, amid the cheering and joy, the gunfire had seemed merely the malign tail-end to some dark age now banished.

Then this evening they'd decided on a rare night on the town. As she'd brushed her hair and made up her face in the small square of mirror in her room, Dominique had experienced conflicting emotions. Above all else there was the heady sensation that the world had opened up again, wide and golden, for all of them. But always such feelings dragged in their wake a train of guilt and dark memories. Daniel. Rosa. Luc. The familiar dull anguish that lay in wait for her like a mournful-eyed companion, ready to cast a pall over any pleasure she had planned.

Tonight she wouldn't let it happen. Resolutely she piled up her hair, securing it with two silver combs, shaded her eyelids with kohl and painted her lips. They were survivors, she and the others. Tonight they'd celebrate the fact without looking back. The grieving would come again. There'd be no escaping. But not tonight.

Now she gazed round the table. This evening the Philo was lit by candlelight. The electricity supply was still unreliable. The tapers, stuck in bottles on each table, lent the club a cosy, intimate air. It was a flattering light, Dominique thought, bringing out the best in everyone, casting soft and interesting shadows. Michel and Guy seemed maturely handsome, André thin and sparky, his black eyes lustrous, Odile had a youthful gravity with her coronet of hair, the lines beneath her eyes smoothed out by the flickering pale glow. Jeanne smiled with a serene, feline prettiness.

Tonight the faces meant so much to her. The bond between them was almost tangible. Momentarily Dominique felt the quick stinging of tears.

To distract herself she passed a finger through the candle flame. 'When I was about five there was this kid up the road who used to do this. He was my hero.' Her arms gleamed with a pearly sheen. She knew she looked striking in the black strapless dress she'd retrieved from her suitcase. She'd not worn anything like it for so long. She felt restless, ready for something exciting to happen.

André smacked her hand. 'You'll frazzle your finger.' She thought he felt the same, jumpy, keen to flirt with her. But she wouldn't. It wouldn't be nice to Jeanne.

She caught the girl's dark eyes. 'What a brute.'

The champagne arrived, and at the same time a youthful three-piece band – piano, sax and drums – took the stand. Its members looked no more than boys, with long hair and wide jackets, *zazou*-style. Without further ado they launched themselves into an up-tempo version of Glenn Miller's 'American Patrol', to the sporadic wheezing of the microphone. As they performed the lively number – rather well, Dominique thought, wondering where Grimaud could have found them – the youths were careful to maintain a cool and negligent air. Obviously the idea of grinning and posturing as they played was anathema to them.

Dominique cooed, 'Aren't they sweet!' She was particularly taken with the drummer, a scowling, curly-haired lad who couldn't have been more than eighteen. She leaned towards Odile. 'The drummer's got star quality, don't you think.'

Odile pulled a face, both motherly and disapproving. 'I bet he's been running round the streets all week toting a sten-gun.' She deplored the wildness of some of the young partisans, who seemed to her to be totally punch-drunk with the power of owning a weapon.

'Exactly! And he's only eighteen.' Dominique jabbed a finger towards Odile to emphasize her point. 'It's the time of his life, poor kid. There'll never be days like this again. It's downhill from now on . . . For us too,' she added mournfully.

'Don't start getting all introspective.' André grasped her wrist and held it. 'We're here to have a good time, remember? Come on and dance. We'll start them all off.'

'Why not?' She led the way to the square of parquet that served as a dance-floor.

With their tense, elated mood they had a go at jitterbugging. It was a dance they'd never actually seen done, but they'd read about it in the Nazi-controlled press which denounced it as decadent and bestial. It sounded fun. Laughing, their moods matching, they threw themselves into the fray, bodies twisting, hands touching. Dominique's skirt whirled around her. André caught her briefly in a rough embrace, then twirled her away again. They giggled breathlessly at their own slapdash experimental style. Everyone was watching them and smiling broadly. Infected by their manic spirits, a stranger pulled Jeanne on to the dancefloor, and the two of them twisted and whirled alongside. Two more couples had a go. As she spun Dominique caught the eye of the young drummer, and he gave her a sweet, shy smile, belying his surly looks.

Eventually she clasped a hand to her side. 'I've got a stitch.' Swaying dramatically, as though she were on the point of collapse. 'I can't . . . go on.'

'Courage. I've got you.' André made a pantomime of supporting her as she staggered from the floor. Both of them were pleased with their simple-minded clowning. They sat down, hot and grinning, fanning themselves with their hands.

'Damnedest thing I ever saw.' Guy smiled at them vaguely, affectionately, and returned to his discussion with Odile and Michel about the political implications of Liberation.

Michel, a touch the worse for drink, was declaring forcibly, 'He's got to be stopped, or it'll be too late.' As a Communist he deplored de Gaulle's high-handed assumption of power. In the midst of the general rejoicing he seemed more sombre than ever, reminding Dominique irresistibly of a dark-jowled bloodhound.

'He'll turn out to be a caretaker, you mark my words.' Guy was unruffled.

'I'll remind you of that ten years from now.' Odile's musical voice took on an edge of sharpness.

André caught Dominique's eye and gave her a look of sly amusement. She was bemused, unable to envisage a time in her life when politics would take precedence over music, champagne, dancing, the sheer joy of living. André poured some more of the Moët. She sipped it appreciatively. It was good stuff. Obviously these particular bottles hadn't been included in Grimaud's label-swapping operations.

There was a commotion suddenly by the door. They turned to look.

'Americans.' Dominique caught André's arm. A group of ten or so had just arrived. She looked across at them expectantly, as though somehow the excitement she vaguely anticipated could have something to do with this new mass-entrance.

To look at, the new arrivals differed wildly from one another. They were short, tall, dark, fair, and everything in between. But to Dominique's eyes they all had some quality in common, which they shared with those she'd already seen on tanks, in jeeps, on the streets. All of them had a kind of loose-limbed negligence, an oddly unmilitary air, which was a million miles from the tight discipline of the Germans. She was intrigued. Somehow they made her think of indulged children and she felt a kinship.

The guests at the tables around them began to clap. They stood up, holding their hands high, as if to demonstrate that this wasn't just polite, routine applause. André and Jeanne and Dominique pushed their way between the tables and shook the hands of the grinning Americans. Other people followed suit. There was a wild, well-intentioned mix of bad English and worse French. The band burst into 'American Patrol' all over again. Grimaud had his waiters push three tables together and he settled the young men there, grinning with foxy bonhomie, clapping them on the shoulders. More free champagne was brought. This evening was costing him a bit, Dominique thought, knowing Grimaud's tight-fisted disposition. The Americans raised their glasses and lounged like lords. They'd be moving on soon – to dust, discomfort, fear, maybe even death. But no one was going to take tonight away from them.

'*Voulez danser, mademoiselle?*'

Dominique looked up as if surprised, though from the corner of her eye she'd seen him coming. The band was playing 'Only a Paper Moon'. The sax had a dreamy, brazen sound. She smiled – an innocent, pleased, slightly flustered smile.

'*Avec plaisir.*' As she stood up with a seductive flounce, she could imagine Guy's sardonic eye on her. The man who'd invited her made her think of an advert for breakfast cereal or toothpaste, something wholesome. He was tall and broad with thick, healthy, black hair, a smooth olive skin. The knowing, seasoned campaigner's grin, with somewhere behind it a trace of diffidence. He danced well and began to quiz her in bad French with the broadest of transatlantic accents.

She cut him short. 'I speak English, you know. Quite well.' She thought he seemed disappointed, as though his fractured French had stood him in good stead thus far with the demoiselles he'd encountered along the way. She knew herself what a handy disguise a foreign language could be.

With the limited time at his disposal certain questions had to be disposed of without delay. There was a steady, calculating look in his eye as he asked her, 'That your boyfriend at the table?'

Dominique shook her head dismissively. 'No, he's with Jeanne, the little dark girl.'

'And the other two. The older guys?'

An elegant shrug. 'Just friends.'

He nodded. An air of satisfied speculation, as though it

343

was worth his while to proceed further. He asked, 'What's your name?'

'Dominique.'

'Funny name.' He smiled reassuringly to show he meant no discourtesy. 'Sounds like a monk.'

'What's yours?'

'Cal.'

'Well, that sounds like . . .' She considered, but came up with no inspiration. '. . . Nothing.' A feeble riposte, but she knew from experience that her timing, her French accent would make it somehow witty. The sort of vapid little joke that some men liked. They laughed together and he took the opportunity to pull her closer. She saw him grin in a cocksure fashion at a friend passing by with a blonde woman in his arms.

'You must be feeling good tonight.' She looked up at him with deliberate flattery. 'Everyone loves you. You're the heroes.' Her words were counterpointed by the hoarse and tender saxophone, insinuating like incidental music in a film.

'I'll never forget it.' He shook his head wonderingly. 'Never.' Momentarily dropping his conscious, soldier-on-the-make mask and giving a genuine, unpremeditated smile. 'I can't tell you, Dominique . . . All those women, the kisses, flags, flowers . . .'

With the fascination of his memories, Cal stopped dancing temporarily, to talk, to explain to her. They stood stationary, face to face, while the other couples circled and the music played. 'I tell you. There was this little old lady in black. So old and ti-i-iny . . .' Stretching the word in his enthusiasm. 'She grabbed my hand and her eyes were like a kid's and she said, "We've been waiting for you so long, but we never lost hope." She had this little croaking French accent. I bent right down and kissed her

344

and I felt so powerful . . .' He hesitated. 'And good, sort of good at the same time . . .'

Listening to him, watching the eagerness on his face, Dominique was touched, and she realized that here was yet another person for whom yesterday, today, tonight would be treasured memories, shining down the years like stars.

Abruptly she wanted to know, 'What do you do? In real life?'

He looked surprised. 'A bank . . . At least I'd just started when . . .'

'And you'll go back to it?'

'I guess.' He sounded a touch bemused. 'But it's hard to imagine right now. Why d'you want to know?'

She flashed her all-purpose seductive grin. 'Reasons.' Shrugging her bare shoulders in a way that couldn't fail to charm. The fact was she wanted to picture him in civilian life, picture his future. She found him sympathetic. A bank. How sweet and ordinary. Yet here he was everybody's hero. How he'd look back and talk about tonight. A mixture of good-will and vanity stirred inside her. She wanted to make the episode even more unforgettable for him, wanted to be remembered herself with tenderness and sentimentality, as a part of the whole magical experience.

Odile was signalling to her across the dance-floor. 'We're leaving now. Are you coming?' They'd agreed to spend the latter part of the night at Le Pessimiste. A sort of glorious family reunion.

'Right away.' Impulsively Dominique caught hold of Cal's hand and dazzled him with a smile. 'We're moving on. To somewhere truly original. I'd really like you to come.'

* * *

'The Germans never set foot in this place,' she told him fiercely, as they walked arm-in-arm through the warm, noisy streets. 'And no collabos either.' She wasn't altogether certain of this second claim. It was rumoured that there had been informers . . . But why complicate things? She wanted to impress on Cal – and two fellow GIs who'd thrown in their lot with his – the specialness of Le Pessimiste. She wasn't sure at all what they'd make of its cavernous gloom. In American films the nightclubs all seemed rather shiny and pale-coloured and plush.

In the event any apprehensions she might have had proved groundless. All of them were sucked into a noisy vortex of laughter, outspread arms, cries of welcome, ecstatic kisses. The three Americans were greeted with almost as much enthusiasm as long-lost Guy and Dominique. In this mass of joyous humanity the shabbiness of the room, the damp, dark walls running with condensation, were supremely unimportant. Dour Serge, the pianist, strummed serenely on the raised platform in the corner, his moody, decidedly unmartial music only audible with the ancient microphone turned up full blast.

Dominique bobbed round the room from face to face, some familiar, some not, though all of them seemed to know her. Some she'd seen already on the barricades, but it was different meeting them here in the aftermath of Liberation. Reunion was right. This evening the Pessimiste regulars were like a close-knit family who'd come through a crisis. The hugs and kisses that greeted Dominique had an emotional, elegiac quality, an awareness of Daniel. But in the singular anarchy of the night it didn't matter that she had Cal by the hand, so that he was embraced too by the same people who offered her words of consolation. Tonight joy and grief were two sides of the same experience, and with his uniform and bemused grin he was one of them by right.

Word got to Ruby that Dominique had arrived. She bore down on her like an Arctic icebreaker, as though the turbulent crowd simply didn't exist.

'Thank the Lord!' To Dominique's amazement there were tears on Ruby's powdered, peach-coloured cheeks. 'My God, I've worried about you, girl!' Dominique found herself crushed against Ruby's black silk bulk, over-powered by her perfume, which had the pungency of incense. Then Le Pessimiste's proprietress held her at arm's length. 'You know we had the *milice* round here asking questions about you. More than once. And they weren't joking either. I tell you, I was glad I knew nothing.' A note of severity in her voice. A meaningful drawing-down of the painted lips. 'When they left the first time I went straight round to Saint Germain church and lit a candle for you.'

'Did you!' Dominique was surprised and touched at this evidence of concern. At the same time she found it hard to picture Ruby doing anything as humble as lighting a candle.

But Ruby had turned her attention to Cal. '*Quel beau garçon!*' She took his face between her hands and shook it quite roughly. 'But all the same, you took your time, you Americans.'

Her French was beyond him. He turned to Dominique. 'What's she saying?'

'Just welcoming you.'

'*Très bien*,' he mumbled vaguely and shook Ruby's hand.

Eventually they met up with the others and found somewhere to sit.

Guy said ruefully to Dominique, or rather shouted

above the hubbub, 'Ruby's in an expansive mood tonight!' His cheek was decorated with the imprint of her plum-coloured lips. Odile took out a clean, folded white handkerchief, spat on it, and began to rub energetically at his face, her tongue protruding from between her teeth. At the top of his voice, in little bursts of French and English, Michel was quizzing one of Cal's fellow GIs, a docker, about the union situation back home. The man, named Eric, seemed quite interested in explaining, though his eye kept wandering towards a long-haired woman at the neighbouring table. Rapt, entwined, André and Jeanne danced, almost without moving, close to where Serge was playing his piano.

Dominique touched Cal's hand, gesturing at the smoky, noisy cellar. 'So you see, this is our local bar. How do you like it?'

'It's remarkable.' He turned his smooth, tanned face towards her with a grin that was now affectionate, as if, in the short time they'd known each other, they'd reached a mutual closer plane of communication. He assumed a mock-critical expression. 'Where's the singer, though? It needs a singer. A sexy singer.'

She shrugged with utmost negligence. 'That's me.'

He laughed. 'I should've guessed.' But there was a confused, questioning look in his eyes, as though he wasn't totally certain she was joking. Dominique decided to let it pass. Singing lay outside the role she was playing tonight. There was a silence between them and Serge's current improvisation spiralled to fill it, delicate, like curling smoke.

Then Cal said suddenly, as if he'd been lost in his own thoughts, 'What about you, Dominique? Don't you have a boyfriend?' Then the phrase she'd known would follow. 'An attractive girl like you.'

348

Dominique gazed ahead of her for a long moment. Then slowly she turned her head, eyes grave and candid. 'Yes, I did have one. I had a boyfriend.' Holding his gaze, demure, dignified. 'But, Cal, tonight I don't want to talk about it.'

'God, I'm sorry.' He recoiled as if she'd slapped him, aghast at what he saw as his *faux pas*. 'Really, I'm so sorry.'

She pitied him and, to show she meant no ill will, tightened her hold on his hand. Secretly she was startled at herself. Cal had taken their exchange to be a moment of honesty, but Dominique knew she'd been acting. The role – the brave, bereaved young *résistante* – was her own, give or take a little interpretation, and yet she'd played it with artful premeditation. She could picture herself on a screen in sombre black and white. The moment had been quietly dramatic, but she experienced just a tug of shame at taking her honest emotions and using them calculatedly for effect.

'Here's that woman again.' Cal had found Ruby rather alarming, but he was glad to be able to change the subject.

She came and leaned over their table, looming dark and mountainous in the dim light. Michel was forced to lean awkwardly to one side in order to prevent his head coming into intimate contact with her armoured breasts. Ruby addressed Dominique as confidentially as was possible in the circumstances. 'They're asking for you, little one. All the regulars. You wouldn't like to give us a song or two?'

'I couldn't.' Dominique looked up at her, eyes wide with a kind of panic. She'd not sung since . . . not for months. 'Honestly, Ruby, I'm completely out of practice.' She held up one hand in a warding-off gesture. Cal watched their exchange with total incomprehension.

Ruby shrugged her beefy shoulders dismissively. 'So what? It's not the Bobino here. You're among friends, *voyons . . .*'

Guy surprised her by lending his voice to Ruby's urging. She'd have expected him to remain aloof from the question. 'Come on, Dominique. You've been telling us all evening that this is the high spot of everyone's existence. I bet you anything you'll feel suicidal tomorrow if you turn down a challenge like this.'

She knew immediately that what he said was absolutely true. Still she answered sharply, 'You keep out of this.'

Under normal circumstances Guy was almost fanatically scrupulous about not influencing friends and acquaintances in their courses of action. Now, uncharacteristically, he persisted. Perhaps he was a little drunk. 'It's a perfect setting for you – all this patriotic fervour and lust for life. Go on. You'll have us all eating out of the palm of your hand.' His grin was half-ironic, half-affectionate.

'You're laughing at me.' She spiked him with her elbow in a way that wasn't quite playful. He knew her too well. The image he presented was powerfully persuasive. It appealed to her vanity. Still she hesitated. It had been so long. But she knew he was right. She'd kick herself tomorrow if she said no.

In the end it was a tiny thing that tipped the balance. She caught sight of Cal's handsome face, bewildered and baffled at their rapid French, and giggled inwardly to think how stupefied he'd be when she walked up there and filled the rapt cellar with her singing.

And, sentimentally, she thought of Ruby's lone candle in Saint Germain Church.

Standing up, she laid a languid arm across the proprietress's dumpy shoulders, surprising herself with this

350

gesture of casual daring. 'You win, boss.' Her heart was beating wildly. 'Lead the way.'

She'd not intended to sing more than two or three songs, informally, for old times' sake, but she'd been unprepared for the potent charge of her audience's response. It was as if the mystery surrounding her absence had bred rumour, heightened memory, woven illusion, so that her reappearance on the low stage had taken on an almost legendary quality. She'd become a symbol – of youthful resistance, flamboyant allure. Her red hair, black dress, smoky, assured voice, held a significance for the audience which went far beyond their simple reality. Almost immediately Dominique sensed the shift in attitude and fed off it.

After a couple of numbers that she and Serge had performed together scores of times Dominique decided to sing Rosa's bittersweet '*Tes Yeux*'. It was in itself a direct and haunting song, but Rosa's absence, their ignorance of her fate, intensified its emotional impact. Dominique made no announcement, but there were plenty of people present who knew Rosa and were aware of the song's significance. The dim faces in front of her were rapt and subdued as the pure line of the melody arched and swelled in the dark cellar. Hands by her sides, grave-faced, she stood in the familiar white spotlight singing with a vulnerable simplicity, knowing that bravura would merely detract from the song's sincerity. As the final words faded there was an electric, almost shocked silence, lasting for seconds before the tumult of applause.

Dominique stood impassively and let it break over her. She'd forgotten how good it felt to be acclaimed by an audience, to have them hang on your words. Her demure stance belied the power she felt. Guy had been right. She

351

had them in the palm of her hand. Tonight whatever she sang would be a triumph.

A bearded man, an actor named Simon whom she knew vaguely, called out the title of a favourite of his. She smiled graciously and without further ado Serge struck up the introduction. Singing, she listened to her own voice, rich and carefree, almost as if it belonged to someone else, marvelling at its ease and fullness. There were other requests, for songs she'd not thought of in months. Yet people had remembered them, found them meaningful. She was exhilarated. After the months of hiding singing felt like freedom.

She wanted to finish on something that would move them. Shamelessly she borrowed a song of Piaf's. '*Où sont-ils tous mes copains?*' About war and those who died in it. As she sang Dominique could see tears in the eyes of the people standing closest, their faces lifted towards her in a kind of rapture. She was crying herself. Probably they thought it was for Daniel. It wasn't. Daniel was a private grief. The tears were for the power of her own performance, at the naked emotion it had released. The song climaxed, chill, impassioned. There was a stunned, prolonged silence, then waves of cheering. She stood dazed and dishevelled, hair partly down, streaming over one shoulder, panting slightly, lips parted, her eyes deep and almost scared.

Then deliberately she broke the spell, whispering something to Serge. Almost immediately he struck up the cheerful, foolish English song, 'We're going to hang out the washing on the Siegfried line'. Dominique leaned on the piano, playful and provocative. The audience bawled the words, drowning her out, and those who didn't know the words bellowed the tune. The noisy optimism of the night returned. Elusive as a cat she slipped from the stage and went to rejoin her friends.

Dominique lay on her back, one arm round Cal, whose head rested on her shoulder. Her small attic window was open. The red-lined curtains flickered from time to time. The night air was warm and sweet, tobacco-scented. Cal's body lay heavy against her. She was passive, peaceful as a child.

A stump of candle illuminated the room which still had the bare, empty look of disuse. Their clothes were a shadowy pile on the floor.

'You awake?' His warm hand shifted a little on her stomach.

'Sure.' She gave him a slow, lazy smile, thinking of his large, dark body, the way he'd whispered to her throatily, urging and caressing. They'd made love under the open window, with voices calling and laughing, good-humoured and strident, echoing in the street below, so that even then they'd been aware of the uniqueness of the night and their part in celebrating it. Conscious as they twisted and twined, narrow-eyed, hard-breathing, that this was a memory in the making.

'Hey, Red.' He'd called her that from the moment they'd been alone. It was probably the name he'd think of her by. She liked its breezy sound. Sort of Hollywood, making her see herself, fleetingly, as someone else.

'What is it?'

'What are you thinking?' Ever since she could remember, men always asked her that. For reasons she didn't understand it never occurred to her to tell the truth.

'Just that I'm hungry.'

In fact she found she'd been musing on some remark of Guy's. After she'd left the stage tonight he'd kissed her and told her he was glad she'd sung. Adding cryptically, and with a smile that seemed serious, 'You certainly weave a powerful illusion.' It hadn't been the right moment to ask him what he meant.

Cal was saying, 'I have chocolate in my pack.' He turned towards her, enveloping her in his solid arms, drawing her into the warmth of his flesh. 'But I'm too lazy to get it. I feel too good.'

She pressed into him, kissing his smooth olive lips, teasing him. 'Why is it that all GIs carry chocolate?'

Before he could give any thought to the matter, they were jolted by the roar of an aeroplane, so loud it must have been flying pretty well at rooftop level. A moment later the strangely muted crump of an explosion. But it was close enough to make the window-frame rattle.

'Must be Germans!' Dominique sat bolt upright, clutching the red blanket against her. What she felt was a fierce and personal fury. 'They're bombing us! I don't believe it! I can't die now when everything's come good again!' A choking rage. Couldn't the bastards see they were finished? Why the hell didn't they now leave well alone?

Cal laughed at her righteous wrath, and pulled her down beside him, covering her with his body. 'What's the problem, Red? You've got to go sometime.'

'Maybe. But I want the next five years at least.' She muttered the words almost to herself, her mouth against his shoulder. 'They're mine. I just feel they're going to be good for me.'

Soon afterwards they heard three or four more explosions. The sky glowed palely with a fire some miles away it seemed. Then there was silence.

33

Ruth hung on to her pain, nursed it. It was all she had left of him apart from a handful of snapshots, the pink pig card his father had sent him from France. When the pain was gone, what would these mementoes mean? Alan was like a stone dropped in a stream, the ripples, marking the spot where he'd been, becoming fainter, fainter . . .

At school sometimes, or in her own room in the evenings, she would deliberately conjure up pictures of him, multiple images like in a film montage, super-imposed, melting into one another. She could see him lying in the sun, his profile taut against the blue, or sitting, thoughtful, chin in hand, in an armchair, listening to something she was saying, or laughing and tussling with the boys, or reading on Maggie's sofa, silent and absorbed, unaware of his surroundings. She embraced each imagined moment, impaling herself on it like a spike, freshening the wound.

At home she felt like a cuckoo in the nest, for all she didn't doubt her mother's love. With Tessa and Monty and Maud it felt crowded. It seemed to her that they'd been so cosy before she arrived, and now here she was, hollow-eyed and pale, an embarrassment, a living reproach. Mostly she hated the sense of her own apart-ness, but there were moments when a perversity crept in, a certain malicious pleasure at the passive power of her grief. She was miserable and cast cold, jealous eyes on the contentment of others.

She had outbursts of tense anger, a focused hostility,

exhilarating at the time and bringing a kind of relief, but leaving her, finally, more alienated than ever.

At school two weeks ago, in English, they'd been studying *Richard II*. She liked the play, feeling an empathy with Richard's passionate, self-absorbed grief. Their teacher was known as Aggie. Her rounded vowels and sticky, plum-coloured lips raised Ruth's hackles at the best of times.

Aggie had smiled round at her small group of pupils – confiding, supercilious – and remarked with a light laugh, 'Of course, we must take Richard's vainglorious posturing in the deposition scene with a pinch of salt.' Her classmates had echoed the knowing smile and dutifully made notes. Ruth had experienced a rush of hot, hysterical anger.

'God!' she'd exploded. 'Is that all you can say? It's pathetic. Holding up his emotions with a pair of sugar-tongs and giving a civilized little smirk. Can't you see he's suffering? Haven't *you* ever suffered? Are you even capable of it?'

At that moment she felt hatred. Tears stung her eyes. The other girls looked at her like stunned sheep. Aggie was speechless, her cheeks blotched red. Ruth was sent to the headmistress, who threatened expulsion if another such outburst occurred.

Afterwards Ruth had remembered Aggie's fastidious grimace with a cold dislike, but she felt lonely, lost, recognizing that her reaction had been unbalanced, leaving her more than ever isolated among her fellows. She pretended indifference to hide her unhappiness. Often she thought the only person she could feel any warmth for was dead. Alan.

The hostility extended to those closest to her. Maud, whom she'd loved as a child, seemed to her a busybody, offering little treats to cheer her up, like home-made fudge – as if that could make any difference – knitting her a lacy-patterned sweater.

'You'll mend, lovey,' she'd say comfortably, as she sat, needles clicking, her heavy legs planted in front of her, placid in thick, brown stockings, irritating Ruth beyond measure. Though, knowing the goodness of Maud's heart, she felt shabby and unkind.

Tessa she saw as an intruder and she resented the endless cooing whenever Monty so much as lifted his little finger. The child sensed her coldness to him and kept away, his fear of her aggravating the situation.

With Sarah her relationship was complex. Her mother was comfort, stability, love. She was also the person with whom she could be herself, with whom she need never pretend. After the years at Maggie's – happy years, admittedly, but a time in which she'd felt the pressure always to present her best face – Ruth took full advantage.

She made no effort to hide her irritations, depressions, anger, no effort to look on the bright side or speak well of people, and she helped around the house reluctantly, ungraciously. She never bothered to make herself look smart, but lurked like a shadow in long skirts and sweaters, always cold, her hair lank on her shoulders. Sometimes she caught a bewildered, stricken expression on Sarah's face and experienced a lurch of guilt. But it changed nothing. She couldn't help herself.

'How can you stand me?' she asked once, only semi-joking, in a moment of relative peace between the two of them.

'I'm not sure I can.' Sarah attempted a humorous, rueful grimace. It failed and turned into a look of naked concern.

* * *

She slept poorly. Lying awake in the Morrison shelter in the bedroom while Sarah was on duty at the Depot she thought about the bombs. Here in London you heard them, saw them. Before, even in the Blitz when her head knew Sarah to be in danger, deep down her heart had never believed it. Now she knew they could kill, really, and not just strangers. Sarah could be killed like Alan. She felt a strange kind of shivering wonder at the thought. If that happened, then she, Ruth, would really have hit rock-bottom. She could give up. No one would expect her to keep on trying. She might even be killed herself . . .

Another thought obsessed her as she lay with her eyes wide open in the dark. She could have been a mother. She could be pregnant now, or even have a tiny, live, feeling creature lying next to her, feeding at her breast. It would have been hers and Alan's, something for her to keep even after his death, keeping his memory alive, making her a grown-up instead of a child, giving her days a purpose.

Now she despised the self that had bowed to convention, frightened of offending the adults around her. She'd thought that she and Alan had so much time. And now she'd never, ever know how it would have felt to lie with him naked, have him enter her. Wretched and restless, she remembered a night when everyone had been out, saw his face next to hers in the twilight, imagined the rustle of his voice whispering, 'Ruth, please . . . Why not . . .?' For a moment then she'd pictured herself succumbing. She was ready. It would have been easy. But her bright-eyed, responsible self had stirred, awakened, made a final effort. Like a fool she'd pushed him away.

The only happiness she could imagine now was linked to Alan. But there had been other kinds of joy. Heavy-eyed in the dark dawn, warm under the thick blankets, she pictured the first time – two years ago – when she'd acted in *Twelfth Night* – as Maria. The lightness and freedom she'd discovered, the possibility of moving people or making them laugh with a tone of voice, a combination of movements. She remembered the curtain call, being cheered by strangers, holding out her white dress, curtseying in the arc of light, mischievously blowing a kiss, wide-eyed and enraptured. She could no longer imagine that person as herself. A sob gathered in her throat and chest. It broke from her in the dark, a choking sound, shocking her with its audibility.

A little later she got up, washed, and pulled on her grey school uniform. She could hear Maud's radio upstairs. Her mother wasn't home yet. She brewed tea and made heavy porridge, leaving the saucepan for Sarah to wash. After a few minutes she picked up her satchel and let herself out into the bleary light of a November morning. The day stretched ahead of her like a desert.

34

The tree-tops swayed dizzily, shedding their remaining few desiccated leaves. The sky was rich with grey, black and silver clouds. Below, in the deep hole smelling of damp earth, the brass-plated fittings on Maud's coffin gleamed, shiny and new. A small group of mourners stood by, looking pale and cold, ducking their heads to counter the wind.

There was a lull. The vicar had finished speaking. His white surplice ballooned round him and some strands of sandy hair, which normally rested on the bare dome of his head, now waved scrappily.

'Maud was someone you always felt better for seeing.' That had been the burden of his oration. Normally Sarah had no time for the dutiful half-truths trotted out on these occasions, and she didn't care for the vicar's prissy, sing-song voice. But for once the official view coincided with her own. For fifteen years, give or take, Maud's good-natured, helpful, energetic presence in the flat upstairs had been a constant in her life, and she found it desolating to imagine that it was gone for ever.

Jim, Maud's husband, stood opposite her, looking sad and dazed in his long bus-driver's overcoat. Seeing him, her tears threatened. She remembered him on the floor on all fours in their stuffy, cosy flat, playing horses with Ruth when she was tiny. Getting her all over-excited before bed, then handing the flushed youngster back to herself or Maud with the cheerful, irresponsible remark,

'Well, I'm off for a pint', while Maud rolled her eyes exasperatedly heavenwards.

They'd been family for her daughter for as long as she could remember, and Maud's sudden death from a heart attack had been yet another proof to Ruth in her closed, distrustful state of mind that human relationships were precarious things, liable to be cruelly snatched away without warning. She hadn't cried for Maud. In some ways Sarah would have preferred it if she had. She'd greeted the news with a low-spirited resignation, as though it merely confirmed her new suspicious outlook on life.

'You coming back to my place for a cuppa and cake, Sarah? There's room in the car.' Ann, Maud's daughter, was large-boned and rosy like her mother had been. She lived in Wandsworth and earned good money, according to Jim, in munitions. With the coming of the V1s her three kids had been re-evacuated to friends in Devon. Her hands, incongruously bright in Fair Isle mittens, clasped the two sides of her grey edge-to-edge coat tight round her. Locks of tinted hair had escaped from the front of her headscarf and flapped in the wind.

Sarah shook her head. 'Thanks, Ann, but I've got to get home. And don't worry about the lift. I feel like a walk.'

Beyond Ann, Maud's son, Ken, in uniform, sobbed uncontrollably, comforted by a grim-faced male relative in a brown felt trilby, pulled well down. Sarah had the sharp suspicion that if she went back for the funeral tea she'd find herself in the same state of blubbering helplessness. She kissed Ann, touched Ken sympathetically on the shoulder, exchanged a few words with Jim, then crossed the damp grass of the graveyard – the iron railings had been taken for scrap – and found herself in the street.

As she walked west, the Fulham Road was like a wind-tunnel. The silk scarf she'd worn as a head-covering in church was blown backwards. She took it off and lowered her bare head into the teeth of the wind.

It'd be Christmas soon. Everyone you met said the same thing. There was no spirit in the air, nothing to buy. It was a job to remember there was anything special about the time of year. Earlier on people had had the bright hope that this would be the first peacetime Christmas, but the damned war draggged on, and the bombing. The V2 rockets were Hitler's latest offering, launched out of sheer malice, since it was obvious he was beaten. There weren't many of them, but they did an awful lot of damage.

Sarah passed a parade of shops with their doleful-looking, threadbare decorations. Maud had been shopping when she collapsed. Her canvas shopping-bag had held the family's meagre allowance of dried fruit ready for a small, home-made Christmas pudding. Sarah had found this detail terribly poignant. Always, Maud had set great store by Christmas.

'I'm not going to the funeral.' Sarah pictured Ruth's white face, the blue-grey shadows under her eyes, the listless, inward look. Sitting hunched by the empty fireplace in a grey sweater, grey socks, a skirt pulled down to envelop her knees and calves. Her voice had been thin and strangely precise. Emotionless.

'Why not? I really think you could put yourself out for Maud – and Jim.'

She'd shaken her head, swishing her hair, which had become lank and lifeless along with the rest of her. 'I can't face the ritual, the play-acting. When people die they should just wheel them away at night and bury them without any fuss. Or burn them. Better still.' She was unemphatic but totally adamant. Guiltily, Sarah could have shaken her to try and wrench some living emotion from her tight, withdrawn figure. They were spending Christmas at Maggie's. Ruth decided matter-of-factly to go on ahead.

Since August Sarah had felt like someone swimming in a stormy sea, straining towards dry land, trying simply to keep her head above water by any means. She longed to care for Ruth, be calm and supportive, to help her patiently back to optimism and a belief in the future. Like everyone, she had a mental picture of what a good mother should be. And yet constantly her feelings towards her daughter swung from one extreme to the other.

When Ruth had turned to her instinctively last summer in the aftermath of Alan's death, she'd welcomed her with a rush of protective love. She could see her now on the journey home, looking so young, so crushed, the tears starting easy and desolate at some chance word or thought. From the depth of her own experience Sarah had felt for her.

But her passionate pity hadn't been proof against the mechanics of living together. There were times when a guilty exasperation was her prime emotion. Ruth had reacted to Alan's death, outwardly at least, with a cold, hard self-centredness. At times she seemed almost to flaunt her suffering like a badge of privilege, so that Sarah was uncertain how to react. Impatience or brusqueness seemed insensitive and out of place, yet it must be wrong to give in to Ruth's absent selfishness, endlessly, uncritically.

She seemed to resent the presence of Tessa and Monty in the house, though since her arrival they'd moved into the small top flat which by chance had come empty. It was as if, in leaving Maggie's, Ruth had felt she was returning to the comfort, the safe horizons of her childhood, and she'd expected to find it unaltered. These intruders had made changes, slept in her bed.

She would make no effort to play with Monty. And in Tessa's presence she was not merely silent, but wore an air of unmistakable hostility. Turning her back and reading, her face rigid and closed, hair falling forward like a curtain, shutting out all attempts at friendliness.

The sky had turned a gunmetal grey. The picturesque clouds of earlier had vanished. Sarah glanced upwards. How drab it was, almost as if the dull sky reflected her sombre thoughts.

At school Ruth's attitude was one of detachment bordering on contempt. The teachers complained. Sarah was summoned to a meeting.

'She's sixteen, Mrs Law.' The headmistress was grey-haired, brisk and cool. 'Might it not be better, under the circumstances, to dispense with these final years? Ruth appears to be deriving little benefit.'

Sarah had disagreed. And to her surprise, later, Ruth had backed her up. 'Why should they have the satisfaction of giving me the boot,' she'd remarked with the petulant air she'd never had before.

Last week Ruth had gone with the sixth form to see Laurence Olivier's *Henry V*. Sarah had had the evening off and she'd spent it with Tessa up in her flat, huddled over a minuscule fire. They'd drunk some sickly sweet sherry – a relative of Tessa's kept her supplied with it from God knew where – and Sarah had talked about her bewilderment and self-doubt in relation to Ruth, her fears that she wasn't doing the right thing, whatever that was, to comfort her daughter, show her the way out of her cold alienation.

'There's no right answer.' Tessa had tried to reassure her with a smile that was affectionate and quizzical and somehow sad – after all, she had her own problems. 'The only thing you can do is keep trying. You're not doing anything wrong. You mean well and you're only human. Just don't give up. Ruth's always been a smashing kid. It'll all come right. She just needs time.'

Sarah had been comforted at the time, but over the days her doubts had returned. She shivered, feeling cold, but low too. Christmas lay ahead and looked cheerless to her.

The red brick façade of home loomed on the left with its scruffy columnar green-black conifer, much too large now for the small paved area at the front. Normally Sarah's spirits rose as she drew close, but today, with Maud gone, Ruth away, the house seemed almost unfriendly, and she knew it would be freezing. She'd swapped shifts to go to the funeral and wouldn't be wanted on duty, all things being equal, till the following night, but the prospect of this unforeseen free time was less than thrilling. She'd almost rather be at work.

At about four o'clock the dusk was gathering fast. A skinny boy in grey flannel shorts, his bare knees looking red and chapped, machine-gunned a couple of his friends, making painful staccato noises in his throat. His victims clasped their guts and staggered picturesquely. Ahead a tall figure leaned against a lamp post almost opposite Sarah's gateway. A man with black, longish hair.

She turned into the short pathway that led to her front door, stopped and felt in her handbag for the key. Her fingers were stiff. She rarely wore gloves. The wind blew her dark hair across her face, hampering vision.

'Sarah.'

She heard a voice and looked round. The tall man was walking towards her. She stared blankly, expectantly.

Since he'd spoken her name it must be someone she knew. She raised one hand to brush the hair away from her face.

'Don't you know me?'

'I can't . . .'

'It's Guy.'

She couldn't take it in at once, staring through the dusk at the boldly-defined features, the strong, black hair, instantly familiar, yet requiring an adjustment of her outlook, so far was she from expecting them. She shook her head slightly as if to dispel illusion. 'You're not a ghost?'

In answer he laid one hand on her wrist, protruding from the sleeve of her coat, and curled his fingers round it. 'Flesh and bone.' The hand was wintry cold, but real enough.

'I'm . . .' She gave a short, dazed laugh. 'I don't know what . . .'

He looked amused, but his shoulders were hunched against the wind. 'Could we think about what to say inside?'

She needed all her concentration to insert the key into the lock, so astounded was she by this abrupt apparition. And for the moment astonishment ousted all other reaction.

He had aged, she thought, when she switched on the light. He was thinner and had a wintry pallor she'd never seen in him. Always, she realized, when they'd been together it had been spring or summer. There was grey in his hair, far more than before. Five years since she'd seen him. Five years of separate experience.

She led him into the living room. His eyes took in the white walls, slate clock, sofa draped with a striped, knitted blanket. He turned to her and smiled. 'Your cave. It's just like before.'

He had on a thick workman's plaid jacket, dark trousers, heavy shoes. All of them worn-looking like her own clothes. They seemed serviceable and familiar, with an air of having become almost a part of him. In wartime you didn't have the option of altering your appearance from day to day. His hair was roughened by the wind. She thought, as she'd thought before, that his gypsy looks were remarkable, effortlessly transcending age, the tarnishing effects of the hard intervening years.

Sarah said seriously, 'It's good to see you. So good.'

She meant it, though she was far from taking for granted that their long separation could easily be breached.

Recklessly she plundered her small stock of coal. They were going to be warm tonight, if nothing else. Guy insisted on laying the fire. 'It'll be a pleasure for me. In Paris I've seen no such thing for three winters.'

Meticulously he set about making firelighters from newspaper, positioning the coal for maximum effect.

Prosaically Sarah brewed tea. In the kitchen it occurred to her to think about her own looks. She stared at herself in the small wall-mirror. The walk in the cold air had brought some colour to her cheeks, but couldn't disguise the lines beneath her eyes, to which under normal circumstances she gave no thought.

Her face was well-shaped but thin, the cheekbones sharply prominent. She had an unselfconscious, preoccupied air as though ideas of seduction or flirtation were miles from her everyday thoughts. Curling dark hair softened her features. She took a brush from her bag and tidied it, but would make no further effort.

When she carried the tea into the next room pale young

367

flames were licking round the strategically placed chunks of coal. Guy had taken off his coat and from a low chair stretched his hands, in a proprietary fashion, towards the incipient blaze.

He looked round with a welcoming grin. 'Come and enjoy, Sarah. A fire feels so good on the skin. I'd forgotten.'

She was heartened. It felt natural to join him and share the warmth, the chill of her body and spirit beginning to thaw.

It wasn't that easy to leave France. Guy had schemed and wangled to obtain his place on the plane. The manoeuvre had taken some weeks.

'If only I'd known,' she exclaimed impulsively, 'I could've killed the fatted calf.' Then reflected that there weren't many of those around nowadays. And on second thoughts she was glad to have been spared the suspense of his impending arrival. Guy's presence, miraculous and unannounced, was infinitely more satisfactory.

'I didn't want to write. If I had and there'd been no reply . . .' He shook his head slowly, and drew down the corners of his mouth. 'I would have imagined such things. I didn't want that. I had to come . . . to know.' He spoke very simply, his eyes holding hers. 'This house was empty. I knocked at the next door. A lady came and she looked suspicious. But she told me you still lived here.' An irresistible, self-mocking smile that she recalled from before. 'I had the idea to kiss her. I was crazy with relief.'

'Lucky you didn't.' A mischievous grin in answer to his. 'That's Mrs Hartley. She's a God-fearing soul. She'd have called the police soon as look at you.'

'I saw her spying through the curtains while I waited for you.' His eyes had an amused glint. 'With a long nose,

368

like a *fourmilier* . . . an anteater. Happily you were not too long. I tell you, Sarah, I was ready to wait for you all night.'

Sarah had bread and the tiny morsel of cheese that constituted the ration. Guy was philosophical. Things were worse in Paris. To sweeten the pill Sarah rifled some of Tessa's treacly sherry – Tessa had already departed with Monty to her mother's for Christmas. She brought it to the fireside.

Guy swallowed a slug and pulled a face. 'In France I'd drink this if I had pain in my throat.'

But it was warming. They began to talk – in broad terms for there was so much to say – about the years between. Guy told her about the army and the time he'd spent wounded in hospital, about Rosa, the Occupation, his own resistance activities, the information network he'd been involved in with a number of others, including Daniel. And finally about Dominique, the killing of Peter Borchert, the months of hiding.

Sarah was agog. What he related sounded like fiction, fantasy. But she refrained from saying as much. For Guy it had been all too real. He'd lived through it moment by moment. It was an experience that would always be closed to her, something she'd never be able truly to share.

And yet Dominique had been intimately involved. The two of them had in common the fear and danger, the close months of hiding. The bond between them must be powerful, ineradicable. Sarah experienced a pang of cold envy. To cover it she asked after Dominique. She'd had a letter from her before the German invasion talking about some kind of singing . . .

Guy filled in the details, cheerfully describing the Philo and Le Pessimiste.

369

'You must have seen her perform. What's she like?' Sarah was curious.

Guy said with confidence, 'She'll have a big career. She's right for Paris now. It's her moment. She is considered a heroine of the Resistance. Her singing is . . . remarkable.' He thought for a moment, seeking the words to explain. 'Not so much the voice, though it's good. But she has conviction and that's what important. She has this picture of herself and she makes everyone believe. And the songs she chooses are unusual. Right for her.' He paused, then said again with a reminiscent smile. 'She's remarkable.'

'And she's happy?'

He shrugged. 'She's successful. She's fashionable. And she has many lovers now. There's a white heat about her that's not relaxing. When she was with Daniel it wasn't the same. They were like two kids. It was good to see. Now she's more complicated.'

Initially her own experience sounded prosaic to her by comparison, but he listened with a rapt, grave attention. There had been bombing in France of course, but nothing on the scale suffered by Britain's major cities.

As she talked about the months of the Blitz and the more recent raids, powerful images rose again into her mind. Of blackened, silhouetted, flame-filled buildings under quivering coral skies, their brightness catching the underside of vast and coiling eddies of smoke. The criss-crossing, arched jets of hoses. The brutal, skeletal outlines of destroyed houses, making the streets alien and desolate. And she knew again, with a sober certainty, that one day, when the war was over, soon perhaps, she'd paint all this.

'I don't know if you can imagine it,' she appealed to

370

Guy. 'But all that destruction had a beauty more . . . fearful . . . than anything I've ever seen.'

He said seriously, 'I'm waiting to see those paintings.'

She tried to explain her own personal battle. At first there had been the coming to terms with the blood and mutilation, the fear, so that she'd be of use. Later, when things were quieter, duller, she'd forced herself not to give up or lose interest. To believe in the importance of what she was doing.

Under these circumstances the people you valued were those who had the same attitude as you, who you could work with. Like, skinny, conventional Joan, who now, as a married woman talked about washing net curtains, turning sheets, with whom she'd once have considered she had nothing in common. To whom she was bonded, because of the nature of their shared experience, the gruelling hours of teamwork, for whom she felt a kind of love. It must be like that for Guy and Dominique, she thought suddenly.

'I feel as if, through this war, I've tried to be useful. Played a supporting role. Renounced my own ego in a way for the greater good.' She laughed at herself. 'Do I sound horribly pretentious?'

'You? Never!' he teased. His eyes were amused, affectionate. He leaned across and brushed her cheek with the back of his hand. It was the first time he'd touched her since they'd stood outside earlier in the freezing wind.

'When all this is over there's so much I want to do. Paint. Travel. Just for me. Be myself.' Though it wasn't only the war. So many things would have to wait until Ruth was whole again.

They'd turned off the light. The room was lit only by the lazily burning red coals. Guy lapsed into his laughable

Edward G. Robinson French-American accent. 'Stick with me, sister. We'll be big-shots again, you and I.'

She grinned. In passing it occurred to her that his words implied a shared future, and that she'd accepted them quite naturally.

She leaned forward and kissed him. It seemed an easy thing to do, as if the last time had been a mere week ago instead of years. The contact of their lips was languorous rather than urgent. Guy pulled her down so that they lay full-length by the fire. It felt simple and inevitable, like coming home.

'If anyone had told me . . .' An image of the funeral flashed into her mind, the bleak, brooding walk in the bitter wind. And now this warmth and ease. This pleasure.

Guy brushed his lips softly, sensuously across hers, his dark figure looming above her. Then slowly he smiled, as if struck by a similar thought.

'I had this picture of me if you didn't come. Frozen to the lamp-post like some faithful soldier.'

They laughed together in the intimacy of their flickering circle of firelight. A cave, Guy had called her room. The emptiness of the house served to underline their isolation in a slow-moving, dream-like world of their own.

In the time intervening her body had unlearned its response to his. The forgetting had happened slowly and inexorably over the months and years, so that now she rarely even dreamed of him. With her work, her day-to-day anxieties, her reactions had been locked in a kind of inertia, which he destroyed at a stroke.

His eyes looked black and deep in the glow of the fire, which warmed flesh-tones, deepened shadow, ironed out detail, so that she could see only the structure of his face and the nakedness of his expression. The rough-smooth texture of his skin on hers, its warmth and livingness were like a prize she'd suffered for, waiting in a kind of limbo. She was free now to run her hands over his body, and she did so, wonderingly.

His caresses, strong and insistent, transported her, making her weightless, drowning her, so that at the point of climax she clutched at her own body, aware of nothing but its shuddering, deep sensations. Then later, moving above him while he lay with his face turned away, as though the responses reflected on it were too powerful to be seen. He came in violent, releasing spasms, pulling her down on top of him and holding her so tight that she experienced the gradual stilling of his body as though it were her own.

They slept by the fire, bringing in an eiderdown, blankets and pillows from the next room, not wanting to leave its warmth for the icy reaches of the shelter. Guy sat up for a while in his cocoon of blankets, hands linked loosely round his raised knees, staring into the flames. Then he turned towards her with a smile.

'Is it you I love, Sarah, or your fire? What's your opinion?'

'Me, I hope. The coal's not inexhaustible.'

He lay down beside her, leaning on one elbow, tracing the line of her arm with his free hand. He said, 'I was scared when I came here. Really scared.'

'Why? What of?'

'Frightened that you'd be dead. Or with another man. Or that I'd see you and we'd be together, and there'd be just emptiness between us. Politeness.'

'Yes.' She lifted a hand and touched his lips. 'It's as if I burnt a candle to you through these last years, and gradually it became meaningless. Just a lone candle in front of a cold stone statue. And I could hardly remember why I lit it. But now you're here I know why, and I'm so grateful that I kept it burning.'

In time they drifted into sleep. At intervals during the night Sarah woke and lay quiet, luxuriating in the wonder of having Guy beside her. It occurred to her drowsily as she turned in their makeshift bed, pressing anew into the warmth of his flesh, that she should mention Robert, that night more than a year ago. And yet it seemed such a small matter. Probably Guy had had such nights, maybe even he and Dominique . . . But what would be the point of probing? Between the two of them there lay the present and the future.

He could stay for only a few days and for two periods of twenty-four hours Sarah was on duty. But they were together whenever possible, talking endlessly, catching up in more detail with the years between, making love, deepening their re-discovery of one another. They made no hard and fast plans for the future, but were blithely confident that from now on their lives would be linked.

Both of them accepted, though, that there would be waiting. The fighting dragged on with no foreseeable end in sight. News was beginning to filter out about a new German offensive in the Ardennes, which seemed likely to slow the eventual outcome even more.

But apart from that, both had private anxieties. Sarah could make no move towards her own happiness while Ruth remained locked in her wan alienation. She must wait, protective and patient, until her daughter had the optimism and the will to make plans for a life of her own.

And Guy harboured repressed nightmare fears for

Rosa's fate. People knew little, but imagined a great deal, and the rumours grew. Rosa had no family now, no lover to search for her. Guy took responsibility for her future unhesitatingly upon himself.

He left just before noon on Christmas Eve. He had a lift lined up to the airport. They said their goodbyes at the house.

They sat in her cold studio, looking out of the long bay window at the white sky, the grey street, waiting for the car to come, talking desultorily. Sarah sent her love to Dominique. She'd already given him a letter to deliver to her. Guy asked to be remembered to Maggie and Ruth.

He sat on the arm of one of her chairs, a small, scuffed leather holdall on the floor at his feet. His hawk-like profile was towards her as he scanned the street. He had on his plaid jacket again, ready for the journey. Like this he seemed to belong to her less fully. She was aware of the life he was returning to, the friends he'd be with for Christmas. Conscious too of the yuletide shift that loomed for her at the Depot, and the Boxing Day at Maggie's that must somehow be made festive in spite of Ruth's leaden-eyed presence.

The last few days had been singular. Set apart. Now both of them were rejoining the mainstream. There was pain in the thought. She'd miss his face and his voice and his body passionately. But ultimately she was strengthened, sure again of the value of what they had between them, certain now that the emotions she'd remembered had not been illusory. The knowledge would be a counterpoint, like secret music, to her everyday life.

He said, 'When I'm back in Paris I can think about you. And now I'll know that you're thinking of me. It's so good, the certainty.'

A jeep pulled up outside and honked. She saw a face look out, high-coloured with a reddish moustache.

'I've got to go,' he said bleakly.

'I know.'

In the hall, before he opened the door, they clung together, clumsily, separated by layers of cold-weather clothes. It was a hug of friendship as well as love. They were allies. The jeep honked again. Letting go was hard.

'Don't keep them waiting.'

Afterwards she couldn't remember his opening the door, leaving the house. But she recalled him stopping on the doorstep, momentarily, and looking back.

Part Three

35

On the nights when she was singing at Le Pessimiste Dominique would wait a while inside the door that led backstage. Next to her was the alcove with the large stone sink where the glasses were washed last thing at night. A narrow passage led to her own cubbyhole of a dressing room and Ruby's office. Standing alone, Dominique took deep breaths. Suppose she walked in now and nobody took any notice and she found her new celebrity had been a dream. Sometimes she felt physically sick at the thought. There were moments when she saw herself as a cork bouncing on a water-spout of popularity and praise. If the water were abruptly shut off she'd fall and be nothing. She tormented herself with thoughts like these before opening the door and entering her smoky domain.

But it never failed. She didn't go straight to the stage, but walked among the tables, chatting and greeting people from her circle of friends which seemed to expand constantly, unmanageably. And the affection, the adulation were there, reliably, banishing her fear until the next night.

Sometimes people that she'd heard of and admired herself would come to see her. One night Camus was there, the writer and editor of *Combat*. Marcel Mouloudji came, a young singer who frequented the Flore. The artist, Dora Maar. A pale and handsome new actor, a Marxist, called Gérard Philipe. She felt a mixture of emotions then. A kind of awe, coupled with the titillating realization that she had become one of them – people who were courted and discussed with envy and obsessive interest. Sometimes there were foreigners, Americans particularly, attracted by the reputation of Saint-Germain-des-Prés and Dominique in particular.

Le Pessimiste was different now. No longer the anonymous family refuge it had been during the years of Occupation, when the attitude and opinions of any regular could be taken pretty well for granted.

Dominique's presence had made it fashionable. Its darkness, uncompromising bleakness, makeshift lighting, unmatched glasses, sweating walls, dilapidated arrogance had become style, like an artisan's cottage transformed in another age to the authentic, desirable residence of a rich man.

Ruby ruled – a grouchy potentate in her mask of pink powder, black mascara, carmine lipstick. Her personality remained ungracious and mercenary. This too became an asset. Celebrities were tickled to find their notoriety cut no ice, and vied with each other to tell tales of her offhandedness. Ruby seemed oblivious. But just once or twice Dominique had seen her give a small foxy smile and remark with a tinge of incredulity, 'They'll take any shit from me.'

Her new clientele didn't drive out the old. If Ruby had favourites she found them among the old guard, people who'd been with her throughout the war. The regulars grumbled sometimes about the flood of upstarts, but secretly perhaps they realized that the newcomers conferred on them a certain status. They were the discerning few who'd recognized from earliest days the singularity of the gloomy cellar-bar, and the uniqueness of its remarkable singer.

* * *

For most people, even now, Paris was a harsh and uncomfortable place. Supplies of all kinds seemed as scarce as ever they had been and the black market flourished. Dominique was partly buffered against the general lack of everything. With her new celebrity people gave her presents. There was chocolate and spam put into circulation by the visiting GIs. And some of her acquaintances, journalists particularly, were beginning to travel. From places like Portugal and America they brought back clothes and food – and cigarettes which she bartered for goods she could make better use of.

There was still a kind of violence in the air. The years of Occupation had divided people and made them bitter and distrustful. Collaborators, known or suspected, were regarded with a hatred that bordered on hysteria. But unravelling the truth about the last four years was a complicated and deceptive game. There were official channels, but it was felt that they were slow and ineffective. And there were people who said that some of the investigators themselves had secrets to hide.

The wilder elements from among the former *résistants* – some of them little more than boys – took the law into their own hands. Weekly there were beatings-up and killings. And there were more insidious forms of revenge. A male dress designer who'd been thick with the Germans – Dominique knew him only by name – had acid substituted for his eye-drops, so that when he came to use them he blinded himself.

Grimaud, Dominique's old boss, hadn't escaped. In the spring he'd been found lying outside his club in a pool of his own blood.

'Poor old devil,' Dominique commented to Ruby. 'He always had an eye to the main chance, but I don't think he ever shopped anyone.' Though you never could be sure.

She went to see him in hospital. Under the crisp white bedding he looked reduced and frail. One eye was swollen blackish-purple, and his ribs were bandaged. His false teeth had been broken in the fray and his mouth had caved in, so that his aggrieved utterances about a man's right to earn an honest living came out as a plaintive, gummy, old man's grumble.

Dominique listened, sitting on a hard wooden chair beside the bed. He'd made a handsome profit out of the Germans, she thought, and he'd paid the price. Wryly she reflected that her own favoured position in Resistance circles was more a question of luck than justice.

People she'd known for years were beginning to call themselves existentialists. To call her one. Dominique accepted the term without comment, not wanting to draw attention to the fact that she didn't know what it meant.

One day, finding herself and Guy the only two customers in the restaurant Chez Brice, she asked him what this new expression signified. With Guy there was no point in pretending. He always saw through her, or she imagined he did.

'It's too complex to explain in a word . . .' He was about to leave and gestured to Brice to bring him the bill.

'Try,' she urged.

'If you insist.' He shrugged. 'In a nutshell existentialists believe that there are no universal values. You create your own through your choice of action.' Grinning at her quizzically across the table, as though debunking the patness of his definition.

'Oh.' She felt none the wiser. Was she one, as people said?

'If you're really interested I'll lend you a book.' Guy smiled up at Brice, passing him a handful of coins. The proprietor seemed an old man now, with a permanent air of depression. His son, Arnaud, had died in captivity in Germany. The restaurant was shabby and gloomy, frequented only by the faithful.

'All right. I'd like that.' She might as well get to the bottom of it.

A couple of days later in Le Pessimiste Guy handed her a house-brick of a volume. 'If you get through this you'll know all there is to know about existentialism.' His eyes held a gleam of malice which she ignored.

'Thanks,' she said briskly. 'I'll give it back as soon as I've finished.' Though the dryness of its title – *Being and Nothingness* – filled her with foreboding. The tome was by Sartre whom she'd seen lots of times in the Flore. A small, bespectacled man who talked with verve and usually had a worshipping disciple or two in tow. She put the book on her bedside table and forgot about it.

In any case, she didn't have much time for reading. Her days were full of people.

With her red hair, her exuberance, the mystery that surrounded her wartime exploits, she was a magnet for journalists. Some of her songs were outspoken, outrageous, redolent of sexual adventure, and this made her even more of an attraction. To the bourgeois press she was an *enfant terrible*, to the avant-garde a heroine. But her Resistance connections conferred a credibility that was valid in both camps.

It wasn't just the press that sought her out. Paris seemed full of songwriters who composed unusual, challenging material and wanted her to perform it. She was overwhelmed with the choice and took on board more songs than she could possibly do justice to. Some she jettisoned quite soon. Others would stay and contribute to her growing legend.

Dominique never doubted that her star was in the ascendant, that she had only to wait a while – until the post-war confusion subsided and life became spacious again – for it to shoot like a comet. She was clear-eyed in her expectations. She could see nothing that would check her.

But alongside, like a she-wolf with her cub, she nursed another ambition. It was for Daniel. She was determined that his talent would shine as brightly as hers. He'd been cheated. In life his career had been bedevilled by war and Occupation. He'd died a martyr to events, but she would see that he wasn't overlooked.

'I'm going to bombard people with his work.' She talked to Guy about her intentions, but no one else, wanting the growing awareness of Daniel's poetry to seem spontaneous, not something engineered by herself. 'It's only fair. He was brilliant. I won't let him be forgotten.'

To begin with Dominique had sorted out twelve of his poems. Some she'd set to music herself in his lifetime. Others she gave to songwriters of her acquaintance. She performed them continuously. Dominique had always used recitation in her act. She chose two love poems, both addressed to her. She spoke them with a raw, controlled intensity. The impact was huge.

Her efforts were beginning to bear fruit. André showed her a favourable mention of Daniel's work in a review called *Confluences*. Inevitably, given his association with Saint Germain, he was referred to loftily as an existentialist poet.

Dominique was tickled. 'He never told me he was one

384

of those. I'm not sure he even knew.' It was encouraging all the same.

The arts magazines were incestuous. They fed off one another. Other mentions followed. A review called *Méta-morphose* published three of his poems. Guy saw a copy of the English magazine, *Horizon*. It contained an article about doomed, war-wasted youth, and, among others, cited Daniel. Dominique was moved by it. That was how she saw him.

She wouldn't be content until there was a published edition of his poems. Secretly she'd earmarked Guy to do some drawings to go with them, although she hadn't told him so yet. But she wouldn't push openly for the volume, or try to bring it into being before its time. She'd wait until the idea occurred inevitably, as if of itself. For Daniel to become a cult. Meanwhile she continued her manoeuvring on his behalf. It was the only thing she could do for him now.

'Shift yourself.' Dominique elbowed the stranger lying alongside her. His leg across her body was beginning to give her cramp. He opened his eyes and sleepily kissed her shoulder.

'Move.' She gave him another push. His name was Patrick, she remembered. A journalist.

Reluctantly he rolled away from her and reached down into the pocket of his jacket hanging on the bedpost, taking out a crumpled packet of Lucky Strikes and a lighter. Smiling and slightly dazed, he offered one to Dominique. She shook her head. He extracted a cigarette himself, lit it and turned to place the packet on the bedside table. His gaze fell on the heavy volume of Sartre that lay there. It had by now gathered a significant film of dust.

'You reading that?' He sounded impressed as he settled back, bare-chested, on the pillow and dragged pleasurably on his cigarette.

'Yes,' she replied, with a careless 'isn't everyone?' air.

He nodded admiringly. 'I had a go, but . . .'

Dominique wasn't displeased with his remarking on the book. It had become such a fixture on the rickety table that she no longer noticed it herself. He'd be sure to bring it into his article – though of course not mentioning the circumstances in which he'd seen it – where it would hint at intriguing depths of studiousness in her.

She'd met Patrick in Le Pessimiste. He'd been in Europe for some weeks, covering the final days of the Third Reich for *Life* magazine. Now, on his way home, he was writing a story of his own on Saint Germain, the existentialists, Dominique . . . He was earnest and thin with wire glasses. She thought him *sympathique*. He had come home with her. Probably she'd never see him again. But there would always be replacements.

She was a prize now, with her striking looks and her success and bravura. It was impossible not to be aware of the fact almost all the time. Sometimes in Le Pessimiste she felt almost abashed by the collective lust she inspired. She imagined herself glowing with a constant low heat, as if in acknowledgement.

It was exhilarating, she admitted to herself, to sit with a crowd at a table in the club and witness a covert battle being fought between the men for her attention. But often it wasn't the best-looking or the most famous that she chose to end the evening with. It amused her to ignore such distinctions and go with some young nobody just because she liked the look of him.

She was half aware of the fact that often she was attracted to a man because something about him

386

reminded her of Daniel. An openness, or a way of smiling, or an inflexion of his voice. She would find herself watching him to catch the fleeting resemblance, taking him home to prolong it. People she knew well were surprised at her after the years she'd spent faithful to Daniel. Some seemed reproachful or disapproving. She ignored them. In any case she was only living up to an image. All the papers said, with a mealy-mouthed prurience, that the habitués of Saint Germain were depraved and promiscuous . . .

She found it hard to relax nowadays, and slept better with another body next to her. Alone she was tense and restless, reliving the excitement of the evening, her performance, her life. And there were still times when she couldn't hold back waves of an agonized despair, a useless longing to see Daniel and hold him and laugh with him like old times.

36

Her canvas was five feet square. Propped against the
white wall of the adobe hut, the colours were startling.
The lower portion of the painting showed black, jagged
buildings, their windows filled with fire. Most of the
canvas was taken up with a sky glowing red, orange,
vermilion and raw umber, swirling smoke that echoed
these pigments, shading to black around the upper perimeter. In the glare of the fire a flock of birds circled,
appearing white with the bleaching effect of the light, just
as she'd seen them in the winter of 1940. Finally, with the
aid of notes and sketches made over the years, she'd set
down an image carried in her head since then.

From the far side of the room Sarah contemplated her
paintings, experiencing a pleasure she'd all but forgotten.
Feeling calm now the work was completed, but with an
edge of excitement at the possibilities it raised. She
became all eyes, forgetting herself.

The room was almost bare. Just a table and two chairs
pushed against one wall, a carpet, an easel, a bench with
paints, brushes, rags. The door was open. Through the
rectangular frame a blue sky showed, reddish earth. In
the distance the white gleam of the Sangre de Cristo
mountains beyond Taos.

She owed the trip to Michael. He'd come to see her one
frosty afternoon just after the New Year, when Tessa was
still with her parents. He was able to stay only a couple of

hours. They sat in the kitchen. He'd kept his coat on, cupping his hands round a mug of tea.

He wanted to thank her, he said, acknowledge the talk they'd had in the pub that summer about Tessa. His eyes were steady and subdued as he looked at her across the kitchen table.

'It's not that it had any dramatic results, and to be honest I still don't really know how things stand between us.' In the cold kitchen his breath steamed as he spoke. 'But I know what I want now, I think. Anyway, I've decided. It's Tessa.'

That afternoon she felt a return of her old affection for him. He looked weary and had laid aside the facetiousness that had irritated her at their last meeting.

Ruth joined them for a short while, then left to go to the local library and study for some school exams that were looming.

'God!' Michael said vehemently when she'd gone. 'Ruth looks terrible – so thin and listless and sort of crushed . . .' He was visibly shaken, as if he'd been caught off-guard.

'It's Alan. Still.' Over the months Sarah had become accustomed to her daughter's pallor, the closed look. Seeing Ruth suddenly through Michael's eyes, she felt a new and painful wave of concern.

'She was always so . . . happy, mischievous.' Michael shook his head. He was very fond of Ruth. Sarah reflected that in the early years he'd been far more involved with her daughter's growing-up than had ever been possible with Monty's.

'She needs a change. Something dramatic,' he suggested.

Sarah was impatient. 'What do you propose? A trip to the seaside?' It was easy for him to say.

389

Michael looked thoughtful. 'It's just possible I could wangle something a bit better than that.'

Through a colleague at Bletchley Park he knew of an American lecture circuit, which, even under present circumstances, seemed to be flourishing. He thought there was a slim chance that he could arrange something . . . Though immediately he blurted a string of disclaimers, fearful of raising her hopes too high.

In the January of '45 the plan had seemed a vision of nirvana, but as spring wore on the European situation became ever more hopeful. In late March the last V2 fell on London. In May Britain celebrated VE day. In early June Ruth took her school-leaving exams. Sarah sold the series of home-front drawings she'd done in the early days of the war to a collector for a favourable price. Michael went ahead with arrangements. The organization obtained the necessary visas. Towards the end of June they left, flying. The January dream became reality.

The months Sarah had spent in New Mexico with Stephen had been intense and memorable. In her brain she still carried pictures of the arid, dramatic landscape, the colours – pink, orange, ochre and blue-grey, and the azure sweep of the sky – that had released in her almost a fever, making her time there the most productive of her life.

Initially they'd travelled to the south-western states to visit Leo, a war-comrade of Stephen's, who worked there on a ranch and lived with Rita, a chic and stylish Spanish-American. The four of them lived close to one another for well over a year in twin adobe cabins, separated only by an expanse of dirt and scrub. Their relationship was never idyllic. Sarah, in particular, found Leo swaggering and overbearing. But the very specialness of their situation formed a bond between them that she believed would still be strong.

After Stephen's death, when she'd been bitter and broken, it was largely with their support that she clawed her way back to a kind of balance. Now her memories of New Mexico were ambiguous. For her it had been a place of extremes. She recalled a light, clear happiness, but also a pain more shattering than Ruth's own.

Rediscovering the patch of reddish scrubland, the hut she'd called home for a year and a half, Sarah felt strangely numbed. Her brain was empty, passive, receiving impressions, closed against reaction. It crossed her mind that this blankness might be an unconscious, self-preserving device.

The cabin looked the same as ever, low and tawny, the angles rounded. Intermittently it had been lived in, renovated. Inside it was almost empty, but freshly painted white.

'We thought you could use this as a studio when you're through lecturing,' Rita said. 'But you'll stay up at the house with us.'

Her memory of Sarah was of someone who painted constantly. 'Eyes on stalks,' Leo laughed to Ruth. She felt an ache at this image of herself and a sudden resentment at the years she'd spent otherwise employed.

'I can't wait to use it.' She smiled at Rita, and had the impression that each of them was searching inside the other for a ghost. Their younger selves. Rita was a handsome matron, with piled, lustrous black hair, silver earrings, full-bodied in a floral summer dress. Sarah felt herself angular and skinny after the years of war. Lacking the gloss of prosperity.

The matching cabin where Leo and Rita had lived was pulled down. In its place was a low, modern, sprawling ranch-house with a refrigerator and air-conditioning. Leo now owned the spread, having bought out his boss, Bill Parsons, shortly before the latter died. He had several hired men and, on top of his basic ranching business, catered for tourists exploring the rugged south-west, though at present, under wartime conditions, these were thin on the ground.

Leo had aged gracefully, she thought. His body was still tightly muscled and his boyish features hadn't altered so much as hardened and set. He had an air of authority, repose. He and Rita were respectably married now and had two boys, Andy and Chris. They were about the same age as Maggie's lads, but to Sarah's eyes they seemed older, stockier, with a casual self-assertiveness.

Leo kissed her soundly, then held her at arm's length. 'You haven't changed, Sal. Not a bit. You're just as pretty as ever.' She liked him, liked his rugged warmth. It would be churlish to dwell on the fact that she also found him just a mite patronizing. She had the impression that if ever they got to talking about politics, or anything serious, their old antagonisms would surface fresh as ever.

The lecture tour was fun, and hectic. Eight south-western cities in a fortnight. She was speaking on the artists of Fitzroy Street. The road, in Bloomsbury, had been a haunt of painters during the first thirty years of the century. She'd lived there herself in the mid-twenties, and had been fascinated by the history of the place.

She'd wondered, privately, why people on the other side of the world would be interested, but most of the lectures were well-attended, and the audience seemed appreciative. They consisted mainly of women, middle-aged to elderly, with a sprinkling of elderly men. America was in the worst throes of the war against Japan and the young were otherwise engaged.

The atmosphere was lively, though, and question time afterwards often became an informal group conversation, straying far from the point. The senior citizens were agog above all to hear about her experiences in the Blitz, and sometimes she felt like a dog with a herd of straggling and wilful sheep, trying to round them up and get them back to the subject she was being paid to lecture on.

She arrived back at the ranch about seven o'clock on a Saturday evening. She was driven on the last leg of her journey in a battered pick-up truck by one of Leo's hired men. Ruth must have seen her coming because she strolled out in the mellow evening sunshine to greet her.

She waved and called, 'Welcome back, Mum.'

To Sarah's eyes the two weeks of absence had physically transformed her daughter. Her long limbs were tanned, her figure rounded out, flatteringly, just perceptibly. The skin of her face had taken on a smooth apricot colour. With the heat she'd tied back the forward locks of her hair. The rest brushed her shoulders, glossy and bleached ash-blonde by the sun. She wore a dusty pink sleeveless dress her mother hadn't seen before. But above all it was her eyes that Sarah noticed. There was an eagerness about them, replacing their habitual bleak, inward expression. The set of her body, too, had an impatience, as though there were things she wanted to tell. She hadn't looked like that for months.

Ruth kissed Sarah, then raised her arms carefully, stretching them out at shoulder height. 'Oooh, I'm so sore. Leo and the boys are teaching me to ride, and I ache all over.' She said it with a childish pride that warmed Sarah's heart.

'Riding! You must give me a demonstration.'

Ruth turned her mouth down, smiling, rueful. 'They've given me the quietest horse. A fat old nag called Playful. She's really patient. We've been exploring all over round here.' Sarah marvelled at the simple pleasure in her daughter's voice.

She grinned. 'Nice dress. Where did you get it?'

Ruth held out her arms and spun round. 'Rita made it. She's a genius. It only took her half a day.' She took Sarah's hand and began to edge her towards the house. 'We've been waiting for you. Rita's cooked this chilli stew. It burns your mouth off. And Leo's fetched some beer.'

They stayed just over a month, waking each day to the strong blue sky Sarah remembered. She got up early most mornings and made coffee and toast, then crossed the scrubland to the cabin where she and Stephen had lived.

In Taos she'd been able to buy the painting materials she needed, and now she set to work with a joyful compulsion, yet with the spacious sensation of having time.

During their stay she completed two large canvases. In some way they almost painted themselves, for she'd planned them in her head over years. First she pictured the burning buildings, the blazing sky, the flight of white birds, working with the same intensity she'd once brought to the landscape that now surrounded her, incorporating layouts and sketches she'd made at odd times and brought with her.

The second canvas was cooler in tone. She recalled driving back from Maggie's after Christmas on a morning of frosty sunshine and blue mist, and passing newly bombed-out houses. The jagged remains of their walls framing the intimate detritus of family life – broken toys, a mantelpiece with ornaments, lace curtains shifting in a slight wind. Fixed in her imagination the image was coldly disturbing, almost surreal. Oddly, Leo and Rita admired these paintings in a way they never really had when her subject matter had been their familiar New Mexico landscape.

She was able to work all day. Leo and Rita positively encouraged her to do so. It confirmed their idea of her, consolidated over years of reminiscing. Sometimes she took a break, sitting outside the cabin by the ungainly prickly pear and gazing out at the landscape she recalled so sharply from sixteen years ago, the reddish earth, the mountains clear in the bright air.

Occasionally Rita would come and sit with her. Worldly and energetic, she surprised Sarah by her nostalgia for the old days. 'Those were good times. It was good living with you and Steve.' Rita turned her smooth, handsome face to the sun. She wore dark glasses, which Sarah thought blotted out expression, so that you could never guess what the wearer was going to say next. 'You always had time. Dreamers . . . People are all so different.'

Sarah laughed. 'I'm only working this hard not to disappoint you.'

Rita nudged her and grinned from behind the black, blank patches of her eyes. 'Liar. You never did anything else.'

Ruth was always occupied, helping Leo or exploring with the boys on horseback. She wore denims and a red shirt and looked blooming. It put Sarah in mind of Stephen and the way these same surroundings had at first transformed him.

An hour or so before supper Ruth would wander down to the hut to watch her paint and talk. It was Sarah's favourite time of day. Here, in these unfamiliar surroundings, it was easier for them to see one another as separate beings and to communicate, without the petty details of home and family life taking priority. Often Ruth was bubbly with news of what she'd been doing. At other times there'd be a quietness about her, a withdrawing, and Sarah would know that the ghost of Alan had caught up with her even here.

Once her daughter asked out of the blue, 'How often do you think of Dad?'

Sarah thought. Then she said evenly, 'I don't think a day goes by without.'

Ruth spread her hands. The movement was broad, sudden, dramatic. 'Well, how do you cope? How *did* you cope?'

Sarah wanted to smile at the gesture, but her daughter's eyes were deadly serious. She shook her head. 'I can't answer that in a word.' Crossing the room and placing her brush into a can of spirit. 'You see, I hated Stephen after he killed himself. I thought he'd done me a wrong. And for a time it ruined all my memories of him . . .'

There was a silence between them. In the white-painted room Ruth's taut figure appeared unnaturally sharp, the red shirt blazing. Her daughter was looking at her. There was a tension about her, as though she craved a truth that she could apply to herself.

'I fought against that, you see. We had such good times together . . . and I made myself remember those. Although it hurt.'

'But it doesn't hurt now?'

Sarah hesitated. 'Just occasionally. But time heals. You won't believe that. It's a cliché, but it's true. And mostly I've got good memories and I can live with them.'

Ruth said plaintively, 'But I don't want time to heal.

It's wrong. If I don't remember Alan and feel pain it'll be as if he'd never existed.'

In the evenings they explored. Sometimes just the two of them, sometimes with the boys. Occasionally Rita or Leo would drive them somewhere further afield. Ruth talked about a place called Eden Rock, an isolated, colourful outcrop quite close by.

Sarah said, 'No. I don't want to go there.'

'Come on,' Ruth urged. 'It's beautiful.'

'Leave your ma,' Leo said sharply. 'She's probably exhausted after all that painting.'

The excuse was paltry. Ruth looked from one to the other, inquiring and suspicious.

Sarah reflected that her talk of good memories rang somewhat hollow. Stephen had killed himself out there at Eden Rock. There were still emotions she hadn't resolved.

37

'Any news?' Each time she put the question unwillingly, fearing the answer either way.

'Not yet.' Guy, who came through most things with an air of control, looked frayed and haggard. He had to clear his throat before he spoke, as though his voice were rusted with anxiety.

There was a dispiriting staleness about asking the same question again and again, but what else could she do?

Dominique touched his shoulder. 'Keep trying.'

He said dully, 'What else can I do?'

As the Allies had pushed into Germany and Poland they'd begun to discover the camps. Vast compounds full of starving skeletons, toothless, shaven-headed, with huge eyes you couldn't meet. They crouched in wooden huts that were putrid with rotting detritus, filth, excrement, the living among the dying, the already dead. Unburied corpses in unbelievable states of emaciation lay naked in casual, tangled heaps.

After Rosa was taken Dominique had blanked her mind, shutting out conjecture. Now there were pictures in the papers like the most unthinkable nightmares. She lay across her bed and stared at them, motionless, her eyes glazed with disbelief. When Rosa had been arrested she'd wept helplessly. But this was beyond tears or even anger. She gazed with a numbed incredulity, an ice-cold awe. Picturing Rosa as she remembered her, generous, with her rich, dark hair and bright clothes, trying to equate her with these wraiths from hell.

As the weeks went by they heard more. Stories of sealed trains, gas chambers, ovens, the daily extermination, the experiments of the Nazi doctors, the dying dragging themselves to their work, the summary killing of those who were too weak, the struggle in the gas chambers to live just a moment longer. Facts so inconceivable they seemed like legends. As the details proliferated Dominique had the impression that she was hearing tales from some black, barbaric mythology, then remembered, each time with the same sickening lurch, that this was true.

Still there was no news of Rosa. Guy went to the Gare d'Orsay each day to find out the latest information, read through lists of names. People began arriving home, many of them received at the Hôtel Lutétia, where Domininique and Sarah had stayed one spring aeons ago.

Dominique knew a woman called Nadine, friendly with Odile Carré, whose husband had been deported for political reasons. Towards the end of April he was repatriated, though he remained in hospital.

She met her one day in the rue Bonaparte. Nadine looked dazed and told Dominique wildly, 'He weighs just over forty kilos. I can recognize him – just – but he looks so . . . strange, so distant, so slow. Sometimes I have this fantasy that someone else has come to live in his body.' She brushed her thick, black, greying hair back with her fingers. As she spoke, her eyes seemed not to focus on Dominique, as though there was a compulsion to talk, but it didn't matter to whom.

She said helplessly, 'I just don't know if he'll ever change. I have an image of him lying there like that, exactly the same, until he's old.'

Day after day Dominique waited for Guy to hear

399

something. Then at night she entered her own world of Le Pessimiste and performed and soaked up the warmth and adulation. She felt a hard-eyed familiarity with the situation. It was what you did. People you loved suffered and died and you carried on living, enjoying living.

She had a secret. The hope that Rosa was dead. That she, Dominique, would never know how she died. She barely admitted it, even to herself. She didn't want to see Rosa monstrously altered, to feel the disgusted, horrified, helpless pity, the shame at being whole. Rosa living would passively accuse her. And yet what could she have done to save her?

Dominique started to avoid Guy. She couldn't face the hopeless repetition.

'Any news?'

'Not yet.'

He'd tell her anyway if he heard anything. Recently she found it hard to be with him. He gave the impression of being elsewhere, of having no time for anyone. He couldn't work. Dominique didn't think he'd held a brush for three months or more. There was a driven look about him, as if his search for Rosa was more real to him than his actual surroundings. Each day he came into contact with the disorientated, emaciated returning deportees, so Rosa's possible fate was constantly in his thoughts. His obsessive fear was that she'd been shot by the Germans at the last moment, with the Allies at the gate, so that dying she'd have known how close she was to liberation.

In June, in Le Pessimiste, Dominique was given a package by a journalist she knew on *Combat*, who'd just come back from the States.

'Here, this is for you.' He skimmed it casually across to

the table where she was sitting with Ruby and André Delarue.

It was from Patrick and contained a copy of *Life* magazine. On the front cover he'd scrawled 'Page thirty-four'.

All fingers and thumbs Dominique began to leaf feverishly through the pages. Quite suddenly she came face to face with her own image. 'Look!' She waved the magazine at Ruby and André, 'It's me!'

To her surprise, instead of a shot by their own photographer, they'd used the snap Michel Carré had taken of her the day Paris was liberated. She was standing on the balcony of his flat, hair blowing across her face, brandishing Guy's sub-machine gun and flashing a dazed, ecstatic smile. Momentarily she contemplated this version of herself. It wasn't a year old and yet she had the impression that she'd been much younger then.

'Show me!' André grabbed the magazine. 'Oh no! It's that picture. It's going to haunt you for the rest of your life, you mark my words.' The photograph had already appeared in a couple of French magazines, enhancing the rumours of her supposed Resistance activity.

'Come on, girl. Translate, name of God!' Ruby spoke no English. Dominique obeyed. The party line on Saint-Germain-des-Prés and the emerging existentialist movement was tight-lipped and vaguely prudish. To a certain extent Patrick had been forced to go along with it, but the article included gratifying puffs for Le Pessimiste, Ruby, Dominique. She was amused to notice that he hadn't omitted to mention the copy of *Being and Nothingness* that resided on her bedside table.

'Not bad, that.' Ruby attempted to purse her lips in a grudging, appraising manner, but a smile won out. 'So, my children,' she remarked with heavy satisfaction.

'We're known in America.' Her eyes shone like a young girl's.

'What's that at the bottom?' she asked. Beneath the article Patrick had appended a handwritten message.

'It says, "I give it eighteen months at the most before you're touring over here".' Dominique grinned, mock-disparaging, while her brain sang. She shrugged. 'He's a bit of an enthusiast, our Patrick.' She carried the article about with her and showed it to everyone.

Two days later in the Place Saint Germain she saw Guy and bounced up to him. 'Look at this!'

But immediately she regretted it, recognizing the preoccupied air that now seemed part of him, and knowing there was no point in trying to interest him in such trivialities. He brushed the magazine aside, vaguely, as though swatting a fly.

'There's news,' he said. 'Rosa's alive.'

She had been in Auschwitz, then, as the Allies advanced, evacuated to Belsen. Belsen had been liberated in mid-April. Since then Rosa had been in an infirmary in north-west Germany, near Celle. He was baffled as to why there'd been no word earlier, but now he was going to move heaven and earth to go and see her.

38

In mid-July there was a party at a neighbouring farm, some twenty miles away. A family called Janssen. Their eldest son had been wounded in Iwo Jima in March. He'd arrived home after a long spell in hospital. They'd invited most of the neighbourhood to celebrate.

'There'll be music and dancing,' Rita told Ruth. She worried vaguely that the ranch was too quiet for a seventeen-year-old.

The house stood in a valley. It was low and plain and spreading, like Leo's, and painted white. In front was a large dirt yard surrounded by trees. It was dusk when they arrived, and as they approached they could see coloured lights shining among the flickering aspen leaves. The air was warm with just the hint of a breeze. Two long tables had been set up, one each side of the yard with candles in jars.

'Look at that.' Ruth leaned forward to gaze out of the car window. 'The lights down there like an island, and the dark mountains all round.' She looked beautiful tonight, Sarah thought, in the pink dress Rita had made, her straight hair pale and shining in the twilight.

The boundary was packed with cars and pick-up trucks. They were pretty well the last to arrive. People were standing in the yard, talking and drinking beer. The scene had a cinematic quality, with the near-darkness and oblique lighting lending a kind of glamour to the guests.

Their hosts were of Scandinavian origin. Will, the husband, had an interesting, long, cadaverous face. His

wife, Eva, was blonde and bonny. She embraced Leo and
Rita and the boys like old friends, and was pleasant and
welcoming to Ruth and Sarah.

Towards herself, in fact, Sarah was prepared for a
certain wariness. Willy-nilly, Stephen's story was well-
known in the region and she had the impression of
entering any gathering here like Medea, with a vague
aura of tragedy. Possibly her dark dress and black curls
accentuated the effect. But usually the feeling dispelled
after a few minutes of earthbound conversation.

Proudly Will introduced Karl, his oldest son. He was
thin-faced and tall, about twenty, a young version of his
father. He'd been awarded a Purple Heart, Leo had told
her, but he seemed slightly abashed here on his own home
ground by this party in his honour. When he crossed the
yard Sarah saw that he still had a slight limp.

Now Eva included them all in a wide gesture of
hospitality. 'Now we can eat. It's just you folks we've
been waiting for. And there's so much. I hope you
brought your appetites.'

Eventually the guests were settled at the two long
tables. They were separated according to age. The young
people – ranging from nine to about twenty – sat on the
right, the rest on the left. There was meat and corn and
butter and bread and potato salad with onion and apple.
There were food shortages in America, as elsewhere, but
it was difficult to go hungry when you had a farm. They
drank beer and toasted Karl in Aquavit. There was a
good nature about the gathering, a sense of durability
somehow, Sarah thought, as though everyone belonged
and took the fact for granted.

From time to time she glanced across at Ruth, who
seemed happy and self-possessed. She sat opposite Karl.
In the flickering light Sarah could see a teasing smile on

404

her face, a look she used to wear often but which had become rare. Then she laughed at something he said and replied to it with a frank, amused grin. Tonight there was no trace of her self-punishing anguish, Sarah reflected with an ache of hope.

'Can you eat something more, Sarah?' On her own table Eva was offering corn on the cob.

She shook her head, smiling. 'It was wonderful, but now I'm full to bursting.'

'My!' Eva wailed with a comic despair. 'We're going to be eating this for a month.'

Afterwards there was dancing to a gramophone, which Karl had made louder by some ingenious device. Mostly the younger children stood round it and changed the records, arguing over what to play next. All ages danced, agile or slow, serious or clowning. It didn't matter. It was fun. Sarah hadn't danced for a long time.

Later, as Bing Crosby and the Andrews Sisters sang 'Don't Fence Me In', and she did a smooth turn of the dirt yard with Will Janssen, he leaned close and murmured, 'Look at the kids.' Nodding his head towards Ruth and Karl who danced casually entwined, looking private and self-absorbed. From somewhere Ruth had acquired a dark mauve, orchid-like, very artificial flower which glowed exotically and eccentrically in her hair. They didn't talk all the time, but when they did they smiled with an air of easy intimacy. The two of them seemed alone in the mêlée of children, neighbours, cousins, grandparents. Sarah was touched by their look of grave pleasure. It occurred to her that perhaps Will, too, had anxieties, and reason to feel reassured at the sight.

Afterwards, in the car, Rita turned affectionately to Ruth. 'Nice boy?'

Ruth was leaning luxuriously and wearily against the

405

dark upholstery. 'Okay.' She was blank-faced, deliberately non-committal. The warm air blowing in through the window tangled the side-locks of her pale hair.

'I've got a suggestion to make to you.' Ruth stared upwards at the sun. She'd borrowed Rita's black glasses and looked fragile and young in them, and a little perverse. 'Think about it before you say no. Count to ten or something.'

'What's that?'

It was a week or so before they were due to leave. Sarah had spent the day taking her canvases to a carpenter to be crated, packing the rest of her materials to be sent. Now she sat with Ruth in the sun outside the adobe hut on the canvas chairs from inside. She was sorry to be going, but her head buzzed with ideas for further paintings and the life she was returning to would be her own, of her own choosing.

Ruth turned her face towards her, warily. 'I want you to come out to Eden Rock this evening . . .' Behind the glasses there was no reading her expression.

'Oh, Ruth . . .' Sarah was ready to demur.

'Don't say anything . . . I know why you don't want to go. Rita told me. But . . . I'd like us to go together.' On a whim she took off the glasses. Her eyes looked suddenly exposed, with an intensity Sarah hadn't guessed at. 'Don't think I'm silly, or not thinking about your feelings, or anything. It's just that . . . well, it seems wrong to be here and not acknowledge my father in any way. It'd be sort of paying respects.'

Sarah felt cornered. Her instinct was to refuse, but the request obviously meant a lot to Ruth. She experienced a moment almost of dread, but told herself it was stupid. Eden Rock was just a place. A part of her, anyway, rejected the superstitious staying away, the idea of a no-go area. Reluctantly she nodded. 'All right. Tonight. I'll go with you.'

The sagebrush gleamed with a metallic sheen, its grey-blue touched with the warm orange of the sinking sun. It was only just over a mile to Eden Rock. They walked unhurriedly, pausing to look at plants, stones, anything that caught their eye. Sarah had a tight feeling in her stomach, a tenseness underlying their desultory conversation.

'You all right?' Ruth asked at one point.

She nodded. 'Fine.' It seemed she was. The mesa loomed small on the skyline, neutral, innocent. Only her mind made it something to be feared.

They walked for a while in silence, then Ruth remarked, 'You know, I'm glad you're like this. Apprehensive.'

'I'm not,' she protested.

'I can see it. And I'm glad you wouldn't go there at first, that you were frightened to. When we talked the other day I thought you had your feelings all packaged up and positive and now I can see it's not that simple.'

'No.' Sarah admitted it.

'You see!' Ruth said with a note of triumph. 'That makes me feel better. It means your memories of Stephen . . . Dad . . . are still alive. They can still hurt you.' She turned to face Sarah, walking backwards momentarily, in denims, a white sweater, her hair hanging anyhow, her face pale and earnest. 'Your feelings about him aren't always under control. But you live with them. And you have a good life still.'

'Yes.' She felt a wave of acute tenderness for her daughter, so painstakingly trying to come to terms with her own mourning.

'Since I've been here I've been really happy sometimes, and it feels so good. And then I'll think of Alan and feel disloyal. I don't want to forget him and stop feeling sad when I think of him.' A trace almost of pleading in her eyes, as though she willed Sarah to understand. 'But watching you I can see that one thing needn't cancel out the other. At night, often, I still lie there and see him and think about him. Then next day there'll be sun, and I'll go riding and feel wonderful. And Karl's nice. I get on with him. But now I'm beginning not to feel guilty about the good things . . .'

Sarah leaned forward and kissed her lightly. 'Ruth, it's so good to see you coming back to life.'

Soon afterwards they approached the base of the mesa. It was red, dramatically shaped, horizontally striped with layers of white and yellow. Behind it was the orange of the setting sun. Sarah held her breath, recalling so many evenings when she and Stephen had watched it go down behind this very rock. It was as if, in this stillness, she could re-enter the mood of those times, remember exactly how it had felt.

'We used to come here a lot. Evenings usually, like tonight. You'd get wonderful sunsets. Such colours. And it was always so quiet.' Her voice was low, she noticed. There she was again. Treating this place as if it were something special, set apart. Had she talked softly, she wondered, when she was here with Stephen?

'I can just imagine you in your twenties clothes,' Ruth teased her.

'I used to wear overalls and things,' Sarah protested. 'I didn't look that much different from you.'

The air was still and warm. It was so peaceful here. It occurred to her that she'd quite naturally remembered the time when she and Stephen had been happy. Now she was here, after all the years between, she realized that was how she thought of the place. It hadn't come to her to picture Stephen with his closed determination, Leo's gun.

'Let's stay for a bit.' Ruth sat down on a rock. Her smooth face was washed with the rich, tawny light. 'The sun'll be gone soon.'

Silently they watched. Within minutes the sun had disappeared behind the mesa, silhouetting its mass, leaving the sky a pale apricot. Absorbed with their separate thoughts, neither woman spoke.

After a while Ruth asked quietly, 'Do you regret coming?'

Sarah shook her head. 'No, you were right. I'd have left still dreading this place. Still imagining there was a kind of taboo about it. Now all I remember is how much I loved it here.'

Walking back in the deepening dusk they talked freely and comfortably, as they hadn't really been able to do for much longer than the year since Alan died.

Like Sarah, Ruth felt free now to plan for the future. Recently, the idea of acting – which she'd shunned since last summer – had surfaced again. She wanted to try for RADA or one of the other London drama schools. It was too late for this year, but Mr Whelpton, her self-appointed mentor from the Alder drama group, had contacts. He'd promised her in the old days that he could get her a job as assistant stage manager in one of two repertory groups with whom he had dealings, and emphasized that the offer wasn't just pie in the sky. Now Ruth was going to hold him to his word.

Tentatively Sarah mentioned the subject of Guy. Even now she was apprehensive of her daughter's reaction.

Ruth knew they'd been writing to one another, but up till now the moment had never seemed right to talk about their hopes for the future.

'He was quite nice as I remember.' Ruth was surprisingly casual. 'I thought something had happened after he visited you. You seemed to have a secret. A part of you wasn't concentrating on me.' Her attitude was cavalier but approving.

As they drew closer to the ranch they stopped to look back. Eden Rock was a tiny black silhouette, barely visible on the skyline.

Ruth said out of the blue, 'You've been so good this last year. Always there. So patient. I *did* notice. I was just so wrapped up in everything.' Fleetingly she kissed her mother's cheek. 'I know I was execrable.' Her voice was light and happy.

'I wouldn't have put it that strongly.' Sarah smiled, with a pretence of wavering. 'Well, maybe . . .' She took Ruth's arm, to walk on. 'But it's past. None of that matters any more.'

39

Ignobly Dominique experienced a sense of relief when Odile told her that Rosa had died. She'd heard by letter. She thought Guy was back from Germany, but hadn't seen him. Someone said he'd gone down to Provence, to his family, but no one seemed sure.

Dominique walked home along the boulevard Saint Michel. It was a hot day. Close. The passers-by looked red and boiled and grumbled to one another. She felt a vague distaste for them. People were so selfish, herself included, so locked into their own skins, their own lives. Millions had died, like Rosa, all over Europe. They were still dying. But the public couldn't focus on it, couldn't keep it in their heads for more than two minutes at a time. The barometer was of far more breathless interest.

She'd said something of the sort to André a little while ago one evening at Le Pessimiste. He'd claimed she was wrong to disapprove. 'It's the strength of the human race,' he asserted glibly. 'If we took on ourselves the suffering of others we'd all have committed suicide years ago. You've got to have a healthy egoism.' He was being provocative. She'd felt his words were aimed at her. They'd had quite an argument. Laughingly he'd proved she was a hypocrite. Probably he was right.

There was a letter waiting for her when she got home to the rue Bonaparte. It had been delivered by hand. She thought the writing was Guy's. She split open the envelope. Sure enough he invited her to drop by at his flat later in the day.

* * *

He looked haggard and tired and touchingly familiar as he opened the door. She felt an ache of affection. They were totally different, the two of them, but linked by so much. She reached up and put her arms round his neck.

'I know. About Rosa. I saw Odile and she told me.'

He held her very tight, as though, if he let go, his composure would disintegrate, as though he didn't want her to see the emotions which showed on his face. Dominique, equally, found it a relief to cling to someone. Not a lover who had to be charmed. Just a fellow human being. 'Guy, I'm sorry. I'm so sorry,' she kept saying.

The words weren't just to comfort him. They seemed her own expiation, for willing Rosa to die, preferring her death to the ordeal of seeing her crippled and wasted. Implicit in the embrace was all of their shared experience. The loss of Daniel, Luc, Rosa. The violation of their home city. A killing. The claustrophobic months of hiding. For a suspended moment all their small antagonisms were laid aside.

Then he led her through into the long room where he lived and worked. Two chairs were placed close to the tall windows which opened on to a balcony. Pale, translucent curtains shifted in a slight breeze. There was a breath of freshness about the day now.

On a small, carved table by the wall stood a bottle of red wine, already broached. He pointed to it, eyebrows raised in a question. She nodded and he poured them both a glass.

She asked carefully, 'Do you want to talk about it? About Rosa, I mean.'

He loomed over her as he handed her the glass. He still hadn't regained the ease of manner she associated with him. There was a strained, closed look to his dark face.

412

He said, 'I want to talk. I feel the need, yes. But I haven't made sense of anything.'

'It doesn't matter.'

'It's all just separate pictures, feelings. I lie awake and my thoughts leap at me . . . Everything's tangled.'

'What did Rosa die of?'

He shrugged, not negligently, but in a tight, hunched fashion. 'They said it was heart failure in the end. But it could have been tuberculosis . . . starvation . . . I don't know . . .' He stared at the floor. 'If you'd seen her . . . I didn't recognize her . . . Only when she spoke.'

There was a heavy silence between them. Dominique took a sip of wine. It tasted metallic to her. She heard someone in the street below calling '*Ça va, Simone*?' A soft summer evening. A peacetime evening.

'She used to hide food in her bed,' Guy said. There was a hoarseness in his throat. 'Bits of bread. A potato. She could never quite believe there'd be more the next day.'

Dominique said nothing. As with the photographs in the papers, indignation, even anger, were paltry and ineffectual.

'She didn't even trust *me*. I'll never know really if she was pleased I was there. Anything like that, emotion, seemed dead in her.' He passed his hand across his eyes. 'It was just survival. For all of them . . . The next food. She couldn't eat much. I fed her seven, eight times a day . . . Just spoonfuls, crumbs. You could see it go down her throat. You could've spanned her neck . . .' He stopped, choked with a harsh sob. She didn't think he was aware that his forefinger and thumb were circled to show how thin . . .

He looked up again, not really seeing Dominique. Like Nadine she'd met in the street, whose husband had come back, his vision was inward. 'There was this skeleton, her

413

body . . .' He paused, waiting, taking breaths, until he was capable of carrying on. 'This skeleton. And on top a head that lived and talked and moved its eyes and asked for things . . .' The precarious control broke down. His shoulders shook with a convulsive weeping. 'Rosa, it was Rosa . . .' He gestured briefly with one hand, as if to excuse his disarray, then lifted it to hide his eyes.

Dominique found tears seeping, hot and uncontrolled, from underneath her lids. There was a burst of light laughter from the street below. Rosa used to laugh like that. She was careless and happy, not marked out for tragedy in any way . . .

'I didn't want to see her, you know. Not changed like that. I was relieved when I heard she'd died.' In the charged silence of the room she felt the confession to be momentous, damning.

Again the tight shrug. Guy was indifferent. 'It doesn't matter. It doesn't matter what *we* feel.'

She thought then that he was right. Her own guilt was supremely unimportant. She got up and knelt down in front of his chair, touching his shoulder. Her sympathy was instinctive. Clumsy and inept. But that didn't matter either. He grasped her hand and held it tight.

Dominique wasn't working that night. Some time later she suggested they might go for a walk beside the river. Outside the air had a warm summer smell. The Seine reflected the pale gold of the setting sun, the whitish pink of the sky. After the sultriness of the day, the evening was idyllic.

'You know, when the Nazis were here I used to think there was a scary, sinister atmosphere to a night like this – like a smile covering treachery.' She glanced at the luminous pale orb of the sun. It glowed on the skin of her

414

upturned face. 'Funny how you forget. Tonight it just seems a perfectly ordinary, lovely evening.'

Affectionately Guy took her arm. He'd recovered himself and seemed temporarily at peace, though sombre and subdued. The pale gravity suited him, she thought. He smiled at her. The smile seemed superimposed on measureless depths of weariness.

'I never got round to telling you why I invited you to drop by,' he said suddenly. 'It was to say goodbye. Since I came back from Germany I've been in Provence, and I've found a house to rent. Near Avignon . . .'

'You sly thing!' she exclaimed, teasing, accusing. Tonight Guy seemed to welcome her efforts at cheeriness, even though both recognized that they were strained attempts to lighten his only partly submerged anguish. 'But why, Guy?' she asked more seriously. 'I can't imagine you anywhere but Paris.'

'Provence is where I come from.'

'I know, but you're a city boy now.'

They paused to lean on the stone parapet of a bridge. Above Nôtre-Dame and the Île Saint Louis, picturesque drifts of high good-weather clouds trailed in the evening sky.

'Look at them. They're hyacinth and gold.' She was quoting, she knew, from some poem they'd done at school, but she couldn't recall what. Dominique turned and leaned her back against the stone rail. 'Provence, eh?' Shaking her head. 'Whatever gave you that idea?' Teasing him gently, humouring him, like someone fragile.

'It was a fantasy of mine. When I was a child I used to hanker after a house near us, with these beautiful sand-coloured walls. Textured with centuries of paint, sun, wind. With a garden that was just a bit of wilderness roped off. With honeysuckle, and a vine . . .'

'Sounds like paradise.'

'After Rosa died, I kept thinking of the place. It seemed to be so much the antidote to everything I'd seen in the hospital. To everything we've lived through these last years.' His eyes lit up briefly with the old self-mocking look. 'I'm getting old.'

'But was the house empty?'

He shook his head, smiling. 'No. That would've been just too perfect. But there was one nearby up for rent. It's smaller. I can afford it, though I'll have to get back to work in earnest to keep it going.' He looked at her sideways and grinned. 'The walls are blue, actually, but the texture's even better.'

'Won't you be lonely?' She turned to him. He looked white and vulnerable against the darkening sky.

'I hope not. I hope Sarah will . . .' To Dominique there was a sudden grace in his expression. It came from within, a subtle shift, a softening, a glow of quiet optimism and unforced affection. Like a boy's, she thought. He said simply, 'I think Sarah'll like it.'

'I'll be able to visit you both. It'll be heaven.' On the way home she expanded on Guy's idea with enthusiasm. 'Easter'll be the best time probably. Before it gets too hot. With my colouring I can't take too much sun.'

To her surprise, it seemed to give him pleasure to encourage her fancies, elaborate on her version of his life. 'You'll be rich and famous by then and cause an incredible stir in the village.'

'Yes.' She was surprised at the bleak note in her own voice.

He looked at her questioningly, but said nothing. They walked on. It was almost fully dark. The streetlighting made the sky appear midnight blue. The hollow tone of her reply seemed to hang between them.

Then Guy asked, 'You're all right, are you? You sounded oddly . . . resigned, just then.'

She smiled brightly and waved away his concern. 'No, Guy, don't try and . . . I'm tired tonight. Emotional. And sometimes . . .'

'Sometimes what?'

In truth, she felt jaded. Guy's account of his time with Rosa and her own reaction had sapped her habitual resilience. She declared half-jokingly, 'Sometimes I feel I'm surrounded by phoniness . . . make believe.' Again, her tone wasn't as intended. She sounded brittle and nervy. She hastened to add, 'Don't misunderstand. I love the singing. It's the best thing . . . And I know I'm good. I've got a feel for a song, better than anyone.'

Guy listened without demur, making no attempt to mock her frank egoism. She knew he had a high opinion of her talent.

She pushed her hair back from her face. The perspiration of the sultry afternoon had curled it more wildly than ever. It glowed, coppery-black in the lamplight, dwarfing the contrasting pallor of her face. Her expression was withdrawn, without the conscious charm she often deployed. 'But sometimes I feel I'm turning into someone I'm not. For instance, the magazines lump me as an existentialist . . .' A flash of mischief lightened her face. 'And, Guy, I'll give you that book back before you go. I'm never going to read it now.'

He smiled, gently ironic. 'Sorry it didn't grip you.'

She spread her hands. 'I tried, I tried . . .' Giving him a humorous, self-deprecating glance, then returning to the thread of her argument.

'You get called something. An existentialist, say, and

417

people treat you as if you are, and it's hard not to go along with it . . . I mean they call me a Resistance heroine.' She'd stopped walking now. Under a lamp, she stood and looked him in the eye, steadily, with a kind of challenge, as though this was something she'd long wanted to get off her chest. 'Obviously, it's good for my career, but you and I know I wasn't interested. I stayed out of it for as long as I possibly could . . .' Her voice trailed off. She scanned his face for a reaction, but he remained inscrutable. 'Sometimes I feel I don't exist. There's just this cardboard cutout the magazines and the audience have invented.' A silence. Further up the street she saw chairs and tables on the pavement, the café brightly illuminated in the surrounding blue darkness. The stars were very clear. It seemed a southern night. There was a painting of Van Gogh's that looked like that. She saw a girl push at her boyfriend's shoulder, playfully reproachful.

'Oh, God.' The words were almost a wail, holding a world of feeling. 'I wish I could talk to Daniel about all this. Sometimes it gets on top of me. If he were here he'd laugh, and put everything in perspective.'

She read a sharp concern in Guy's eyes. He reached for her hand. The gesture of sympathy sparked something inside her. She smiled shakily, visibly pulling herself together. 'Oh, Guy, take no notice. I'm just being morbid. I'll feel good about everything again tomorrow.'

40

The world seemed full of Dominique. Yesterday two letters had arrived from her simultaneously. Today, as Sarah drank a cup of coffee in her garden and leafed through *Picture Post*, she came across an article on post-war Paris, with a picture of Dominique in shorts, waving a gun, and wearing the rapturous, life-loving smile she remembered. The image was so vivid that Sarah was momentarily transported back to the last time she'd seen the French girl, glowing with her plans to conquer the city she'd decided was her spiritual home.

Her letters, equally, had bubbled with her doings. New songs she'd discovered, the people she was seeing, a short break she'd taken with a boyfriend in an unspoiled coastal village called Saint Tropez. She'd visited Guy, she said, in his new house near Avignon.

'He's set on the prospect of you and he living there till you're old and grey, happy ever after,' she added, in a negligently scrawled postscript. The words, though obviously written with scant thought and a little satire, kept drifting into Sarah's mind.

Ruth had been home last weekend and Sarah had mentioned Guy's impending visit to London. Ruth smiled carelessly, mischievously. 'Your handsome prince, eh?' Then launched into some bit of gossip about a notorious, fading British actress.

Both remarks had been coined in passing by two people happily wrapped up in their own lives. Yet they'd disturbed Sarah. She'd taken them, she knew, too literally.

She wanted to answer back, to say, 'They're clichés you're foisting on me. Real life's not that simple.' But both Ruth and Dominique would have been amazed and disconcerted at being taken so seriously.

'We're all going to live happily ever after now,' Robert had claimed when he'd come to see her a couple of weeks ago. He'd been stretched out on the grass in the sun – she'd done away with her wartime vegetable patch. He'd said it with a sideways, kidding glance, his thin face droll and fox-like, but essentially he meant it. Sarah was touched by his boundless faith in the new Labour government and the egalitarian society they hoped to build.

He was studying hard for the degree he'd missed before the war, in his disarray over Dominique, and spent every available spare moment working for the party. He dismissed people who grumbled about the current lack of food and housing as gutless whiners.

'It's all a question of faith,' he told Sarah with a fervour that wasn't unmixed with personal ambition. 'The future's so close, and it's going to make everything worthwhile.'

He'd been sombrely impressed when she told him that she and Ruth had heard the news of Hiroshima and Nagasaki, and the new wonder-weapon, the atom bomb, just a few days before they left New Mexico.

Sarah's latent differences with Leo had surfaced briefly, but sharply. He thought the new bomb was a boon, a speedy and efficient method of resolving the closing stages of the war, and nothing more.

Sarah saw the issue as less clear-cut. She felt that its use had probably been experimental rather than strictly necessary, and that in some way the prime aim of the exercise had been to flaunt the destructive power of the weapon at the Russians. The implications of this alarmed her, and all the grains of information she'd gleaned since about the bomb had only increased her misgivings. She and Leo clashed bitterly, their old hostility rising like an evil genie from a lamp. Rita spent a distressing day or two as pig-in-the-middle.

In the end, though, both sides made conciliatory approaches. Neither Sarah nor Leo wanted to part bad friends. There was too much affection and too much history between them. And Sarah was deeply grateful to both he and Rita for their kindness to Ruth.

The farewell embrace between herself and Leo was warmhearted, but they'd been frank about their differences. 'Bloody good thing we live five thousand miles apart, Sal, ' had been Leo's parting shot.

Sarah tipped her head back so that the lazy early-October sun caught her face. The garden's colours were mature and mellow, the grass straw-pale, the trees from neighbouring plots fluttering their yellowed leaves against the blue of the sky. One late pink rose bloomed valiantly on a bush, whose leaves had a dry, late-season look, but the reliable crimson fuchsia would go on right into November if she was lucky. Recently she found she had an odd, elegiac feeling about this house and garden. Almost as though she were the caretaker, and her life here was all behind her.

In fact, with Maud dead, Jim moved to live with his daughter, Tessa back with Michael, and Ruth to all intents and purposes independent, it was hardly surprising. Yet the flat and the small square of garden were still home, still dear to her, housing memories and friendly, familiar shades.

With Guy's imminent arrival she was taking time off.

Otherwise her days were well-occupied, her life even and happy. Each morning she awoke with renewed exhilaration at the prospect of her day's work. Her own work.

Since arriving back from the States, she'd completed two more, larger, canvases on war subjects. They hadn't been exhibited anywhere – there'd not been time yet – but she'd shown them to friends and interested parties. They were variously loved and hated. A private collector had offered her a sum that had surprised her for the surreal, misty, blue painting. She had a shrewd idea that the four canvases would cause a modest stir in critical circles.

Disappointingly, Michael had taken against her choice of subject matter.

'You're turning back the clock,' he said. 'You might almost as well be painting crinoline ladies with watering cans.' He'd flashed a sidelong smile to show he was exaggerating, but the criticism remained. Oddly, she hadn't been hurt, though she'd always taken Michael's opinions seriously. She thought his comments beside the point. The subject matter had been baggage for so long. She'd carried it in her head – rather like a snow scene inside a glass ball, it sometimes struck her – throughout the duty-bound years at the Depot, and nothing was going to stop her from bringing it into the open. But the series of four canvases had pretty well ridden her of her obsession.

Guy had invited her to spend the winter with him in Provence. The prospect seemed sheerest luxury. And laying aside her purely personal pleasure, she hoped that the stay would provide her with a totally new kind of inspiration.

* * *

Last weekend, referring to Guy, Ruth had remarked carelessly, 'Your handsome prince, eh?' Then her mind had hopped away to some completely unrelated subject. That was how she was nowadays. Quick and skittish, almost feverish at times.

She came home irregularly, and always without warning. Mr Whelpton had been as good as his word, fixing her up with an ASM job with a repertory company in Bedford. There, it seemed, she worked like a slave, kept late hours, lived in gruesome digs, and was rewarded with a pittance and the odd opportunity of appearing on stage.

She seemed older, suddenly, and restive, wearing bright make-up and smoking, brandishing her packet of Capstans with a casual-defiant air. On each visit home she had a different callow youth in tow, whom she treated, so it seemed to Sarah, with a breezy contempt. A contrast to the undisguised calf-love of her manner with Alan. But the youths seemed not to mind.

To the job itself, Ruth brought a touching gravity, a total identification with the small, self-centred world of the company. During her flying visits she regaled her mother with the sayings and doings of her colleagues, people Sarah knew only by name.

'Diane says Noel Coward is just so old hat nowadays,' she'd confide, between inexpert puffs at her cigarette.

'Peter was such a bastard to me last night.' Her speech was peppered with expletives, which she used with an innocent gusto. 'Afterwards he apologized. I forgave him . . . He's got so much on his mind.'

She was more determined than ever to take RADA by storm the following autumn.

Each time she saw her Sarah was flooded afresh with relief and wonder at this new, busy, involved, self-opinionated persona. She watched the more disquieting aspects of her daughter's growing independence with an amused, but vaguely anxious tenderness. Yet all in all Ruth seemed happy. And after the year of desolate apathy that was all Sarah really cared about.

'Just as long as they're only callow youths . . . Now an ageing lounge lizard would really be something to worry about.' Tessa was unfailingly optimistic when Sarah mentioned her maternal misgivings.

She and Michael had managed to find a pretty, red-brick house in Caterham, with stone fireplaces, a cottage garden and beechwoods nearby. From the word go Sarah found its atmosphere oppressive. 'I don't know what it is. There's a sort of carefulness about it. An air of determined good behaviour,' she confided to Maggie, but couldn't pinpoint what it was exactly that made her feel this way.

Tessa was pregnant again, and in the hot weather seemed permanently uncomfortable and lethargic. Monty was bright and talkative, but still very wary of Michael.

Tessa said, 'Sometimes I think Michael's constantly repressing irritation with Monty. Then I'll decide he's simply hurt because Monty doesn't want to show him things or talk to him much . . . But Michael isn't very patient with him.' Her eyes were defensive, and her voice had a dying fall.

Michael was working freelance, writing criticism and articles and sitting on the committees of a couple of galleries. Sarah could see that he felt he was working at half-cock, and that he really wanted to get his own magazine, *Liaisons*, off the ground again. But for the moment at least he lacked finance, and anyway, the time just didn't seem right.

Both he and Tessa were sincerely trying to re-establish

their relationship. When you visited their cottage the atmosphere of worthy effort was almost tangible, hanging in the air above the good oak furniture inherited from Tessa's side of the family. You felt that anger could erupt at any time but they knew it mustn't.

Once, in passing, Michael mentioned to Sarah that he'd run into Dinah, his wartime mistress, at the opening of an art exhibition.

'Did it set you hankering after old times?' she asked, negligently, thoughtlessly. Immediately she could have bitten her tongue. There'd been a time when such a casual, frank inquiry would have been routine between herself and Michael. But things had changed and now the question sounded glaringly indiscreet.

But Michael seemed not to take offence. 'The question's purely academic,' he replied, with a crooked, faintly jaundiced grin.

Sarah looked at her watch. Half past four. She heard the sound of the front door being opened, slammed. Footsteps on the stairs. It'd be the son from upstairs back from school. He always looked like Just William when he got home, with his socks concertina'd round his shins, cap resembling a pimple on a haystack, as his mother told him with monotonous frequency. The family had moved into Maud and Jim's flat some four or five months ago.

'That you?' It was his mother's voice. Bessy.

'Who d'you think?'

'You're late!'

The door to the flat slammed shut.

It couldn't be long now before Guy arrived. She was semi-incredulous. He still seemed an almost mythical creature in her life, they'd spent so little time together. There were irrational, disconnected moments, when she

425

almost doubted his existence. But soon he'd be here in the flesh, tall and smiling, and exactly as he'd always been.

From behind half-closed lids she squinted at the sun back-lighting the skeletons of the yellowed leaves. Her eagerness to see Guy was tempered now with an edge of unease. Last December they'd talked expansively, happily, of living their lives together, but at the same time they'd known that no concrete steps could yet be taken. They'd both had private difficulties to contend with. Now nothing stood in the way of some kind of decision, and she was torn.

She looked forward, with a child's wondering impatience, to the prospect of spending time with him in Provence. But would he ask her for a more permanent commitment? And was she ready to give it? Dominique's scrawled 'happy ever after' had focused her mind. Her life here was as comfortable and congenial as an old shoe. There was risk involved in exchanging it for the unknown. Though also, she conceded to herself, a powerful temptation.

And there was Ruth. It wasn't that Sarah imagined that she played a particularly central role in her daughter's life nowadays, hovering in London and feeding her and her friends whenever they happened to drop by. Even so, to remove herself bodily to France on any long-term basis was pretty drastic . . .

Then again, on her last visit Ruth had said in the offhand, outspoken way she affected recently, 'I can't wait for you to go and live in Provence. All my holidays'll be taken care of . . .' Glancing through her curtain of pale hair with a vaguely speculative look, as though to assess what the chances were.

* * *

Guy grinned at her with frank amusement. 'I'm wooing you with photographs.'

He sat forward on the slatted garden bench, elbows resting on his knees, passing her the snaps one by one, explaining their contents. Sarah sat on a rug on the grass. The photographs were black and white, but razor-sharp, with the clear, bright Provençal sun.

'The house is just . . .' She shook her head. Words like beautiful and gorgeous sounded dutiful, and didn't express her genuine enchantment.

It was square and solid, with a shallow, tiled, pitched roof, and shutters that hinted at a cool darkness within. A thriving bush of rosemary flanked the doorway, and the back wall supported a flourishing vine. The sun caught the edges of the leaves, turning them transparent. Heavy, dark grapes nestled among them.

'The grapes are the best . . . Look.' He pointed eagerly. 'In the morning I drink coffee, see, just here . . .' He indicated a wrought-iron table and chairs at the foot of the vine. 'And then I pick grapes . . . I tell you, it's such a good breakfast.' She was amused and touched by his proprietorial pride.

He reached out and hooked his fingers in her dark hair, his thumb stroking the back of her neck. He grinned, meeting her eyes with an air of mock-inquiry. 'Well? Have I seduced you yet with my snapshots?'

Smiling, she admitted the possibility. 'I feel a certain weakening.'

It was so good to have him here at last, vivid and solid in the flesh. He leaned against the slatted back of the bench, stretching out his long body in dark shirt and trousers, sleeves rolled to show his tanned forearms, his bold face animated below the thick, greying hair. She felt his presence as a positive force. And she *liked* him so

427

much. Absence bred doubts and cowardice. Now he was here, everything seemed simpler.

Earlier she had asked him how he was managing now in the aftermath of Rosa's death. He hadn't replied immediately. He seemed to consider, to be sure of giving an honest answer. He'd spoken soberly. 'I dream often. Nights are bad sometimes. But then in the daytime I cope.' A dismissive movement of the shoulders. 'I'll get over it. It's not my right to suffer, to talk about suffering. It's Rosa's tragedy, not mine.'

Then he smiled slowly, as though mocking his own earnestness. He said, tongue-in-cheek, 'I'm like Thoreau now, you know, Sarah. Solitary. Getting my consolation from nature. But I invite you to share my wilderness.'

'I'm working so hard again. For a time I really thought it was gone, that I wouldn't be able. And I'm experimenting with things I was painting as a young man, but it's so different now.' His voice was low and confidential in the darkening garden. He'd put on a sweater, but it was still mild enough to sit outside. 'There are ruins, with these incredible shapes, and twisted olive trees, and rolling earth, and black cypresses against the pale fields. They've always been there. I grew up with them. But suddenly I see them as if I never saw them before.'

He paused. From upstairs they could hear faintly the strains of Bessy's radio playing 'String of Pearls'. There was a light in the upstairs window, a smell of bacon. Somehow this evidence of domestic activity in the house emphasized their intimacy, their aloneness here outside. She was conscious of a calm but active happiness. And a feeling of peace.

'I'm so impatient, Sarah, to show you the landscape. To have your reaction to it.'

428

She didn't know how long they'd been out here, talking unhurriedly, without feeling the need to unpack, or eat, or drink. Tasting the pleasure, the leisure of being together.

Sarah said slowly, 'I'd have to keep a place over here. Not this flat. Somewhere smaller. Ruth could use it when she's at drama school. I'd have to be back and forth a lot . . . There's Ruth, and my friends . . .' The thoughts emerging almost without her being aware of having formulated them. It seemed that, subconsciously, her ideas were falling into place.

It came to her suddenly, with total clarity, that the prospect of living with Guy was inevitable. Simple and miraculous at the same time. That with the war over, Ruth grown, now, if ever, was the perfect time to change her life, that if she hung back she'd regret it for the rest of her days.

'I know you have doubts.' Guy leaned towards her. 'But, Sarah, I don't want to shut you off, for you to lose your life here. I'd like to share *this* life with you too. Share Ruth and the people you know . . . We have double the possibilities.' With a sweeping gesture he indicated the wideness of their horizons. 'At the same time I want us to be committed to each other. I've wanted it all these years . . . I think our life together can be so good. You should give it a chance, Sarah. What do you say?'

She reached across and laid a hand on his forearm, its solidity and wiriness beneath her fingers a sensual pleasure. She nodded. 'Yes. I say yes.' She smiled at him, slightly dazed, and gave a small, expressive shrug. 'I think the decision took itself. And no, Guy, I haven't got doubts.'

As she spoke, the streetlights came on. The sky lightened to a luminous grey-blue. The stars showed, seeming low tonight, accessible. Sarah caught the scent, faint and elusive, of the lone, last rose.